SAMUEL

GADIANTON'S FOE

SAMUEL

GADIANTON'S FOE

A NOVEL

CLAIR POULSON

Covenant Communications, Inc.

Cover illustration by Matthew Judd

Cover design copyrighted 1994 by Covenant Communications, Inc.

Published by Covenant Communications, Inc.
American Fork, Utah

Printed in Canada
First Printing: February 1994

14 13 12 11 10 09 08 07   10 9 8 7 6 5 4 3 2

ISBN 978-1-59156-916-9

In loving memory of my father, Kermit Poulson, and Ruth's father, Jackson Tucker. No two men could have taught us more about fighting the Gadiantons in our lives than did our dads.

CHAPTER 1

Ophera knew terror.

She was huddled with her little son in a dank, dark closet near the back of the old house. Shouting from outside penetrated the thick walls. Someone was calling Samuel's name. There was a loud crash and the sound of splintering wood. Footsteps resounded on the floor. Her child trembled.

"Shh. You mustn't make a sound," she whispered, pulling a rough woolen blanket quietly over them both. The darkness was intense but offered comfort.

"He's got to be here," a raspy voice called. "We'll check every room."

"Are you sure this is the right house?" a thin, mousy voice shouted.

"Got to be," answered the raspy one.

Terrified, Ophera listened. Six-year-old Jath whimpered. "Shh . . ." his mother whispered, her face pressing the soft warm flesh of his cheek. His tight little muscles felt ready to explode. "Please, Jath, they'll be gone in a minute," she urged hopefully.

He stifled the storm, but she still felt the thump, thump, thump of his brave little heart against her breast. Love for him surged from deep within. The age-old instinct of a mother to protect its young was over-powering, and she gripped the knife she held until her palms sweated.

Someone entered the room, moving rapidly to the closet where they were hidden. The door rattled. It held fast. A curse preceded the deafening ax-blow that sent splinters spraying down on their blanket. Ophera held her breath. Another blow followed, and with a thud the door fell in. Jath jerked and Ophera held him tighter.

The blanket slipped; time stood still. "Don't see anybody," the intruder shouted. Jath jerked again. The owner of the voice and the ax did not move.

An eternity passed. Finally, "Empty here," he shouted and moved away.

Ophera took a quick breath and listened again. "I tell you, the house is empty, Herdon." The speaker's footsteps left the room as he spoke.

The raspy voice of the one called Herdon was muffled by several walls. "I'm sure this is the right place. This fellow Samuel, he was a friend of Pahoran, God rest his soul, ha, ha. He's thick with Captain Moronihah and Helaman, too, they said. Kishkumen thinks he'll try something if we don't get him first."

"It'd help if we knew what he looks like," the ax-man responded, his voice also muffled now.

"Well, if any of the Brotherhood knew, they'd have told us. None of them have ever met him, but I'm sure he's the one who caused my brother, Teor, to be hanged. He just recently came to Zarahemla, but word is, he was a good friend of Chief Judge Pahoran, and will likely try to find his killer, they say." Their footsteps had receded to the front of the house and Ophera could barely make out Herdon's parting words. "We'll get him. Let's report now and come back later."

Ophera waited for a minute before shedding the oppressive blanket. Safe for the moment, she carried Jath from the closet, still clutching her knife in one hand.

She froze.

Someone was entering the house. She scrambled back to the closet, fumbling blindly with the blanket.

"Ophera! Ophera, where are you?" Samuel's voice was unusually loud and strained.

"Sam! We're here," she cried, bursting from the closet, the knife dropping to the floor as she ran.

Samuel gathered his wife and son into his powerful arms. Only after they had both stopped trembling did he say, "I was scared out of my wits for you two. I saw two men leave the yard, and . . ."

"They were looking for you, Sam. They know you were a friend of Pahoran's. They said some man called Kishkumen was afraid you'd do just what you are!" Her blue eyes flashed with anger as she spoke.

"Meaning what?" Samuel asked, suppressing a smile.

"Going out and trying, all by yourself, to avenge the murder of the chief judge. They don't know what you look like, but they know you have more courage than good sense," she said in frustration, wiping her eyes.

"I was careful, Ophera, but I was afraid for you, so I hurried back. The whole city is in an uproar over the murder. It is still hard to believe that Pahoran is dead after only a few months as chief judge. I hear that his brother Pacumeni will probably be appointed to take his place soon, even before the year is over. Three chief judges in one year. The fortieth year of the judges has been a hard one," Samuel reflected.

"But that's not our problem, Sam. Let's get out of Zarahemla while we can," Ophera said. "Let Moronihah and his men worry about catching the guilty ones. Jath and I need you."

"You're right," he said, kissing her forehead and hoisting his son in the crook of his arm. "We'll leave for Gilead immediately."

Gilead, the village where Ophera and Samuel had grown up, was just a few hours ride from Zarahemla. They had seen little of the quiet town since their marriage several years before because Samuel loved to wander and Ophera had promised to follow wherever he went. His father and her mother, who had married after both had lost their spouses during the great war, still lived there and their home served as a place of refuge whenever Samuel and Ophera needed it.

They picked their way through the forest, avoiding the road, as they trekked toward Gilead. "Sam, I'm so glad we're leaving Zarahemla. It's just too dangerous for you there."

He glanced over at her and her heart sank. She knew that look. She mouthed his words as he said, "I'm going back." He went on. "I just wish Gadoni were here."

Gadoni was Samuel's closest friend. Once a bitter enemy, the sturdy Lamanite had come to know God and had saved Samuel's life on more than one occasion, as Samuel had also done for him. For several years they had been inseparable, but Gadoni had taken his beautiful mixed-blood wife, Laishita, to meet and stay for a time with his family in the city of Nephi, the capital of the Lamanite nation. There was a strained peace between the Nephites and Lamanites and Gadoni had felt it would be safe to visit. Samuel had heard nothing from him for almost a year.

Ophera bristled, but choked back the angry words she wanted to hurl at her husband. She remembered the covenants and promises she had made when she married him. She had accepted him and loved him for what he was. Even now, knowing the danger he would be in upon returning to Zarahemla, she could not ask him to do otherwise. She had loved him for many years and had learned to worry and pray in silence. She just wished that he would pray more and depend upon his own strength less. He couldn't see it, but he was not as close to the Lord as he had once been and it worried her.

* * *

Word of the death of Pahoran had spread rapidly. Oreb, Samuel's younger brother, received the news in Gilead before Samuel and his family had arrived. Like his brother, he was angry and wanted to avenge his leader's death.

Impetuous and headstrong, Oreb had forged his way through twenty-one busy years. Ruggedly handsome, with dark brown hair and bright green eyes, he had not married—many broken hearts floated in his wake. He had exceeded Samuel's six feet plus and was built like a young bull and often acted like one.

True to character, he was astraddle a bay stallion and stampeding out of the village, intent on riding to Zarahemla and who knew what, when he met Samuel.

"Where are you headed in such a hurry, Oreb?" Samuel asked with a twinkle in his deep blue eyes.

"Zarahemla. The chief judge has been murdered. I want to help find the men who did it. Why are you here, Sam? I thought you'd be hunting for them, too. Wasn't Pahoran a friend of yours? You should be there," he said, jumping, as he often did, to an erroneous conclusion.

"He's only bringing Jath and me here to safety. Already men are looking for him. Why don't you go back with Sam," Ophera suggested, knowing in her heart what a great help he would be to her husband.

"I'd like that!" Oreb said quickly. "Is that okay with you, Sam?"

"Of course it is. Let's get Ophera and Jath settled, then we can plan our strategy. We'll ride back early tomorrow morning, after we come up with some sort of plan," Samuel suggested sensibly.

"Sure, Sam. Whatever you say." Oreb had always looked up to his older, more experienced, and admittedly, more clear-thinking brother. He seldom questioned Samuel's judgment or his decisions. To go with Samuel on a mission like this would be nothing short of high adventure.

When Oreb and the others rode up, Latoni, Samuel's kindly father, limped from his shop, wiping his forehead with a dirty rag. "Sam. Ophera.

What a surprise! It's sure good to see you. And how's my little man?" he asked, taking Jath in his arms and hugging him fondly.

Kamina hurried across the street from the house, her face bright with love. "What are you three doing here?" she cried, fondly taking her grandson from Latoni.

"The unrest in Zarahemla, it . . ." Samuel began.

"I'm glad you got out of there," Latoni said. "It's much safer here in times of unrest. Maybe you can convince your brother to stay out of the conflict there."

"Father, Sam and I . . ."

"Oh, no! You two aren't going back there, are you?" Latoni asked, lines of worry creasing his aging face.

"Yes, Father," Samuel said. "We're going to help identify the rebels."

"Oh, boys. How I wish we could have lasting peace." There was sadness in Latoni's voice. "Can't you wait here a few weeks and give the authorities time to find the guilty ones? Then, if they fail, you might try without putting yourselves in so much danger."

Latoni had been severely injured while serving under Captain Moroni when his children were young, leaving him crippled for life. Sarah, Samuel's mother and Latoni's first wife, had died following a stressful period of captivity at the hands of the Lamanites. Kamina's first husband had died in defense of his people in the same long and bloody war. Further worry while Samuel and Gadoni fought in the final battles had taken its toll on him. Now there was the current conflict—one more insidious in nature; this one was apostasy and mutiny.

Ophera and Kamina sided instantly with Latoni. "They will be less concerned about you and it would be safer if you waited," Ophera urged.

After much discussion they were finally persuaded. The two brothers left early one morning about two weeks later after hearing that no one had been charged with the murder. They carried bows, arrows, swords, and knives. Both were dressed in leather and wore strong sandals on their feet.

"I'm glad you're coming with me, Oreb," Samuel said as they wended their way through heavy timber, alive with the sounds of awakening animals and birds. "We are dealing with dangerous men and must use caution."

"Where are we going first?" Oreb asked.

"To Captain Moronihah. We must let someone know of our plan—the chief captain is the best man I can think of."

When they arrived at the army's headquarters, Moronihah welcomed them warmly. "So, you're back. I heard you had disappeared after the murder of Pahoran," he stated. "This band of robbers is gaining numbers daily. They are a bigger threat to the peace of the nation than the Lamanite armies. Helaman was here earlier and we discussed strategy, but we still don't even know who they are. It's impossible to fight an enemy you can't identify."

"I know the names of two of them," Samuel said, smiling at the surprise on the chief captain's face. The son of Moroni, the most famous soldier in Nephite history, Moronihah had inherited his father's massive stature and undying faith in God.

"You do? How did you learn them and who are they?" he asked. Samuel told him of the intrusion at his home a couple of weeks before. "One of the men in my house called the other one Herdon. He heard that I testified against his brother, Teor, several years ago after the Kingmen uprising. They also mentioned a man named Kishkumen."

"I've never heard of either one of them, but Sam, it sounds like they are after you, so you better be careful," Moronihah cautioned.

"They only know me by name and reputation and we've given them a couple of weeks to quit worrying about me. That's why I think my idea will work," Samuel said a little boastfully.

"And what idea is that?"

"My brother and I plan to infiltrate the robbers. That's why we're here, to seek your blessing and make you aware. We'll only make contact with you when it's safe."

"Sam and Oreb, this is a brave thing you want to do. It's also very dangerous. Are you sure?" Moronihah asked, his brow creased with concern.

"Yes," Samuel said emphatically, "in the memory of Chief Judge Pahoran."

"What names will you use? You surely don't plan to use your own?"

"I will be Sarl. Oreb will be Oran," Samuel said.

* * *

As Samuel and Oreb were meeting with Moronihah, another meeting was taking place in another part of the city—a sinister and secret meeting.

"Samuel has fled. There has been no sign of anyone at the old house he was supposed to be living in for many days," Herdon was saying.

"He may be a friend of Moronihah and Helaman, but he is also a coward," Kishkumen said with a wicked laugh. "Forget him, he poses no threat to our grand cause."

"Forget him? Never! Because of him my brother was hanged," Herdon said in a rage. "He testified against my brother, Teor, many years ago, and as a result the judge had him hanged. Only recently did I learn that it was this same Samuel. He deserves to die."

"I see. Well, in that case, when he shows up you know what to do with him. No one need be the wiser."

"Thank you, Kishkumen. I'll find him and avenge the death of my brother," Herdon said with an evil grin, displaying filthy yellow teeth and black gaps of ones no longer there.

Herdon was a big man with a surly disposition. He let his long dark hair hang in greasy mats and was forever scratching at the lice that homesteaded there. His face was badly scarred beneath dark eyebrows that shaded his deep sunken eyes. Protruding beneath them was his nose, short and unnaturally squat, the result of a fight sometime in his villainous past. A dirty, graying beard hung long and unkempt from his broad chin.

Kishkumen, the leader of this secret band of conspiring and avaricious men was a stark contrast to Herdon. He was clean, with shorter, lighter hair, a medium complexion, and a deceptively honest face. He wore no beard. To judge the true character of this evil man, one had to look deep into his hazel eyes where there lurked evidence of a man devoid of conscience; Kishkumen was full of hatred and unholy lust for power.

Other men sat in the shadowy room. Next to Herdon was his good friend and almost constant companion, Javis. He was also dirty and unkempt, the lice on his head even more crowded than their kin on Herdon. Not that there were more, just that he was a very small man with a tiny, pointed head, bald over better than a third of the area where black hair once grew. His eyes were unusually big for such a small man and one of them was continually making its way toward his nose, leaving the other one to look ahead by itself. His beard appeared partially plucked and his face bore few scars—he had learned over the years to hide behind his big friend when the going got rough.

"Men, we need to recruit more members, but remember, I must personally approve each one," Kishkumen was telling them. "We are a brotherhood, and no one can be given our secrets until he has proven himself. You all know the penalty for anyone who joins and then acts the fool . . ."

He left the statement dangling—as much a threat to those in the room who might ever change their minds as to others who might later enter into their secret society and not prove loyal to their satanic designs.

Kishkumen arrogantly announced a series of carefully planned crimes and made assignments. Each was designed to bring wealth to the brotherhood and invoke fear in the citizenry. He stressed the importance of each member keeping up appearances in the community by continuing to work at gainful employment.

Herdon and Javis, both married men, worked as builders. They were lazy when it came to physical labor, but somehow managed to get jobs doing menial chores at construction sites. However, they preferred theft over labor and had been easily recruited by the secret band of Kishkumen.

They left the meeting together. "Let's check Samuel's place one more time," Herdon suggested. "We haven't been there for several days."

* * *

After leaving Moronihah, Samuel and Oreb had also decided to head for the old house where Samuel and his family had been living. When they approached the house they heard voices inside and quickly hid. Two men, scummy and filthy, emerged a few moments later.

The smaller one said, "It looks like Sam is afraid to return, Herdon."

Samuel and Oreb glanced at each other. "Let's get them," Oreb urged.

"No we don't. We want to infiltrate, remember?" Samuel scolded mildly.

"But they were in your house, Sam!"

"Which means they're probably part of the secret band. Let's follow them and see where they live. We may be able to use them if we are careful."

"Hey, that's a good idea!" Oreb agreed eagerly.

Samuel and Oreb followed the men at a discreet distance. They were led deep into an old, run-down section of the city.

"Fits those two," Oreb observed. "Kind of a shabby place, isn't it?"

"I suppose they live here, all right," Samuel agreed.

A minute later, Herdon entered a crumbling stone house. Javis continued across the street and into an even worse one. "Well, I guess we better change our appearance if we're going to try to make friends with those two," Samuel said, wrinkling his nose.

"Ugh," Oreb agreed with a shudder.

Just then, a girl emerged from Herdon's house. At first glance she appeared to be a walking bundle of rags. Both men faded into the shadows and watched her. "Wow!" Oreb exclaimed in an enthusiastic whisper as she drew closer. "She can't be that man's daughter. She's far too pretty."

"Settle down, Oreb," Samuel whispered. "We have work to do."

"I know, Sam, but . . ."

She was almost to them. The two brothers faded deeper into the darkness of the grove of ancient mangrove trees. She passed within twenty feet of them. She appeared to be about seventeen or eighteen years old, quite tall, and slender with glistening brown hair that hung nearly to her waist.

She walked rapidly, looking straight ahead, her hips swinging rhythmically in her clean but ragged dress. When she was out of voice range, Oreb exclaimed, "Wow!"

Samuel put his hand on his brother's arm and said quietly, "Let's stay put until dark, then slip closer and see if we can learn anything about those two."

Oreb offered no resistance and they sat down to wait. It had been fully dark for almost an hour when the girl passed again. When she stepped into the doorway of Herdon's house, a faint glow from inside silhouetted her willowy frame. She was carrying a package under one arm.

"Let's get closer," Samuel whispered, leading the way.

Hunkered beneath a window, they listened. Oreb poked him with an elbow at the sound of a sweet, but agitated voice.

"What's in this, Father?"

"None of your business, girl," a raspy, gruff voice responded.

"That's not fair, Father. If I have to run errands for you in the dark, the least you could do is tell me what I'm picking up. This might be dangerous for all I know. I don't like the way your friends look at me or talk to me," she said in a plaintive voice.

"Kapilla, as long as you live under my roof, you will do what I say! If you want out of your little job, then get married and let some other poor man feed you."

"Who would I marry?" she asked, her sweet voice taking on a sharp edge. "One of your friends? They're the only men I ever see, and I'd die before I ever married one of them!"

"Fine. So keep running my little errands and be quiet about it," Kapilla's father rasped.

"Herdon. Kapilla. Come join us for supper." The summons came from deeper in the house. Samuel had never heard a voice more filled with sadness.

He whispered to Oreb, "Not a very loving father, is he? Let's find a closer window. I want to hear more."

Light was flickering from a window behind the house. The sad woman spoke. "Did you and Javis work today?"

"Yes," Herdon lied, his raspy voice coated with sugar.

"Are you still working on the new synagogue?"

"Yes, dear." Samuel glanced doubtfully at Oreb. Not just anyone was allowed to work on a structure of such importance.

"Are you going again tomorrow?" she persisted, her thin voice breaking.

"Yes. Why do you fret so about what I'm doing?" The sugar was gone. "It's none of your business where I work or when."

A strained silence prevailed for several minutes. All that could be heard was the smack of lips and clack of wooden utensils on wooden plates. Finally, the woman spoke again. "All you do is work all day and all night. And they sure must pay bad, because you don't bring much home. Anyway, I need some help around here. When will you have some time off?"

"I don't know!" Herdon thundered so loudly the shrubs shook beside Samuel's face. "Shush, woman. Your cooking is difficult enough to eat without having to listen to you moan all through the meal."

Silence prevailed again except for the chewing, smacking, and clacking. Samuel cautiously peeked inside. Seated at a rough wooden table, beneath a candle in a brass holder on the wall, were Herdon, his wife, Kapilla, and two dirty, skinny boys—they looked about eleven or twelve.

Samuel crouched beside Oreb again. "Take a peek," he whispered, "then we'll go over to the other man's house."

Oreb looked.

"She doesn't fit there, Sam," Oreb said gruffly as they slipped across the street a moment later.

"Oreb, forget her!" Samuel said impatiently. "It's her father and his friend Javis that we're interested in."

"But she is so . . ." Oreb began.

"Enough," Samuel ordered. "You know better girls than her, anyway."

Oreb was sullen as they crouched beneath another open window. All they learned was that Javis had a husky wife and two small children. He and his family snuffed their oil lamp and went to sleep quite early.

Samuel and Oreb, who had become unusually quiet, spent the night in an abandoned stable just a few hundred paces from Herdon's place. They slept poorly and by morning it didn't take much to make themselves appear dirty and shoddy before hiding all the weapons but their knives and following Herdon and Javis.

The two robbers led them to an area where some corrals and sheds were being built. Oreb grew impatient as he and Samuel hid among the spiny branches in a thick stand of campeachy trees and watched the two men working with a crew of about twenty others. "They're leaving, Sam," Oreb whispered early in the afternoon. "Let's get out of here and find something to eat."

"No, let's go see if we can get a job," Samuel said evenly.

"What? We don't need a job—especially not here. I thought . . ."

"Follow me," Samuel ordered briskly and strode out of the trees before Oreb could complete his protest.

Ten minutes later, they were sweating alongside several other men, heaving big poles atop a long shed. They never quit until it was nearly dark. "You men are good workers," the foreman told them. "Come back tomorrow and you may work again."

"Sure will," Samuel said, ignoring Oreb's disapproving glare.

"Why are we working there, Sam?" Oreb asked angrily as they headed toward Herdon's house once more.

"Because we want to meet Herdon and Javis," he said reasonably. "Can you think of a less obvious way than that?"

Oreb stammered, then dropped his protest.

It didn't take long to discover that Herdon, who had left work before they did, was not home. The first thing they heard from the window in the back was the sad woman complaining to her fair daughter and silent sons that their father would be late again. "He said they would be at the synagogue until very late tonight."

"It's dark, Mother," Kapilla said sensibly. "They can't work in the dark."

"They must have large flares," her mother reasoned.

"Who cares?" Kapilla said. "When he's there at night, or wherever he is, I don't have to be his errand girl. Mother, his friends are awful. I detest them!"

"They're probably just poor people like us," her mother reasoned. "There's nothing anyone can do about that. The rich folks, the Church, and the government all look down on the likes of us. You must learn to be content with your station in life, girl, as I have. You're no better than the rest of us, and don't you forget that!" she scolded.

Kapilla said no more. The two boys said nothing. Samuel wondered about them. They seemed so dull and . . . well, dejected, he decided.

The morning sun had barely cleared the tree tops and smothered the work site with its hot rays when Samuel and Oreb arrived at work several days later. They had stayed at the stable, watched Herdon's house and become familiar faces at the work site. It was two hours before Herdon and Javis showed up that morning. The tired, haggard look on their dirty faces evoked a comment from Oreb. "They must have been out late again last night," he said with a chuckle.

Samuel grinned but kept working. Today, he and Oreb had decided, was the day to try to get acquainted with Herdon and Javis. After a couple of hours he managed to sidle close to the smelly pair. He said nothing as he labored alongside them. Finally, Herdon said to him, "You and the young fellow are kind of new around here, aren't you?"

"Yes. My name's Sarl, and that's my brother, Oran," Samuel said. "Rotten job, isn't it?"

"Yes, but somebody has to do it," Javis observed, eyeing Samuel suspiciously. He seemed to eye everyone suspiciously as his bad eye wandered.

"This is Javis," Herdon rasped. "He's not the real ambitious sort." He chuckled, slapping Javis on the back so hard the smaller man nearly choked. "By the way, my name's Herdon."

"Hey, you lazy oafs get to work." The foreman had strode up. "Don't be like these two," he said, addressing Samuel. "They're not worth much."

Samuel bent and picked up a big rock that needed moving. He had deposited it several feet away before stepping close to Herdon again. "Who does he think he is?" he asked, scowling.

"Just ignore him. He can't find many people to do the kind of stuff we will, but he'll ride you if you don't look busy," Herdon said. Samuel smiled a knowing smile and a friendship of sorts was born.

That night, a storm moved in. The old shed leaked, and by morning, Samuel and Oreb were wet and miserable. Oreb grumbled all the way to the work site. "If we have to work, why can't we at least do it in the parts of the city where they have streets of rocks or concrete instead of mud," he complained.

"Just be patient, I'm getting somewhere with Herdon, now," Samuel said.

"You look like you spent the night in a stable. Where do you live?" Herdon asked Samuel later in the day.

"You were right; we live in a stable. We don't have a home. Got run out of Manti a few weeks back," he said slyly. "Government leaders don't like me."

Herdon grinned, exposing his mouthful of rotting teeth and gaping holes. "There are some people I think you'd like to meet. If you want money, they'll show you how to get it, and the government can't do a thing about it," he said secretively, his squat nose only inches from Samuel's face.

"That would be nice," Samuel responded, barely able to tolerate the sickening smell of his new friend, but inwardly gloating over his success. He had little doubt who Herdon planned to introduce him to—the secret band of robbers!

CHAPTER 2

Several years had passed since the Lamanite armies had been defeated and driven from Nephite lands. Their king, a diabolic Nephite defector, was rebuilding his fighting force and stirring the hearts of the Lamanites to anger against their brethren. Many Lamanite men, both young and old, flocked to the land of Nephi to join the growing army.

During the period of uneasy peace there had been some travel back and forth between the two nations. It was during this time that Gadoni had taken his beautiful, part-Lamanite wife, Laishita, and his children to his old home in the city of Nephi to meet his family.

Laishita had grown up in the Nephite capital of Zarahemla. Her father had fought in the Nephite army against the Lamanites. Her mother was the daughter of a Nephite man and a Lamanite woman. Laishita had inherited the black hair, dark eyes, and to a certain extent, the dark skin of the Lamanite people.

Being a good natured and vivacious young woman, she got along well with people wherever she went. So, when Laishita first met Gadoni's mother, the old Lamanite woman had cheerfully accepted her, despite the Nephite blood that coursed through her veins.

Gadoni was the youngest of many children. His father had died at war when Gadoni was just a baby. Most of his brothers had also died fighting the Nephites. His aged mother lived in the home of his only surviving brother, and it was there that Gadoni and his family had lived for nearly a year.

Gadoni spoke little of his experiences among the Nephites. His family held to the general hatred of their people toward the nation of white men. He had tried to share with them his love of a God that they never understood and of his looking forward to the birth of a Savior, but they would not hear it. They would only let him stay in their midst if he refrained from speaking of the Nephites or their religious beliefs.

Gadoni and Laishita often discussed returning to Gilead or Zarahemla, but had kept putting it off. The journey between the two lands was not easy. They would have to descend many miles through rugged mountain ranges and a wilderness teeming with wild beasts. This would be difficult with their three young children—girls ages seven and four, and a handsome, six-week-old baby boy.

The increasing talk of war made them nervous, though, and one evening it all came to a head. Laman, Gadoni's older brother, said, "It's time we joined the army, Gadoni. I think we'll be invading the Nephite lands again soon. We can finally avenge the deaths of our father and brothers."

Gadoni struggled to conceal the shock he felt. He would never serve in the Lamanite army. Years ago he had made a covenant of peace with Captain Moroni. He had been accepted and loved by his friend Samuel and the Nephites. Their God was now his God and they were now his people.

"Come on, little brother, what do you say?" Laman urged with a wicked glint in his eye.

"Not just yet," Gadoni said, desperately trying to buy time. "They won't be fighting for many months."

"You're wrong, Gadoni. I think an invasion is being planned soon. If you don't join with me, I'll know you're a coward or a traitor or both."

Gadoni's chest tightened. His relations with Laman had been strained the past year, but he thought he had been accepted as he was. Now he knew he had made a terrible misjudgment and that he and his family were in grave danger. He had to stall. He must get Laishita and the children away.

"Tomorrow morning," Laman said firmly, his black eyes blazing with anger. "If you don't, I will report you as a spy and traitor." Laman stormed away, leaving Gadoni trembling with fear for his little family.

Laman, his brother, had been named after their ancestor from over five hundred years ago. That earlier Laman had led a rebellion against his righteous younger brother, Nephi. He had taken many of the family as followers and God had marked them with a dark skin to distinguish them from the people of Nephi.

Laman had called his people Lamanites, and over the centuries the lies he fostered of wrongs done to him by Nephi had been passed down from generation to generation. Most Lamanites readily believed the ancient tales and imagined many continuing injustices being heaped upon them by Nephi's descendants.

This modern Laman, proud to bear the name of his forefather, hated the Nephites. He knew well of his younger brother's change of heart, but because of his mother's tears in Gadoni's behalf he had been silent—until now. The current unrest that had turned many hearts to war again had made him intolerant.

That night, Gadoni spoke urgently to Laishita. "We must leave Laman's house tonight and travel into the wilderness. Laman swore that if I didn't join the Lamanite army tomorrow, he would declare me a spy."

Laishita, despite having given birth to five children (two had died at birth), was still the vibrant beauty that Gadoni had married. Their years together had deepened his love for her. His bold heart ached at the fear and concern that now darkened her face.

"Gadoni, Laman frightens me so. How will we get away from the house without him knowing?" she asked. Laman's home was an ancient house built of stone by the Nephites before the Lamanites had driven them from the city of Nephi and claimed it as their own.

"We'll go through the window in the dark of night. Get the girls ready and bundle little Enos up while I gather a few provisions," he said urgently. "In a few minutes I'll walk past Laman and outside. If he tries to stop me from leaving, I'll try to convince him that I'll accept his offer to join the army."

When all was in readiness, he left their small room at the back of the house. "Where are you going, Gadoni?" Laman demanded as he headed for the door.

"Out for a walk. I want to be by myself for awhile and consider what you told me earlier. Laishita and the children are sleeping. I'll be ready to go with you in the morning, I think."

Laman smiled, but before he could reply, Gadoni hurried out the door. He walked in the warm night air, gazing at the clear, starlit sky, his heart heavy with worry. When he returned, Laman could not be seen at the door and there was no light in the house. He approached the window where Laishita was ready and waiting. She rapidly passed the provisions,

Gadoni's weapons, and their three children to him. Then he helped her through the small opening and she followed as he led the way to the city's edge.

The city of Nephi, built by Nephi's people hundreds of years ago, was surrounded by a massive stone wall, but it was in a bad state of repair. Gadoni knew of several places where his family could pass through the wall without going to a gate. It was to one of those weak spots that they now fled.

Seven-year-old Limre, the dark image of her pretty mother, struggled gamely to keep up. Gadoni carried four-year-old Zera while infant Enos was in a backpack on his mother's back. Because of the necessity of carrying the children, they had taken few provisions. Gadoni owned horses, but they were with Laman's animals, and he decided not to risk going after them.

The glorious dawn found the little family, scratched, bruised and exhausted, resting in a thicket near the edge of a deep canyon, several miles from the city of Nephi. "Father, I'm very, very tired," Limre complained, her dark eyes dim with exhaustion. "My feet hurt and I'm hungry, too."

"I'm sorry, but we've got to reach the wilderness before we take time to eat or sleep. Laman may follow us."

"Is he mad at us, Father?"

"Yes, Limre. He's very angry. He wants to take your father away from you. I couldn't bear that," he said, holding her close.

Zera and Enos were asleep. Laishita gave Gadoni and Limre a tired smile. "Looks like we're off on another adventure, Gadoni," she whispered.

"Yes, but I hope it proves not to be a dangerous one. We really can't rest here long. Laman will be coming soon, I'm sure," he said gravely.

Gadoni led them deep into the forest, avoiding established paths.

Several miles back, a small band of Lamanites, led by a seething Laman, were studying the ground intently for tracks. Laman had awoken in the middle of the night with a nagging suspicion. His fears were confirmed when he checked their room in the middle of the night and found Gadoni's family missing.

Laman had gathered help in a rage, but they were hours finding the direction the little family had gone. Now they were in pursuit. Laman vowed that his treacherous brother would pay with his very life!

Gadoni was uneasy. He was certain Laman would be after them by now, but what worried him most was how many other men were with him. He couldn't possibly defend his family against very many. He made a hasty decision.

"Laishita, we must find a place for you and the children to hide for a little while. I want to see if we're being followed. If we are, I'll try to steer them onto a false trail and then come back for you," he told her.

A densely wooded area led almost to the rim of a vast green canyon. The sides were nearly vertical. Gadoni listened for a moment to the sound of running water somewhere below them. Using a strong vine, he descended over the edge. In a few minutes he scrambled back over the rim.

"Laishita," he said excitedly, "I found a perfect spot. I'll take Limre down first, then Enos, then Zera, and then you."

Laishita did not argue. Gadoni worked quickly, and soon the family was snugly situated on a shallow ledge that ran back into a crevice beneath the edge of the canyon rim. A small spring flowed from within the wall and along the edge of the mossy ledge before plunging a hundred feet or more to green, gentler slopes and flowing on to the river that raged far below.

He left the provisions and a knife and small ax with Laishita. He also left a long, coiled length of vine that she could use in an extreme emergency to lower herself and the children to the banks of the river in the unlikely event he did not return.

Gadoni led his family in prayer. "I'll be back sometime tomorrow," he said after they had finished. Kissing Laishita lightly on the forehead, he reached for the vine and in a few seconds was over the rim.

He pulled his makeshift rope up and hid it some distance away. Then he carefully backtracked, covering their tracks wherever they could be seen. Next, he left plain signs leading in the opposite direction for a couple of miles, then expertly doubled back, leaving no discernable evidence of his passing. He then left more tracks as he retraced the trail he had just created, hoping it would appear that his family had passed that way. Then he went in search of his enemies.

He found them early in the afternoon. He silently crept within earshot. "They can't be going very fast with small children," one of them said.

"We'll catch them soon, but don't underestimate my treacherous younger brother," Laman said angrily. "He is a traitor and will not hesitate to do harm to any of us. We must be very careful and avoid an ambush."

Gadoni was thinking how much he did not want to ambush them. He wished Laman no harm. His only desire was to lead his family safely back to the land of Zarahemla. He followed the men until they came to the end of Gadoni's false trail.

When the tracks vanished, the small band of dark-skinned men drew up and discussed the problem. "Where have they gone?" one man asked, puzzled.

"Well," another said stiffly, "they aren't here, so they've gone somewhere."

"Gadoni is clever," Laman reminded them again. "He has started to cover their trail, but he can't do that and move quickly. We'll continue this way. They'll leave tracks again. Spread out and move forward," he ordered.

Gadoni moved swiftly now, leaving tracks that they would be sure to intercept in a mile or so. He ran in a great arc that, by dark, had him traveling straight back to the city of Nephi. It was late when he arrived there. Cautiously, he entered the city and proceeded to where Laman held his few animals. Gadoni caught his two horses, loaded them with provisions from the room he had vacated the night before, and fled once more.

He rode hard under a brightly starlit sky until he was a safe distance from the city. He was taking a different route. He had no desire to meet up with Laman and his band. Finally, so tired that he could go no farther, he stopped and slept. He was up at dawn and on his way again. Laishita and the children were rested but anxious when he finally dropped his vine over the canyon rim and descended to their damp hiding place.

Laishita smiled when Gadoni explained what he had done. "Oh, Gadoni, thank you for getting the horses. My feet feel better just thinking about them."

"And my back," Gadoni said with a chuckle. "I only did it so I wouldn't have to carry Zera anymore. Let's get back on the rim and ride out of here. When Laman discovers that the horses are gone, he'll be in a murderous mood."

Laman had already figured out Gadoni's deception. Shortly after daylight he told his men, "Something's wrong here. We're headed back to the city of Nephi. I don't like it. Let's cut back to where the tracks disappeared."

No one argued with him, so the Lamanite band turned cross-country until they came across Gadoni's old trail and followed it again. Suddenly one of Laman's men shouted, "Horse tracks just came onto this old trail."

"This is no coincidence," Laman said, wrinkling his broad forehead. "This is a big wilderness and we're not on an established trail. Gadoni's gone back to Nephi and taken his horses. Hurry, men, they'll be difficult to catch now."

They hadn't gone more that another mile before the horse's tracks veered to the right toward the rim of the sweeping green canyon. Laman smiled smugly. "Gadoni thinks we're stupid. His family is hidden somewhere near here. Faster, men," he urged, following the fresh horse tracks.

Gadoni settled everyone on the horses along with the provisions and weapons. Laishita rode a bay mare, Zera in front of her. Limre rode with Gadoni on his sleek black stallion. Tiny Enos was tightly bound to his father's back.

Just as they turned to ride along the grassy canyon rim, Gadoni caught a movement in the trees from the corner of his eye. "Laishita, ride hard!" he shouted in alarm, kicking his heels into the black horse's belly.

The vicious band of Lamanites, led by Laman, burst from the dense forest, stringing arrows in their bows just as the horses thundered into the nearby woods. The little girls swayed dangerously while clinging to their parents with all their strength.

Arrows flew, but the dense forest deflected them. Gadoni pushed on faster than was safe, hoping that his horses would not lose their footing. They hadn't gone far before the horses became lathered and were tiring, but Gadoni forced them on through several miles of dense rain forest.

Suddenly, Laishita screamed. Gadoni twisted and looked back just in time to see the bay mare hit the ground. Laishita and Zera flew forward, landing in a heap against a rotting log. Gadoni swiftly jumped from his stallion, leaving Limre holding it, and ran to their aid, little Enos bouncing on his back.

Laishita was on her feet, but the injured horse had pinned Zera against the log. When it struggled, she cried out in pain. Working with lightning speed, Gadoni examined the injured mare. It had stepped in the hole of some rodent and broken a front leg. The horse struggled again and Zera screamed. Gadoni plunged his long knife into the mare's heart, putting her out of her misery while stilling her so she wouldn't do further damage to Zera.

Gadoni worked frantically to free the little girl. He cut down a small tree and made a pole to pry the leaden weight of the horse until they were able to pull Zera free.

A quick examination of his four-year-old daughter revealed a broken leg and many bruises and minor cuts. Gadoni quickly splinted the leg and loaded her behind Limre on the black stallion with all the provisions. With Enos on his back again, the brave father led the horse while Laishita, shaken, but otherwise unharmed, followed behind.

Laman drew his ferocious band of men to a stop. "We're losing ground," he lamented. "With all of them on horses we'll never be able to catch them. We will return home." He paused, his dark eyes flashing with anger. "Gadoni will pay for his treachery. He is no longer my brother! Someday I will find him and he will pay!" he threatened. His dark, nearly naked companions grunted their agreement.

They camped, too tired to travel farther. They ate and they slept. After darkness closed over the wilderness like a black mist, they could hear wild beasts screaming and fighting nearby, but none approached their fire. The next morning they prepared to return to the city of Nephi.

A scant hundred yards beyond their camp the wild beasts were slinking away from the skeletal remains of Gadoni's bay mare. They had picked it clean of every ounce of flesh. Had Laman only known . . . but he did not.

CHAPTER 3

Tonight you will meet others," Herdon said in his raspy voice. "Kishkumen was impressed with you the other night. He says we need strong young men like you in our cause."

Samuel shuddered inwardly, but his face was as stone, hiding his true feelings from Herdon. A few nights earlier they had met a few of Herdon's friends, including the man called Kishkumen who appeared to be the leader of the robbers and whose eyes betrayed a decadent soul. Samuel was ill at ease in his presence.

After meeting him, the two brothers had talked. "He's a dangerous man, Oreb," Samuel had said of Kishkumen.

"Yes," Oreb had replied. "I wouldn't be surprised if he killed Pahoran with his own hands."

"Nor would I," Samuel had agreed.

Herdon spoke to Samuel again. "You and your brother Oran will stay with us now. My wife has consented. Since you will be joining our band of brave men, you cannot live in an old stable unfit even for animals."

"We don't want to crowd you," Samuel said, preferring his present quarters.

"We'll move the twins out back, Sarl. I insist that you come and sleep in their room."

Samuel wanted to protest further, but Oreb broke in with a silly grin. "Thank you, Herdon. We'd like that very much."

Samuel shot him a sultry look, but said no more. Instead, he began to work again. It would not be wise to upset Herdon.

That evening, the brothers ate with Herdon's family. Samuel chuckled to himself when he noticed Oreb smiling at the ragged but very attractive Kapilla. Even though she did not return his smile, she cast him frequent furtive glances. Herdon's wife asked, in her unusually sad voice, "Are you going out tonight, Herdon?"

"Yes," he said sharply. "I want to introduce Sarl and Oran to my friends."

"His friends are villains!" Kapilla erupted, her pale green eyes suddenly flashing with anger.

"Shut up, you foolish girl. These men are my friends, too. Are they villains as well?" Herdon asked, his face purple with rage.

"If they're your friends, they must be," she snapped.

"Shut up!" Herdon shouted.

"You asked me a question, Father."

"Leave the table!" he ordered. The room shook and ugly purple veins stood out on his temples.

Samuel glanced at Oreb. The young man was ready to fight. Samuel poked him with his elbow. Oreb relaxed—barely. Kapilla fled, her head ducked and tears streaming down her face.

"The girl has a nasty tongue," Herdon said in the wake of her escape. "I wish she had no tongue at all, like the boys. They never talk back to their father."

Samuel and Oreb exchanged glances with stony faces before busying themselves with the bland meal before them.

"What are their names?" Samuel inquired after the tension had eased.

"Whose names?" Herdon asked stupidly.

"Your sons'."

"Oh, those two idiots! We call the taller one Kim and the other one is Kib. They're twins."

The boys glanced at their father at the mention of their names, but quickly resumed shoving food into their mouths as if they might not have another chance to eat for a long time.

"I really hate to take their room," Samuel remarked, watching Herdon's expression carefully.

He didn't look up, just snorted. "Nonsense, they don't need a room anyway. They just eat our food. They're like dogs. They were born idiots and idiots they'll always be."

Samuel looked over at Kim. Their eyes met. He saw sadness and hurt, but there was a spark of intelligence in the pale green eyes. With pity, he wondered what it was about the twins—idiots they were not, he decided, but something was amiss. A suspicious thought lurked in Samuel's mind. He couldn't brush it away.

When the meal was concluded, Herdon said, "We'll go now." Samuel and Oreb followed him obediently into the next room where Kapilla was hunched on a rough wooden bench, sobbing quietly. "You stay home tonight," Herdon said without looking at her. "I won't need your help."

Kapilla nodded, but made no attempt to raise her head or brush back the long straight locks of light brown hair that veiled her stricken face. Samuel felt a rage building within him. He had never witnessed such cruelty from a parent. Herdon despised his own flesh and blood.

With an effort, he contained his anger and signaled for Oreb to do the same. They went outside with Herdon where Javis joined them. The four men tramped through the gathering darkness along the dusty Zarahemla streets.

Several minutes later, Samuel and Oreb were ushered into a large stone house. They entered a room lit by a single oil lamp that sat in the center of a long wooden table. The eerie light reflected from over thirty sets of hard, unforgiving eyes around the table. At the door stood two giant men. Except for the movement of their eyes, they might have been armed statues. Kishkumen rose to his feet at the head of the table.

"Men," he began, his voice low and menacing, "we are gathered in secret tonight. Ours is an important mission. Anyone here who is not willing to do whatever is asked may leave now." A few eyes flitted toward the statues. No one moved. Kishkumen smiled.

Somehow, Samuel knew that turning back at this point could prove fatal and for the first time doubted the wisdom of his undertaking. Kishkumen went on. "Once you have united yourselves with our brave band the penalty for leaving or even divulging our secret mission to others is death!"

There was a somber silence followed by the introduction of each new prospective member in the room. Samuel and Oreb, introduced as Sarl and Oran, were two of ten. All were required to take an oath of secrecy. His stomach was knotted, but despite his misgivings, Samuel, using his false name, took the oath, silently denying it in his heart. Oreb, as tense as a taut bow string, followed suit.

At the opposite end of the table from Kishkumen sat an especially malefic man. Even Kishkumen looked to him for approval as he conducted their sinister business. The small lamp barely threw enough light to that end of the table to enable Samuel to make out the dark beard, wide-set eyes, broad nose, and firm mouth. In turn, the man's stark eyes considered each of the newcomers, his face like granite. Only after Kishkumen had explained the secret combinations to the new confederates did he finally recognize and introduce the fearsome man as Gadianton.

Gadianton rose to his feet, bowed, and sat down. He was over six feet tall, with broad shoulders and narrow hips. Long black hair hung past his shoulders. His voice was so deep it seemed to rise from the depths of his black heart. "It is good to know you, brothers," was all he said.

Kishkumen, after a short, heavy silence, said, "Pahoran's brother, Pacumeni, has just been appointed chief judge of the land. Pacumeni is not an improvement over his brother. He must die. Some of you will see to it. When you have completed your task, you will report to me." His eyes drifted ominously over the group, finally stopping. "Herdon, the assignment is yours to plan and lead this execution. You have one week." He paused, studying the faces that surrounded the table. "You will be assisted by Javis, Sarl, and Oran," he said at last.

Samuel felt as if the breath had been bashed out of him. Pacumeni was his friend. He couldn't . . .

"As in the execution of Pahoran," Kishkumen continued, "it is forbidden to mention the name of Pacumeni's executioners. Any man here who breathes the names of any of the four who carry out this assignment will himself be executed."

Samuel's heart sank. No one would mention who had killed Pahoran. These men, he now knew, were serious about their evil business and their secrets would be revealed to none. Of one thing he was now certain, though; Gadianton, Kishkumen, and this band were collectively responsible for Pahoran's murder.

Later that night, Samuel and Oreb lay side by side in the stuffy room usually occupied by the twins. When Herdon's contented snores finally rumbled through the open doorway, they whispered quietly to each other.

"Oreb."

"Yes."

"We must get a message to Captain Moronihah. Only we can save the life of Pacumeni."

"But who killed Pahoran?" Oreb asked. "We still need to find that out."

"We're wasting our time. You heard them. All are sworn to secrecy. No one who knows will ever tell the guilty name. I believe it was Kishkumen, though."

"Or that man called Gadianton," Oreb countered.

"I believe he's the devil himself," Samuel said, "but I still think Kishkumen is the killer. Another thing, I think that unless this band is destroyed, Gadianton will soon be their leader, not Kishkumen. They all fear him, it seems to me, more that they do Kishkumen."

"Gadianton robbers," Oreb said in a whisper so quiet Samuel could barely hear him.

"Yes," Samuel replied, "Gadianton robbers. We must put an end to them or they will destroy our people."

Both men fell thoughtfully silent. After a few minutes, Oreb spoke again. "What's wrong with Kim and Kib?"

Samuel thought for a moment before answering. "Their father, I think. My guess is that he has abused them badly. I wish we could help them."

"Me, too. And Kapilla—she knows her father is bad. We must find a way to help her, too."

Samuel grinned in the darkness. "She's cast quite a spell on you, little brother," he said. "You'll find a way, I'm sure. We better sleep now. Tomorrow I'll make an excuse at work that will give me a chance to slip away and talk to Moronihah. I want you to stay close to Herdon, if you can. We must not let him get suspicious."

They slept.

"Hey, you two, wake up. We have a job to do." It was Herdon's raspy voice. His baneful assignment had him in an especially jaunty mood.

They crawled from the verminous bed. Samuel scratched at the lice he was sure had found themselves a new residence when he saw Herdon digging at his head. Oreb scratched, too.

Breakfast was ready, but only Kapilla and her emaciated mother joined the men for large bowls of pasty pottage. The boys must still be asleep, Samuel thought to himself. The meal was finished quickly, with no conversation to lighten his mood.

Herdon rose. "I'm going after Javis," he announced. "I'll be right back."

Samuel nodded and rose from the table. He wandered outside where he soon discovered the twins in a foul, rat-infested shed out back. They were awake. He sat down beside them on the floor and spoke soft, reassuring words to them. Their eyes were big and focused on his face. There was apprehension evident in their pale depths. He put his strong arms around their shoulders and continued to speak quietly of the clear morning and beautiful day ahead. He was not sure how much of what he said they understood, but they relaxed in his show of love, which he portrayed with his voice, his eyes, and his smile. He was sure that they had felt little of that virtue from any other man. When he stood and walked toward the house, they shyly but silently followed him.

Inside, Oreb approached Kapilla. He was mesmerized by her captivating green eyes. "Have you always lived here?" he asked.

"Where else?" she snapped.

He flinched. "I don't know. I just wondered." He gazed at her. She returned the gaze, then dropped her eyes.

"You're a beautiful girl, Kapilla," he said boldly. "Why do you stay here? You seem so unhappy."

"Where else could I go?" she snapped, her eyes dropping to the filthy floor at her feet. "I'm Herdon's daughter. Even in this part of the city people avoid me because he is my father."

"Do you want to leave?"

"Of course."

"Then I'll help you."

"Oh, sure you will!" she said doubtfully. "Look at you. You're no better than my father. It's your kind I want to get away from, but can't."

Oreb's heart ached for her. He yearned to tell her who he really was, but he couldn't—not yet. And the way he looked now, he was disgusting.

"Kapilla, give me a chance, please," he pleaded.

"Then you'd think you owned me. I will belong to no man the way my mother belongs to my father. Anyway, I won't leave without Kim and Kib. I'm the only one in the world who cares about them. They'd die if I wasn't here."

Samuel entered as she spoke. Kapilla turned and, seeing the two boys trailing him, held out her arms. They rushed to her, and Oreb saw in her eyes a light that wasn't there a moment ago. She kissed them lightly and led them into the next room. Samuel and Oreb followed.

Kapilla's insipid mother was nowhere to be seen, so she spooned out some of the pottage for her brothers. Before they had finished their breakfast, Herdon stomped in, followed by his shriveled little shadow, Javis.

"Get them out of here, girl," he growled. "We have important business to discuss."

Meekly, she ushered the boys from the room as a mother hen might gather her chicks about her and lead them to safety. From the doorway she glanced back at Oreb. He smiled. She frowned and left.

"When we get this job done, Oran," Herdon said to Oreb, his ugly teeth and glaring gaps exposed in a wide grin, "you may marry her. But you have to take the idiots, too." He laughed heartily, spewing foul spray in Oreb's direction.

Oreb grinned and said, "She's very pretty."

"I mean it. She's yours if you want her, but the boys go too. I couldn't tolerate them around if she was gone."

Suddenly, Kapilla reappeared in a storm. "Father, you have no right!" she shrieked. "I'll never marry any friend of yours!" In a flurry she was gone, whipping up the stale air as she left. Oreb heard her call the boys and a moment later they left the house.

"Offer still holds, Oran," Herdon chuckled. "Now, about our assignment. The four of us are in this together, but I'll do the job itself," he said with relish. "The rest of you will help me set it up. We have a week. I want to get it done sooner than that."

"What can I do?" the pitiful Javis asked, slobbering in his excitement.

"I'm coming to that, Javis," Herdon snapped.

"Aren't we going to work today?" Samuel asked.

"Hadn't planned to."

"We better make things look normal, hadn't we?"

"Guess you're right, Sarl. Tell you what. You go to work and tell them the rest of us are sick—ate spoiled meat or something. Oran, you go see if you can learn where Pacumeni will be in two nights," Herdon ordered.

"How do I do that?" he asked.

"I don't know, just do it! Or can't you handle it?"

"I'll handle it," Oreb vowed meekly.

"Good. Javis, you see if Captain Moronihah is in the city. We don't want him messing things up for us. He's close friends with Pacumeni, I hear."

"I'll do it," Javis said cheerfully. "What are you going to do today?"

"Sharpen my sword and think. I don't want anything to go wrong. This is my chance to prove myself to the brotherhood." He smirked, pulling at his beard with one sordid hand while scratching his greasy head with the other.

Javis, Samuel, and Oreb left Herdon's house together. They hurried, side by side, for a short distance, then Samuel said, "I've got to get to the work site." He winked at Oreb and turned down the street that led to the stables.

Samuel made the excuses for the others, feigning sick himself. "You better go home, too," the foreman said. "You're no good to me in your condition."

He didn't argue, but left slowly, dragging his feet and holding his belly. As soon as he was out of sight he began to run. He was an excellent runner and soon spotted Oreb who was now alone. He overtook him quickly. "When did Javis leave you?" he asked.

"Just a few minutes ago. He's going to go by the headquarters of the army. How are you going to talk to Captain Moronihah without Javis seeing you?"

"I'll try to catch up and follow him, then I'll figure something out. Oreb, you go right to Pacumeni and warn him. Establish a place where he'll be in two nights and tell him I'll have Captain Moronihah contact him. Maybe they can set a trap for Herdon."

Samuel soon spotted Javis. He was plodding along slowly, stopping every few minutes to wipe his forehead and look nervously behind him. The sun cast blistering rays over the city. By noon it would be almost unbearable. Samuel followed Javis at a discreet distance. Javis walked right to the large stone headquarters building and conversed with a guard that stood beside the massive entrance. After a minute he turned and walked away, passing Samuel who had slipped behind the trunk of a giant palm tree. Samuel could only hope he was going home now. After Javis had disappeared around a street corner, Samuel headed for the large door. He identified himself to the guard who sent for Moronihah's aide.

"Hey, I can't just stand around out here. I might be seen by someone who would . . ." Samuel started to protest when told he would have to wait.

The guard cut him off. "You don't look like any friend of Moronihah's to me. You'll wait right here like I say!"

Nervously, Samuel did as he was told, conscious of how ragged and filthy he was. Suddenly, he observed a figure coming their way. From the size of the man and his choppy stride he was sure it was Javis. Samuel bolted past the guard and ran inside.

"Hey, get back here!" the guard called as he pursued him.

Inside the building there were long corridors. The guard's shouts blended with their echoing footsteps. Moronihah and the prophet Helaman appeared in the corridor and Samuel nearly collided with them. The guard grabbed Samuel roughly and blurted, "I'm sorry, Captain, he just bolted past me. I'll . . ."

Moronihah cut him off with a smile. "It's all right. I'll take care of him. How are you, Sam? My, but you do look bad . . . and smell even worse."

The guard, red-faced, backed quietly away. Moronihah stopped him and said, "Well done, soldier. Anyone would have thought this man was a bad one." Turning to Samuel, he asked, "What's on your mind, my friend?"

"One of them is outside. He knows me."

"One of who?" Helaman asked.

"The secret brotherhood. Those responsible for the death of Pahoran."

Moronihah's broad face grew dark. "Describe him."

Samuel did.

Moronihah turned to the guard. "Don't let that man enter."

"He may be the same one who was here earlier, sir," the guard volunteered. "He inquired about you."

"Very well. Return to your post."

"Yes, sir," the young guard said and hurried back outside.

"You infiltrated them, then?" the chief captain asked after escorting Samuel and Helaman into his private quarters. "I was just explaining to Helaman what you and Oreb are doing. I was getting worried. It's been several days . . ."

"Yes, we are in," Samuel interrupted with enthusiasm.

"Be very careful, Samuel," Helaman said with a frown. "You have selected dangerous company to keep."

"Yes, but I can handle it," he said confidently.

Helaman cast Moronihah a doubtful look then asked, "Who killed Pahoran?"

"I don't know. They won't even allow the members of their secret society to talk about it to each other, but I think it was Kishkumen. He's the leader of the band, although I think a powerful and evil man named Gadianton would like to be."

"What else have you learned?" Moronihah asked.

"They plan to murder Pacumeni."

Moronihah shot to his feet, his blue eyes blazing with anger. "When? Where?" he demanded.

"In two nights. Oreb is meeting with the chief judge right now, I hope. He was to find where he would be that night. Herdon was assigned to be in charge of the execution. Oreb, Javis, and I were ordered to help him."

"Javis?"

"The man outside."

"We must act quickly," Moronihah said.

"Men, do not underestimate the power of our adversary," Helaman cautioned.

"I have an idea that will work fine," Samuel said and told them of his idea of a trap.

"I'll go now and meet Pacumeni," Moronihah responded. "You leave by the back way. You've done us a great service."

"And remember who you are dealing with, Sam," Helaman cautioned. "We don't want anyone hurt."

"Oreb and I can handle it," Samuel said. "And we will be careful."

Helaman placed a hand on his shoulder. "May the Lord go with you."

After leaving by the back, Samuel circled the building and spotted Javis several hundred feet down the street, plodding slowly along again. He followed him. Javis went directly to Herdon's house.

Javis was only inside a moment before he came out—alone. Samuel wondered where Herdon was. Maybe he was still inside, but Javis would surely have stayed in there longer if his friend was at home.

Remembering the repeated warnings of the prophet, Samuel left in search of Oreb. He was relieved when he spotted him a few minutes later.

The streets were nearly abandoned in the oppressive heat of the day. Samuel watched to be sure Oreb wasn't being followed and then joined him.

"How did it go?" he asked.

"Just fine, Sam. Pacumeni is most grateful. He'll meet with Moronihah."

"Good." Samuel paused as some strangers passed by. "I'm worried, Oreb."

His younger brother gave him a searching look before asking, "Why?"

"Javis doubled back on me and almost caught me going in to see Moronihah. In fact, he may have recognized me. I followed him back to Herdon's, but I don't believe he was home."

"We'll just have to be careful," Oreb said with a casual grin. "I'll go back first. You come later," he suggested.

Samuel hid and watched Oreb enter Herdon's house a few minutes later. He came back out after about thirty minutes and headed down the street. Samuel joined him after he had gone several blocks.

"Was anyone there?" Samuel asked.

"Yes, but not Herdon. Kapilla said he left just after we did and she hasn't seen him since."

Samuel was thoughtful for a few minutes. Finally, he said, "Let's be there when he gets home."

They waited too long. Herdon entered the house as they came into view late that afternoon. They hid in an abandoned house a block away for a half-hour before entering Herdon's home together just minutes after Javis went in. Herdon and Javis were in the kitchen talking. Kapilla lifted her hand when the brothers entered. They stopped. Fear filled her pale green eyes, but a smile brushed across her face. She stepped near and whispered, "Father followed you, Oran. You aren't really one of them, are you?"

Samuel and Oreb looked at each other in alarm. Samuel answered for Oreb. "No," he whispered, "but you mustn't let them know that. We'll be very careful."

"Please do," she answered urgently, her eyes glued to Oreb's handsome face.

His heart pounding, Samuel entered the kitchen. Oreb stood beside Kapilla for a moment, boldly grabbed her hand and squeezed, then followed Samuel.

"Well, there you are. Come sit down," Herdon said amiably. "How did it go, Oran?"

"Just fine," he said. "Pacumeni will be in the palace the next two nights. He has moved in there already." Samuel hoped Herdon didn't detect the slight quiver in Oreb's voice.

"Good. This shouldn't be too difficult, should it? Have a good day at work, Sarl?"

"No," Samuel responded, his eyes locked with Herdon's. "There isn't such a thing as a good day at a rotten job in sultry weather." Herdon and Javis both chuckled. They began to quietly discuss their plans. The fact that his family was in an adjacent room didn't seem to bother Herdon. Samuel guessed that he figured they were so afraid of him that they wouldn't dare say anything if they heard something they shouldn't.

"I've been sitting here all day, thinking," Herdon lied. "Now, here's what we'll do . . ."

Samuel and Oreb exchanged glances, then sat back on the rough bench, leaning against the dusty rock walls of the old house and listened. Samuel tried to appear interested in every word, but was distracted by nagging doubts and the repeated cautions of Helaman.

CHAPTER 4

Zera's sobbing awoke Gadoni with a start. the sun was already high in the cloudless sky. He had not meant to sleep so long. Exhaustion had overcome him and he had bedded his family down for a short rest. He wondered how long he would have slept if Zera hadn't started crying from the pain of her broken leg.

Gadoni hastily awoke the rest of the family. While Laishita nursed little Enos, he gave them a quick breakfast of dry fry-bread and jerky. While they choked it down, he began loading the black horse.

He feared that he had given the ferocious band, led by Laman, time to about catch them. Gadoni was fuming at himself for being so careless. Laman had already demonstrated that he would show them no mercy.

"I'm sorry!" he snapped later when Limre complained that they were going too fast. "We slept too long. We can't afford to take our time or rest long until we have reached the safety of the Nephite lands. If I could be sure when we have lost Laman . . ."

"Gadoni," Laishita interjected calmly, "we'll be okay now. I'm sure Laman has turned back."

"What makes you so sure of that?"

"I just feel it. We can go a little easier now."

So confident were her words that Gadoni slowed the pace. He had learned never to argue when Laishita felt something. She had proven over the years to be amazingly accurate. He had discovered since joining the Church that most righteous women were more in tune with the Spirit than their husbands when it came to matters of the family. Laishita was humble and he knew that her feelings were influenced by the Lord. She had often been the source of his inspiration. So he listened now and felt relief.

They traveled slowly for several days. High in the wilderness mountains, they began a steep descent early one afternoon. The forest had thinned out as they gained altitude, and the ground was a maze of hard, jagged rocks. The climb had been gentle, but the path ahead was narrow and descended rapidly; it was treacherous.

Gadoni carried Zera and led his spirited stallion. Limre and Laishita followed on foot. Enos was bound on his mother's back. "Keep your eyes on the trail, Limre," Gadoni called back. "You'll get dizzy if you look over the edge."

"Why can't I ride, Father?" Limre asked.

"Because your feet are more sure here than the horse's. Now, please be silent and concentrate on where you're going."

Gadoni had learned to use horses from Samuel. Many Nephites used them to pull chariots and carriages as well as for riding. The Lamanites, on the other hand, used them much less.

Latoni, Samuel's father, was a farrier by trade. He shod many of the Nephites' horses. Samuel had spent his younger years caring for the horses his father worked with. He had grown to love and respect the powerful animals. Gadoni had come to share that respect.

Samuel had emphasized the shortcomings of horses as well, though. Much of the land was not conducive to travel by horseback and those who depended on them soon learned to avoid those areas. Swampy jungles were often impossible for horses to travel through. Steep, rocky mountainsides and narrow trails were good to avoid, if possible, but if not they required caution.

Gadoni thought about that as he led his horse down just such terrain. Looking ahead, he could see no improvement for several hundred feet.

He noticed with concern that the blue sky had turned to gray. Gadoni's worries increased when a cool drop of rain gently pecked his bare arm. He looked up. Dark, heavily saturated clouds loomed about the towering peaks. He was only too familiar with the serpentine nature of the storms those kinds of clouds could deliver.

"It's going to rain," he shouted to his family, not wanting to alarm them but hoping to stress the need for more caution should the rocky trail become wet and slick. "Go very slowly and hug the edge of the mountain," he urged.

He had barely mouthed his warning when a powerful lightning bolt tore the bottom from the clouds and the rain fell in a thunderous downpour.

Within seconds the storm unleashed its full fury. Sheets of water were driven against the weary travelers by a savage wind. Gadoni stopped and leaned against the cold rock, sheltering Zera the best he could with his own body.

The horse whinnied in terror as lightning ripped through the pouring rain. Gadoni held tight with one hand to the lead rope. Suddenly, large rocks, loosened by a lightning strike above, began to fall. They bounced on the narrow trail just ahead of them, startling the frightened animal. With a loud neigh, he reared, jerking the rope from Gadoni's clenched fist.

Screams filtered through the clamor of the storm as the dark figure of the stallion vanished over the edge of the trail. The screaming continued. Gadoni inched his way back up the slippery trail, holding fast to Zera. He found Laishita on her knees, anguished cries pouring from her without a break. Limre stood near, swaying dangerously in the blowing rain, also screaming at the top of her lungs.

Gadoni's heart jumped into his throat when he saw Laishita's empty back. "Where's Enos!?" he shouted.

She looked up, her face terror stricken, and pointed over the edge of the mountain. The screaming intensified. The most chilling horror Gadoni had ever known clutched his chest, nearly wringing the breath from him. Clinging tighter to Zera, he crawled closer.

Laishita lifted her tortured face and shouted, nearly choking on the words, "The horse knocked me down. I dropped him." Her terrified wailing resumed.

Gadoni pictured her removing the precious infant from her back to shelter him with her body. When the horse reared, it must have knocked both her and Limre against the wall of the trail. He moaned in anguish as he envisioned his little son slipping from his mother's arms and tumbling down the deadly mountainside after the horse.

Gadoni prayed.

He felt as though a chunk of heart had been torn from his chest and hurled down the steep mountain. Only God could bring it back. His tears mixed with Laishita's and, diluted by the rushing rainwater, flowed over the mountainside as if in search of their son.

As suddenly as it had begun, the storm passed. Gadoni peered over the edge of the rain-slick trail. Below, he spotted the horse lodged against the mountainside by a tiny, twisted juniper tree that grew at the edge of a narrow, sloping ledge. It was dead, its neck twisted in grotesque fashion beneath its muddy body.

Several small stones had landed on the horse and were resting against the side of the mountain. One of them stirred. With a start, Gadoni realized it was Enos, muddy, but alive. Laishita shrieked, "Get him, Gadoni! He's alive!"

Without a thought for his own safety, Gadoni started down. Inch by inch he lowered himself down the almost vertical incline. His fingers bled as they dug for each small handhold. His leather sandals kept slipping as he put his weight on them, unsure of the wet rocks his feet were searching out.

Each time a foot would slip, his fingers tightened on their scant handhold and he would hold himself in place until his foot found something solid. Enos cried as his father descended imperceptibly toward him. For Laishita, time was frozen. Terror filled her heart as she waited and prayed, her little girls whimpering and clinging to her arms.

Gadoni finally reached the dead stallion. Tentatively, he placed one foot on it, then the other. It shifted slightly, the little tree bending further under the increased weight. He reached for Enos with one hand while holding firmly to a small bush with the other.

His bleeding fingers gripped the sodden leather wrapping the child was clothed in and lifted. As he did so, the horse's body slipped farther, bending the small juniper until it was almost horizontal. Gadoni swiftly pulled the child to him and placed one foot onto a small outcrop of solid rock. No sooner did he shift his weight to that foot than the tree snapped and, with a sickening roar, the dead horse, packed with all their provisions and weapons except their knives, plunged to the bottom of the ravine.

For a breathtaking moment, Gadoni swayed perilously, only one foot planted and one hand clinging to a bush. His other foot searched for and finally found a solid place to rest and he leaned into the rock face of the mountain and rested, holding tightly to his precious bundle.

Several minutes passed during which Gadoni secured his hold on his infant son. After his aching body had rested he finally found the strength to call out to Laishita, who was waiting and praying thirty feet above.

"I can't climb and hold him," he shouted. "You must make a rope and lower it to me."

"From what?" she called down, her voice full of desperation.

"The cloth Enos was bound to your back in. Tear it in strips. Tear clothing too, if you need to, but be quick about it!"

The sun broke through the clouds and steam rose like ghoulish fog from the rocks as they dried. Laishita worked feverishly, cutting the cloth into strips with her small knife. Finally completed, she lowered one end to Gadoni. It was several feet short. "Add to it!" he called again as his legs, feet, and hands screamed for relief—a change of position.

Laishita pulled the makeshift rope back up and added strips cut from the bottom of her long skirt. This time it reached Gadoni. He repositioned his feet ever so slightly and, leaning hard against the steep slope, let go of his handhold with his left hand. He balanced there precariously for several seconds.

Using extreme care and exercising all the patience he could muster, Gadoni secured the end of the dangling rope around the infant's chest, beneath his little arms. That accomplished, he called out again. "Pull slowly. We mustn't bounce him against the rocks. Keep him just above my head and I will follow."

Gadoni selected a handhold for his left hand again and slowly lifted the child with his right while Laishita pulled. "Okay, that's enough for now!" he shouted above the child's incessant crying.

With Enos pressed against the rock, his weight born entirely by Laishita, Gadoni groped for another handhold with his right hand. The rocks were drying rapidly in the bright sunlight and his handholds were more secure. He inched his way up until his head was even with the crying child again. Then, while his wife pulled, he steadied the cherished bundle. For thirty strenuous minutes they worked until Laishita safely pulled the baby over the edge of the trail.

While Laishita nursed and calmed her son, Gadoni, using the last of his taxed strength, pulled himself back onto the trail and collapsed. While he rested, he thanked God for miraculously preserving the life of his son. After examining Enos and finding only a few bruises and scratches, the little family again worked their way down the steep, narrow trail. Not until they were safely down from the mountain and into the immense rain-forest below did anyone mention hunger.

"What can I have to eat, Father?" Zera asked.

"I'll find something," he assured her.

Limre chipped in. "What can you find here, Father? You don't have a bow or any arrows. You can't shoot an animal."

"Roots," he said, smiling at the anticipated frown.

"Ugh," both girls chimed in unison.

"When you get hungry enough, you'll be glad for anything," Gadoni predicted.

They continued downward through the gently sloping forest. When they stopped to rest in a grassy clearing, Gadoni went in search of something to ease their pangs of hunger. He found several plants that had non-poisonous, nourishing roots. He gathered an ample supply.

His daughters stuck their delicate noses in the air and declined to eat, so he and Laishita had an unsavory, but life-sustaining meal by themselves before continuing on. The girls complained constantly about their empty stomachs and finally agreed to try a root. They pulled faces and spat, but managed to choke enough down to give them some strength.

When darkness approached, the little family made camp for the night. Gadoni started a fire by vigorously rubbing two sticks together. For their evening meal, they ate more roots, roasted over the fire, making them more palatable.

Only Limre got a good night's rest. Zera and Enos kept Gadoni and Laishita awake most of the night as they cried from the pain caused by their accidents. Finally, as a lurid dawn made its appearance through the dense green foliage overhead, exhaustion overtook the children and they slept.

Gadoni smiled at his wife and said, "Let's sleep. We're in no hurry now anyway. What we need most is rest."

She returned his smile, nodded, and closed her dark eyes. It was noon before they stirred again. They munched on more roasted roots, then Gadoni fashioned a makeshift spear using a straight stick and his knife and went in search of small game. He did not come back empty handed and they enjoyed a nourishing meal of roasted rabbit before continuing on their journey.

CHAPTER 5

On the surface, there was nothing to indicate that Herdon was planning anything beyond the murder of the chief judge, but Kapilla's warning and Helaman's caution kept running through Samuel's mind. Somehow, he knew that he and Oreb were in danger.

They had spent the night in Herdon's house again and then worked the next day. That night, Herdon ordered a trial run. "We'll walk through our assignments tonight," he said. "I want to be positive we each are very sure of our part in this. I don't want anything to go wrong."

Samuel's mind raced. There had been nothing about any trial run when Herdon laid out his plan the night before. What was he up to? Did he plan to slay Pacumeni tonight? Or, did he plan to do something to Oreb and him? Somehow, Samuel was certain that one or the other, if not both, was the case. Pacumeni must be warned, for he and Moronihah were expecting the attempt the following night. And how could he and Oreb protect themselves if they were targets? He ran Herdon's plan through his mind and his uneasiness grew—he and Oreb would be split up. But, he reminded himself, he had handled dangerous situations before, and he could do it again.

Herdon was still speaking, eyeing Samuel suspiciously. "Oran, you and Javis are to cover the back of the chief judge's palace. Do not allow anyone to enter the door there, and watch for anyone who tries to leave that way, too. If you see someone leave in the middle of the night, you are to assume I was seen and they must be killed. You two will do that."

He turned to Samuel.

"Sarl, you'll be with me. Your job is to stop anyone who might pursue me after I have finished my task. There must be no living witnesses. Tonight we'll do everything, including entering the palace, but we'll turn back after I have done that. We want to learn the layout of the palace and see if anyone comes or goes that time of night and how heavily guarded it is."

There was a long pause. No one spoke. Samuel was worried. Things just did not fit. He glanced at his brother. Oreb was pale and sober.

"Very well, then. We'll leave in the middle of the night. Each of you get a few hours sleep first," Herdon urged, his purple lips curled into an ugly half-smile beneath his squashed nose.

Samuel shuddered, but was grateful for the few hours. It gave him a chance to whisper some instructions to Oreb. They didn't sleep, but pretended to be dozing when Herdon entered the room to awaken them.

"Let's go, boys," he said jovially.

The brothers sat up, rubbing their eyes and acting groggy. "Already?" Samuel asked.

"Yes, we haven't time to spare. Outside, quickly. Javis is waiting," Herdon urged.

Not another word was uttered until the four men were well away from the house, walking in a tight group under a partly cloudy, very dark sky. "Everybody got his knife?" Herdon asked.

There were mumbled assents. Each man wore a leather scabbard containing a long, razor sharp knife on his belt. These were the only weapons they would carry either night, Herdon had ordered.

"Are you all clear on what you're to do?" Herdon asked.

Mumbles again. Herdon walked faster. Samuel and Oreb trailed a little way behind Javis who was marching after Herdon like a good soldier.

"Do you smell anything?" Samuel whispered to Oreb.

"Yes, I smell guava blossoms," Oreb whispered in response.

"Not that kind of smell!" Samuel snickered, but he couldn't help but notice the sweet fragrances of the night. He smiled in spite of himself.

Oreb caught on. "Yes, I think those two are too cheerful."

"That's what I . . ."

"Hey, shut up, you two!" Herdon interrupted. "We've got to have complete silence." His raspy voice was anything but silent, but Samuel and Oreb ceased whispering.

The night grew more ominous. The air was heavy and humid, carrying the threat of storm, but the darkness never impeded the fast pace Herdon set. He led them right down the middle of the deserted streets. Not until they had reached the area where the palace of the chief judge was located did they slow down.

Herdon veered off the street and began a stealthy approach the last few blocks. The residence loomed large in the night, lit by brightly flickering torches at the corners which cast eerie shadows through the large, plush gardens surrounding it. Ducking as they ran, Oreb and Javis entered the grounds to the left and disappeared, heading toward the back.

Herdon and Samuel waited in the shadows across the street until the others had been allowed sufficient time to reach their positions. Herdon signaled for Samuel to follow and darted across the empty street and entered the palace grounds to the right.

Samuel dropped to his knees and crawled past aromatic flower beds, staying close to the surrounding shrubbery, hidden from the lone sentinel at the front entrance by heavy shadows and dense foliage. From the position he selected, Samuel watched Herdon scale the wall by climbing large vines that reached clear to the roof and enter through a high window.

As soon as Herdon disappeared inside, Samuel, his heart pounding and palms sweaty, approached the guard, holding one hand above his head, the other signaling the guard to remain silent. The guard held a long, razor sharp spear which he pointed menacingly toward Samuel as he approached.

He allowed Samuel to get close enough to whisper, "I am Samuel. I've come to warn Judge Pacumeni that the attempt on his life by the robbers that was planned for tomorrow night has been changed. An assassin is in the palace. He entered by a window around there," he said, pointing urgently.

The guard reacted swiftly. "What's your code name?"

"Sarl."

"I'm Larcus. Follow me," he ordered as he whirled and entered the spacious palace. He alerted other guards who spread rapidly through the palace in search of the deadly intruder.

"Is Pacumeni here?" Samuel asked as he followed Larcus.

"No. He's in hiding. We feared something like this might happen." Samuel's heart beat slower and he breathed a sigh of relief. The judge was safe. Now, Herdon must be captured. Shouting rang out from far back in the palace. Samuel and Larcus dashed that way.

By the time they arrived in Pacumeni's sleeping room, the fight was over. Herdon was gone, but a young guard lay mortally wounded on the polished stone floor, a dark red pool mushrooming around his body.

"Quickly," Larcus shouted, "Check the windows and doors. After him!"

Samuel made a mad dash for the rear of the palace while others flew in all directions. He knew the way, having been in the palace many times. "Oreb!" he shouted as he burst through the doorway.

"Here, Sam!" his brother cried. He spotted him in a desperate struggle with two shadowy figures in the garden.

Samuel charged down the broad stairway, taking three and four steps at a leap. Someone appeared from a grove of fruit trees to his right, wielding a long sword and shouting obscenities. Samuel's adrenaline flowed and he exploded out of the reach of his angry pursuer.

He grabbed the first figure he came to in the flickering light and, with a savage thrust, threw the scrawny man into the path of the robber to his rear. Both men fell, cursing, in a heap. Samuel struck a blow at Oreb's other foe with his knife. The robber collapsed at their feet.

Oreb and Samuel spun in unison to face the two Samuel had left sprawling. There were three! In the dim light of the torches, Samuel recognized the twisted, angry face of Herdon, who had joined the others. For a fleeting moment Samuel wondered where he got the sword he was wielding. He also recognized the faces of Javis and Gadianton, who were coming at them.

Gadianton swung his sword, catching Samuel a glancing blow to the left shoulder as he tried in vain to ward if off with his knife. Herdon tried to duck in under Gadianton, but Oreb kicked savagely, splitting his lip and snapping his head back violently.

Gadianton thrust again with savage force. Oreb grunted and fell. At that moment, shouts arose as Larcus led the other guards in a mad charge down the stone path toward the fighting men.

Herdon, who was holding his bleeding mouth and kneeling in pain on the ground, saw the approaching guards. "Run!" he screamed and, struggling to his feet, set the cowardly example.

Gadianton and Javis followed swiftly. Several guards pursed them, but soon returned, having lost them in the ebony night that prevailed beyond the palace gardens.

"Oreb," Samuel moaned softly, kneeling beside his fallen brother. He paid no heed to the blood that oozed from the nasty, gaping cut on his own shoulder as he regarded the ashen form of Oreb. "Can you hear me, Oreb?"

No response.

"Help me get him inside," Samuel said in a cracking voice to Larcus, who was also kneeling nearby, checking the one robber who had not fled.

"This one's dead," Larcus said without emotion as he moved to help Samuel pick up his stricken brother.

They laid Oreb on a clean bed in the palace. Samuel was relieved to find that his brother was still breathing, although his breaths were shallow and labored. He tore open Oreb's vest and gasped. The sword of Gadianton had pierced deeply into his stomach, turning the skin near the wound a sticky crimson.

Servants gathered and began to clean and dress the wound, applying healing herbs. Samuel prayed silently for his gallant young brother, refusing to be treated himself until all that could be done for Oreb had been done.

The pale face and ominous stillness of his young body brought vivid memories from the deep reservoirs of Samuel's mind. Oreb had always been active and full of mischief. He was frequently running brashly off on some reckless venture or another. Many happy times they had spent together: Samuel, the big brother who could do no wrong, and Oreb, the little one, always trying to mimic him.

Samuel was angry with himself for letting Oreb receive such a serious injury. He wished he had insisted on him staying in Gilead—as if Oreb would have agreed to that.

"Sam," the strong, clear voice of Captain Moronihah echoed in the room. "What went wrong? I thought you said tomorrow night."

"I did," Samuel answered softly, rising to face his friend. "They were on to us—changed their plans."

"Who's hurt?" Captain Moronihah asked, pointing toward the bed surrounded with bustling Nephite women.

"Oreb." Samuel could barely force out the name. "Gadianton stabbed him with a sword."

"How bad is it?" the chief captain asked, concern creasing his broad face.

"Real bad," Samuel said, sinking to the floor by the bed.

"Sam! You're wounded too!" Moronihah exclaimed. "You're drenched in blood and your shoulder is bleeding badly."

"I'm okay."

"Someone, dress this man's wound," Moronihah ordered in a voice that was accustomed to obedience.

Two servants left Oreb's bedside and helped Samuel to a woven chair and began to clean the blood from his wound. They hadn't finished when the chief judge strode in, surrounded by a dozen heavily armed men.

Again, Samuel had to explain what happened. Pacumeni's face grew dark as Samuel's story unfolded. "They'll be after your brother and you in earnest now, Sam. You can identify them. They are determined and ruthless men and care none for the feelings or welfare of others," he said with an intensity Samuel had never felt from him before.

"That's true, I'm afraid," Moronihah said solemnly. "Their master is Satan. Their secret combinations were first given to Cain before he slew his brother, Abel. As long as men's lives are filled with greed and sin, they'll be susceptible to Satan's influence and will be his followers. We're not engaged in combat with mere men, but with the very author of sin himself."

Samuel listened intently to his two great friends, then said solemnly, "I'm not through with them. I'll hunt them down and destroy them if I can. And if Oreb lives, he'll be just as angry and determined as I am."

"Now Sam, you two have done enough. Remember what Helaman said. The danger now is even greater. You need to rest and be healed of the wounds of tonight's battle. You'll be safely guarded here in the palace. I'll triple the guard and provide you with the best care available until you are both well, then you better find sanctuary somewhere far away until we bring these men to justice," Chief Judge Pacumeni said.

"If Oreb . . ." Samuel began.

"No *if*, Sam," Moronihah interrupted. "He will be on his feet in no time," he said confidently. "Now, you rest, my friend."

"I'll have the servants prepare a room," Pacumeni offered.

"Thank you. However, I do need a favor. Near Herdon's house are some old stables. Oreb and I stored our clothes and weapons there. Would you send someone for them?" Samuel asked.

"I'll dispatch men at once," Pacumeni promised.

* * *

Herdon stumbled into his house, caked with dry blood and mud. The blood was mostly his own from his lip and a few superficial wounds he had received that night. The mud was from stumbling and falling repeatedly on his speedy flight through the city. Rain had come following the short battle at the palace. Herdon, in trying to avoid the paved roadways for fear of being apprehended, had run blindly through gardens, stables, and backyards in his desperate flight home.

Safe there now, he sat fuming. He vowed to get his revenge against Samuel, for he was sure that was who he was. Oran had called him by name. Oran, whoever he was, had already received his payback for breaking the oath of the brotherhood—Gadianton himself had dealt with Oran.

Kapilla entered the room, rubbing the sleep from her pale eyes, as the shrill whistle and constant chirping of dozens of birds announced the end of the storm and the dawn of a new day. "Father, what happened to you? Where have you been?" she cried in shock as she surveyed her father's muddy, bloody clothes. Her eyes drifted to the blood stained knife and sword he had hung on a peg in the corner of the dimly lit room.

"None of your business, but Oran . . ." he sneered.

"What of Oran?" Kapilla interrupted in a rising voice. "Where is he? What have you done?"

"He won't be coming calling, I can promise you that," he said with a chuckle. "Not with a sword clear through him!"

"Father, did you . . . ?"

"No, but someone did."

"Who?" she screamed.

"Well, if you must know, he was killed by one of the palace guards, my fair daughter," he said with contempt on his dirty, bearded face. "Now, get out of my sight!"

Kapilla rushed for the door, her hands over her face, great sobs racking her slender body.

"Kapilla!" Herdon shouted.

She stopped.

"Fix me some breakfast!"

"But you just said . . ."

"Fix me some breakfast. You hear me, girl?" he shouted again. "I've had a hard night and I'm hungry."

Just then, Herdon's wife came in, her frail body hunched over like someone twice her age. Her sad eyes blinked rapidly. "What's all the shouting about?" she asked, her voice low. Kapilla brushed by her and out of the room. The frail woman gasped. "Herdon, what happened to you? Are you hurt?"

She stepped toward him, but he came to his feet, blind with fury at Kapilla. His wife reached for him, but he seemed not to recognize her and with a savage thrust, he threw her against the stone wall and began screaming at Kapilla to return.

Kapilla returned—with a knife in her hand. "Father, you stay away from me. You'll never do to me what you did to Kim and . . ." Her words caught in her throat when her eyes fell upon her frail mother, lying inert on the hard floor. The knife dropped and she shoved her way past Herdon and knelt, cradling her mother's bleeding head tenderly in her arms.

Herdon, realizing what he had done, backed from the room, feeling no remorse, but sick of the sight of any of his family. Mumbling his contempt for a weak wife, idiot sons, and disobedient daughter, he left the house without a backward glance.

"Father," Kapilla said.

When there was no response, she looked up to discover him missing. She needed help. In a panic, she lowered her mother's head to the floor and ran across the street to the home of Javis. She pounded at the door. Javis' wife finally appeared.

She was a stout woman, with strong, hairy arms and a huge bosom. "What is it Kapilla?" she asked in a voice that was almost gentle. "Is something wrong?"

"Yes, it's mother. Father threw her down. Would you and Javis please come help me?" she pleaded, her chest constricted with fear.

"Certainly, I'll come, but as for that weasel, Javis, he's been gone all night. I don't know when he'll be home."

With a tenderness that was in stark contrast to her appearance, the wife of Javis examined Kapilla's mother. It was only a minute before she stood and faced Kapilla. Big tears streamed down her wide face. "I'm so sorry, Kapilla, but your mother is dead," she said softly.

Kapilla was stunned. She couldn't speak. She knelt by her mother's body.

"What will happen to the twins?" Javis' wife asked.

Without looking up, Kapilla choked back a sob and said, "I'll care for them."

She could contain the grief no more and let it pour from her aching soul. Kapilla had just suffered the loss of her mother . . . and Oran, the one man who had begun to mean something in her life.

CHAPTER 6

The past few days in the wilderness had taken its on Gadoni and his family. The injured children were doing fairly well, but the strain of carrying them through the rugged mountains and teeming forests and jungles was very tiring on Gadoni and Laishita. Limre complained of sore feet, tired legs, and pain from the many bruises and cuts she was accumulating from stumbling and falling as she grew weaker from the strain of hiking in the rugged terrain.

"Father," Limre said one afternoon as they rested and chewed on some fresh dried meat Gadoni had made from small game he had snared.

"What is it, Limre?" Gadoni asked.

"Are we lost?"

"No." He paused. "Well, not exactly, anyway. I know about where Manti is. I'll find it, so don't you worry."

"Where is it, Father?"

"That way," he said, pointing.

"How far?" she asked, her dark eyes searching his face.

"Well, I'm not really sure. But I think that we can be there in a couple of days, even as slow as we're going. From there it isn't a bad trip to Gilead. We can follow the Sidon River most of the way," he explained.

Two days was a good estimate. They limped into Manti shortly before dusk the second day. Gadoni located some old acquaintances from the days he served in the Nephite army. The family was welcomed with open arms and given the first adequate nourishment and rest they had received in many days.

Gadoni's Nephite friends coaxed him to stay longer in Manti, but he was anxious to return to Gilead where he hoped to find Samuel. If he and his family weren't there, Gadoni was sure Latoni would know where he could find them.

The use of a horse for the trip down the Sidon River was offered, but Gadoni refused. He was losing faith in horses and preferred to trust his own legs and strong back. Laishita agreed, so they set off again on foot.

The young family traveled slowly, feeling secure now that they were back in Nephite lands. Gadoni was carefree and relaxed, and the bubbly laughter had returned to Laishita. Gadoni hadn't seen her so cheerful since they left a year ago for the city of Nephi. Happiness like he had not known in that year returned to him.

They stopped early the second day out of Manti and set up camp in a grove of bulky trumpet trees. Monkeys chattered and entertained the children with their crazy antics among the flashy leaves of the bulky trees. Birds sang cheerful songs and scattered splashes of color through the grove as the sun set.

Malefic eyes watched!

The little family slept.

Gadoni awoke with a start. Through the heavy branches he saw a smattering of stars shining in the heavens. A gentle breeze rustled the leaves and swayed the massive branches. He shivered.

A new bow and quiver of arrows acquired in Manti lay near him. He reached with his left hand to draw them close. Without knowing why, he pulled an arrow from the quiver and fitted it on the string of the bow. It was dark and he could barely even see his hands.

A twig snapped. He jerked the string back on his bow and waited, every nerve in his body on edge. He peered in vain into the darkness. The hair stood up on the back of his neck and little bumps rose on his dark brown skin.

A dark form moved, indistinguishable from the trees except for the motion. It could be a low hanging branch swaying in the breeze. Movement again—closer this time. He had the impulse to let an arrow fly—stifled the urge, unsure of his target.

He strained to see through the mist of black, being careful to make no movement. The form moved again—in his direction. Another twig snapped. He heard breath being expelled. He thought he could make out a dim glow, as from a pair of eyes only a few feet away. They disappeared—instantly reappeared. A blink?

There was movement closer. Gadoni pulled the string a little tighter. He studied the form. It's outline became clear.

A deer.

Gadoni moved and the deer whirled and vanished. He laughed quietly, setting the bow on the ground beside him.

"Gadoni."

He jumped. "Laishita, you scared me. I thought you were asleep."

"I was but you woke me. What was that?"

"A deer."

"Gadoni!"

"Laishita, what is it!?" He felt for her in the darkness.

"Enos! He's gone!" she screamed.

"But he was right here between us."

"Mother, what's happening?" Limre cried, intense fear in her little voice.

Gadoni was searching the ground frantically with his hands. Enos was not there. "Laishita, hold the girls while I search. He must be near."

"Gadoni!"

"What now?"

"I can't find Zera either!"

Ice encased Gadoni with the cold hands of fear. His arms and legs refused to move. Terror reigned in the darkness.

Daylight found Gadoni still searching the ground near their camp sight. There was no doubt. Two separate sets of sandal tracks led away from the camp in the direction of Manti. One clear mark of the cloven hoof of a deer had been planted after the sandal tracks, right on top of one.

Gadoni set out. Limre and Laishita followed, their tears cried out, only numbness in their bodies now. The tracks veered to the right. Gadoni said, "It must be Laman and one of his men. These tracks aren't going toward Manti now."

The young father's heart was heavy. He wanted to pursue his unseen enemy and take his children back, but they were traveling much faster than he. Gadoni needed help, and Gilead wasn't far. With Laishita consenting, the three of them left the faint trail they were following and sped for Gilead, praying that Samuel would be there.

With Samuel's help, Gadoni was confident they could overtake the abductors in the wilderness. Meantime, Laishita and Limre would be safe in Gilead.

It was with relief that Gadoni spotted Samuel's son, Jath, playing in front of Latoni's blacksmith shop. "Grandfather," the boy cried with excitement, "it's Gadoni! He's coming down the street. Come see, Grandfather."

Latoni needed no coaxing. He burst from the shop as fast as his crippled leg would allow, a broad smile lighting his face.

The smile faded when he saw the grim faces of Gadoni and Laishita. "What's wrong, Gadoni?" he asked.

"They took Zera and Enos," Gadoni stated flatly.

"Who's Enos?" Latoni asked as he put his arms around the shoulders of the distraught couple.

"Our baby," Gadoni said.

"Who took them?" Latoni asked.

"My brother, Laman. They're not far ahead of us. I need Sam's help. We can overtake them," he said as Ophera burst upon them with open arms.

"Laishita. Gadoni. You're back. It's good to see you. Where . . ."

Latoni interrupted. "Gadoni's brother has stolen little Zera and their new baby boy, Enos."

Ophera gasped and took Laishita into her arms. The two young mothers sobbed quietly.

"Samuel's in Zarahemla. Oreb's with him," Latoni responded to an inquiring look from Gadoni.

Kamina had arrived and reached for Limre. Gadoni watched them silently for a moment, no emotion on his face. "Will you keep Laishita and Limre? I'll find Sam," he said decisively. "May I borrow a horse?"

Latoni looked away.

"What is it, Latoni? What haven't you told me?"

"Sam and Oreb went to search for the men that murdered our chief judge."

"Pahoran?" Gadoni asked in alarm.

"Yes. They may be hard to locate," Latoni said, turning and looking into Gadoni's worried eyes.

"I'll go. If I can't find them, I'll return and pursue my wicked brother alone," Gadoni said with resolve.

"It's almost dark. Come rest and eat first," Latoni invited.

"I can't wait."

"Well, come eat at least."

Gadoni reluctantly agreed. Only the gnawing in his stomach and the weakness of his limbs allowed him to be persuaded. He wolfed his food down, kissed his frightened wife and daughter, mounted the horse Latoni had waiting, and rode hard in the direction of Zarahemla.

It was the middle of another dark night when he entered the walls of the Nephite capital. No sentries were at the gate, and he rode into the city unhindered. He went on until he pulled his lathered horse to a stop in front of the large stone building that served as the army headquarters.

The guards there greeted Gadoni coldly. "I am a friend of Captain Moronihah. I must see him at once. It is a matter of the utmost urgency. I am looking for my friend Samuel. The captain may know where I can find him."

The two guards lowered their swords and looked at each other in the soft flickering light of a pair of glowing torches. They softened. "We cannot awaken the chief captain, but we'll tell him you're here when he arises at sun-up. You may wait," the older of the two said.

Gadoni protested the delay, but to no avail. Finally he said, "I'll rest here."

His body exhausted, he relaxed against the stone wall and was asleep instantly. One of the guards awoke him a few hours later. "The chief captain will see you now," he was told.

The sun was up and shining brightly in Gadoni's eyes. He bounded to his feet, shaking the drowsiness off and following the guard through the large doors. Inside, the halls echoed with the sound of early morning activity. Soldiers were going everywhere, like a swarm of bees. The guard stopped at a solid wooden door and tapped with the bronze handle of his sword.

The guard shoved the heavy door open. Inside, several soldiers were seated around a large table. One of them stood and greeted Gadoni warmly.

"How good to see you again, Gadoni," Moronihah said sincerely, embracing the sturdy Lamanite. "You're a welcome sight to behold. We have just been discussing the Lamanites. Some believe they are preparing to attack again. You must have just returned from the Land of Nephi. Maybe you can help us."

"That's right. I'm here because I fled when my brother pressed me to join their army. I refused and they seek my life," Gadoni said.

"Then they are planning an attack," Moronihah said more than asked, his wide-set eyes narrowing.

"Yes, sir, but I don't know when."

"Do you think it'll be soon?"

"I don't think so. They have barely begun to amass an army again. But I'm not sure," Gadoni said, telling them as much as he knew.

Every eye in the room was on him. He was nervous, but anxious to get to the question at hand—the whereabouts of Samuel and Oreb. Moronihah spoke again. "Thank you for your help. I'm sorry. You must have something else to talk to me about. We will discuss this later," he said to his men. "Gadoni, do you wish to speak with me privately?"

"Please."

Gadoni followed Moronihah into an adjoining room. "I'm looking for Sam and his brother," he blurted, fighting to control his emotions. "Do you know where they are?"

"I'll take you to them. What's happened, Gadoni? This must be more than just your brother seeking your life. You're as safe here as any of us," Moronihah said.

"Someone has stolen my two youngest children. It could only have been my brother, Laman. I'm afraid they're headed back to the city of Nephi."

"Let us go now," Moronihah said and summoned his guard.

In a few minutes they were at the palace of Chief Judge Pacumeni. Moronihah had explained to Gadoni about the fight at the palace and the injuries received by Samuel and Oreb. Gadoni was relieved to learn that Samuel was recovering very well and should be able to assist him.

"Gadoni, you're back!" Samuel exclaimed, embracing his dark-skinned friend.

"How is Oreb?" Gadoni asked, putting his own pressing concerns aside for the moment.

"He'll recover," Samuel said. "He had a close call, though. For two or three days it looked like he might die, but he's strong and determined. Would you like to see him?"

"Yes."

Gadoni followed Samuel. He found Oreb, propped up in bed with luxurious pillows. He was thin and his face was drawn, but he flashed a big smile at the sight of Gadoni. "You should have been here, Gadoni!" he exclaimed. "We had some fight."

"I wish I had been. Maybe if I'd left Nephi sooner . . ." His voice broke.

"Sam," Moronihah said, "Gadoni needs help."

Samuel put a big hand on his friend's shoulder and looked deep into his eyes. "What is it, Gadoni? How can I help?"

Gadoni quickly regained his composure, then quickly related the tale of his escape from the city of Nephi and the loss of his son and daughter several days later in the wilderness.

"Where did this happen?" Samuel asked.

"Between Manti and Gilead—the night before last. It's been almost thirty hours now."

Samuel turned to Oreb. "I must go with Gadoni. Will you be all right?"

"Of course. I just wish I could come, too," Oreb said gravely.

"So do I," Samuel responded. "You're a brave man and an able fighter. We should be back soon, though. You get well and then we'll finish this business with Herdon and Gadianton."

Oreb smiled weakly and Samuel and Gadoni bid him farewell and left the palace with Moronihah and his guards.

"You two be careful," the chief captain said, as they mounted the horse Gadoni had borrowed from Latoni. "Gadoni, make sure Sam keeps a clean dressing on his wound. He still has a little healing to do, himself."

"I'm fine," Samuel protested, "but please make sure Oreb is taken care of while I'm gone."

A few minutes later, Samuel and Gadoni were on their way, traveling rapidly, in hopes of overtaking the kidnappers before they reached the land of Nephi.

CHAPTER 7

Kapilla sat on a wooden bench beneath a sprawling mangrove tree near the house with one arm around the thin shoulders of each of her brothers. Together, they watched the coral sky slowly fade over the majestic mountains in the distance as another lonely day drew to a close. She talked sporadically as her thoughts lurched from one heartache to another. The boys' faces were turned up to hers, listening to every word she said, occasionally looking away fearfully to see if their father was coming. She knew they understood most of what she was saying and was sure that they felt her emotion. She drew them close and lapsed into silence.

As for Herdon, he had not returned since his wife's death. Javis never had come home that fateful night. His wife and other neighbors had seen to the burial of Kapilla's mother and they had checked on her and the boys frequently at first, but after a few days they seemed to forget about them.

A meager and rapidly dwindling supply of food was a worry to Kapilla. She was using it sparingly but had no idea how she would feed the boys when it ran out. She thought sadly of Oran. She was sure that even if he had lived, he would not have come around again.

The sound of an approaching horse, its feet pounding the dusty road on the far side of the house, brought her to her feet. She was surprised when the beat of the horse's feet stopped. She started around the house, her brothers trailing behind her.

A well-dressed man was dismounting near the front door. Kapilla stopped at the corner of the house and watched him. He spotted her and beckoned. She approached nervously. He was dressed too well for people in this part of the city.

"I'm looking for a young lady named Kapilla," he said, smiling. The kindness in his voice eased some of her tension.

"I'm Kapilla," she said, encircling her brothers with her arms.

"I am an aide of Chief Judge Pacumeni," he said. "I have a message from Oreb. Or maybe you knew him as Oran."

Kapilla's heart leaped. She opened her mouth to speak. Only an embarrassing squeak managed to come out.

"He wants to see you," the messenger said, still smiling.

"But . . . but, I thought Oran was dead," she said with effort.

"Dead? Oreb? What made you think that?"

"My fa . . ." She stopped.

"Where is your father?" he asked, the smile leaving his face and his hand darting to the hilt of his sword.

"He's gone. He said Oran was dead. Stabbed." Kapilla was trembling.

"Not so, but his name is really Oreb, and his brother is Samuel. Oreb was stabbed all right. And he was in pretty bad shape for awhile, but he's going to recover." The messenger was still looking around nervously.

"Father really is gone," she said, the shock wearing off and her courage returning. "He left several days ago and I haven't seen him since."

"Oreb would like you to come see him," the messenger said. "Would tomorrow be okay?"

"Oh, yes," she said, trying to repress a smile but failing. "But . . . but . . . I . . ." She lowered her eyes.

"But what?"

"I can't leave my brothers," she said with an effort.

"Can't your mother watch them for a few hours?" he asked, looking puzzled.

"No . . . she's dead." Her head was hanging and her eyes watching the dust play on her bare feet.

"I'm sorry. I thought Oreb mentioned her. I guess I misunderstood."

"She died the night Oreb was stabbed. My father . . ." She couldn't go on.

"Did your father kill her?" the messenger asked, his eyes narrowing suspiciously.

"He didn't mean to. He was angry with me. He shoved her and she fell."

"I'll be back before noon tomorrow. You and your brothers be ready. I'll take you all to see Oreb."

Kapilla said nothing, her head still drooping miserably. When she finally looked up, only a cloud of dust remained; the stranger and his horse were gone.

As promised, he returned the next morning. This time he was in a fancy covered carriage. He helped Kapilla and her brothers climb in and drove them to the palace.

Kapilla brushed her hair with her hand and straightened her plain, badly worn dress after alighting from the carriage. She was suddenly self-conscious and keenly aware of how out of place she and her two little brothers were in this wealthy part of the city. She felt as if the eyes of everyone in the area were looking down on her. Awkwardly, she took Kim and Kib each by the hand and trailed inside, fighting the impulse to turn and flee.

Never in her life had Kapilla seen such splendor. The palace was huge and beautifully decorated. Colorful woven rugs lay on polished marble floors. Gold was everywhere—lanterns, door handles, decorated plaques, and small statues. Beautiful paintings adorned the walls and not a speck of dust could be seen anywhere.

In awe she walked through the spacious palace. The awe was swept away when she was led into the room where Oreb lay, pale and thin, on a large, soft bed. His face was turned toward her, and he smiled, but the pain in his eyes made her stop and stare.

He stretched a hand toward her with a grimace. "Hello, Kapilla. I'm glad you came." He beckoned with a finger.

Timidly, she moved toward him, conscious of her two ragged brothers only a half-step behind. She stopped at his bedside. Oreb reached for her hand. She took it and he weakly pulled. She knelt at his side.

"They told me about your mother," he said tenderly. "I'm sorry."

Kapilla nodded. Her eyes filled with salty water. She tried to speak, but choked up instead. She was vaguely conscious of servants withdrawing from the room. After a long, strained moment she looked around. Only the twins were still with them. They looked stunned and gaped at the sight of Oreb, sickly and bedridden.

"Thanks for coming," Oreb said at last. His dark green eyes were searching her face. "I've missed you."

Kapilla found her voice. "I never thought I'd see you again." She tightened her grip on his hand.

He smiled weakly. "What?" he said, a mischievous glint lighting his eyes. "You didn't think a little band of robbers could stop me, did you?"

"My father told me you were dead. I didn't know until yesterday that you were still alive."

The glint left his eyes at the mention of Herdon. "Where is your father?"

"I don't know. He and Javis are both gone, hiding I suppose. After what happened to you here, they probably don't dare come home for fear of being recognized or something. I don't think Father even knows he killed my mother." She paused, then said with venom that surprised herself, "I hope they never come back. They're no good."

"You can't stay at your house, Kapilla, for they may. And you've got to get Kim and Kib away, too," Oreb said, concern furrowing his pale brow.

"And where would we go?" she asked helplessly. "I have enough worries just figuring out what we're going to eat without trying to find a new place to live."

She started to pull away from Oreb's grasp. He held tight. "If only I could get out of this bed," he said in frustration. "I'd take you away from there."

"You would?" Kapilla asked in wonderment, a feeling of warmth flooding over her like she had never felt before.

"Certainly. I love you. Can't you tell that?"

Kapilla's face turned scarlet. She ducked her head, her long brown hair falling in cascades around her pretty face.

"Kapilla," Oreb said slowly, "I mean it—I loved you from the moment we first met."

"But . . . but I'm from such a bad family. My father is a rob . . ."

Oreb interrupted. "What your father is means nothing. You're a special person. I love you for being what you are in spite of your father." Kapilla leaned forward and shyly pressed her lips against Oreb's forehead. He put his arm around her and pulled her head down until their lips met. The twins never moved, watching the strange actions of their sister without emotion.

After a long time, she finally pulled herself gently from Oreb's grasp and said, "And I love you, Oreb. Please get well fast. I'm afraid. Afraid for the twins and me."

"I'll think of something, Kapilla," Oreb said, gazing fondly at her. She smiled in return, her heart so full she felt it might burst. "Oreb, where's Sarl, or Samuel?" she asked suddenly. "Is he all right?"

"Samuel was hurt too, but not seriously. His old friend, Gadoni, a Lamanite, came for him. He went to help him."

"A Lamanite," she objected with alarm. "Why would he go with a Lamanite?"

"He's actually a Nephite by choice but a Lamanite by birth. He and Samuel are as close as two friends can be. Someone stole Gadoni's two youngest children. Gadoni thinks it was his brother, Laman. Anyway, they're trying to catch him before he reaches the land of Nephi." Oreb closed his eyes and took a deep breath.

Kapilla could see that his energy was nearly gone, but she was confused and Oreb patiently explained how Gadoni had been visiting his family in Nephi. "I guess when he decided to come back, his brother objected," he concluded.

Oreb's eyes closed again. His hand lost its grip and Kapilla gently pulled hers away. "You must rest, Oreb," she said softly. "I'll try to come back soon."

Oreb's eyes opened briefly and a weak smile crossed his face. "Thank you," he whispered. And then with immense effort he said, "Take good care of the boys."

She smiled. Her love grew. No one had ever shown concern for her unfortunate brothers before like Oreb did. He was so good. She gathered them with tears in her pale eyes and led them from the room.

Late that afternoon, Kapilla was surprised when a large two-seat carriage pulled up in front of the house and stopped. Two men jumped out and approached the door.

"Kapilla," one of them said, "the chief judge sent us. He wants you to come work for him at the palace. You are to live in the servant's quarters."

She was stunned, but her thoughts turned to Kim and Kib. "But my brothers; I can't leave them," she said apprehensively.

"They may come, too. We'll help you pack. Where are the boys?"

"Playing out back," she said. "I'll get them."

The twins were frightened, sticking to Kapilla like two shadows as the men from the government loaded their few belongings in the big carriage. Kapilla tried to help, but the men waved her aside. She gave up and stood watching, her arms around her brothers.

She tried to explain what was happening. The apprehension in their faces faded at her soothing words. They nodded when she told them that everything would be all right and that they were going where their father could not find them. By the time they climbed into the carriage, smiles lit their thin faces.

The servants at the palace, except for the supervising ones, lived in a long stone building behind the palace gardens. That is where Kapilla, Kim, and Kib were settled that evening. Kapilla's duties were outlined by a supervising maid. She would be expected to clean, serve meals, or do whatever other chores became necessary. The twins would be allowed to be near her when she worked if they caused no trouble. Kapilla promised that she would make sure they behaved properly.

Later in the evening, Kapilla and the ever-present twins peeked into Oreb's room. He managed a fairly broad grin and said, "Hello. Come on in."

"How did this happen?" Kapilla asked, indicating the clean, colorful dress she was wearing and the new leather vests and skirts the boys wore.

"You mean your clothes?" he asked mildly.

"And the job and living here."

Oreb's grin widened and his green eyes sparkled.

"You had something to do with this, didn't you?" she asked, reaching for and squeezing his hand.

"You do a good job, now, won't you?" he said, his grin still growing.

"I'll work real hard," she assured him seriously.

They talked together for several minutes. Then suddenly Kapilla said, "Oreb, I forgot my mother's necklace! It's the only really nice thing she ever had that Father didn't sell or trade when he wanted something for himself. It was her mother's and her mother's before that. Mother never stood up to Father very often, but she wouldn't let him touch that necklace. She finally hid it. I'm the only one she ever told where it was."

"Then you better get it tomorrow."

"Do you think that would be okay? I don't want to offend Judge Pacumeni."

"You won't. I'll arrange it for you. The boys can sit here with me while you go. I'd enjoy the company," he concluded.

Kapilla worked hard all the next morning. Despite her parentage, she was not afraid of hard work. The twins pitched in and helped scrub the polished stone floors of the hallways. By noon the work was finished. Kapilla was given the rest of the day off.

After seeing to the twins' lunch, Kapilla scooted them into Oreb's room in the palace. Kapilla was amazed at how much better he was looking and told him so.

"It's because you're here," he said.

She knew he meant it and felt her face redden. "I'm going after the necklace now," she said, smiling awkwardly at his adoring face.

"Oh, not yet," he said. "The carriage will be available in a few hours. If you go now you'll have to walk. I've made arrangements."

"That's okay, Oreb. I know the way. It's not all that far. I'll hurry. You will let the boys sit here with you?"

"Of course, but why don't you wait? You could sit here, too."

"I can sit here when I get back," she said with a smile. She couldn't tell him that she simply couldn't stand any more charity right now. It made her feel dependent. She didn't want to be dependent. She had learned to take care of herself in a cruel world and didn't want to lose the ability or the incentive.

Turning to the twins, she said, "You two take care of Oreb for me while I'm gone. He's so sick. I'll be back soon."

They nodded.

She strolled to the door . . . hesitated . . . turned and walked back to the bed and kissed Oreb tenderly and departed without another word.

Kapilla hurried along the cobbled streets, her heart light, humming a happy tune. Only when she turned a corner and found herself on a dusty road in the poorest part of the city did her spirits sag. This was where she had spent her life. Other than errands for her father, she had seldom gone beyond these dusty streets. The people she had met on those occasions were acquaintances of her father—evil men. They were men with some power and influence who sought more. They were greedy and immoral. The thought depressed her.

Before she knew it, she was home. For a moment she paused and studied the run-down house and cluttered yard. It was a far cry from the palace. She felt a twinge of guilt, shrugged it off, and hurried inside.

She wasted no time in finding the treasured necklace. It was hidden beneath a loose stone in the floor of her parents' bedroom, stored in a plain earthen jar. She pulled it out of the jar and dropped it in a deep pocket of the colorful dress she was wearing.

Kapilla heard footsteps enter the house. She hurriedly brushed the dust from her knees and went to see who was there, expecting Javis' wife, for she had visited often since Kapilla's mother died. The color drained from her face and she had to lean against the doorway to keep from fainting when she saw her father standing in the middle of the room. He was holding a little Lamanite girl with wide, frightened eyes and one leg in a crude splint. Behind him were Javis and another man, one she had never seen before.

Herdon spoke with anger. "Kapilla, what is that dress you're wearing?"

She stammered. "I have a job," she said at last. "They gave it to me."

"You lie!" he thundered.

"No, I had to make money to feed the twins. You were gone and we ran out of food," she said, unable to keep the anger from her voice.

"Kapilla," he said in a threatening tone that made her tremble with fear. "You know what happens when someone lies to me," and he struck out hard and fast with his empty hand, slapping her face a wicked blow.

She stumbled backward into the wall. "Where are the idiots?" he demanded. The little girl he held was drooping like a rag doll in his hand.

Kapilla blurted out the first thing that popped into her head. "They're playing up the street somewhere." Then she felt guilty. She was lying and that went against her nature, but if she told him the truth, she knew his wrath would be uncontrollable. She had no doubt that he was capable of killing her in a rage.

"And where is your mother? Is she up the street, too?" he mocked.

"She's dead. You killed her," she blurted.

"Why you . . ." Herdon struck out again, dropping the little girl to the floor. Kapilla ducked his blow but he caught her arm with his other hand, jerking her around and shaking her viciously. "If she's dead it is so much the better, but now you are going to have to take care of this little girl."

"Father, she looks like a Lamanite!" she exclaimed. "And she's got a broken leg."

"Well, so she does," Herdon said with a snarl. "Her father is a friend of Sarl, the brother of your friend Oran—you know, the one Gadianton killed. Actually, they are not who they said. The brotherhood learned they were really Samuel and his brother Oreb. Since their treachery the night Oreb died, Samuel has not been seen. This little one will bring him to us."

Javis grinned and the stranger chuckled. Kapilla reached down and picked the little girl tenderly off the floor. She instantly felt a tugging at her heartstrings and held the trembling child close.

Herdon said, "Javis and I have to leave for a little while. Ammdoni will stay with you. We will be back soon. Feed the child, Kapilla. And don't say a word to anyone or I'll send you to see your mother. There better be something ready for the rest of us to eat, too." With the threat hanging like a cold mist in the air, he left.

Kapilla was shaking uncontrollably. She was deathly afraid of her father. He had beaten her before—not as bad or as often as he had the twins, but enough that she had learned never to disobey him. She had no doubt that he would kill her if she did not have things ready when he returned as he had ordered. The man called Ammdoni leered at Kapilla. He was young, but small in stature. "Where have Javis and Father been?" she asked.

"Around," the young robber said evasively.

"Did you know Sarl?"

"We met once. He was very foolish," Ammdoni said, advancing toward Kapilla.

"Father said his name was really Samuel, is that true?" She was talking to give herself time to think.

"Yes. Samuel is a friend of the leaders of the government. Several years ago he caused the death of your father's brother, Teor. Your father and our friends want him out of the way, permanently."

"But how did they learn who he is?" she asked, not that it mattered, but she wanted to put Ammdoni off guard, for Oreb and the safety of the palace awaited her if she could get away from him.

She held the child close and forced a smile. She felt the little girl relax in her arms.

"Your father is a smart man, Kapilla. He knew this Samuel and his brother were up to no good, so he had some of us do some checking. He heard Oran, his real name is Oreb," he said with a malicious chuckle, "call him Sam one night in a fight. From there he figured it out, I guess."

Ammdoni moved closer. Kapilla turned and walked into the kitchen. He followed. "I guess I better get fixing something to feed you," she said, knowing there was not food in the house, but desperately stalling while she figured how to get away. She reached into a cupboard. Her hand fell on a knife. She clutched it in her fist and held the child tightly.

Ammdoni was only a step away. "What do you have there?" he asked suspiciously.

"Just this," she said and whirled, burying the knife deep in his shoulder. He screamed and grabbed for the knife. Kapilla fled through the house and out the door. She darted across the street and began running through back yards and alleys. Kapilla stumbled repeatedly in her haste, and the little girl began whimpering. She didn't want to injure or frighten the child, but desperation drove her on. Several times she looked back and saw Ammdoni, but he was bleeding badly and losing ground. Finally she could see him no more, but still she ran, although much slower now, for she was exhausted.

It seemed like an eternity before the palace came into view. Kapilla was stopped by the guards at the main entrance, but one of them recognized her and they let her pass. She stumbled through the great hallways and burst into Oreb's room, tears of relief streaming down her face, and collapsed beside his bed.

Oreb's eyes popped wide in surprise and he jerked up in his bed so fast he screamed with pain. The twins jumped to their feet and cowered together. Servants gathered at the door, astonishment on their faces.

"Oreb, my father had this child. He said I would die if anyone found out." She was speaking rapidly, between deep, choking breaths. "He left me with Ammdoni. I stabbed him and got away but he still pursued me."

"This is Gadoni's daughter!" Oreb exclaimed, his face contorted in pain. He paused, shifting to ease the hurt and then said, "Zera."

The child's eyes grew wide at the mention of her name and she cried.

"Kapilla, where is the infant?"

"They said nothing of the other child. He handed this one to me and said to feed her. He struck me and he threatened me," she said, sobbing in anguish. "Oh, Oreb, what should I do?"

"We've got to stop Samuel and Gadoni," Oreb said, lying back down. "They are after Gadoni's brother—headed for the land of Nephi. They think Laman took the children." He clutched his stomach in agony before concluding with, "But it was the Gadianton robbers."

"What's going on here?" the strong voice of Chief Judge Pacumeni demanded.

Kapilla turned to see him surrounded by his guard. Before she found the words to answer, he demanded, "Who is the child, Kapilla? Why have you brought her here?"

Kapilla felt her face redden, tried to speak but began to cough. Oreb answered for her. "Sir, this is Zera, the daughter of Gadoni. The robbers had her. Kapilla risked her life to bring her here."

The judge's face softened and he regarded Kapilla respectfully. "How did you do this, young lady?" he asked. "Those men are desperate. How did you come to find the child and make good your escape?"

Kapilla lifted her head and slowly explained. The judge and Oreb listened intently, then Pacumeni ordered a maid to care for Zera, two guards to summon Captain Moronihah, and two more to find the prophet, Helaman. Still more were sent to search for Ammdoni.

"Sir," Oreb said, trying in vain to sit up again. "Samuel and Gadoni . . ."

"They'll figure it out, Oreb. They're expert trackers. They probably already know the Lamanites didn't take the children. Our concern now is for the infant boy—Enos, isn't it? Kapilla, do you have any idea where he might be?"

"No."

Pacumeni stepped forward and placed a hand on her shoulder. "Thank you for what you've done, Kapilla. You're a brave girl." Then he said to Oreb, "You get some rest, young man. All this excitement isn't good for you.

"We'll alert the guards at the servant's quarters," he said, addressing Kapilla again. "Better yet," he said thoughtfully, tugging at his long black beard, "we'll move you and your brothers into the palace. Yes, that would be best. Go quickly and bring your things."

A wave of the hand sent several of the servants scurrying to help. Kapilla beckoned her brothers. They had sat motionless during the whole excited exchange. Now they obediently followed her.

She glanced silently at Oreb before leaving the room. Pain creased his brow. He tried again to sit up, but fell back helplessly onto the plush pillows. Tears filled his eyes, and behind them, anger burned deep.

* * *

Herdon was in a rage. Never had Kapilla dared to defy him, but he had returned to find the place abandoned. Learning that Kapilla had fled with the twins and Gadoni's daughter was too much. Ammdoni had returned and he knocked him violently to the floor, upended the table, and threw an oil lamp against the wall. Then he kicked a chair, bruising a toe and cursing. He grabbed every piece of pottery in the house and smashed them against Ammdoni and the wall. Knives, clothing, and everything else he could get his hands on, he threw and stomped on. Not until the contents of the house were ruined did his rage subside.

"She will pay for her treachery," he said aloud as he surveyed the damage he had done.

Ammdoni lay silent, badly injured. Javis cowered in the door while Herdon's rage ran its course. "I want her found! I want the city searched until Kapilla is found," Herdon shouted. "How dare she defy her own father? Come, Javis, we will summon the brotherhood."

An hour later, Herdon stood with Kishkumen, Gadianton, and a dozen others in the large stone house not far from the south wall of the city. Gadianton, his dark eyes blazing, said, "One child is enough, Herdon, but your daughter must be found and soon! And bring that fool Ammdoni to me. He must die. I will not stand for fools!"

Herdon winced, but wisely said nothing, for it would not take much to turn the men against him, and his life would be worth nothing. He would bring Ammdoni to them and he and Javis would find Kapilla.

"We still have the infant son of the Lamanite," Gadianton went on, more calm now. "Your friend Samuel will do whatever we order to secure the release of the child. Samuel will be made to pay for his crime against the brotherhood."

"No one will live who is a traitor to the brotherhood," Kishkumen vowed, pounding his fist against a stone pillar. "No one!"

"No one!" Herdon repeated fiercely and with Javis at his heels went for Ammdoni.

CHAPTER 8

The haunting cry of wild beasts disturbed the night deep in the vast wilderness that separated Nephite lands from those of the Lamanites. Samuel and Gadoni found the familiar sounds strangely comforting. They were camped for the night, darkness having made tracking impossible.

They became uneasy when the beasts grew silent. The air was muggy and the stars vanished. "I hope it's not going to storm," Gadoni said glumly, recognizing the feel in the air.

"It doesn't look good," Samuel said. "Tracking could get real tough."

"That's my fear," Gadoni agreed and lapsed into a worried silence.

The storm began with a few scattered drops here and there, but within minutes it was raining in torrents. There was no let up for several hours. When it did finally diminish, a light rain continued to fall.

The men slept fitfully during the long, stormy night. Daybreak brought the bad news they most feared; all sign of the men they pursued had vanished. With no sign to follow they had to make a decision. They did so.

Nighttime found them deep in the wilderness, pressing closer by the hour to the Land of Nephi. They rested only long enough that night to renew their strength, then traveled on, climbing ever higher. Samuel's sword wound ached, but he was feeling stronger the harder he pushed, so he went on, ignoring the pain.

Nothing slowed the pair down, and after just a few days they approached the run-down walls of the city of Nephi late on a stormy night. Despite occasional sheets of lightning, they entered the city.

Samuel was tense with anxiety as they slipped up to the old stone house of Gadoni's brother. If Gadoni's children were here, they would recover them. Swiftly and silently, Gadoni checked the windows while Samuel stood watch. "I can't tell anything from out here," he whispered to Samuel. "We'll have to go inside."

They chose the door. It was just an empty hole. Sticking together, they eased through and entered the room where Gadoni expected Laman and his wife to be sleeping. Laman was snoring loudly on his mat in a far corner, his large wife at his side.

Gadoni pulled his knife and pressed the point lightly against Laman's neck. "Don't move, big brother," he hissed.

Laman awoke with a groan. "Gadoni? What are you doing here?" he asked groggily.

"As if you don't know!" Gadoni said, louder than he had intended.

"Laman, what's happening?" his wife asked sleepily.

"It's Gadoni. The fool wasn't content with his escape to the Nephites. He's come back to stir up trouble, I guess," Laman said angrily.

"You know why I'm back, Laman. Now where are they? I have no time or patience to waste," Gadoni said, his voice cold as ice.

"Where's who? If you mean the rest of my band of warriors, you really are a fool. Trying to find all of them will cause more trouble than you can even imagine." Laman started to sit up, but relaxed when Gadoni pressed the knife a little harder.

"Laman, I'm in no mood for your games. If you want to live, tell me where my children are. Now!" he ordered, his voice husky with emotion.

"Woman, light a candle so I can see my insane little brother," Laman said to his wife.

She hesitated. "Gadoni, is it all right if . . ." she began.

"Please do," Gadoni interrupted.

Samuel was conscious of the rain coming down hard outside. No one spoke inside until the Lamanite woman had a candle glowing, sending a dim, eerie light through the room. Laman demanded, "Who is that?"

Samuel stepped out of the shadows near the door. "This is my friend, Samuel," Gadoni said. "He's come to help me get my children back. Now, where are they, Laman?"

"Oh, my foolish little brother. I don't have your children. The last time I saw them they were with you, riding into the trees—fleeing in fear."

"I don't believe you, Laman," Gadoni said with uncertainty, pulling the knife away from Laman's throat.

"Gadoni, I vowed that you would no longer be my brother. I disowned you. Now you come back and accuse me of stealing your children. Well, no matter what I say, you're still my brother. And no matter what you believe, I don't know anything about your missing children."

"Gadoni, I think he's telling the truth. We better leave," Samuel said quietly from his position across the room.

Gadoni backed toward him. "Not until I check the house. Watch them, Sam, while I look."

His mother was with him when he came back a few minutes later. "Gadoni, my son, you must go in search of your children among the Nephites—you have an enemy there. Laman did not take them. Please, hurry and find my little grandchildren," she urged.

Samuel instantly liked the good woman. He could see why Gadoni was such a fine person. Her eyes glowed with pain but were filled with love for her youngest son.

Gadoni embraced her fondly. "Thank you, Mother. We'll go now. Come on, Sam. We must hurry. Someone else has the children." His voice was quivering. Samuel's heart went out to him as he asked in anguish, "Who could it be?"

Samuel shook his head sadly and backed out of the door, his eyes never leaving the twisted, angry face of Laman. Gadoni followed. "If you make it out of our lands alive again, Gadoni, don't be the fool and come back another time. I don't like having a stinking Nephite in my house. You have insulted me once too often," Laman said, his anger rising. "One day I will kill you."

Gadoni's mother stood by the door as they went out. A tear rolled down her wrinkled cheek. She started to speak to Laman, but did not. Instead, she simply grasped Gadoni's hand briefly and said, "Go safely, my son."

He tried to smile at her and followed Samuel into the pouring rain. "Will he follow us?" Samuel asked, shouting to be heard above the fierce storm.

"I suppose he will," Gadoni shouted back. "Stay close to me. I'll have us out of the city in no time. Laman will never catch us."

By the time they left the city, they were not only wet, but muddy. The rain never let up; it just came harder. Not far beyond the city walls was a small stream that ran down a wide, grassy gully. As they neared it, Samuel was conscious of a dreadful roar that hadn't been there earlier.

"A flood!" Gadoni shouted.

"Can we cross?" Samuel asked, straining to see the raging torrent in the darkness.

"I doubt it. When it rains like this . . ." Gadoni stopped. The water was rising so fast that it reached their ankles where they stood. "This way, Sam," he shouted.

Samuel followed him back toward the city walls, trying to escape the rapidly rising water. They huddled against the rough rocks of the wall. Samuel shouted, "We can't wait here long, Gadoni."

"I saw the stream do this once when I was very young," Gadoni responded. "We can't go forward. We are trapped unless we go through the city and out the other side. We better wait here. Maybe it'll go down soon."

"I hope the storm keeps your brother inside. If he finds us here, we're in trouble," Samuel said, looking about him in the darkness and listening for any sound that might indicate someone was near.

Without warning, a sheet of lightning revealed the angry face of Laman and several other men only a few feet away, silently making their way around the city wall. "Come!" Gadoni shouted.

They scrambled onto the wall at a point where it had crumbled and fallen. Samuel heard the Lamanites behind them on the wall. They fled, treacherous holes and jagged, jutting rocks making the flight along the wall difficult. They had to use care to keep from stumbling and falling to the ground where they would almost certainly be injured and allow their unforgiving pursuers to catch them.

By the time they came to another spot where the wall had deteriorated badly, they had outdistanced the Lamanites. Gadoni led the way down and ran for the stream again. It was raging higher than ever. "We'll have to go back in the city and hide," Gadoni shouted. "We don't have a chance here."

Samuel saw that there was no alternative, so he said, "Whatever you say."

There was enough light from the early pre-dawn that Laman and his friends loosed a volley of arrows at them as they zig-zagged along the outside of the wall. They found another place where, by Samuel legging Gadoni up and Gadoni pulling Samuel, they were able to cross into the city. They fled into a maze of run-down, abandoned dwellings, finally turning into one. Inside, they huddled together, gasping for air.

When Samuel had caught his breath, he said, "They'll probably be here soon, Gadoni."

"Maybe we lost them and can stay here until the stream's had time to subside."

"By then it will surely be full daylight," Samuel said with ever increasing worry.

"We'll have to trust to luck," Gadoni said, shrugging his shoulders. "I'm sorry I got you into this, Sam. I was sure Laman had taken the children."

"So was I, my friend. We'll get away yet," he whispered with more optimism than he felt.

They heard voices outside and looked at each other grimly. Laman's voice boomed. "We've got you surrounded, Gadoni. You and your Nephite friend better give up now or we'll come in after you."

"So much for luck," Gadoni said. "If we give up, they'll kill us."

"Then we'll fight," Samuel said. "Let's see if we can tell how many men are out there."

They separated, carefully checking outside through cracks in the wall of the decaying old building. They met again in the center room. "Five that way," Gadoni announced quietly.

"Only four in back," Samuel whispered with a forced grin. "That makes it two against nine."

"Did you see Laman?" Gadoni asked.

"He was shielding himself behind a tree a few feet from the back."

"Let's attack the ones at the front first. Maybe we can reduce the odds," Gadoni suggested.

Samuel agreed, knowing that Gadoni somehow hoped they wouldn't have to fight his brother. They crept forward and found cracks in the rock wall where the mortar had crumbled away that were wide enough to send arrows through. They fired simultaneously. Two Lamanites dropped. The others scrambled for cover, but only one made it. He cried for help.

Three Lamanites from the back hurried to his aid. Two of them dropped from arrows loosed by Samuel and Gadoni. "Let's try the back," Samuel suggested.

"Laman is alone there, now," Gadoni whispered, his face betraying his emotions more than usual.

"I'm sorry, Gadoni, but it's our best chance now."

They hurried through the house and stopped near a window. Samuel peeked through. "Gadoni, look out!" he warned. "Laman's heading for the door."

Gadoni spun around just as Laman charged in. He had a drawn sword in his hand and his face was contorted with hatred. Gadoni did not have time to string an arrow. He pulled his knife.

Samuel lunged forward and struck Laman in the side of the head just as Gadoni expertly deflected the long sword. Laman slashed at Samuel who ducked, the blade slicing the air just over his head. Gadoni's knife struck Laman's sword arm, biting deep into the flesh. The sword fell and Samuel threw his arm around Laman's neck and pulled him to the floor.

Gadoni held his razor-sharp knife to his brother's throat. "Go ahead, you little Nephite dog," Laman hissed, "kill me."

"I don't want to see you dead, Laman. We just want to leave in safety," Gadoni said sadly.

"Even the elements are against you. You'll never leave alive," Laman taunted.

"Tie him up," Samuel said, anxious to finish the fight and get on their way. The storm had worn itself out, and he was sure they would soon be able to cross the swollen stream.

Quickly, Gadoni put his knife in its sheath. He checked the cut he had inflicted on Laman's arm. It was deep but not bleeding badly, so he bound his arms tightly behind his back. Then he tied his legs securely. Samuel kept watch outside. The two surviving men out there could not be seen. "Let's go, Gadoni. I think the others have gone for help," he urged.

"I'm ready," Gadoni said, scrambling to his feet. He paused, looking sadly at Laman lying bound and bloody on the floor. "I'm sorry it came to this, Laman. I mean you no harm. Good-bye, my brother."

Laman spat at him. "I will kill you someday, Gadoni," he threatened again.

Gadoni turned without another word and followed Samuel to the back door. The rain had stopped and a bright ray of sunshine stabbed its way through the clouds and lit a small grove of graceful mahogany trees with its glow. Samuel and Gadoni ran to the trees and hid there long enough to survey the surrounding area.

"I don't see any reinforcements," Samuel whispered, "so let's get back to the wall."

They ran swiftly through the wet grass and muddy streets. Not a soul stirred in the run-down houses they passed. At the city wall, Gadoni looked back. "Samuel, they're coming," he cried.

Samuel glanced over his shoulder. A large band of heavily armed men were running in their direction. Samuel and Gadoni scrambled over the tumbled rocks that formed the wall at that point and charged into the receding stream as the Lamanites began to pour over the wall themselves.

They were soon waist deep in the swift, muddy water, dodging debris and fighting for their balance. By the time they were chest deep, the Lamanites were almost at the edge of the gully, stringing arrows into their bows.

"Go under," Samuel shouted.

Without waiting for a reply, he took a deep breath, grabbed Gadoni's arm and ducked beneath the boiling surface. Samuel made no effort to swim. He just walked, stooped over, fighting to keep the current from sweeping his feet from beneath him. Gadoni kept pace. After a minute, they surfaced, gulped more air and went under again as a host of poorly aimed arrows flew their way.

Samuel veered upstream, still clinging to Gadoni's arm so they wouldn't become separated. When they surfaced again for air, the Lamanites were looking downstream. They hurriedly worked their way to the bank and out of the flood. They were not observed again until they were fading into the forest several hundred feet beyond the stream.

A few arrows fell harmlessly short before they were out of sight of the Lamanites. They stopped running and walked back to where they could see what the Lamanites would do. Several of them had entered the stream. The first one was struck by a log, and he stumbled and disappeared beneath the rumbling brown water. He never came up. The others turned back, appeared to argue for a minute, then started wading again.

"We better not wait around. We made it, and so can they," Samuel said.

Gadoni took no coaxing and began trotting through the heavy timber behind Samuel. They kept up the mile-eating pace until sheer exhaustion forced them to stop.

The freak storm had caused widespread flooding. Mud-slides and muddy lakes impeded their progress. The mountain passes were treacherous, and Samuel and Gadoni had to backtrack long distances and search out detours when their way was blocked.

They never saw the band of Lamanites again, and reached Gilead several days later. They were greeted with the good news of Zera's return. Laishita and Limre were not there, having been escorted days before to the palace of the chief judge in Zarahemla to be with Zera under the protection of the government.

Samuel and Gadoni stayed only long enough to eat and rest briefly before Samuel bid Ophera and Jath farewell again. "We'll get little Enos back," he assured his worried wife.

At the palace the next morning, they were greeted by Kapilla. She shyly accepted the thanks heaped on her by Gadoni as she escorted them to the elegant room now occupied by Laishita and the girls. Samuel left his friend there and went in search of Oreb.

He was surprised to see Kim and Kib at his bedside. Oreb was propped up by several plush, duck down pillows. He was speaking so intently to the twins that he failed to notice Samuel standing beside Kapilla in the doorway. They listened and watched in wonderment.

Oreb was recounting a hunting adventure. The boys listened as if they understood every word of the story as it unfolded from Oreb's lips. Samuel glanced at Kapilla, struck by her beauty. Tears of joy flooded her flawless face. In her pale green eyes he detected a deep love for her brothers and the gallant young storyteller who held them spellbound.

She reached to wipe away the tears. The movement caught Oreb's eye and he looked up, a big smile lighting his face. "Come on in, you two. Glad you finally decided to come back, Sam," he said with a mischievous glint in his eyes. "You took long enough. Old Herdon must have led you in quite a circle."

"So he did," Samuel said as he approached the bed. "What are you telling these boys? Sounds like a tall tale to me."

"Maybe just a little; they make a good audience. They never question a thing I say," he said with a chuckle.

"So how are you feeling?" Samuel asked.

"Much better. I'm going to be ready to go after the robbers pretty soon," he said. "I guess by now you know they have Enos?"

"Yes. Gadoni and I'll be leaving soon to find him."

"Without me?" Oreb asked in surprise.

"I'm afraid we can't wait."

"Help me up, Sam. Maybe if I just moved around a little . . ."

"Don't be crazy, Oreb. You're lucky just to be alive. You stay put and we'll keep you informed. Meantime, keep the boys entertained. You're the best thing that's happened to them in a long time, I suspect." Samuel turned to Kapilla. "You make sure he takes care of himself, Kapilla."

"I'll do that. I don't want him running off again," she said protectively.

Oreb reddened. "I wouldn't be running off. I only want to help stop these men before they hurt little Enos and other innocent people," he said forcefully.

"I know that, Oreb," Kapilla said, reaching for his hand. "But it's nice to have you near. The boys and I need you."

Oreb's red turned to scarlet, but his eyes betrayed his pleasure at the attention of Herdon's beautiful daughter.

"So, tell me what took you so long, Sam," Oreb said, changing the subject.

Samuel pulled up a stool, sat down, and filled the young couple in on the recent trip to the land of Nephi. Kim and Kib, sitting cross-legged on the floor, never took their eyes off Samuel's face as he spoke. It was as if they too wanted to share in the adventure. Samuel smiled at them. They smiled back.

CHAPTER 9

Samuel and Gadoni were eating breakfast with Chief Judge Pacumeni after a night of much needed rest. They were discussing how to best go about searching for Enos when a palace guard interrupted.

"Sir, there's a messenger here from Captain Moronihah. He says it is very important."

"Show him in," the chief judge ordered.

A minute later, a tall, handsome young man entered the palace dining room. "You are from Captain Moronihah?" Pacumeni asked. "Deliver your message, please."

"Yes, sir," the polite courier said with a slight bow. "This morning this parchment was delivered to the army headquarters. It's addressed to Samuel. I was told I would find him here, Chief Judge Pacumeni."

"This is Samuel," the judge said, nodding across the heavy wooden table.

The messenger stepped forward as Samuel arose. "The man that left it said it bore a message of grave urgency, both to you and to your friends in the government," he said to Samuel. "Captain Moronihah was anxious to have it read."

Samuel studied the rolled and sealed parchment suspiciously, turning it over and over in his hands. Finally, he peeled off the red wax seal and unrolled it. His face burned as he read the inscription to himself. Gadoni asked, "What does it say, Sam?"

Samuel looked up and said with an acid tongue, "It's from the Gadianton robbers."

Gadoni's eyes narrowed. Pacumeni ordered tersely, "Read it." Tension drew his lips back together tightly. There was a subconscious flicker of his eyelids over cold, angry eyes.

Samuel read. "Samuel, we have the boy, Enos. We know he is the son of Gadoni, your friend. No one will ever know who killed him, but his little body will be deposited where you cannot miss it unless you and your brother surrender to us. Further instructions will follow. The brother of the late Chief Judge Pahoran is not to interfere. Instruct Captain Moronihah likewise. Any efforts by them to intercede on your behalf will result in the boy's certain death."

Samuel lowered the parchment. His eyes met Gadoni's, then settled on Pacumeni. "It's signed, 'The Secret Band of Deliverers,'" he said with seething anger.

An intense silence permeated the hot air of the brightly lit dining room. Gadoni wore a look of despair, Pacumeni one of worry. The young courier stood like a statue. Finally, he broke the silence. "I would like to help," he said quietly.

"Help?" Samuel asked, regarding him quizzically.

"Yes, I want to help. I am Nemti. My father died at the hands of the robbers. I'm sure Captain Moronihah will approve it," he explained, his dark brown eyes staring, unblinking at Samuel's face.

Samuel was drawn to the young man as he stood awaiting an answer. He was nearly as tall as Samuel with muscular arms and legs. Loose brown curls fell almost to his shoulders. He was medium complected with an intelligent, honest face. He appeared to be about the age of Oreb. He did not squirm under Samuel's intense scrutiny.

"As a matter of fact, we could use some help. I'll go with you to speak with Moronihah," Samuel said and turned to Gadoni. "I'll return shortly. Be ready to leave. We'll find little Enos and bring him back safely from wherever he is."

An hour later, Samuel returned, accompanied by Nemti. He was greeted by Gadoni who was even more somber and sorrowful than when Samuel had left. "We will succeed, Gadoni," Samuel said with a grim smile.

"Another message arrived while you were gone, Sam. Your brother-in-law, Sheam, is dead. He died of fever several weeks ago," Gadoni said in a wavering voice.

Samuel stood in shock before searching for a seat and sinking with his head in his hands. The image of his dark and beautiful sister, Nonita, filled his tightly closed eyes. She had been radiantly happy when she married Sheam two years ago and accompanied him to the city of

Bountiful near the East Sea. He had seemed like a good husband for her, although he was much older, and her barely beyond childhood. His death and her sorrow cut deep into Samuel's heart. She would need him. She would want to return to Gilead to be with her family, but he couldn't . . . Little Enos needed him, too.

As if reading his mind, Gadoni said, "Go for her, Sam. She asked that you come. She wants to return to Gilead."

"I can't do that, Gadoni. "

"But who will . . ."

"I'll ask Pacumeni for one more favor. Maybe he'll send someone. Does my father know yet?"

"Yes, he saw the messenger first."

"Where is the messenger?"

"He's eating," Gadoni said.

"I'll speak with him and the chief judge. Nemti and I will join you in a few minutes. We have much to do," Samuel said.

The chief judge agreed to send a servant to bring Nonita back and take her on to Gilead. The messenger, a relative of Sheam's, agreed to return to Gilead and give Samuel's father word, then accompany Pacumeni's servant back to Bountiful.

Samuel and Nemti joined Gadoni and the three discussed the task they faced. "Herdon is the key," Samuel told the others. "We must first find him and make him talk. Javis is another possibility, except that I'm not sure he'll know much. He's not very bright and I'd be surprised if he's allowed to know many secrets."

"What about the man they call Gadianton or even Kishkumen?" Nemti asked.

"They're the leaders. They'll be hard to find without help. We must find Herdon and make him lead us to them," Samuel replied thoughtfully.

The sun had settled gently over the majestic mountains and the final pink hues of daylight were barely lingering as the three men approached Herdon's house. No lamps burned within. The place appeared deserted. A cursory check confirmed Samuel's suspicion that Herdon was not living there, but there was dried blood on the floor with the debris from the wrecked house.

"Someone sure tore this place up. What do we do now?" Nemti asked.

"We'll see if Javis is at his place. That's it over there. He'll lead us to

Herdon, I think," he said, unable to keep a trace of uncertainty from his voice.

"There's a light in the house," Gadoni observed.

"You two stay outside. I'll go in and see if he's home," Samuel said.

Samuel had never met the large woman that invited him in. A quick assessment told him she must outweigh her skinny robber husband by nearly double, but she had a kindly face. "I need to speak to Javis," Samuel told her without introducing himself.

"The lazy man," she lamented. "He hasn't come around since Herdon killed his wife." There was bitterness in her voice and her eyes were filled with sadness. "Poor Kapilla. Do you know her?"

"Yes, beautiful girl."

"She's gone, and so are the twins. Left in a fancy carriage." She glanced toward the window where a trace of the recent sunset still lingered. He nodded his head and she went on. "How are those poor little boys?"

"They're doing fine."

Her eyes narrowed and she shifted her bulky frame closer. With a secretive voice she asked, "Where are they?"

Samuel ignored the question. "It's very important that I speak with Javis," he insisted.

"He'll be around sometime," she said, sounding as if it didn't matter one way or the other to her. Then she leaned so close he could smell the caustic odor of her breath. "Where are the children?"

"They're someplace safe and doing fine," Samuel answered, taking a step backward.

She wasn't satisfied. "Tell me, please," she said, closing the distance between them again.

He shook his head firmly. "Where can I find Javis tonight?"

She again moved closer. Samuel stepped back. "I don't know, but he does come home occasionally and bring some money so the children and I can eat. We're grateful for that," she said.

"When do you expect to see him again?"

"Tonight, maybe. You never know, though." She stepped closer.

"Thank you," Samuel said and spun toward the door, intent on getting out before she started asking more questions.

"We'll wait," Samuel said to his two colleagues after joining them in the deepening shadows. "It's as good a chance as we'll have, I suppose."

It paid off. Near midnight, a small dark form shuffled from the trees near where they waited and turned toward the door of Javis' home. The quarter moon that had just risen threw enough light on the shadowy figure to convince Samuel it was Javis.

A signal to Gadoni and Nemti was followed by a short scuffle and then Javis was carried, gagged and kicking, into Herdon's deserted house. Samuel spoke to him in the darkness of the interior. "I am Samuel. These are my friends. We'll take the gag off when I'm convinced that you'll make no unnecessary noise. We need some information from you."

A muffled mumble was the response. Gadoni carried Javis to a window where a tiny bit of light from the new moon was peeking in. Nemti slowly removed the gag. Samuel stuck his head so close to Javis that he thought he would choke from the odor. "Let me introduce my friends," he said in a menacing voice. "Nemti just removed the gag from your mouth. The muscular fellow holding you so gently is Gadoni, the father of the children you kidnapped."

Javis jerked, and unmistakable fear crossed his face. Samuel had only guessed that he had assisted Herdon in the kidnapping. Now, with his face only a hand-span away, he knew. He pressed his advantage. "Little Enos—where is he?"

Javis spoke in a voice that cracked. "I don't know what you're talking about."

Samuel went on, unrelenting. "Javis, Gadoni wants his son back and will not allow you to stand in his way. Where is the child?" he asked in a loud, angry whisper.

Javis stared at him for a moment, then threw his head back against Gadoni's chest so hard he must have scattered a hundred tiny bugs from his scraggly hair. "If I knew I wouldn't tell you!" he hissed defiantly.

"Where is Herdon?" Samuel asked so fast Javis didn't have time to readjust his thinking.

"With the others and . . ." He cut himself short as his mind caught up with his mouth.

"Where?"

"None of your business," Javis said with growing defiance.

"On that you're wrong, Javis," Samuel said distinctly. "Enos is our business and even if the other robbers don't trust your feeble mind enough to keep you informed of his location, they do trust Herdon." He paused and Gadoni began to squeeze Javis with his powerful arms. "Javis, they used you, can't you see that?" Samuel asked, his voice more forgiving.

"Herdon trusts me," Javis said in defense of the attack on his character.

"No he doesn't. He knows you messed up the attempt on the life of the chief judge. You lost his trust—that's why he won't tell you where the baby is," Samuel said, pressing his face ever closer to the little robber.

Gadoni, whose only reaction to this point had been to squeeze the bony body, said, "Javis, I want my son back. I will succeed, with or without your help." His voice was cold, almost sinister, as he went on. "I am a Lamanite by birth, but have chosen to live as a Nephite. I am dedicated to making life better for all of us here, especially my family. You and your kind will not stand in my way. I'll see you destroyed from the face of the earth unless you help me find my son."

Gadoni tightened his grip and Javis gasped. A cloud drifted beneath the moon, plunging them into almost total blackness. A somber silence settled over the room. Gadoni increased the strangling pressure on Javis. Samuel and Nemti stood like stones in front of him. When the moon was freed, its light revealed a weakening face.

Samuel leaned close again and asked slowly, "Where is Herdon?"

"He's not in Zarahemla," Javis said weakly.

"Where is he?" Samuel pressed.

"It's his turn to watch . . ." He stopped in mid-sentence.

"Enos?" Gadoni finished, releasing his tight hold and spinning the little robber around like a top.

"I didn't say . . ."

Gadoni grabbed him with both hands on his greasy vest. With powerful force he lifted him off the floor and held him close to his face. "You know where my son is!" Gadoni said, his voice sparking with anger. "Tell me!"

"I don't know. He's not in the city . . . I mean, I don't know anything." Javis' voice squeaked with fear.

Gadoni swung him around and smashed him against the stone wall then dropped him. Samuel as quickly stepped in and picked him up. Javis' feet dangled nearly a foot above the floor. "Take us to Herdon, Javis, or else!" he threatened in a tone that could not be mistaken.

"I don't know where he is," the weasel faced robber said, terror-stricken.

"Then find out."

"How?"

"Don't be stupid," Samuel said, slamming him against the wall with almost as much force as Gadoni had used, then letting him drop to the floor again.

Javis began to whine. Samuel bent over him, pulling his head up by the long, greasy locks that grew below his bald top. "We'll follow you. You find someone who knows. Tell them you must see Herdon at once. Be convincing. Your life may depend on it, Javis," Samuel said.

Gadoni helped Javis to his feet. His anger was controlled. "We will go now," he said.

Another whimper was his only response. "We haven't time to waste," Samuel said decisively. "You lead the way."

For the next several minutes Javis led them through the dark streets of Zarahemla. Samuel wasn't surprised when he stopped in front of the large stone house where he and Oreb had previously met with the robbers. "Don't try to go inside, Javis," Samuel warned. "Deliver your message and make arrangements to meet Herdon, that's all. And make it quick. We'll be waiting . . . and watching, with our bows," he threatened, pulling an arrow from his quiver.

Javis approached the door with faltering, frightened steps. For a moment, Samuel thought he might run, taking his chances with Samuel rather than incur the murderous wrath of the robbers.

Gadoni and Nemti moved with stealth to dark positions around the house. Samuel crouched in the shadows in front. At the door, Javis looked nervously around. Finally, he lifted a hand and knocked.

The door didn't move. He knocked again, harder. Samuel was close enough to hear when someone responded.

It was a gruff voice that came from inside the closed door. "Who is it?"

"It's me—Javis."

"It's the middle of the night, you fool! What are you doing coming here, anyway?"

Samuel feared Javis might bolt, but he didn't. Instead, he blurted, "My wife's awful sick. I need Herdon's help. I think she's going to die." The trembling of his voice added credence to his urgent message.

The door opened. The man standing there was deep in shadow. Samuel couldn't make out his face. "It'll take time," he said.

"Please hurry," Javis pleaded.

"Be patient, you foolish man. I'll have to send someone to take his place with the child in the morning. Don't expect him for three or four days at least."

Javis started to speak again, but the voice from the gloomy doorway interrupted. "Enough. Go to your sick wife. Away with you, now!"

The door closed with a groan.

"We'll follow whoever they send after Herdon and that may lead us to the baby," Sam said after Javis had rejoined them.

All that night they watched the house, but no one ever came out. They sent Javis home with a stern warning about what might happen if he tried to leave. Then for three more days they waited and watched both Javis' home and the stone house. No one either came in or went out of either house. Samuel was puzzled.

Finally at dusk on the fourth night, as Samuel, nearly done in with exhaustion, sat in the trees near Javis' house, someone approached it. It was not Herdon. He entered and stayed only a short time before coming out with Javis firmly in tow. The man was obviously angry and berated Javis with fury as they headed up the street.

Samuel followed at a discreet distance, but rapidly, as Javis and his angry companion were wasting no time. They went directly to the big stone house where both Gadoni and Nemti were hidden, trying to stay awake. Samuel joined them as Javis was ushered unceremoniously through the front door. Samuel had Gadoni and Nemti watch the back while he watched the front. An hour passed and no one reappeared. Samuel was getting nervous. He waited a few more minutes. The door finally opened and Javis came through, stumbling and falling.

Samuel held his breath. Javis struggled to get to his feet, finally succeeding, but held his stomach as he shuffled down the walk. He fell again when he reached the street. He was a long time getting up. Samuel dared not approach him until he was farther away from the house for fear someone was watching from one of the many windows.

Javis was crawling. He finally managed to get to his feet again and walk a few steps. For several minutes Javis struggled up the street, finally collapsing and making no further effort to rise. Darkness was closing in.

Samuel looked up and down the street. Seeing no one, he rushed out of his hiding place, gathered the little man up in his arms and ran back into the trees beside the road. He soon discovered why Javis was having so much trouble; he had been badly beaten. "Javis, talk to me," Samuel urged.

His eyes opened, and he looked up at Samuel, seeming to study him.

"Who did this, Javis?" Samuel pressed gently.

Feebly, and with his head lowered, Javis finally spoke. "He saw that my wife wasn't dying."

"Who?"

"I can't tell you."

"Javis, can't you see that they don't care about you? Why do you protect them like this?"

"I made an oath. They say I broke it. They wanted to kill me, but Herdon wouldn't let them. I'm never to speak of them again or . . ." he said, his voice so soft Samuel could barely make out his words.

Herdon had failed; Javis was dying. Samuel was angry, but even in his anger, he felt pity for the despicable little robber. He held him gently in his arms until the thin body relaxed in death. Samuel placed him on the ground and sped back to find Gadoni and Nemti. After explaining what had happened, he asked, "Has anyone else left?"

"No," Gadoni answered.

"Should someone go in?" Samuel asked slowly, "or should we wait for someone to come out and follow them?"

"I'm tired of waiting. It's getting us nowhere," Gadoni said impatiently. "There's a light in there. I'm going in. If I listen I may learn something."

"How will you get in?" Nemti asked uncertainly.

Gadoni pointed. "Those high windows. It's dark now, so I'll use those vines that grow up the side of the house to scale the wall"

"Nemti, you stay here and keep watch while I go with Gadoni," Samuel said. Gadoni went first, swiftly pulling his way up the stout vines and disappearing through a window. A few minutes later, Samuel joined him. It was dark inside and they had to feel their way around, groping like blind men.

After locating a stairwell, Samuel and Gadoni crept down. The steps were of stone and revealed no sound beneath the soft leather soles of their sandals. At the bottom, they carefully pushed a heavy wooden door open a few inches, swords drawn. Samuel peered through. All he could see was a dimly glowing lamp on the very table where he and Oreb had met with Gadianton, Kishkumen, and their secret band. The room was deserted.

They listened. There were no voices. Cautiously, they searched the entire house. There was no one in it. "This can't be," Gadoni said, frowning. "Nobody left this house after Javis did."

"Unless they left when we were climbing in, or while I was with Javis and not watching the front." He scratched his head. "But I didn't see anyone on the street, either. Let's go talk to Nemti."

They walked out the front door. "Are you certain?" Samuel asked Nemti a moment later.

"Well, quite sure. I kept moving around. I don't think anyone could have left by either the front or the back without me knowing it," the young man said.

Samuel stroked his chin thoughtfully. "Let's go back inside. I want to look that place over more carefully."

The young soldier nodded. "I'm sorry, I . . ."

"You're doing fine. There's something strange here. Come on, you might just as well come with us."

With the aid of the robber's oil lamp, they lit three torches they found lying in a large pile in the big room. For the next several minutes they searched the house from top to bottom—three stories in all.

Samuel, in frustration, slapped a wooden wall near the back of the house on the ground floor. It moved. "Gadoni, Nemti, come here," he shouted.

They appeared from neighboring rooms. He was busily poking and pressing when Gadoni asked, "What is it, Sam?"

"This wall feels loose." He sniffed. "And there's a musty smell—like a cellar. The smell of dirt, even."

"But there's no basement in this house," Nemti observed, poking at the wall.

"Maybe or maybe not. What if there's a hidden lock of some kind. This loose section could be a door," Samuel said, his spine tingling as he spoke.

For the next few minutes, they searched frantically for a clue. Finally, Gadoni stepped back and surveyed the room while the others watched, their torches burning brightly. His eyes slowly covered the stone floor they stood on. Suddenly, he walked over to a far corner. "This rock," he said, "it's a little different color from the rest in this floor."

Samuel started toward him as Gadoni pressed the toe of his sandal on the off-colored stone. With a creak, the loose section of wall began to rotate. Gadoni pressed harder and it opened wider. By the time the secret door was fully open, the rock was depressed six inches into the floor.

All three men stepped forward. The light from their torches revealed a steep, narrow stone stairway that led down until it faded into blackness. An ingenious set of ropes and pulleys connected the door with the stone.

After briefly studying the complicated contraption, they moved single file down the steep stairs into a deep, dark passageway. Nervously, Gadoni, who was in the lead, pulled his knife. Nemti, following closely on his heels, followed suit. Samuel brought up the rear, watching nervously behind him as they went.

The passageway was rocked in, both walls and ceiling. They followed it for several hundred yards before they finally came to another steep stairway that led upward. Nemti stepped beside Gadoni and the two of them took the final step before the stairs. Samuel stared in shock as they disappeared through a gaping hole that suddenly opened beneath them.

Samuel dropped to his knees and crawled to the edge. Both torches still burned, but were lying at the bottom of the hole, about twelve feet down. Gadoni and Nemti stood up and brushed themselves off. Samuel shouted, "Are you hurt?"

After his voice quit echoing, Gadoni answered. "Just bruised, Sam, but we can't get out. You've got to help us."

"Gadoni!" Sam heard young Nemti shout in terror. "We're not alone down here."

"What do you mean?" Samuel called down.

"Skeletons," was the chilling reply. "Lots of them."

Samuel rose to his feet. "Hang in there and I'll be back. I'll find a rope or something. I'll have you out in no time."

He ran back up the long tunnel, his heart pounding and fear constricting his chest. The robbers were not to be underestimated. He had to hurry and get Gadoni and Nemti out of that deadly dungeon. There was no time to be wasted if they were to ever find little Enos.

CHAPTER 10

Nonita's mount plodded along the trail, lagging several steps behind her escort. Her heart was still heavy with grief. She had been happy with Sheam. She couldn't understand why he had died and left her, still only in her late teens, so desperately alone.

She had been sorely disappointed when Samuel, the big brother whom she had always thought could do anything, had failed to come for her. She had put off asking Sheam's family to send word to her own, but she had been so desperately alone that she finally knew she had to return to Gilead. After hearing the terrible news about Gadoni's family she was anxious and fearful and wanted all the more to be reunited with her own people.

The dense forest she was passing through was filled with sights and sounds of beauty, but she was so deep in her troubled thoughts that she was oblivious to it all. Her mind was weighted down with heartache and worry. She thought of Oreb lying injured and shuddered. He had always been invincible. Only a few years older than her, he had fancied himself her protector. He was the only one in the family who had resented her marriage while so young to an older man, a stranger from far off Bountiful. Feelings of guilt and betrayal toward Oreb were the main reason she had grieved alone and waited so long to send word of her husband's death.

A stunned shout jerked her from her sad reverie. With a start, she realized she had lagged farther behind her escort and he was out of sight. With a fierce pounding in her chest she rode around a curve in the trail ahead.

She stopped abruptly, both hands flying to her face. The man who was taking her to her family lay face down on the ground in front of her, an arrow protruding from his back. His horse was loping down the trail. Her long dark hair flew as she threw her head around, searching for the unseen assailant.

Her first thought was Lamanites, but she knew it was highly unlikely that they would be so near the city of Bountiful. They had not been in this part of the land since Captain Moroni and his armies had defeated them several years before.

Her frightened mind had not had time to conjure up any other possibilities before two men, Nephites, emerged from the thick trees and shrubs at the side of the trail and grabbed the reins of her horse. Their faces were split with menacing grins.

Nonita dug her heels into the horse's sides but was too late. The men held fast as two more appeared behind her. From the evil glint in their eyes she knew these men weren't there to offer aid. She was jerked roughly from the horse's back and sank to the ground, her trembling legs refusing to support her.

One of the men pulled her to her feet. "This one's a beauty!" he exclaimed.

Nonita reacted by spitting in his leering face. With an oath, he jumped back. His companions laughed. "She don't choose you, Kerlin," one of them said.

"She'll change her mind when she gets to know me," the one called Kerlin hurled back.

He reached for Nonita again. She spun away but he grabbed her roughly by the arm. She scratched his face with her free hand so deep that blood oozed. He slapped her and she bit his hand viciously, but he was strong and held her tight while the others bound her arms securely behind her back.

"Where is my horse going? Why are you letting it just run off?" Nonita demanded.

"Where we're going, horses can't make it. There are no trails, only a jungle full of bogs and streams," Kerlin answered with a chuckle, pushing her into the dense foliage beside the trail.

"Where are we going?" she demanded, determined not to let these men have their way with her.

"To join the other women."

"What other women?" Nonita asked, not really wanting to hear the answer.

"The ones we're collecting as wives," he said frankly, pulling absently on a short, neatly trimmed beard. "You are a godsend. We didn't expect to . . ."

"I'll never be . . ."

"Hush," he ordered, his faded brown eyes flashing from a rugged face. "You're not in a position to say what you'll do. We need wives for the men of our brave band. You'll be grateful to us one day."

Nonita realized with nauseous fear that these men must be part of the band her dead escort had called the Gadianton robbers. They were ruthless, greedy, power-hungry men, following leaders who were inspired by the devil. She lapsed into gloomy silence as the stark reality of her perilous situation hit her.

After several hours of strenuous travel, the band prepared to spend the night. There, beneath the bulky shelter of a huge mangrove tree she endured the foul mouths of the robbers all evening. Kerlin, though she tried to ignore him, was always nearby.

She found herself tightly bound before her captors settled down to sleep. "Why are you doing this, Kerlin?" she protested.

"So you won't wander off."

"Are you crazy?" she asked boldly. "I wouldn't start off in this jungle by myself for anything. I'd never make it."

"I don't doubt that, but all the same, we won't take any chances." He gawked at her in the light of the small campfire as he spoke. She watched him angrily in return. He wasn't more than a couple of inches taller than she but was powerfully built. "Sure wouldn't want to let you get away," he said after she had endured an uneasy minute. "You're a mighty pretty young woman, and . . ." His voice trailed off.

Nonita shuddered. Her thoughts kept turning to her dead husband. With all her heart she longed for him. If only he hadn't died, she thought bitterly, I wouldn't be in this terrible situation.

"Go to sleep, girl," Kerlin ordered brusquely. "We have a long way to travel tomorrow and you need the rest."

* * *

Samuel's face was long as he stood beside Oreb's bed. "I'm afraid the robbers got them," he explained. "I wasn't gone long, but when I returned to the hole in the tunnel, it was empty and the trap reset. I jumped over it and hiked up the long stairway beyond only to find a locked door."

With a grimace, Oreb swung his legs over the edge of the bed and started to rise. Samuel reached a big hand out and gently restrained him. "What are you doing, Sam?" Oreb demanded.

"The real question is, what are you doing?" Samuel countered.

"I've been getting around some. I'll never get well if I don't get out of this bed. Anyway, you need help, big brother, and it looks like I'm about all you have left." Oreb brushed Samuel's hand away and stood shakily, bravely holding a straight face, but unable to conceal the pain in his eyes. "There, you see, Sam, I'm all right. I'll help you," he announced.

"Oreb, you can't!" Kapilla had just entered the room, her twin brothers trailing behind her.

Oreb smiled at her fondly. "Kapilla, I must. Sam needs my help. He . . ."

Kapilla's pale eyes narrowed and sprayed Samuel with anger. "Sam, can't you see he's not well yet?"

"I didn't . . ." Samuel began.

Oreb finished for him. "I want to go, Kapilla. Sam's on your side. He thinks I'm not up to it yet, but I am."

Kapilla was not persuaded. "I just don't see why you want to get yourself hurt again," she scolded. "Gadoni and Nemti can . . ." Oreb cut her off with a wave of his hand. Sudden understanding appeared on her face. "They're hurt," she said.

"They're gone," Samuel corrected softly. "The robbers have them."

"Oh, no! I'm sorry," Kapilla said, shaking her head slowly back and forth. "Did my father do it?"

"I don't know exactly who did," Samuel said and explained what had happened. Kim and Kib had stood at the door during the brief exchange. Samuel jerked his head toward them in surprise when Kim said, "We'll help."

Oreb laughed and sank back onto the bed. "He means it, Sam."

"But they're . . ."

"What? Not smart enough? Oh, Sam, they're smart all right. They just need a chance to prove it."

Kapilla spoke up, the anger gone from her face, and her pale green eyes glowing with joy. "Oreb is the difference," she said. "He's spent hours talking to the boys and telling them stories. They love him almost as much as I do."

Both boys were smiling broadly. The frightened look was gone from their eyes. "Herdon is the reason they've been so silent. He used to beat them, even when they were babies, just for making any sort of noise or anything. They can both talk just fine when they want to, can't you?" Oreb said, smiling at them.

"Yes," Kim said.

"I can, too," Kib followed.

Their faces were lit like candles. Oreb stood up again and approached them, his face not nearly as contorted with pain as it had been a minute ago. "They've been able to talk all the time, but only did so when no one was around except the two of them. I think fear repressed them. They're fine now that they've learned their father can't hurt them anymore."

Samuel stretched one of his long arms around each of the boys and said, "Well boys, the best way you can help right now is by looking after your sister. Will you do that for us?"

"Yes," Kim said.

"Yes," Kib agreed.

Samuel turned again to Oreb. He had been watching him closely. He was much stronger than he'd thought. "Oreb, there is something you could do."

"There is?"

"Yes. You'll have to be very careful, but there is a way you can help me."

Kapilla's proud smile faded, but she lodged no further protest. Instead, she said to Kim and Kib, "I'm counting on you two. You won't let me down, will you?"

"No," said Kim.

"No," echoed Kib.

"Oreb, get some more rest. We'll talk later and leave after dark," Samuel announced. Then, turning to Kapilla, he said, "We'll be okay. And tell Nonita when she arrives that we're all right and will be back soon."

When Samuel met Oreb in the giant hallway of the palace that evening, his younger brother was looking pale and thin, but his eyes were lit with excitement. Without a word he followed Samuel outside, his sword buckled on and his bow and quiver of arrows slung over his shoulder.

Samuel had arranged for horses. He didn't want to inflict anymore wear to his brother than was absolutely necessary. They did not dismount until they were near the big stone house. "Remember this place?" he asked Oreb, pointing at the ghostly structure, lit only by a slender finger of silver moon and a host of twinkling stars.

Oreb nodded.

"The entrance to the tunnel is in there. We'll tether the horses in the trees and go in. I hope there's no one home," Samuel said, trying to sound cheerful.

No candles, torches, or lamps burned inside. The two men drew their swords as they entered, Samuel taking the lead. He felt his way in the darkness until he located the stash of torches in the empty meeting room. With the aid of his flint and steel he soon had one burning brightly. He lit a second one from the first and handed it to Oreb.

The secret door was as Samuel had left it hours before. He opened it, peered through, and then said, "You stand guard, Oreb. All I plan to do is step off the distance to the other end of the passageway. I'll be right back."

"You better be," Oreb said nervously, forcing a grin.

Samuel moved swiftly but cautiously down the long tunnel. When he reached the trap at the base of the stairway at the far end, he turned and retraced his steps. When he walked through the secret doorway he found Oreb emerging from the shadows and retrieving his torch. "Follow me," Samuel said after closing the door.

He led Oreb outside, leaving their extinguished torches behind. He boosted Oreb onto his horse and handed him the reins of the other one. "As near as I can tell, the tunnel goes that way," Samuel said, pointing southward.

He stepped into the deserted street and looked the houses over before starting off, Oreb following with the horses. He marched, counting his steps, directly down a cobbled street. When he finally stopped, Oreb pulled up beside him. "This it?" Oreb asked.

"Five hundred and ninety-two steps," Samuel mumbled, looking about him in the dimly lit night. "There. That stone house over there that is built on a mound. The tunnel must end there."

"That's bigger than the other place," Oreb observed as Samuel helped him off the horse. "And there is light in there. Do you think Gadoni and Nemti . . ."

"They could be in there. Stay here," Samuel said, pointing to a massive pine that Oreb slipped behind. "I'll hide the horses and then we'll have a look around."

A minute later, Samuel and Oreb worked their way close to the big stone structure. "Oreb, keep a watch out here while I go in," Samuel whispered. "I'm going to try that window."

"What are you going to do in there?"

"Just have a look. I want to know who's in there."

Samuel left Oreb waiting again. It only took him a few seconds to enter and he moved silently inside, following the sound of raucous laughter that came from the center of the massive house. He passed through a maze of rooms and hallways before coming to a closed door with light seeping beneath it. The laughter and loud voices came from just beyond. He shoved gently on the door, easing it open just enough to peer inside.

Several men were sprawled around the room in various stages of inebriation. A vast table was covered with the untidy remains of a feast. Wine containers were strewn on the floor, some shattered, the purple contents staining the floor.

Fierce anger surged through Samuel when he recognized the raspy voice of Herdon coming from beyond the table. His words were slurred and Samuel had to strain to decipher what he was saying over the laughter and rude noises of the drunks. Shortly, the noise gradually subsided and his ears perked at the sound of his name.

It was Herdon's voice again. He said, "I'd sure like to have seen Samuel's face when he discovered his friends missing." A round of chuckles swept over the room before Herdon belched and went on. "Yes, sir, he's going to come to us like a fly to fresh dung now."

Another robber said with a slur, "And then we can take him to the hideout in the wilderness. He'll wish he had never messed with us." Samuel listened a few more minutes, but nothing more of interest came his way, so he rose to his feet and started back toward the front of the house. He was feeling his way down a large hallway when a distinct creaking startled him. It came from a room to his right. He stopped and pressed an ear to the door.

Footsteps were coming his way. He slipped into a room across the hall, leaving the door cracked slightly, and peered through. Two men entered the hallway, the lead one, someone he didn't know, was carrying a torch. The other was hard to see and Samuel couldn't make out his features, but his walk was vaguely familiar.

Samuel slid out of his hiding spot and cautiously followed. The man with the torch shoved open the door where the party was taking place. The voice of the other man rang out in anger. It was the voice of Gadianton!

"What is going on here?" he demanded. "You bunch of drunken swine! Who is standing guard? Do you think we can whisk Samuel's friends away and expect him to do nothing? For all you men know he could be in this house at this very moment!"

Gadianton paused. The room grew still. The power of the outlaw leader penetrated the woozy brains of even the drunkest of his band. "Get yourselves organized," he ordered. "I want this place secure in minutes. I am returning to our headquarters now."

Samuel waited to hear no more. He hustled back down the hallway and left the house, joining Oreb outside.

"You had me worried, Sam. What took you so long in there?" his brother asked anxiously.

"Herdon's in there. So are lots of others. They're drunk. Gadianton came in and told them to be on the lookout for me." "How did he get in? I didn't see anyone . . ."

"The tunnel . . . or a tunnel. I suspect this house is connected to more than the one we just came from. Gadianton said he was returning to their headquarters, so he must have come from there, wherever it is. I'm sure it's not the house we were in earlier. It could be that Gadoni and Nemti are at this headquarters he mentioned. One of the others mentioned a wilderness hideout and that they would take me there when I came running to them. We've got to find it, but not with them taking me there."

"Okay, maybe tomorrow," Oreb said weakly.

Samuel was alarmed. Oreb had sunk to his knees and was holding his head in his hands. "Oreb, let's get you back to the palace so you can rest. I should never have made you come in your condition."

Oreb started to protest, but Samuel firmly guided him back to their horses and helped him aboard. Back at the palace, Samuel had a guard wake Kapilla. She tenderly cared for Oreb.

Samuel waited no longer. He had a servant care for the horses and left the palace on foot, running swiftly through the darkened streets of a slumbering Zarahemla. He went directly to the large stone house he had so recently left.

He approached with extreme caution. Gadianton's order had not been ignored. Several sentries stood, or sat, around the house. The advantage was Samuel's. He knew they were there and he knew they were drunk. Their reflexes would be slow and their wits sluggish. He moved with stealth and approached one of the sentries from behind. With one end of an unlit torch, he rapped the man sharply on the back of the head, catching him before he fell. After carrying the unconscious man into the deep shadows, he bound and gagged him and left him in a clump of fragrant bushes.

One by one, each of his colleagues met the same fate. There were five in all, and with them out of the way, Samuel entered the house again. He hung his torch from his belt, adjusted his bow and quiver to a more comfortable position on his back and drew his sword. Not bothering to check the house for the other robbers, he moved through the darkness by memory and feel toward the room Gadianton had appeared from.

Samuel entered and felt his way around the walls. Satisfied that there were no windows or other doors, he jammed a large wooden bench against the door. He now feared intrusion in the windowless room only from the secret passage he was sure existed. He lit his torch and chuckled to himself. Whoever had designed the system of secret doors and tunnels lacked diversity. The door and the catch were identical to the one Samuel was familiar with in the other house.

He wasted no time in pressing the stone and watching the hidden door swing into the secret passageway. He removed the bench from its propped position against the door to the hallway before easing into the secret corridor and closing the section of wall behind him and starting down the stairway.

Samuel soon confirmed his suspicion that this was not the same passageway he had followed earlier. There had to be another entrance to the tunnel that connected this house with the first one. One marked difference appeared after traveling only a few steps from the bottom of the stairs—the tunnel veered sharply to the right. From there it went on for close to a half-mile, then it forked.

He stood undecided for a minute, studying the two routes. He finally decided to follow the one to the left. Ever alert for a trap, he moved as quickly as he dared along the musty underground passageway.

This maze beneath the city was not of recent construction. Samuel wondered who had spent the months it must have taken to first dig, then rock up the long corridors. He suspected there were still more. The robbers must have discovered them somehow and now used them very effectively for their own sinister purposes. He even wondered if these passages dated back to the days of the Mulekites who had first established this city many hundreds of years ago.

The rock houses and secret doors were of more recent vintage, probably designed by the robbers. Samuel's thoughts were interrupted by a sudden gush of cool, clean air. He flattened himself against the wall, extinguishing his torch, thinking someone had opened a door into another hideout ahead somewhere.

His heart pounded and his palms sweated as he waited, expecting a violent confrontation at any moment. No one came, but the breeze continued. Afraid to move without light for fear of traps in the tunnel floor, Samuel finally pulled out his flint and steel and relit his torch. Cautiously he moved forward once again. He was surprised as the tunnel turned gradually upward. He was even more surprised when he found himself stepping out into the warm night air. Sam stood in a deep, heavily foliaged stand of trumpet trees. The shield shaped leaves were so thick he could not see the thin moon or stars above. He worked his way out of them and stared at the dark, ominous wall of Zarahemla, barely discernable in the distance. It took a moment before he realized that he was standing, not inside, but outside of the city!

He spent several minutes orienting himself with the terrain until he was sure he could find the opening again if he ever had to. He forced himself to finally re-enter the dank confines of the secret tunnel. He felt like a caged animal in there, with nowhere to turn if danger presented itself.

Once underground again, Samuel decided to see where the other fork led. It proved to be short and ended at another long stairway, not unlike the others he had encountered. After checking carefully for a trapdoor at the foot of the stairs and finding none, he began the ascent.

He found the catch on the back side of the door before extinguishing his torch. He had to pull hard before the door began to swing toward him. He stopped, waited, heard no one inside, and pulled harder. The door complained with a dull screech, but swung open, admitting him to a small, cool room. He closed the door and felt his way around the room. It was empty and had only one legitimate door. Just to reassure himself, he felt for and found the loose stone in the corner that opened the door—just like the others.

Samuel carefully opened the door that led into what he was sure must be the headquarters of the robbers that Gadianton had referred to. It swung smoothly, without all the racket he had just endured. He stepped into a hallway so narrow that his shoulders nearly brushed both walls at once. He reached above him and cracked his knuckles on the unexpectedly low ceiling.

He turned to his right in the hallway, discovering that it ended in solid rock only a couple of feet past the door. He went the other way with more success, but stumbled and fell, painfully bruising his knees, when he ran into an unexpected stairway, leading upward. Groping his way in the stifling darkness, he made his way up. It was long, narrow, and turned gradually as it ascended.

At the top, he found another door which he opened quietly. He slipped through and stared into the total blackness of another room. The darkness played on his frayed nerves as he began to feel his way around the room, keeping one hand against the rough rock wall.

Samuel sensed a presence in the room. He quietly shoved his unlit torch into his belt and drew his sword. He strained to hear the almost inaudible sound of someone breathing. He must have disturbed someone sleeping in this room, but that other person, whoever it was, was aware of Samuel's presence and was making every effort to be silent.

A chill came over him and his fist tightened on the hilt of his sword. He took shallow, silent breaths, feeling the minutes tick by like hours. He couldn't stay where he was all night, so he finally took a tentative step away from the wall.

A hoarse scream filled the room, echoing from the rock walls. Swift steps came at him. Samuel deftly hopped sideways just before his invisible attacker reached him. Something sliced neatly through his vest, barely brushing his skin. The man screamed again, as if trying to frighten Samuel into immediate surrender. The scream was intimidating, but not near as frightening as the sword Samuel's enemy wielded.

Terror struck when the echoing of the scream was replaced by the unmistakable sound of pounding feet somewhere deep in the building. He grappled with the fear, trying to keep his mind clear. Had he shut the door when he entered the room? He did not think so. He must find it again.

He listened to the other man's labored breathing and smelled the sickly sweet odor of stale wine permeating the air. He tried to figure about where the door was from him. Fifteen feet, perhaps, and to his enemy's right? Samuel intentionally scuffed one foot on the floor and swiftly sidestepped as his attacker lunged with another ear-shattering scream. Without stopping, Samuel raced for the door, slamming painfully into the wall, little bits of light flashing in his head, but his right hand discovering the empty doorway.

Shaking off the pain, Samuel slid through, reached for the door, and slammed it shut just as a flash of light appeared from across the room. He ran down the dark stairway, willing his feet not to miss a step. The door above him opened and light flooded the stairway as he rounded the curve.

Men were shouting and cursing, running down the stairs after him. He reached the bottom unexpectedly and sprawled on his face on the rock floor. His knees and elbows were skinned, but he regained his feet and ignored the pain as he sprinted down the hallway, slamming into the wall at the end. Light from his pursuer's torches filled the hallway as he found the door, pulled it open, and lunged in, shoving it shut behind him.

Samuel's heart raced. Unless he could open the secret passageway and get through it and close the door behind him before the robbers entered, he was a dead man. He leaned against the door, gasping for air when he felt a thick, loose board against his chest. He grabbed it and twisted. It came around and fell into a catch of some kind. Men reached the door from the other side, but it held fast.

Suddenly remembering his wife's wise counsel, Samuel offered a silent prayer of thanks and a plea for further help. He had neglected to pray as he should and reflected on all the difficulties that had come to him the past few days. He had depended on his own strength and it came to him that that was not enough.

As the men slammed their bodies against the door, Samuel moved again and pressed on the hidden stone, opening the creaking secret door. He bolted through and pulled it shut just as the crude lock broke with a loud crack, allowing the robbers to flood into the room behind him. He spun to start down the stairs but fell. He caught himself before rolling down more than a couple of steps. The secret door started to creak again. Almost as if pushed by an unseen hand, Samuel lunged back up the stairs, slipping behind the door as it opened.

A flood of men and light surged through and down the stairway. "He can't be far ahead. We must catch him," one voice shouted above the din.

"Run faster," another commanded.

At least twenty men disappeared into the tunnel. Samuel waited until only a faint glow from their torches remained before re-entering the room. He went to close the secret door, but changed his mind, and slowly made his way back into the headquarters of the secret band of robbers, a repentant prayer in his heart. Samuel recognized with a guilty feeling that only with the help of God could he and his friends and loved ones get out of the perilous situation they were in.

As he walked slowly through the house, Samuel left each door in the position he found it. If any of the robbers in the tunnel returned, he did not want to tip them off that he had not escaped through the underground passageways. For several minutes he felt his way from room to room, searching for any clue as to the whereabouts of Gadoni, Nemti, and Enos, hoping beyond hope that they were near, not in the wilderness hideout. He realized after a few minutes of unsuccessful exploring that it would be nearly impossible to find the passageway again in the darkness. He would have to find another way out of the building.

Alert for more robbers as he explored, Samuel finally heard voices ahead of him. Despite his fear of being discovered again, he wanted to hear what they had to say. He already knew that he was in a large building. He suspected it had more floors above him. He searched for a stairway, wondering as he did about the absence of windows. Perhaps he was still underground, but after climbing two flights of stairs from the level of the tunnel, that seemed unlikely.

He shoved the puzzle from his thoughts when he found another stairway and climbed it. At the top a warm breeze brushed his face. He looked around and spotted an open window, faint light illuminating its outline against the night sky. He approached and looked out. To his surprise, he stood only a few feet above the ground. He could easily climb through and escape.

That was not his design—yet. He was satisfied, though, that much of this building was concealed beneath the ground. He suspected that it was not really a very tall building when viewed from the street.

He was suddenly startled and jumped back from the window as a voice cried out from just a few feet away, "Who goes there?"

"I just came up to get some air," he answered, trying to sound nonchalant above the roar of his hammering heart.

A shadowy figure stepped near in the dim light of the window. "You know that no one is to come up here unless he is on duty as a sentry. What is . . ." the voice was saying.

Samuel cut him off. "I'm sick. I need fresh air. I'll go back down in a moment." He inched toward the guard as he spoke.

"You haven't identified yourself yet!" the guard hissed angrily.

"I'm . . ." Samuel began as he lunged at the sentry. They struggled for a moment, then Samuel was able to deliver a powerful blow that connected with the robber's face and he collapsed. Samuel dragged him to the window and shoved him out. He scrambled out himself and carried the unconscious man into some dense shrubbery where he left him bound and gagged. Moments later, Samuel re-entered the building.

Being more careful, he searched out a room where he hid in a closet, directly over the mumble of voices from below. By pressing his ear to the floor, which at this level in the building was made of rough wood, he was able to listen to the conversation taking place down there.

Nothing of interest was said until a commotion erupted. "So you're back. Where's your prisoner, or is he dead?"

"Got away," someone said.

"What? Twenty of you couldn't catch one person? How did he get away?"

"He ran like the wind!"

"Did he have a torch?"

"No."

The first voice sounded incredulous when he asked, "Do you mean that he ran faster in the darkness than you could with light?"

Other voices chipped in, angry and frustrated. Someone said, "I think it was a spirit!"

"Or black magic," said another.

On and on the noisy argument raged. Samuel chuckled to himself, but his humor faded when an only too familiar voice spoke and all the others stilled.

Gadianton said, "Enough, the lot of you! Am I cursed with nothing but fools? Nobody outran you. There was no magic. You've been outsmarted." He paused for effect. When he continued, he spoke softer, but with intensity. "It was probably Samuel looking for our prisoners. Did anyone look behind you? No, I daresay you all ran wildly after him, never once looking back. The rest of you just sat here chattering like monkeys and let him walk right back into our headquarters."

The hair stood up on the back of Samuel's neck. He wanted to get to his feet, but forced himself to relax and listen to what else Gadianton had to say.

"I'm sure he's found his way out of here by now, but he'll be back. Put more men on guard. I'm leaving for our wilderness hideout in the morning. I plan to question the prisoners. When I get back, I don't want to learn that you have allowed that treacherous man in here again without capturing him." His voice was shrill and angry. "So get to it, you lazy pack of dogs," he said, and silence prevailed below.

Samuel mulled over the words he had just heard. Gadoni and Nemti were not in this place, nor was the baby. They were in the wilderness! He was wasting his time here. He had to find that hideout, and soon.

Samuel was cautious as he headed for the window, the shortest way out from where he was. He eased around a corner, prepared to make a dash for the window, but flattened himself against the wall, holding his breath at the appearance of two sentries. He had not been seen, but his path to the window was blocked.

It was soon apparent that it was these robbers' intention to stand guard at the window to prevent, ironically, the intrusion of an enemy from outside. He was the enemy they watched for, and all he wanted was to get away.

If there were two here, he was sure there would be two at any other doors or windows. And the more he moved about the more likely someone would hear or see him. He had to go now if he was to escape, but he knew he could not overpower these two alert robbers as he had the earlier sentry. Samuel had no desire to kill anyone. He had taken many lives in battle, but it was something that always brought sorrow to his soul.

He thought of little Enos and of Gadoni and the brave young Nemti. He could not let them down. Silently he prayed for guidance.

Laban.

The name entered his mind and Samuel reflected on the story told from the writings of his ancestor, Nephi. That great man, though young, had been commanded to obtain the plates of brass from Laban, a wicked relative who lived in Jerusalem. The record was essential to the spiritual well-being of Nephi's posterity when they entered the Promised Land. The Lord allowed Laban to fall into Nephi's hands, and when he shrank away from the awful prospect of taking his life, the Spirit of the Lord commanded him to do so. Nephi had obeyed.

Now, over five hundred years later, Samuel faced a similar grim task. He knelt in a darkened corner of the hallway. He must leave now and find a way to help his friends or they would lose their lives. He prayed for strength to do what must be done.

He still carried a short bow and several arrows. He eased the bow from his back. It was specially designed for the kind of mission Samuel was on now. It allowed freedom of movement while being readily accessible when needed. He fitted a sharp, short arrow into the string of his bow and took deadly aim in the dim light from the window.

When the first robber fell with a cry, the second pulled his sword and peered into the darkness, confused. Samuel shot again and a moment later leaped through the window and into the bushes outside as footsteps rang through the halls of the building.

Later, Samuel watched the somber sky turn golden from his hiding spot near the exit of the tunnel beyond the great gray walls of Zarahemla. His body ached and cried for rest, but he was determined to follow Gadianton into the wilderness, if he came this way. He had almost nodded off when voices alerted him. Gadianton and several other men suddenly strode from the thick grove of trumpet trees that concealed the mouth of the tunnel. A rush of energy filled his exhausted body, pushing him to his feet. Silently, he followed as they struck out in single file through the forest.

CHAPTER 11

The sun bore down unmercifully on the robbers' high wilderness hideout. Kishkumen wiped his brow with his hand as he smugly introduced himself to the women captives seated miserably on the hard ground in front of him. "I am Kishkumen, leader of a brave band of men who have been wronged by their own people, the Nephites. You have been chosen to join us here in the wilderness to cook and care for us while we prepare to avenge the wrongs that have been inflicted upon us by unjust judges in Zarahemla and other cities." He paused, his dark eyes sweeping over the unhappy group before resting on Nonita, his face twisting into an approving smile.

Nonita watched him, her mind full of defiance and courage. During the long march through the wilderness, several other women, all young, had been forced to join the group she was in. Now they were here, slaves, it seemed, to a mysterious band of outlaws.

"Each of you," Kishkumen continued, "will become the wife of one of our brave men. You will bear us children here in the wilderness." His eyes narrowed and his speech slowed with emphasis. "You will not resist or complain. Being chosen by one of my men is the highest honor that could ever come to a young Nephite woman."

From the sobs around her, Nonita knew she was not the only one who found no honor in his proposal. Her eyes were glued to Kishkumen, but she controlled herself as his eyes fell on her again.

"You," he said, almost shouting as he thrust his arm in her direction, making her flinch, "will come with me. I have a special assignment for you."

"Kishkumen, I have chosen her," Kerlin said from his position behind the women.

"I haven't said it is time to choose yet!" Kishkumen thundered.

"Yes, sir, but when you do . . ."

"Enough! I will decide who will choose the first wives. Now, say no more!" he ordered.

Nonita looked back. Kerlin was angry and determined. She was afraid of him and wondered what he was thinking as he stood silent and red-faced after his rebuke. He would, she was sure, defend her if the circumstances were right, but not for the right reasons. Ironically, the thought gave her some comfort in this serene place of horror.

"Come," Kishkumen ordered. Nonita glanced once more at Kerlin, then turned to follow the man who had declared himself the leader.

The robbers' hideout was located deep in the wilderness. They had tents of various sizes pitched on a rugged bench that sat beneath vertical cliffs on the west and overlooking endless miles of velvety green jungle from all other sides. Large boulders were scattered across the area, concealing the carefully placed tents from any who might happen to look from the jungle floor toward the towering mountains. Only a few trees managed to get a toehold in the rock and send down enough roots to support their craggy forms from tumbling on the robbers' camp. Grass and shrubbery was scrubby and sparse.

Nonita was led through the maze of boulders to a large tent that was pitched so close to the cliff that it almost touched the black rock that rose like a giant shadow to dizzying heights overhead. Kishkumen opened the flap that served as a door and motioned for her to enter the tent made of the hides of wilderness beasts. She felt her composure slipping as she thought about what this wicked man might desire of her once inside. She could only pray and hope.

"Here is your replacement," Kishkumen announced to a simple looking little man that sat with his back to Nonita on a pile of soft hides. He swiveled and Nonita gasped when she saw a sleeping Lamanite baby in his hairy arms.

"Take care of the child," Kishkumen ordered. "He is your responsibility until we need him no more."

"Yes, sir," she mumbled, as the full impact of what was happening hit her like a whip. She was being given charge of Enos, the son of Gadoni and Laishita. It had to be him—it could be none other.

"What is your name, girl?" Kishkumen demanded as she tenderly took the child from the simple man's arms.

"Nonita," she stammered, fighting to hold back a flood of tears that were threatening to overflow.

"Nonita, you are to be with him constantly. His life is your responsibility. Do you understand?" Kishkumen asked.

"Yes." She dared not say more.

"Very well," he said as he ushered the simple one from the tent. He stopped and poked his head back inside. She faced away from him, but felt his eyes like fire on her back. "And don't do anything foolish. A guard will be posted outside your tent at all times," he said and the flap swished shut.

Nonita let the tears flow and held the precious child close. She silently swore that she would protect him with her very life and thanked God for bringing her to this unholy place and giving her charge of little Enos.

When the baby awoke crying, Nonita soothed him by rocking him gently in her arms and singing a soft love song. When he persisted, she found a pasty white mixture in a gourd on the floor. She fed him, wondering at how someone so small could look so healthy without the benefit of his mother's milk. The food satisfied him and he was soon in a playful mood. Nonita devoted her full attention to him.

As the long, hot day wore on, sunlight filtered in through a small crack where the crude stitching that held the hides together had torn. With Enos in her arms, Nonita placed an eye to the hole and peered through. Men moved here and there around the few tents that were within her limited view. None of the women could be seen. A tall, heavyset man strolled past her peephole. Instinctively she drew back.

Within minutes she was at the little hole again. It drew her like a moth to a flame. She found security in it. The simple act of viewing her captors without them knowing it gave her a psychological boost that bolstered her courage and determination.

Across the camp from Nonita, sheltered by a huge boulder, was another tent, a much smaller one. Its two occupants were not free to move about as Nonita was. Their muscles ached and their wrists and ankles were chafed and sore from the rawhide cords that bound them. The air reeked of unwashed bodies.

Outside, never less than two heavily armed guards paced back and forth. The captives inside listened to them as they laughed and spoke of the evil designs of their wicked band.

The pair of suffering men whispered when they spoke to each other to avoid attracting the attention of their captors. "They are stealing women now!" Gadoni said, his quiet voice filled with anger. "Do they have no conscience at all?"

Nemti didn't answer for several minutes. When he did, he simply whispered what they both felt and had expressed before. "They must be stopped."

"But how? What can we do?" Gadoni lamented. "They'll kill us when they get Samuel, and they almost certainly will." He fell silent for a moment, his eyes on the hard rock floor. When he spoke again, it was with resolve. "No, he will not be captured. Samuel is too clever for them. We must put our trust in him and in the Lord."

Nemti nodded his assent.

Gadoni went on. "I'm sorry, Nemti. I'll try not to be so negative again. We must keep up our spirits and not lose hope."

"You are a man of great faith," Nemti remarked, his dark brown eyes drawing Gadoni's from the floor. "I admire you. How do you do it? If I had a son and . . ." He stopped, his face downcast. "I'm sorry, I shouldn't have mentioned him. I know how much it must hurt to be reminded . . ."

"Nemti, he is never off my mind," Gadoni interrupted. "I feel he is close, perhaps somewhere in this very camp. And I believe that for now, at least, he is being well cared for. What concerns me is how long that will continue."

The tent flap opened, allowing a breath of fresh air to circulate. A robber stepped in, wrinkling his nose. "You," he said, pointing a long, curved sword at Nemti's face, "come with me."

"Where . . ." Nemti began.

"No questions. Just come."

Nemti tossed a despairing glance at Gadoni, then struggled to his feet. The robber didn't offer to help, just smiled when Nemti grimaced with pain as the rough cords cut into his tender skin. He finally managed to shuffle to the exit. He glanced once more at Gadoni, who sat motionless, his face like granite and his dark eyes closed.

The bright sunlight made Nemti squint. Momentarily blinded, his toe caught on a rock and his cramped muscles refused to respond. He fell face forward on the hard ground. Blood spurted from his nose. He was jerked unceremoniously to his feet. By the time he had regained his balance, his eyes had adjusted to the bright light. He shuffled ahead, a slow stream of blood mixing with the dirt on his leather vest.

Nonita was standing at her little peephole. She gasped when she saw a bloody, badly beaten young Nephite stumbling past the tents and boulders, a sword-wielding robber prodding him along. She watched with morbid interest as they drew closer. He appeared to be about Oreb's age and was tall and strong. She wondered what he had done to prompt the beating he had received.

The young captive was ushered to within ten feet of Nonita's tent. She saw in his dark brown eyes a strong resolve. He held his battered head high and proud as he passed by. Her first thought had been that he was one of them who had been errant, but his eyes told her he was an innocent captive, as she was. She wondered for what purpose he was being held. Why, she asked herself, do these evil and conspiring men force their will on others? She knew the answer; Satan, the author of their evil combinations, was himself miserable and wanted all men to share in that misery. These robbers, miserable in their sins, followed the same course as their chosen master.

A tug on her long dress interrupted Nonita's thoughts. She glanced down at the baby's dark, curly head and smiled.

* * *

Nemti was alone that night, far across the camp from Gadoni. No explanation for his move had been given, but he assumed that someone felt he and Gadoni posed a threat if held together for too long. Maybe they were right, he thought bitterly as he squirmed around on the hard ground, trying to make himself less uncomfortable.

He found it hard to fight discouragement without Gadoni to lift his spirits. Apart from the devout Lamanite, he wasn't sure if he could handle his confinement. But he remembered that he had volunteered for this assignment and had to make the best of it. Maybe he could yet, somehow, be of assistance to little Enos. After all, that was what his mission was all about.

The next morning, Nemti was ushered outside and taken to a fire to eat. He had been fed in the tent with Gadoni twice a day, but for some unknown reason his captors had decided to feed their prisoners all together—probably because there were getting to be quite a few, he surmised.

A stern warning was given to him to not communicate at all with the other prisoners. Gadoni was already seated near the fire when Nemti arrived. The rest of the prisoners—seven in all—were, to Nemti's astonishment, young women. All were young and attractive, but looked dejected and hopeless. Each was bound as he and Gadoni were, with hands in front and feet so close they could barely shuffle.

There was a short, silent wait, then Nemti saw another woman approaching from the same direction he had come. She was not bound, but escorted closely by a husky young robber with a heavily bearded face. The young woman was beautiful beyond belief. She held her head high, and her dark eyes flashed as she drew closer. Her long dark hair fell in gentle curls down her back.

Nemti pulled his eyes from the vision and glanced at Gadoni. His Lamanite friend looked shocked for the briefest moment, then quickly molded his face into granite again, all emotion erased.

Nemti looked at the beautiful young woman again. She was bare-foot and walked slowly, but with dignity, over the rocky ground. Not until she was near the fire did she look right or left. When she did, her eyes fell upon Gadoni. Surprise registered on her face, but, like Gadoni, she controlled it so quickly that he almost wondered if he had imagined it. Those two know each other, he thought, and the knowledge sent his heart racing with new-found hope.

The young woman's eyes swept over the other women. She smiled at them. Several gave weak smiles in return. Nemti, not wanting to appear to be gaping, looked away. If she looked at him, he didn't know it.

The guard behind her waved to a spot on the ground. She gracefully lowered herself. Once seated, she said, "Thank you, Kerlin."

The robber's face was hard and he watched the young woman with leering eyes. He possessed a strong, rugged face, bushy but trimmed beard and faded brown eyes. He was short but stocky, with shoulder length hair. Though he looked to be several years older than the girl he was not an ugly man, Nemti decided, and certainly better groomed than most of the other robbers. But his eyes and face betrayed his character.

The robber in charge repeated the warning that none of the captives speak or otherwise attempt to communicate with one another before a bland breakfast was served. The prisoners, all but the beautiful dark girl, were forced to eat with their hands bound. The women were terribly embarrassed when food spilled on their already soiled clothes as they fumbled with the crude wooden utensils they were given. One of them, younger than the rest, got sick all over herself. The guards laughed and she cried.

Try as he might, Nemti could not keep his eyes off the dark-haired one. Gadoni, on the other hand, never looked her way. Once, Nemti glanced at the girl and caught her studying his face intently. For a long moment their eyes were locked. He read deep anguish but fierce determination in her clear brown eyes. Something about her seemed vaguely familiar, but he wasn't sure what it was. She smiled, a perfect set of gleaming white teeth appealingly exposed. He smiled back, feeling his face flush, and their eyes parted.

Later, back in his stifling little tent of crudely tanned hides, Nemti could think of nothing but the pretty girl. That smile and those aching eyes haunted him. If he never saw her face again, it would be forever etched in his memory.

Again, the picture in his mind of her face reminded him of someone, but who? As Nemti thought again of Gadoni and the look of fleeting recognition he had seen on his dark face, he reasoned that she must remind him of someone as well, someone they both knew.

Suddenly, it hit him like a thunderbolt. Samuel!

The straight, narrow nose, and even white teeth. When Samuel smiled, his teeth were only slightly exposed, as were hers. His was the same smile only on a lighter complected face. But, he argued, she couldn't be kin to Samuel. It just wasn't reasonable.

The look of hurt and anguish in her eyes came to him again, and with it a realization of who she might be finally dawned on him. Nonita, the sister Samuel so desperately loved and wanted to help. She had lost her husband several weeks ago, after a short marriage, Samuel had told him. Gadoni had urged Samuel to go for her in Bountiful, but he had sent a servant of Pacumeni instead.

* * *

Nonita held little Enos close. How she wished she could carry him across the compound and present him to his father. She loved Gadoni like a brother, and wanted desperately to find a way to let him know that his son, this delightful little boy, was okay. She must think of a way. The waiting . . . waiting for whatever was to come would be more bearable to him if he only knew what she held in her arms.

Tears moistened her eyes. Tears, not for herself, as her own tragedy seemed suddenly so far away, but tears for those who still lived—tears for those she loved so much and who were suffering such unbearable anguish. She thought of Laishita, the spirited, part-Lamanite, part-Nephite woman who was mother to the child she held. The fear and agony she must feel would be almost more than one could bear.

Her thoughts turned to Samuel: gallant, brave, honorable Samuel. The brother who had so many times unselfishly laid his life on the line for those he loved. Where was he now? What was he doing? Her hopes, and the hopes of them all, rested on his broad shoulders. What weight he must feel.

Nonita prayed. God could grant Samuel the wisdom and open the way. She would put her trust in Him, she resolved, even above the trust she had in her brother. She smiled and gently rocked the sleeping child, stroking his curly hair and pressing him lovingly against her bosom.

* * *

Gadoni was mentally exhausted. He had spent the afternoon trying to sort through things. Seeing Nonita here in the robbers' camp had nearly unraveled him. It had taken superhuman effort not to look at her again, afraid that if he did, he would give a signal to his captors that he knew her. That, he was sure, would only cause her more pain.

He marveled at the control Nonita exhibited. And he wondered why she alone, of all the captives, had no restraints. Guilt swept that thought away. If Samuel had gone for her instead of helping him, perhaps she wouldn't be here now—then again, maybe she would.

Gadoni wondered where Samuel was. So much depended on him—more than Samuel had any idea, he was sure. If anyone could bring them out of this mess, it was Samuel. But could even he? Not without help!

Gadoni prayed.

CHAPTER 12

Ophera rose from her knees. Word of the disappearance of Gadoni had rocked the little town of Gilead that morning. Her husband, Samuel, would now be trying to rescue both Gadoni and little Enos. He faced an insurmountable task. The robbers sought his life. He could not possibly get near them without the help of God.

It was that divine help she had been, for the past hour, so earnestly petitioning. Now, feeling some relief, she rejoined her distraught friend, Laishita.

"I know it's hard," she said a few minutes later, "but our men will be depending on us. They need our faith, our prayers, and our love."

Laishita wiped the tears from her face and nodded. "I know you're right, Ophera. I know you're right, but . . . but . . ."

Ophera reached for her hand and the tears flowed freely as they stood and embraced. After a couple of minutes, Laishita pulled away, straightened her jet-black hair, dried her reddened eyes, and spoke. "Thank you, Ophera. I could never make it without you. No one ever had a better friend."

The two were silent again. Ophera broke the silence next. "Samuel will find them," she said confidently. "I just wonder where he is right now."

* * *

Samuel glanced at the sinking sun. It was a crimson ball hanging precariously over the western mountains, ready to surrender to their majestic heights. The darkness it promised was what Samuel waited for. He had followed Gadianton and a small band of robbers for two days.

He had learned their habits and knew they would be camping for the night across the large clearing from him.

He had no fear of losing track of them. They were not following any clearly defined trails through the jungle, but left clear signs for him to follow as they forced their way through the dense undergrowth. He took his time working around the swampy clearing, taking great care not to expose himself to his enemy.

The robbers were noisy, seldom ceasing from their raucous laughter and loud, boastful talk. Samuel chewed on a piece of dry meat as he lay in the bushes and listened. He took a drink from his water bag to wash it down and wiped his mouth with the back of his hand. The short growth of hair on his face felt strange. He rubbed his hand over his face again, then reached for another piece of jerky.

Beards were foreign to Samuel. He never allowed the hair on his face to grow more than a day or two if he could help it. Even when out in the wilderness, he kept his knife honed so sharp he could easily scrape the stubble off.

Gadoni grew very little beard and had no trouble keeping a clean face. Samuel envied him, but tonight as he waited and listened in the growing darkness, he smiled with satisfaction and rubbed his face again. The stubble was getting quite long after several days of intentional neglect. He wanted it to grow and willed it to grow faster, giving him a look no one would recognize. A beard was a good disguise.

Samuel suddenly froze in his position on his belly in the bushes when something touched his bare leg. He knew that cool, scaly feeling and did not like it. He had encountered snakes many times in the wilderness. He had never been attacked by one, but they always injected him with an unreasonable portion of fear.

He tried to calm his pounding heart as the snake, a very large one, slithered up the full length of his body. Samuel held his breath when its head brushed his cheek. He did not exhale until he felt two or three feet of the long monster pass off his body.

A minute later it was gone, as silently as it had come. His hands were clammy and he wiped large beads of perspiration from his forehead. He felt almost ill from the close encounter and was trying to shake off the effects of the fright when a loud, masculine scream shattered the jungle night. It came from the robbers camp not many feet beyond him.

"What the . . ." Samuel heard Gadianton start to shout.

"It's a snake," one of the other men cried.

"Well, kill it," Gadianton ordered with disgust in his voice.

A scuffle followed, accompanied by much cursing and shouting. When the disturbance finally began to subside, Samuel heard someone say, "I think it's dead."

Then another voice exclaimed, "That's the biggest snake I ever saw!"

Gadianton's voice was next heard to say sensibly, "Well, now that we have it, let's roast it."

It was relatively quiet as the men skinned their quarry, but a frightened voice interrupted a moment later. "Jarsus is dead."

"What? How . . ." Gadianton began.

"Snake bit him," the other man interrupted.

Samuel felt the sweat break out all over again. He had the urge to jump and flee his hiding place, but controlled himself, and after a few minutes was finally able to concentrate on the conversation of the robbers again.

The demise of the unfortunate Jarsus was soon forgotten, forcefully reminding Samuel of how cold-blooded these evil men were. If the life of one of their own did not matter enough to them to at least mourn his death, then how much less must the lives of their enemies mean? The thought was not a pleasant one, but it served to impress on Samuel the urgency of his mission.

Later, Gadianton ordered the men to go to sleep. Samuel was amazed at how quickly the small band of robbers reacted to Gadianton's order. Their chatter and laughter ceased at once. Again he was impressed that the real leader among the robbers was Gadianton, not Kishkumen.

The next morning he again dined on jerky, sipped a little water, and prepared to follow the slightly diminished band. They were on their way shortly after daybreak as the jungle came alive with birds and small animals, singing and chattering their joy over the new day. Samuel's spirits were lifted until he stepped into the abandoned camp of his enemy and saw the dead body of the one they called Jarsus, lying unburied near the smoldering fire-pit.

The trek was taking Samuel deeper and deeper into the wilderness. By noon, the ground started to rise and he could see the beautiful mountain peaks looming closer. He wondered how far into the rugged mountains the robbers' camp was.

His answer came by mid-afternoon. Sentinels met the small band led by Gadianton. Samuel was close enough to hear the password used by Gadianton before he led his men up a narrow, boulder-strewn path. "Conquer," he said as he approached the sentinels.

Samuel stayed in the trees where he couldn't be seen while he figured his next move.

Samuel, though he couldn't see it from where he was, reasoned that the camp must be situated on a plateau or bench. Beyond, not too far, sheer granite cliffs rose high in the air. Samuel observed the sentinels. He counted seven and there could well have been more. They were positioned so that it would be extremely difficult for someone to sneak into their camp, especially in the light of day. It would be hard in the darkness, but Samuel pondered that possibility.

This was not to be the night, though. Samuel needed to do some scouting first. Sundown found him far to the southwest of the camp and high above it in the mountains. By dark, he had learned what he had hoped for. Though extremely rugged, a man could reach the top of the granite face that descended vertically to the robbers' camp, far below.

After spending the night up there, Samuel worked his way to the very edge of the cliff the next morning. He peered over, fighting the dizziness it caused. It was straight down for at least three or four hundred feet. He soon gained control of his equilibrium, however, and settled in to study the layout of the camp below him.

Little activity was taking place, but his heart sank when he saw how large the compound was. He had expected a small hideout, not the big, sprawling encampment he was overlooking. Several men were busy cooking over an open fire. People occasionally exited or entered tents. Not until breakfast was ready did he see many people. His interest perked when he saw a bound prisoner being escorted from a tent below him to a central eating area.

Even at this distance, he was sure it was Gadoni who plodded, head erect, in front of two sword-wielding guards. Next, he was shocked when he saw several women being herded like dumb animals to join Gadoni from a different part of the compound. Their hands were loosely bound but their feet unshackled. They were clearly not there of their own will.

After wondering and worrying about Nemti for several minutes, another prisoner emerged from the far side of the camp. He couldn't be sure it was Nemti but he suspected that it was; he certainly hoped it was. Now, he had only to learn where little Enos was being held.

The men who stood guard around the prisoners seemed to be waiting for something. Their voices drifted up to him, but he could only make out a few words. He thought someone said, "Beautiful girl," but couldn't be sure.

He soon learned that he had heard right. A woman with long black hair stepped from a tent pitched against the face of the cliff, only a hundred feet or so from Gadoni's tent. She moved with grace toward the others. The guard that escorted her seated her facing the granite cliff. Something about her seemed familiar, but her face was lowered and he never got a good look until she had completed her meal, then she looked up at the towering precipice. Samuel pressed tighter against the rock. Although he was sure he was concealed, with only part of his head exposed, he felt like the young woman was staring right into his eyes.

An uneasy feeling crept over him. He did not know why, but the presence of that girl, unbound, but a prisoner, nonetheless, upset him. He wished he were closer so he could make out her features and see if he could recognize her. He turned his thoughts to other matters, but her presence haunted him.

After the morning meal was finished the prisoners were herded back to their tents. A few minutes later, a small group of men left the encampment and trekked into the wilderness. Samuel assumed they were headed back to Zarahemla. He wondered if Gadianton was among the group, not that it mattered particularly. He supposed they came and went on a regular basis.

All that day, as Samuel continued to scout the surrounding mountains, the mysterious presence of the dark-haired woman disturbed him. He even awoke during the night, dreaming of innocent girls being taken captive by the evil band of Kishkumen and Gadianton.

The next morning, even though he still didn't know which tent Enos was in, Samuel had firmly implanted in his mind a course of action. He could not save his friends alone; the security was too tight in the compound. He prayed that they would be protected until he could bring help. As much as he hated to leave them now that he had found them, he consoled himself with the fact that a few more days of growth for his beard would help his disguise, then reluctantly, he did what he felt was best. He hurried through the wilderness, back toward Zarahemla.

It had taken Gadianton and his little band nearly two days to make the journey. Samuel could make it in less. Time was of the essence, so he traveled as hard as his endurance would allow, fierce determination pushing him on.

CHAPTER 13

I'm feeling much better now, Kapilla," Oreb insisted as they lounged on a bench in the colorful palace courtyard. "I hope Samuel shows up again soon, because I'm ready to go with him now and be of some help."

"Oh, Oreb," she responded, gazing fondly into his eyes, "you always think beyond yourself. You still need more time to heal. It's been less than a week since you tried before, and look how sick that made you."

"I know, Kapilla, but I really do feel much better. Honest, I can help now. I just wonder where he is and why he's been so long."

"I think he'll be back soon, with Gadoni, Nemti, and even the baby, Enos, all safe. This nightmare will be over then and you can quit worrying about going and helping," she said, sounding quite positive but not looking it.

"I wish, but I think not. Samuel needs help. I can just feel it," Oreb stressed, punctuating his feelings by slamming one fist into the other palm. "And I am going to be that help."

Kapilla said no more. She reached for him, and he took her hand in his. They sat in silence for several minutes, neither wanting to be disturbed. But they were. A servant intruded and announced, "There is a messenger here to see you, Kapilla. He says it's urgent."

"What could it be?" she asked Oreb, wrinkling her brow.

"I have no idea. I'll come with you and we'll soon know, though."

"No, you find Kim and Kib. It's time for you to give them their lessons. I'll be back in a minute," she told him.

Oreb had been teaching the boys twice a day, every day. Their progress was remarkable. A bond had grown between the three, and he looked forward to each session, excited to see the boys' development. He found them in the most distant corner of the grounds, sitting beneath a huge flowering tree filled with singing birds. They were content as they reclined in the deep grass, their faces smiling.

Kapilla rushed into the palace and through the long corridors, her sandals clacking on the stone floor and echoing from the high walls. Waiting for her near the front entrance was a poorly dressed woman and her son. Kapilla knew them well; they were neighbors and the woman was a close friend of her mother and the wife of Javis.

"Javis is gone. He hasn't been around for days and his wife is very ill," she said, coming right to the point. "She asked if you would come see her before she dies. Please come with us. I'll have you back in two or three hours."

Kapilla hesitated. The old neighborhood held only bad memories. She had no desire to return there, but Javis' wife had helped and comforted her when her father had killed her mother. She could not refuse her request. Slowly she turned to Pacumeni's servant who stood behind her. "Please tell Oreb where I've gone. I'll be back in a little while."

"Are you sure, Kapilla?" he asked, his face creased with concern.

"Yes, I'm sure. She is a good woman and has been good to me. I'll be all right. Please tell Oreb not to worry."

An old carriage parked in the street near the palace was waiting. Kapilla scrambled in, and they rode quickly through the streets of Zarahemla. When they arrived at Javis' house, the woman got out and Kapilla started to follow her, but the young man grabbed her arm.

"Not so fast, Kapilla," he said. "There is someone who wants to see you."

At that moment, her father ran from the door of Javis' house and swung in beside her.

"Father," she screamed, "what are you . . ."

"Shut up, girl. You're going with me," he growled.

"Never! I'm getting out," she shouted and tried to climb over him, but he struck her cruelly in the face, knocking her back into the seat. The carriage was started up with a jerk and rolled quickly down the street, swaying back and forth crazily.

"Where are you taking me?" Kapilla demanded, holding her hands over her bleeding mouth.

"You'll see soon enough. Now be still," he ordered.

She screamed her defiance, and he grabbed her, clamping a strong hand over her mouth. She quit struggling, her heart terrorized. The carriage slowed and Kapilla watched as people on the street moved aside for it to pass, oblivious to her desperate plight.

They pulled up in front of a stone house. The two men ushered her inside and forced her through the house and into a damp, smelly room. Herdon put a rough hand over her eyes and held her while the other man walked across the room. She heard the sound of something scraping and squeaking, like a balky door. When Herdon moved his hand, the other man held a torch and a section of the wall stood open before a gaping black hole. She struggled again, but Herdon's grip was too tight. He roughly shoved her ahead, through the opening and down a long stone stairway. Panic filled her and she screamed. The men laughed.

"No one will hear you down here," Herdon said, "so save your breath."

Oreb, oh Oreb, she thought as she walked through the long, cool tunnel. She silently berated herself for being so foolish. She should have known it was a trap. It had only been a few days since she had seen Javis' wife and she was as robust and healthy then as a woman her age and size could be.

Oreb had told her about the tunnel. This must be it—the one Gadoni and Nemti were in when they disappeared. They soon reached another stairway, were ushered into another house, through a series of rooms and hallways, then into another room with only one door. Again Herdon covered her eyes and a secret door opened and she was shoved into another tunnel.

"Father, where are you taking me?" she asked after passing a fork in the tunnel.

"To your wedding!" he said, thundering with laughter, accompanied by chuckles from his young friend.

The corridors bounced the laughter endlessly back and forth and Kapilla covered her ears, trembling with fear at her father's words. Finally, getting control of herself, she screamed, "I will marry no one but Oreb!"

"Oh, you little fool," Herdon said. "Oreb will never be your husband. He should have been dead, and soon will be. You will marry one of the brave men of our mighty band. The choice is not yours. We are selecting wives for the men to choose from. Even I will get another—much younger and prettier than your mother," he said with contempt.

She stopped, spun around, and slapped his face with all her strength. His face was hideous under the flickering yellow light of the torch. Never had she detested a person so much in her life. "You killed her! I hate you!"

Herdon struck her so hard she fell. Roughly he jerked her to her feet. "I still should send you to your mother," he hissed. "And I would if I hadn't been told to bring you to be the wife of one of our brave band of men."

"Never! I will never marry a Gadianton robber!" she cried.

"Gadianton robber?" her father's friend asked with a laugh. "What is a Gadianton robber?"

"You are. All of you and your awful friends are!"

"But where did you hear such a name? Our leader is another man," her father said smugly.

"Kishkumen? Ha," Kapilla said with satisfaction at the surprise on their faces. "Oreb and Samuel told me of him and of Gadianton. They say Gadianton is the real leader. Everyone is calling you Gadianton robbers."

Both men laughed heartily. "Dangerous sounding, isn't it," Herdon's friend said, "but I don't think Kishkumen would like it. Best we not repeat it."

Herdon slapped Kapilla again. "Turn around and get a move on, girl. We haven't time for your nonsense," he said angrily.

The next stairway led them into still another small room and from there a long, narrow hallway took them to the foot of a winding stairway. After climbing to the top, they passed through another room and another. There were no windows and the damp smell of a cellar filled Kapilla's nose, and she shivered. Finally, the men shoved her into a fairly large room. Several other women were huddled together near the far wall. An oil lamp burned on a small table. The only door was the one she had just come through.

Herdon pushed her roughly toward the other women and followed his friend from the room. The big wooden door slammed shut. Kapilla rushed toward it.

"It's no use, my dear," a kindly voice said. "It'll be locked."

Kapilla stopped, staring at the door for a long moment before slowly turning to face the others. They all watched her, their faces full of terror—haunted.

A woman who looked about thirty approached her. "I am Dara," she said, putting an arm around Kapilla's shoulder.

Dara's voice was full of compassion, and Kapilla allowed herself to be held close and comforted. She was obviously a prisoner herself, but Kapilla had never met anyone quite like her. She was an attractive woman with flowing brown hair and deep blue eyes.

"We'll help each other," Dara said. "We have all been brought here for an evil reason, but we have each other and we have God." She then introduced Kapilla to the other six women, all in their teens or early twenties. None of them smiled, but they all nodded in acknowledgment. "And your name, my dear?" Dara prodded gently.

"Kapilla," she said, her voice trembling.

Dara wiped the tears that ran down Kapilla's cheeks. "That's all right, girl. You go ahead and cry. It'll make you feel better."

Her tears renewed the sadness and fear in the others and soon all but Dara and one other were crying and sniffling. One by one, Dara consoled and comforted them. She was the oldest of the captive women and cared for the others as if they were her children.

The youngest, a pretty girl of about fourteen, talked about dying. She would rather die, she told them, than be the wife of some evil person she could never love.

"We know why we have been taken, or chosen, but who are these men?" another pretty captive asked. "Do you know?"

"They are the Gadianton robbers," Kapilla sobbed.

"Who are the Gadianton robbers?"

"They are a band of lawless men who seek to overthrow the government. They were responsible for the murder of Pahoran, the chief judge. They will stop at nothing to get what they want. Even my . . ." Kapilla said and stopped, choking and rubbing her eyes.

"What?" Dara urged.

"I'm so sorry . . . my own father . . . he is one of the ones that brought me here!" she said, her words stinging at the end. "He killed my mother and he is after a new wife, too."

Dara put her arms around Kapilla's shoulders and urged her to sit down. "It's not your fault that your father has done this. We must all be brave and look for a chance to escape."

During the long afternoon, Kapilla unfolded, bit by bit, the story of Samuel, Gadoni, Oreb, and little Enos. Dara was touched and told the others that maybe God would let them be of service to their fellow captives if they would just set their minds to it.

Dara encouraged the women to talk of the nightmare of their own abductions. The telling seemed to make each who spoke feel better. By the time it grew late and sleep tugged at drooping eyelids, they seemed to feel better just in the telling of their stories. A kinship and mutual respect developed.

After all had spoken but Dara and one other, Kapilla coaxed Dara to share her story, and finally she did. "I was married once," she began, "many years ago. I was seventeen at the time. My husband, a kind and loving man, was killed while fighting in the army of Captain Moroni near the East Sea during the war with the Lamanites. I have spent my life since then caring for orphans." For the first time she choked up. "They . . . these men took me from the orphanage. My children . . . my poor little homeless children . . ." A touch of bitterness appeared in her voice but faded quickly.

"My children will be okay," she said hopefully. "There are others there to care for them, but I do worry about my aged mother. I hope someone will care for her as well."

Kapilla viewed Dara with awe. Here was a woman who had suffered tragedy as a young woman, but had chosen to not let it destroy her. Instead, she had spent her life unselfishly comforting and caring for others in need.

Dara smiled. "If it's wives they want, they shouldn't have chosen me. I am not young and beautiful like the rest of you."

"Oh, but you are beautiful," Kapilla said as she gazed at Dara. She was indeed a woman who bore her years well. She was tall and stately, but her features still held their youthful beauty and grace. What stood out most about Dara, beyond her physical beauty, was her pure, loving soul. Kapilla was grateful to be with one so strong in character. She would be a great comfort as they all faced a terrifying future.

The last of the group refused to speak of her experience. She gave her name as Moreal, but would say no more. There was a coldness about her and Kapilla felt an uneasiness each time she looked at her. She wished she would talk and let them get to know her. She hadn't even cried. It would be better if she talked as the others did, as the eight of them would need each other, but Moreal said nothing and her dark eyes remained tearless.

Kapilla never saw her father the next morning when four men, all of them strangers, herded the eight women back into the tunnel after feeding them a meager breakfast. When they exited, Kapilla was surprised to find that they were no longer in the city. With horror, she realized that they were being taken someplace else, to some other city, perhaps.

All that long, hot day they traveled through the jungle, following no clear trails. It was apparent that they were not headed for some other city, but rather to the hideout in the wilderness that Oreb had mentioned. That would explain why Samuel had been gone for so long. A numbing fear crept over Kapilla. She cried, as did all the others but Dara, who was so strong, and Moreal, who was aloof.

The robbers who escorted them kept the women's conversation to a minimum as they walked. This proved to be almost more torture than the grueling march. They needed one another's support.

A storm came late in the afternoon. It poured with such intensity that it became muddy and so difficult to walk that the women stumbled often and were soon covered with mud. Moreal complained the loudest, and the men finally agreed to seek shelter. They found some refuge beneath heavy foliage, but the women were already so soaked and cold that they suffered greatly. They huddled together for warmth and comfort as they prepared to endure the remainder of the fierce storm. Their guards sat near, soaked, but watching them with lustful eyes.

CHAPTER 14

It had been a long, grueling trip back to Zarahemla, but Samuel had made excellent time. He went directly to the palace of Chief Judge Pacumeni. Soaking wet from the afternoon storm, he approached the guards who did not recognize him until he spoke. His beard was growing fast and coming in a shade darker than his hair, making him look strangely different. If he could fool them, he could fool his enemies, he thought, encouraged by his disguise.

He stepped inside the hallway and tried to clean his muddy sandals on the grass mat there. He looked up in surprise when he heard Oreb's voice, accompanied by running footsteps. "Sam! Sam!" he shouted.

"I can hear you, Oreb," he said sternly. "Now calm down and tell me what's troubling you."

Oreb was so upset he could hardly talk. "They . . . took . . . Kapilla! They stole her!"

Samuel's stomach turned sour. "When?" he asked. "How?"

"Yesterday. They . . . they said Javis' wife was dying. She wanted to see Kapilla." Oreb cradled his head with closed fists. "Why did she go? If only she had told me!"

"Are you sure that's where she's gone?" Samuel asked with little hope.

"Yes. I've been to Javis' house. His wife told me. Herdon left her tied to a chair. Kapilla's gone. They must have her in one of those stone houses. Let's go and . . ."

"Not so fast, Oreb," Samuel interrupted. "I found their hideout in the wilderness. They are probably on their way there with her. They are holding other women there as well as Gadoni and Nemti. Little Enos is probably there, too. I need some food, then I'm going to find Captain Moronihah."

"Okay, but I'm coming, too!" Oreb thundered.

"But you're . . ."

"I'm fine, Sam. I'm much better now. I can go anywhere you go," Oreb said, his broad face a study in determination.

"Well, not quite, but I could use your help," Samuel said with a tired smile. "Come, let's see if there's any food to be had in the palace dining room."

While Samuel was eating, Oreb gathered his weapons. When he returned, Kim and Kib were with him. They were dressed to travel.

"Where are the twins going?" Samuel asked suspiciously, wiping his mouth and pushing away from the table.

"With us," Oreb stated flatly.

"No. That won't do," Samuel said quickly.

"Please, Sam," Kib said. "Kapilla is our sister. We can help find her."

Samuel was mildly shocked. Kib, who had been so silent, talked as normal as anyone. He looked at the twins with a critical eye. Both had put on a little weight, and their eyes sparkled. Before he could lodge another protest, Kim spoke up. "Oreb's been teaching us how to use these knives," he said, fingering a long, shiny weapon that hung from his belt. "And he's been showing us how to shoot a bow and arrow."

"And they do very well, Sam. And you ought to see them use a sling. They won't be in the way. Anyway, they have a right to help," Oreb argued.

Samuel gave in. "Okay, but you must promise to follow my orders."

"We will," they chimed in unison, their faces lit in smiles that Samuel was sure their abusive father had never seen.

"How is Nonita?" Samuel asked, as he led the way from the palace. "I assume she's gone on to Gilead."

Oreb's round face bore a puzzled look. "I don't know, Sam. I haven't seen her. Should she have been here by now?" he asked.

Samuel whirled. "Easily! She was to be brought directly here by Pacumeni's order. Where could she . . ." He cut off his own sentence as the grim facts came together in his mind.

"Sam, are you sure they didn't take her directly to Father?" Oreb asked, his face clouded with doubt.

"Oh, Oreb," Samuel said, sinking to his knees on the floor, his face in his great hands, his body trembling.

"What is it, Sam?"

"I know where she is!" He shuddered, and then said more to himself than his brother, "It was her. They have taken her, too." He looked up almost choked with anger. "I saw her, Oreb. She's a captive in the wilderness."

Thunder cracked and the rain pounded.

* * *

The storm was raging in the wilderness, too. Nonita held Enos and paced back and forth in the tent. She was humming, but the sound of her voice was smothered by the rain washing over the tent in torrents. Kerlin sat inside where he could stay dry. His eyes followed every move she made.

His presence infuriated her, but she tried not to show it. He was frequently assigned duty at her tent, by his choice, no doubt, and she did not want to make him angry. She had nothing to say to him, and he in turn spoke little, referring to her, however, as his woman when he did speak.

She had no intention of ever being his wife and would die first, but she felt no danger in his presence now. As long as the baby was there and Kishkumen and Gadianton had not given her to him as his wife, she felt that he would keep his hands off her. He would not do anything to bring their wrath down on him.

The bad weather had forced the feeding of the prisoners in their tents. Nonita had come to look forward to the short, silent periods in the presence of Gadoni, the other young women captives, and the tall, soldierly looking young man whose name she had yet to learn. Gadoni's strength and resolve flowed across the space between them and uplifted her even though their eyes seldom met. The handsome stranger, when his eyes caught hers, transferred a silent courage that filled her soul with peace. Glancing at the hulking form of Kerlin, she prayed for the weather to break before morning.

* * *

Kapilla awoke with a start, disoriented. Tiny streams of sunlight filtered through the heavy leaves and reflected from puddles of water on the jungle floor. With a wave of nausea, she remembered where she was.

Her eyes met Dara's, who lifted a finger to her lips in a gesture of silence. The other women were still sleeping. By the time they had all fallen asleep the stormy night had nearly worn itself out. They were exhausted. Even the guards were tired. Three of them were asleep near their captives. Dara pointed to them and touched her lips again.

Kapilla glanced around, but could not see the fourth man. Dara pointed into the jungle. Looking in the direction she indicated, Kapilla saw where someone had recently exited their little refuge.

Dara had busied herself picking mushrooms that grew all over in the damp area. Kapilla liked mushrooms but was afraid of them. She had always experienced difficulty in distinguishing edible ones from the poisonous varieties. Dara popped a succulent chunk into her mouth before silently offering some to Kapilla. Gratefully, she ate it, savoring its unique flavor.

By the time the others were awake, Dara had a couple of piles of mushrooms broken up on the grass beside her. She offered some to the other women. They all munched hungrily.

"We'll have some, too," one of their captors ordered.

"I picked these for us," Dara said, sheltering her little mounds with her body.

The guard's eyes flashed menacingly and he started toward Dara. She crouched lower around the mushrooms. He grabbed her shoulder and jerked her up straight. "Stupid woman," he hissed.

"All right, I'll share. Just don't hurt me," she feigned. "Here, take these." She scooped up one of the piles and he rudely snatched them from her.

Without a word of thanks he began stuffing his mouth. He offered some to the other two men. They too began to chew and swallow noisily. By the time the fourth robber returned, the mushrooms Dara had picked were all gone.

"It's time to go, women," he announced and handed them some moldy dried meat. They obediently followed, saying nothing. Kapilla chewed on her meat with distaste. She had enjoyed the mushrooms but knew that she needed the substance of the meat to give her the strength to keep up the pace set by their captors. She could not help but notice Moreal. She wore a sour face and kept turning to watch the three men who brought up the rear. She also was chewing the meat, but seemed preoccupied.

None of the other women paid any attention to the men during the next two or three hours as they plodded ahead. Each, Kapilla knew, harbored their own fears. When she heard a feeble groan from behind her, Kapilla turned and saw one of the robbers bending over, holding his stomach. His face was a sickly shade of purple and he was retching uncontrollably. He sank to his knees, still retching. His arms supported him for a few moments, then buckled, and he fell face down in his own bile.

Everyone had stopped and was watching him, spellbound, as he suffered. The other robbers gathered around him, encouraging him to get up, but he just lay there moaning, too sick to respond. Several minutes passed. The other men discussed his sudden illness.

Dara said, "If you aren't going to help him, then I will. We can't just let him lie here and suffer."

Gently, she turned him over and called for some water to cool his burning face. So engrossed was Kapilla in the scene that she never noticed Moreal step back and watch the group warily.

One of the other men began to complain that his stomach hurt, too, and then a third. Within minutes, they, too, were violently ill. That left only one of the robbers on his feet. He cursed and asked, "What's happening here?"

"It was her!" Moreal hissed, pointing an accusing finger at Dara. "She caused it!"

The women all looked at Moreal in surprise—all, that is, but Dara and Kapilla. Their eyes met and Kapilla understood.

"What do you mean?" the healthy robber asked.

"Mushrooms. She fed them poison mushrooms!"

The other women gasped. One said, "We ate them, too!" She turned accusingly toward Dara, who was kneeling on the ground beside another of the stricken men.

"Help me, Kapilla," Dara said, as if oblivious to the accusation against her. "I can't care for these sick men by myself."

Moreal spat words again. "She only gave the poison ones to the men. She fed us good ones."

With an angry face, the unaffected robber pulled his sword and stepped toward Dara. She said under her breath, "Move aside."

Surprised, Kapilla stood up and backed away. Dara leaped deftly to her feet, a long knife gleaming in each hand. The robber stopped in his tracks, his eyes flitting to the empty knife sheaths of his downed comrades. "So you think you can fight a skilled swordsman with a pair of puny knives," he said, crouching as if he was about to attack. "You should at least have taken their swords," he taunted.

"I can use these, and I will if I have to," Dara threatened. There was no fear in her voice, only confidence.

The robber snorted in contempt and closed the distance between them, waving his sword. The women parted, leaving a clear path between the two adversaries. Kapilla, her heart beating wildly, watched spellbound.

Moreal never moved, but a wicked grin spread across her face. The others froze, watching the confrontation, fear of the inevitable outcome in their eyes. The robber continued to advance. Dara's eyes were glued to his face. When he was about ten feet away, one of Dara's arms flicked faster than the eye could follow, and her knife appeared, as if by magic, embedded deep in his chest. He swayed, a look of shock on his face, then fell to the ground, dead.

Dara waved the other knife at Moreal. "You are one of them. I suspected it from the beginning. You will stay and care for these sick men. The rest of us are going to return to Zarahemla," she said.

Moreal spat at her and cursed. Dara said, "Kapilla, get the rest of their weapons. You others help." She gestured with the knife.

They moved as if emerging from a trance. Dara stepped beside the dead robber, rolled him over, and pulled the knife from his chest. She wiped the blood from the blade in the wet grass and handed it to Kapilla. Then she removed his knife from his belt and the sword that was still gripped in his lifeless hand. She handed them to Kapilla as well. Her eyes flitted frequently to Moreal. Finally, she stripped the body of the bow and quiver of arrows and stood up.

"Quickly," she ordered again, her face impassive and cold, "help me gather the food from their pouches." The women, all but the youngest, pitched in. She was on her knees throwing up, sickened at the sight of blood and death.

Dara moved with efficiency, helping the women strap on the weapons and divide the food. She dropped part of the provisions at Moreal's feet, and said, "If you take good care of these men, they will recover. Boil some sarsaparilla root and make them drink it. It will offset the effects of the poison. They'll be as good as new in a day or two."

Moreal spat again, hitting Dara in the face. Dara calmly wiped it off with the back of her hand and said to the others, "Let's go now."

Moreal started after them, the hatred in her eyes mixing with fear. "You can't just leave me like this," she wailed.

Dara said, "We can, and we will. You go care for your friends. They'll get you home alive. Without them you'll die here and feed the hungry beasts with your carcass. You know what to do. Their lives and your own are in your hands."

Moreal hesitated, then turned back. In a short while the seven women were alone, surrounded by the beautiful vastness of the wild jungle. They stopped for a rest and Kapilla noticed that Dara was looking pale.

"Please excuse me," she said and stepped behind the gnarled trunk of a sprawling mahogany tree. Kapilla heard her retching.

When she rejoined the others she said simply, "I'm sorry. I have never had to do anything like that before." She waved in the general direction they had come from. "I couldn't let the Gadianton robbers do to you what they would have done. I hope God will forgive me if I have done wrong."

CHAPTER 15

Samuel, Oreb, and the twins rested and ate in a thicket of palm trees, large fronds waving gently above them. They were on their way to the robbers' wilderness hideout, but Samuel had cautiously chosen a roundabout route. He did not want to accidentally run into any Gadianton robbers in the wilderness.

Before leaving Zarahemla, Samuel had spent some time with Captain Moronihah. Their discussions had been intense, but in the end the chief captain assured Samuel that his requests would be carried out.

A good night's rest had followed before the four of them set out, well before daybreak. They had not traveled as fast as Samuel would have liked because the twins and Oreb were not in prime condition. He had to exercise patience and be content with the progress they were making.

"Will our father be there?" Kib asked as they discussed the layout of the wilderness hideout.

"I don't know, Kib. If that's where they're taking Kapilla, then he very well could be," Samuel answered, noting a flash of anger on the boy's face.

"He better not hurt Kapilla," Kib went on, his voice taking on a threatening tone.

"He killed our mother," Kim stated, stepping beside his brother. "We won't let him kill Kapilla, too."

"Now wait a minute, you two. Don't go getting the idea that you'll take on your father. He has lots of friends—mean ones. You will do as I tell you, remember? You can be a big help to Oreb and me, but not if all you think about is how angry you are at your father," Samuel cautioned.

The boys hung their heads. Samuel hugged them both. How his heart ached for them. The years of terror and pain that Herdon had

inflicted on them they had held bottled up inside. The love and friendship of Oreb had allowed the terror and much of the pain to leave,
freeing their bright minds and active bodies. Hate, though, would do
them no good. Samuel wanted them to learn to forgive. He and Oreb
must help them hold their anger in check.

Oreb smiled at them. "Sam's right, you know. You must only use
your weapons to defend yourselves and others." Turning to Samuel, he
said, "They really are quite good." He addressed the boys again. "Show
Sam how well you can use a sling."

The twins brightened and produced their weapons. They each
selected a smooth, round stone. Oreb pointed at a big knot on a tree
trunk over fifty feet away. "See that knot?" he said. "Aim for it."

Almost in unison the two swung their slings in a long, graceful arc,
then with a loud snap they each released one string. The stones whistled
through the air and hit their mark, less than an inch apart.

"Wow!" Samuel exclaimed, genuinely impressed. "Where did you
two learn to do that?"

"When Father used to put us in the shed behind the house we'd
sneak out. Our uncle made us the slings before he died, and we kept
them hidden outside. Father would have taken them away if he'd seen
them," Kim said.

"We'd go into the woods and practice a lot when Father was not
home," Kib finished for his brother.

"Their practice paid off. They really are good, aren't they?" Oreb
said, as proud as if they were his own children.

"Yes," Samuel agreed with a smile. "I'll be glad to have you boys near
to protect me if I get in trouble. It's time to move again. Let's go."

They had many miles of swampy jungle to traverse that day and
rugged mountains ahead the next. For the twins, it was an immense
adventure, but for Samuel and Oreb it was a mission of immense risk.

Two days later, the sun broke through the dark, heavy clouds that
had been dousing the wilderness for days. Kim and Kib crawled from
beneath the overhang of mossy rock that had been sheltering them and
joined Samuel and Oreb at the edge of the granite precipice overlooking
the camp of the Gadianton robbers.

Many men were moving around below. "The wilderness must be
crawling with robbers," Samuel noted. "I would guess that the number of

robbers down there has doubled since I left the other day. I suspect more are on the way, too."

"What are they up to, Sam?" Oreb inquired.

"I believe they're trying to build their own secret society here and then plan to infiltrate Nephite society in our major cities. They must hope to undermine our government by corruption and murder, then take over."

"Can they do it?"

"Unless they're stopped before they get too strong, they can."

"Why are they kidnapping women?"

"I think they hope to persuade many of them to be wives for robbers living here in this camp. Uncooperative ones will probably be made slaves or killed," Samuel said.

The twins were taking it all in, their eyes wide with wonder at the scene below them. Tents dotted the large plateau and men congregated in groups as the sun warmed the area.

Upon seeing a group of women being moved from a large tent, the twins became especially alert. "I wonder if Kapilla is there," Kib said in a loud whisper.

"That's what I intend to find out," Samuel said grimly.

"How?" Kim asked, his eyes wide with excitement.

"By going into their camp."

"They'll catch you, Sam. You can't do that," Kib protested.

"I hope they don't. Anyway, I don't see any other way. Oreb, you know the plan. Keep a sharp lookout while you wait up here. Boys, you do exactly as Oreb tells you. I'm counting on you. My safety and that of your sister, if she's down there, could depend on you," Samuel stressed.

"Yes, sir," Kib responded, looking very serious.

"You can depend on us," Kim affirmed.

Samuel slithered back from the edge of the cliff, gathered his weapons, and headed south along the rugged mountainside. It took him several hours to work his way to a position below the heavily guarded plateau.

He tugged at his short beard. Oreb had assured him that he was virtually unrecognizable. In Zarahemla he had purchased clothing similar to that worn by many of the robbers, and his beard was dark and bushy. Praying that he was ready for his brazen attempt, he came out of his hiding place and started boldly up the rock-strewn trail toward the camp.

"Who goes there?" a heavily armed sentinel demanded from his post beside a big rock on the steep incline.

"Who wants to know?" Samuel responded.

"I do," the guard said, stepping into full view, an arrow trained on Samuel's chest.

"I am here to conquer," Samuel said, hoping the password hadn't changed.

"Then you've come to the right place," was the response. "Where do you come from?"

"Manti," Samuel lied.

"Good. You're the first from Manti, but why are you alone? You shouldn't have been able to find this place without an escort."

Reacting quickly to this unanticipated twist, Samuel said, "There was another man with me. He got a fever but managed to get me close enough to show me where to go. He died during the night."

That answer seemed to satisfy the sentry. "When will others follow from Manti?" he asked.

"In a few days," Samuel said, hoping he wouldn't say the wrong thing. "The brotherhood is getting strong there now," he went on as he walked past the guard, who lowered his weapon.

"Pass on, brother," the sentry said, stepping back.

Samuel heaved a sigh of relief. He recognized the man from his very first meeting with the band in Zarahemla, but he gave Samuel no hint of recognition. Encouraged, he hurried up the trail.

Samuel passed two more sentries before gaining entrance to the camp. Once admitted, he wandered around, trying to orient himself. No one seemed interested in him, so he was content to be seen by as many men as possible, as that would diminish the chance of someone becoming suspicious later.

He was surprised at the loose organization that prevailed in the stronghold. He decided they must have a lot of faith in not being discovered. He was soon conversing with different men as he wandered about. They were all uncouth, unkempt, and foul-mouthed, but spoke to him as if he were truly one of them. He had no trouble finding the tents where the prisoners were being held. By nightfall, he had met many of the robbers and was able to strike up a conversation with one man whom he had noticed beside the tent where the girl he suspected was his sister, Nonita, was being held.

"My name is Kerlin. Did I hear you say you were from Manti?" the short, stocky robber asked.

"Yes. We're not as well organized as you are down in Zarahemla, but we're getting there. We want to be more involved in the brotherhood. That's why I'm here," Samuel explained. "My name is Sarenti," Samuel went on, using the name he and Oreb had selected earlier.

The two talked for several minutes. "How long will you be here?" Kerlin asked after awhile. He seemed relaxed with Samuel, and though his face was sullen, he did not act suspicious.

"Until I have learned enough to enable me to return to Manti and build up the secret band there. Since I am going to be here for awhile, can I help you men? What is your assignment, anyway?" he asked Kerlin.

"I am in charge here, Sarenti," a large, sour-faced man said from behind Kerlin. He stepped around him and said, eyeing Samuel carefully, "I am Tarnta. Follow my orders and you will work for me."

"That's fine with me," Samuel said.

"Help Kerlin," Tarnta said. "He takes over at dark in guarding the tent of one of the captive girls." He winked at Kerlin as he spoke. "She's a pretty one, but Kerlin has spoken for her, so don't get any ideas unless you want a knife in the back."

Samuel nodded and wondered how many women had been kidnapped and what their full purpose was. He knew there were many evil women among the Nephites who would willingly join with the robbers in their secret combinations and wicked designs. Where were they? Why had the robbers resorted to stealing women? He wondered if they were planning a whole new society here in the wilderness, separate from the families many of them had in the land of Zarahemla.

He sighed. Whatever the reasons, if all went as planned, his beautiful sister, if she was here, and all the other young women they were holding here would soon be free. If things did not go as planned . . . He shuddered at the thought and shoved it from his mind.

Later that evening, Samuel followed Kerlin to their post. He had to control his anger at the lustful way the young robber spoke of the captive girl who might be Nonita. "This is where we spend the night, Sarenti," Kerlin announced as they approached the tent. Addressing the guards they were relieving, he asked, "How's the prisoner?"

"She's doing just fine, Kerlin. So is the baby," one of them said.

Samuel was stunned and had to fight the impulse to charge into the tent. Could it be Enos? Could this girl, the one he thought to be Nonita, actually be caring for Gadoni's son? The thought made his head spin.

A few minutes later, after Kerlin had nervously paced around the tent, he said to Samuel, "You stay out here. I had better check on the girl and baby inside." He was through the flap before Samuel could respond.

"Hello," he heard Kerlin say inside. "I have help tonight, so I can spend more time in here with you."

Samuel listened with intense interest for the voice of the prisoner. He was not disappointed when he heard his younger sister say, "Kerlin, the baby needs more milk. Would you get it?"

"Sure, anything you ask. I'll be right back," Kerlin said and exited the tent. To Samuel, who had quickly stepped several paces away, he said, "The baby needs milk. I'll be right back. We have some goats. We use their milk for cheese, but I have been getting some for the baby. Don't let anyone in that tent, understand?"

Samuel nodded in the near darkness and began to pace as Kerlin disappeared. Without any further hesitation, he slipped into the tent. A small candle burned, lighting the tent so that he could see Nonita, her back to him, rocking the baby in her arms and humming. She turned and looked at Samuel. He could see well enough to recognize that the baby in her arms was a beautiful, dark-skinned Lamanite child.

Nonita spoke with no hint of recognition. "You must be the other guard. Am I so dangerous that it takes two of you now?"

"No, little sister. I have come to take you home," he said in a whisper.

Nonita gasped. "Sam, is that you?"

"Shh. My name is Sarenti, here," he warned.

"Oh, I prayed that you'd come, but I didn't dare hope," she whispered, laying the baby on a pile of furry skins. She embraced Samuel, the tears flowing freely down her careworn young face.

"I mustn't stay. Is Gadoni all right?" Samuel asked.

"He's fine, but he doesn't know I have his baby. What will you do?"

"I'll tell you later, little sister. Don't let on that you know me." Samuel paused, then holding her away from him, he said, "I'm so sorry about Sheam. And I'm so sorry that this . . ."

"It's okay, Sam . . . I mean, Sarenti. Right now little Enos needs me. How I envy Laishita. He is such a beautiful baby."

"Be careful, Nonita. Kerlin seems to think you are his. He can be very dangerous, I suspect."

"Yes. I know, Sam. How glad I am that you are here. But you need to watch him. He is very jealous." She shuddered.

Samuel cut her off gently. "You're right. He mustn't catch me in here. I'll be close by," he said and returned to the darkness outside, his heart full and his mind churning. He offered a silent prayer of thanks to God for leading him to Nonita and Enos and pleaded for help in freeing them, as well as Gadoni, Nemti, and Kapilla. He wished he could just whisk them all away tonight, but that was too risky. He must follow the plan he had set in motion.

Kerlin startled him when he suddenly appeared out of the darkness and said, "I got some." He held a small jug in his hand. After Kerlin had entered the tent, Samuel walked around behind it and leaned against the cool granite cliff. From there he could listen to Kerlin inside the tent without fear of Kerlin suddenly leaving the tent and seeing him standing close.

"Thank you, Kerlin," Samuel heard Nonita say.

The robber grunted, then it was silent for several minutes.

"Nonita, I will make you very happy. Kishkumen told me today that as soon as they have no further need of the baby he and Gadianton will allow me to have you for my wife."

Samuel tensed when Nonita flared. "And what will happen to the baby?"

"That baby is being used to entice an enemy and traitor. When he comes looking for the baby, Samuel, that's the traitor's name, will be hanged, and then the baby will be taken care of."

Samuel shuddered. The hatred of the secret band for him was certainly potent.

Nonita was very angry. "Kerlin, what do you mean by this child being taken care of?" she demanded.

"Killed, woman! What did you think I meant? He is a Lamanite. There is no reason to let him live. The child's father is the Lamanite you see at meals. He will also cease to be of any value when we get Samuel, and we will. He is bound to come," he said with a chuckle, "because he has no better sense."

"Kerlin, leave this tent," Nonita said. "I will never be your wife, and no one will lay a hand on this child while I live. You are . . . are despicable!"

"And you are beautiful, Nonita, and you will be mine," Kerlin said with a growl.

"I want to go to sleep now, Kerlin. Please leave," she said firmly.

"I think she likes me. Nobody's ever looked at me the way she does. She'll make a great robber's wife, don't you think?" Kerlin said to Samuel after he stepped outside.

Samuel restrained the impulse to attack the man. Instead, he said, "How would I know? You never even let me see the girl. Tomorrow, why don't you introduce us? I give you my word that I won't fall for her, too. But I could give you an opinion." Samuel forced a chuckle before going on. "I heard the baby cry. Is it her baby?"

Kerlin growled. "No. You are rather nosy, aren't you?"

"I was just curious. I didn't mean to upset you," Samuel said.

"If you must know, he's a hostage," Kerlin said angrily.

"I see."

"But it's kind of a secret, so don't say anything."

"I wouldn't dream of it," Samuel said. "Whose baby is it? Its father must be a pretty important person."

"No, his father is a Lamanite. The baby was taken to entice a traitor to come looking for it so we can kill him," Kerlin said secretively.

"Who is the traitor?" Samuel asked, trying to sound impressed.

"Samuel is his name. He's a dangerous one. The baby's father is called Gadoni, and he's being held here, too. He's dangerous, also."

Samuel lapsed into silence. He did not want to ask so many questions that Kerlin became suspicious of him. Kerlin drifted near the tent. Finally, he sat down with his back against a rock and went to sleep. Samuel kept watch during the long night, and when Kerlin awoke, the first golden streaks of dawn were appearing over the sea of trees that carpeted the jungle floor. Within half an hour a relief guard appeared and Samuel walked back to the guard's quarters. Kerlin stayed at the tent.

Samuel ate with most of the other men that morning, then positioned himself as inconspicuously as possible near where the prisoners were fed. Nemti passed close by and Samuel caught the young soldier's eye momentarily, but he gave no sign of recognition.

Kerlin escorted Nonita from her tent and stood behind her as she ate, so Samuel avoided looking her way except for a few brief glances. On one of those occasions he caught her eye and for a fleeting moment a smile brushed her face. The last prisoner brought to the eating area was Gadoni. He was tightly shackled and looked frail, but he still held his head high, a look of defiance on his dark face. Samuel shifted a little so he could look directly at Gadoni. The Lamanite had become a common sight and most of the robbers that were near paid him little attention.

Gadoni's dark eyes swept over the throng of men and handful of women in the circle. His eyes stopped briefly on Nemti and he tipped a smile his way, causing the younger man's face to light up. He also let his gaze rest on Nonita and she gave him the same fleeting smile she had sent Samuel's way.

As Samuel followed Gadoni's gaze he suddenly realized that Kapilla was not among the women prisoners. He wondered where she could be. If they were bringing her here, she should have been here by now. He worried about how Oreb would react if she did not show up here.

When Samuel looked toward Gadoni again, the dark Lamanite eyes were staring, unblinking, at him. He looked deep in those familiar eyes and studied the impassive face for a hint of recognition. A faint, fleeting smile crossed Gadoni's face before he looked away. He was not fooled by Samuel's disguise. A moment later their eyes locked again and a silent understanding passed between the two friends. For the rest of the meal, Gadoni's head seemed to be a little higher and his defiance toward the robbers more pronounced. He radiated total trust and confidence. Samuel could not let him down.

A few minutes later, Tarnta assigned Samuel a tent to sleep in. "Thank you," Samuel said politely. "I could sure use some rest, but I think I'll go get a drink of fresh water at the spring before I go to sleep."

Tarnta pointed toward the south end of the granite cliff. "It's over there," he said.

Samuel nodded and headed in that direction. The spring gushed from the base of the cliff, forming a small stream that glistened and gurgled as it passed through the rocks and shrubs, cutting its way to the edge of the plateau where it gracefully fell from view.

Earlier, Samuel had spotted the spring from above. Near it was a huge boulder that had the uncanny appearance of a cat's head. Once he was sheltered by the boulder from the camp, Samuel stopped and looked toward the top of the towering granite cliffs. He moved his right arm in a pre-arranged signal. Movement in a crevice above could only be seen from this spot. An arm waved back at Samuel in a slow arc. He moved his left hand this time, then went on to the spring.

The hidden post above was manned by one of the twins. Samuel had left explicit instructions that someone was to be in position all the time during daylight hours so that he could communicate with Oreb and the twins. His signal was to tell them that he needed more time—all was not yet ready for the execution of their daring plan.

CHAPTER 16

The jungle, a place of wild beauty, had become a wilderness of terror for Kapilla. After escaping from the Gadianton robbers, she and the other women had struggled in vain to find their way back to Zarahemla. They were hopelessly lost, and with each hour the chances of surviving long enough to find their way back to civilization were decreasing.

The more they searched for a way out, the more confused they became. Wild beasts prowled nearby, driving fear deep into Kapilla's heart. All the young women were afraid and losing hope. But they were not hungry. Dara, reasonably adept with a bow, killed wild animals for meat, and they all picked mushrooms, dug roots, and found wild fruit.

Their lives were in constant danger. Early one afternoon, while working their way out of a dense, swampy area, they stumbled onto a trail made by jungle animals. They followed it because it was easier to walk there. It led them onto a peninsula almost totally surrounded with stale, foul-smelling water. Afraid to cross through the stagnant swamp for fear of what might be in it, they backtracked.

Kapilla spotted what looked like an easier path leading across a sandy clearing. She stepped ahead of the others and was well across the area when she suddenly started sinking. The moist sand sucked at her feet, and the more she struggled the harder it pulled. Within seconds her ankles disappeared beneath the oozing quagmire and the jungle was filled with Kapilla's terrorized screams.

Dara quickly began spreading large palm fronds over the ground to where Kapilla was helplessly sinking. The others joined in the effort, bringing the largest, heaviest fronds they could find. By the time a suitable trail was built, Kapilla was waist deep in the quicksand.

Using her knife as a makeshift shovel, Dara crawled beside Kapilla on the firm green trail and began furiously scooping the sand away. She made so little progress that she abandoned the idea and called for the young women to cut strong vines which she fastened around Kapilla's chest.

Everyone pitched in, pulling for all they were worth while Dara dug again. After what seemed like an eternity, Kapilla, her voice breaking, said, "I think its working. Pull harder!"

They did, and finally Kapilla, exhausted and shaking, crawled onto the leaves and from there to solid ground where she lay sobbing for nearly an hour.

"I have never felt so helpless," she told the others through her tears. "The more I tried to get out, the harder I was sucked down."

"We'll know to watch for such traps in the future," Dara warned. The exhausted women made a crude camp that night near the quicksand. Kapilla's dress had been torn from her in the struggle, so Dara made makeshift clothes for her using palm fronds fastened together with wiry grass. It was uncomfortable, but protected her so well from the sun and bloodthirsty insects that they made similar outfits for everyone, replacing their torn and tattered clothing.

By early the next afternoon, they tried again to find a straight course from the jungle. Once again their efforts ended in failure. Tears flowed and Dara spoke futile words of comfort and encouragement. One by one they sank to the ground, defeat written on their soiled, careworn faces.

Kapilla, as discouraged as any, thought of Oreb and her two brothers. She longed to hold them close and tell them how much they meant to her. Oreb was the first hope for true happiness she had known, and she had no desire to lose him now. "We can't give up," she said forcefully. "Dara is right. We'll stick together and stay alive until we find our way out of here."

The very utterance of the words lifted her spirits and boosted her confidence. She could not shake the fear of the jungle, but she was able to control the terror. Her resolve, added to Dara's faith, calmed the others, and together they promised to keep trying until they found their way back to Zarahemla.

* * *

Samuel was assigned to guard a large tent containing the women captives. He spent much of the night pacing restlessly around it. The rest of the time he perched himself on a rock in front of the tent where he could listen to some of the conversation from inside.

"What chance do we have?" one girl asked. "Who will ever rescue us?"

"I'd rather be dead than stuck with one of those despicable men," another retorted.

"I'm not so sure that we will have any choice," still another said. "I think we better make up our minds to get along with them."

"That's easy for you to say," the second girl replied hotly. "You're not married. I have a husband to think about. I love him, and I will never belong to another man!"

"I guess we'll see," another chipped in. "This can't go on forever. They'll be making demands of us soon."

"I wonder what they're doing with Nonita," one said. "She seems afraid of that one called Kerlin, but I think she's as good as his already."

The voice of the third one was louder this time. "I wish he'd choose me. I'd go with him. Maybe I'll give Nonita some competition."

A young woman who had remained silent until now spoke up. "Hush, all of you. This talk is dangerous. They might be out there listening this very moment," she scolded.

Samuel smiled to himself. Little did they know that the one listening was their only hope of escape, with the Lord's help, of course. The voices faded to whispers until they finally went to sleep. Frustration gnawed at him. His time was being wasted guarding this tent. He needed to alert Nemti, talk to Gadoni, and spend some more time with Nonita. He had to find a way.

He was relieved at dawn. He ate an early, makeshift breakfast and retired to his tent. After sleeping soundly for several hours, he awoke, sweat pouring off him like rain. The sun was high and the little tent was roasting. Samuel stepped out into the bright sunlight and walked toward the spring. Beside the cat-head boulder he stopped and signaled, "No change," to the twin on duty in the crevice above.

"All is well here," was signaled back.

Samuel wandered aimlessly around the growing encampment. The robbers' ranks continued to swell a little each day. He was disheartened to learn that several more kidnapped women had been brought into camp that morning. He wondered if Kapilla was one of them. He even saw the first woman in camp who was not a prisoner. Moreal was her name and she came with two men in the late afternoon. They looked very tired and their tale of near death by mushroom poisoning spread quickly through the camp.

He learned that they had been escorting a group of captive women who had escaped in the wilderness, leaving two robbers dead, one from mushroom poisoning and the other from a knife wound. Samuel wondered if that was why Kapilla had not appeared. Maybe she was safely back in Zarahemla.

Samuel drifted over to the area where Gadoni was being held. The guard assigned to watch the tent complained of a fever. An idea sprang into Samuel's head and he asked, "Do you need someone to relieve you?"

"Yes. Would you ask Tarnta to send someone? I can't stand to sit out in this heat any longer," he complained.

"It is extra hot and muggy today," Samuel said slyly. "You go on back and lie down. I'll cover for you. If you'll tell Tarnta I'm here and have him send someone else in an hour or so, I'll watch the Lamanite for awhile."

"Thanks, Sarenti," the man said gratefully. "I'll speak to Tarnta. Keep a close eye on this one, though," he said, poking a dirty thumb toward the tent. "He's dangerous."

"I'll do it. Now, you get feeling better," Samuel said to the back of the departing robber.

Gadoni's tent was not close to any others, and was pitched behind a boulder. Samuel looked around. The robbers had sought shade from the few stunted trees that attempted to shove their roots into the rock in search of water and nutrients. He could not see anyone who might be close enough to observe his movements. He certainly could not be overheard. He slipped to the tent flap and pulled it open.

"Hello, my brother," Gadoni greeted him affectionately. "What took you so long?" The dark Lamanite face broke into a wide grin.

"It's good to see you, Gadoni. It wasn't easy finding this place, but we'll have you out of here before long. How do you feel?"

"Weak, but I'm all right," Gadoni answered, his face growing serious. "Have you spoken with Nonita yet? I don't know why they have her here or how they caught her."

"They're stealing beautiful young women and bringing them here as wives in this wilderness hideout. Nonita has a special assignment right now though, she . . ."

"She needs to be very cautious," Gadoni interrupted. "The one they call Kerlin has laid claim to her."

"I know. I spoke with her," Samuel said, pausing to look around and make sure they were still alone.

"Sam, my worst fears are still for my son," Gadoni said earnestly. "Have you learned anything about him? That worry, above all, is killing me."

"He's fine, Gadoni. Nonita is caring for him."

"What! He's here in this camp?" Gadoni asked, shocked. "I must see him!"

"No, Gadoni. We can't risk it yet. But it won't be long. We . . ."

"Who's going to help you?" Gadoni interrupted again. "You must have a plan."

"Yes, I do. Oreb and the twins are waiting at the top of the cliff," Samuel started to explain.

"The twins! But they . . ."

"They are good help," Samuel said and hastily explained about them and the plan he had set in motion. As they talked, Samuel handed Gadoni the knife.

"I'll be ready," Gadoni said as Samuel helped him conceal the weapon beneath his clothing where he could easily reach it with his bound hands and cut the rawhide that bound both his hands and feet.

"Good. We'll make it," Samuel assured him, letting the flap close. "I see men moving around again. I better be careful."

"Thank you," Gadoni whispered. "What name are you using?"

"Sarenti," he said and casually walked a short distance from the tent.

After being relieved a short while later, Samuel began looking for a way to speak to Nemti. He had a knife for him, too, and needed to explain what was going to happen. If his luck would just hold out a little longer, then Nemti could be alerted, too.

High on the towering granite cliff above, Oreb stood watch. He was fast growing impatient. Samuel had signaled nothing about Kapilla and he was sick with worry. Kib had gone back to the tent to sleep after Oreb had relieved him an hour before. Kim stood watch higher up to protect the camp in the unlikely event unwelcome visitors should come nosing around.

Kim found the assignment exhilarating. After being abused and repressed all his life, the responsibility vested in him now was enough to keep him going for hours on end. He kept his eyes peeled. Not so much as a bird flitted in the trees that he didn't see. He caught a movement in a thicket. It was indefinable, and though he looked closer, he could see nothing to alarm him further.

His eyes drifted over the entire area again. Oreb sat like a rock in his crevice about seventy paces from the thicket. Kim's eyes covered it again. There was something there—the leaves near the ground rustled. Kim's spine tingled and he tensed. His eyes were glued to that one spot. A touch of color, like flesh, appeared. It was the arm of a man!

Kim forced himself tighter against the rocks at his back. He did not dare move. The arm did, and it was attached to a body. The body crawled forward. The intruder's face was pointed toward Oreb. He crawled closer, glancing upward only momentarily. If he saw Kim, he gave no indication of it.

The stalking man carried a bow which he held in front of him as he rose to a kneeling position. He drew an arrow from the quiver on his back. Kim watched, terror stricken, his sling hanging slack in his hand. Not until the man began to pull back the string, aiming at Oreb's exposed back, did Kim react.

That was Oreb who was about to be killed, the man who had treated him kindly and showed him that life was worth living. He couldn't sit and watch him die. He rose to his feet and deftly swung the long sling. The small round stone that he had placed in the pouch hours earlier flew swiftly and silently through the air. Deadly accurate, even at that distance, the stone found its mark. It struck the robber in the temple. He tumbled forward, his arrow striking the ground harmlessly in front of him.

Oreb whirled from his hiding place. In seconds he absorbed the scene on the slope above him and knew that Kim, bearing a grin as wide as the Sidon, had saved his life. He lifted his hand to silently acknowledge his thanks when the smile disappeared and Kim gestured wildly toward the same thicket. Three heavily armed men stood there.

Before Oreb could react, several more men stepped into view on the ledge above Kim. He froze.

Samuel made one more trip to the cat-head boulder. He was surprised and a little angry to see no one there. He waited a minute, then walked to the spring, spent a few minutes, then returned to the boulder. The crevice was still vacant and the daylight was slipping away. Samuel's eyes went higher where dark, heavy clouds loomed, threatening to release the liquid load that had been forewarned by the muggy heat of the day.

Where are they? Samuel mouthed the words in frustration.

"See something up there?"

The unexpected voice made him jump. He turned to find Kerlin standing behind him. "Yes," he said, trying to mask his surprise, but suddenly grateful that no one was on duty in the crevice. "Clouds, and heavy ones at that. I think we are going to get wet tonight."

Samuel looked up again, but away from the cliffs this time. Kerlin followed his gaze. "I'm afraid you're right, Sarenti. You are assigned to watch Nonita's tent again tonight. You better go." There was no hint of suspicion in his voice.

"Right," Samuel said, unenthusiastically. He followed Kerlin away from the rock, afraid to glance up again. If he had, he would have seen a figure move silently into place there.

Samuel had hoped to be given the assignment to guard Nemti tonight. He had hinted, but it was not to be. Worry gnawed at him. He had to get to Nemti. And Oreb. Where were Oreb and the twins? It was not like Oreb to let up in his duty. Impetuous and impatient, yes, but Oreb was also conscientious.

As Samuel paced back and forth in front of Nonita's tent, he could not relax. He had visions of his carefully laid plan shattering right in front of his face. And he wondered why Kerlin was not with him tonight. He was worried. He started to pull the tent flap back and let Nonita know he was near when he heard something.

"Psst."

Samuel's head snapped around. The rain and clouds hid even the stars; it was pitch black. He could see nothing.

"Psst."

There it was again. Whoever was out there was close. Samuel's hand fell to the sword he had strapped to his side and pulled it from its sheath. He strained to see. A faint glow of light came from Nonita's tent as her candle illuminated the hides it was made from. In that faint light he finally spotted a motionless form beside the rock he had been sitting on earlier. He drew his sword and stepped toward it.

Oreb stood up. "Sam, it's me, Oreb. We've got to move now!" he whispered breathlessly.

Samuel looked anxiously around him, but could see no one else. "Where were you?" he asked angrily.

"I'll explain later. The robbers discovered that we were there. I don't think they got word down to the camp, but we can't take a chance. We can't wait any longer."

"The twins?" Samuel asked in alarm.

"They're fine. I owe my life to Kim. Help came just in time. We're all set," Oreb whispered.

"I haven't armed Nemti yet, but let's . . ." Samuel was saying.

"Sarenti, you traitor!" Kerlin shouted, lunging from the darkness with a drawn sword.

Samuel whirled and their swords met with a clang in the darkness. Oreb jumped forward and Kerlin, outnumbered, fled into the darkness. "He will alert the others. I'll go free Gadoni while you get Nonita and Enos . . ."

"Where are they holding Kapilla?" Oreb asked.

"She's not here. I think she escaped and returned to Zarahemla along with several other women. I'll explain later."

"Good. Go then," the young man said lightly. "I know what to do." Relief was apparent in Oreb's voice despite the need for haste because of Kerlin.

The rain was coming harder as Samuel stumbled in the dark toward Gadoni's tent. "Stop! Who goes there?" a deep voice asked from the wet darkness.

"Sarenti," Samuel answered. "Tarnta needs you, Onti," he lied.

Word had not spread this far yet, Samuel realized with relief.

The robber stepped close enough for Samuel to make out his features. "What does he want?" he demanded.

"I don't know. He didn't tell me, but he wants you now!"

"All right," the unsuspecting guard muttered. "I'll be glad to get out of the rain for awhile."

Samuel waited until he had stepped past before hitting him. Onti collapsed and Samuel pulled him into the tent with Gadoni. "A change of plans, Gadoni," he announced, dropping his burden and cutting Gadoni loose.

Gadoni tried to loosen his cramped muscles. "We must hurry, they know about us. Take these," Samuel said, shoving the robber's weapons to his friend. "You may need more than that knife I gave you."

"Are we going to get my son now?"

"Oreb is there. We must find Nemti first. This weather's perfect. I just hope the others don't have trouble with the wet coming down." He opened the flap as he spoke. "It's still clear. Let's go, and stay close to me," Samuel warned, leading the way into the stormy night.

A fire lit the center of the encampment and there was excited activity there. Samuel and Gadoni circled around, but became disoriented in the darkness and pouring rain. He sought his way back to the main camp, but stopped when he heard shouts. He crept closer. Men were buckling on their weapons.

He heard Kerlin shout, "They're gone! They took Nonita and the baby!" as he stumbled with two companions from the darkness into the glow of the fire.

"You fool!" Tarnta shouted. "You should not have gone alone before! Go find them!" They left and he shouted again, "What about the Lamanite?"

"He's gone, too. Onti is unconscious in the tent," another man answered as he too ran into the light of the fire.

A different voice shouted, "The rest of the prisoners are secure."

"They can't be far. Find them!" a voice that Samuel recognized as that of Kishkumen erupted with a volley of angry oaths.

Samuel and Gadoni waited no longer. They tried again to find Nemti's tent, praying that they were not too late. Men bustled everywhere, carrying sputtering torches and waving swords in the downpour.

Samuel finally found Nemti's tent. Two guards, one holding a torch, patrolled around it. Samuel and Gadoni attacked. Surprise was on their side and both robbers dropped without a struggle. Gadoni picked up the dropped torch and Samuel slashed the tent open with one stroke of his sword.

"It's Samuel," he said as he deftly cut Nemti loose, handed him the sword of one of the fallen robbers, and stepped out. Stiff and awkward, Nemti followed.

"Hey! You there! Stop!" a voice commanded.

Samuel didn't stop. He led Nemti and Gadoni into the wet darkness toward the cliffs. Torrents of rain covered the sound of their retreat. They didn't stop until they reached the sheer granite wall. Samuel, gasping for air, explained to Nemti what was happening.

Suddenly he could hear something above him on the face of the cliff. Seconds later a heavily armed Nephite soldier lit beside him. Samuel greeted the man. Nemti embraced him, calling him by name. A few seconds later another came, then several more. Soon soldiers lined the cliff front and still more ropes were lowered, dropping more men.

Samuel and Nemti worked their way along the ledges, greeting soldiers and searching for Oreb and the others. Several unlucky robbers, blindly searching for Samuel and the others, stumbled into the amassing troops. Each in turn was taken captive, dying only if he resisted. Some shouted warnings, but the shouts were swallowed up in the torrential downpour.

With relief, Samuel finally discovered Oreb, Nonita, and Enos safely behind the line of amassing Nephite soldiers who had made the dangerous descent over the face of the cliffs and awaited the order to attack.

A squad of soldiers was detailed to keep the prisoners secure. The rest, under the command of Captain Calno, an experienced fighter, prepared for the battle ahead.

* * *

The storm raged on and on in the jungle that night. Kapilla tucked her bare knees tighter against her chest and shivered. A moan caused her to turn her head. One of the other women was stretched out beneath a makeshift shelter to her left. The branches and palm fronds did not stop all the water from reaching the fevered body. Dara was kneeling beside her, providing what comfort she could.

Tragedy had struck the little group of lost women. Fever had afflicted two of them. One died earlier that day. The other, fifteen-year-old Eva, stood little chance of faring better as she moaned and coughed beneath the dripping shelter.

They had tried to find a good place to camp before darkness came and the storm struck, but had failed, and were subjected to the full wrath of the downpour. Eva coughed violently and Dara stood and threw more wet wood on their pitiful fire, then returned to lie by the sick girl. Kapilla thought about Oreb. She wondered if he was out in this storm, cold and wet and lonely.

The night seemed endless. Kapilla drifted in and out of troubled slumber. The rain let up after a few hours, but her comfort increased only slightly. She finally stood up and moved around a little. The fronds that were her skirt were cold and wet. She felt worse.

Kapilla finally knelt beside Eva. Dara had fallen asleep. The sick girl's breathing was heavy and labored. She placed her hand on Eva's forehead. It was not as hot as it had been.

Eva stirred. Kapilla took the girl's warm hand in hers, forgetting her own misery as she whispered words of comfort. To her surprise, Eva's grip tightened. Then she spoke. "Is that you, Kapilla?"

"Yes."

"Am I going to die?"

"Don't talk that way, Eva. You must not think of dying. Think only of getting well so we can go home."

"But we are lost. How can we find our way out of here?" The fear and discouragement in the young girl's voice was heart rending.

"I don't know, Eva," Kapilla said honestly, but trying to sound cheerful. "We will make it, though. Oreb will find us. We just need to be patient a while longer." She wondered at her own words. She hoped desperately that Oreb was searching and that he would find them. As futile as it seemed, she made herself believe it.

"Kapilla."

Eva pulled her from her reverie. "Yes," she said, looking at her thin face in the flickering light of the meager fire.

"I'm very thirsty."

"I'll get you a drink," Kapilla responded and rose to her feet. The early light of dawn was turning the underside of the clouds silver, faintly lighting her way. She found a water-bag and helped Eva sip slowly from it.

"Thank you," Eva whispered. "That helps."

Kapilla touched Eva's forehead again. The worst of the fever had passed. She said so to Eva.

"Is it really?" the frail girl asked.

"Yes. You are getting better and the storm is nearly over. Go to sleep now and get some rest," she said with a tenderness born of years of caring for her brothers.

Kapilla held Eva's hand until her breathing became even as she dropped off to sleep. Then she stood and walked to the edge of their camp. She absently studied the huge outline of the trees, twisted, stark and tall in the growing dawn.

A short one moved! Then another! A scream rose from her throat and shattered the stillness of the jungle. The stark forms were men! They moved toward her, swords outstretched.

CHAPTER 17

Captain Calno, an experienced, self-assured soldier, had given the order to attack. The robbers, though they now knew an enemy was in the camp, had not expected hundreds of Nephite soldiers. They had fallen easily at first to the powerfully-wielded swords of Calno's men, but finally seemed to gather strength from fear and fought like cornered animals. The battle had raged for hours, fought in the dark with the aid of torches.

The women captives were freed and taken to safety behind the lines as, gradually, the soldiers had driven the men of Gadianton and Kishkumen to the very edge of the plateau. Several robbers, in pairs or small bands, had deserted their comrades and fled down the boulder-strewn slope and into the jungle. Of those who did not flee, many died.

Finally, the last few men had surrendered and were taken back to the cliff to join the other captives. Calno, the dawn having arrived, ordered a systematic search of the entire hideout. Samuel helped in the search as he had helped in the battle.

Gadoni and Nemti had volunteered to fight, but Calno had refused to let them, due to their weakened conditions. They had stayed behind to help protect the women and baby Enos, instead.

It was Samuel who discovered Moreal hiding in a tent, covered with blankets. She attacked him, kicking and clawing, when he threw the covering off her. However, she was quickly restrained and he hauled her back toward the other prisoners.

As they passed Nemti, Gadoni, and the others, the girl cried out, "Nemti, help me, please!"

Surprised, Samuel glanced over and saw Nemti watching her, a look of shock covering his face. He stepped toward her and asked, "Moreal, what are you doing here?"

Before she could answer, Samuel asked Nemti, "Do you know this girl?"

"Yes," he answered haltingly. "We were friends." His brown eyes were filled with sadness.

"Friends!" Moreal yelled. "We were more than friends." Her face softened and she said in a childlike voice, "Nemti, I have missed you so. I still love you. Please, tell this man that you'll care for me. Please."

Nemti stepped closer and Samuel released his grip on the girl. She dove forward, throwing her arms around his neck, and began to sob uncontrollably. Slowly, almost trance-like, Nemti forced her away.

He held her at arm's length, looked her in the eye and asked sadly, "Why, Moreal? Why?"

Her face grew dark and she hissed, "You stopped seeing me!"

"That's no excuse for taking up with the Gadianton robbers."

"At least they respect me as a woman," she said, throwing her head back in anger.

"So did I, it's just that you were not the one for me." Nemti said. "We are too different. But this . . . this is awful. You have ruined . . ."

Moreal slapped Nemti's face and Samuel quickly restrained her. "Come, you better go now. I don't think Nemti has anything more to say to you."

As Samuel dragged her away, she screamed. "I loved you, Nemti. I still do. It could work for us if you weren't so . . . so . . . . so righteous!"

Nemti said nothing, but he watched her for a moment before shaking his head and turning away. Samuel, as soon as Moreal was placed under guard with the other prisoners, began to organize the freed women for the trip back to the city of Zarahemla. He also sent someone after Kim and Kib, who were still on the mountain above them, and ordered still others to collect what supplies they could from the robbers' camp, then pile everything else to be burned.

Captain Calno ordered soldiers to carry the bodies of the dead robbers to the center of the plateau and pile them in a heap on the hard ground, it being impossible to dig graves. Among the dead were seven Nephite soldiers. They were carried down into the jungle and buried. The wounded were cared for in the larger tents.

That night, the towering granite cliffs glowed somber red, reflecting the light from the large fires that consumed the property of the Gadianton robbers. The grisly pile of dead men, left as a wretched warning to others who might come here with evil designs, appeared in the artificial light as just another boulder.

* * *

The day had finally passed for Kapilla. The pair of Gadianton robbers who had chanced upon the hapless women that morning had filled them all with unspeakable terror. They collected the weapons, and threatened and bullied the young women and Dara throughout the long day, forcing them to dig roots, pick wild fruit, and prepare the food for them to selfishly wolf down.

Eva was mostly ignored that day. Kapilla and Dara gave her what attention they could, but the two men threatened them each time they bent over her. Finally, after dark, Dara whispered to Kapilla, "Eva will die if we don't do something for her real soon. She was doing better this morning, but tonight she is much worse."

"What do you think those two will do?" Kapilla asked. "Surely they're on their way to the hideout. Maybe they'll just leave."

"We'll wait a little longer and see," Dara said. "But if they don't leave by morning, we'll have to do something. In the meantime, I don't think they'll bother us about caring for Eva during the night."

"Hey, you two quit whispering," one of the robbers growled. "You make it hard to trust you when you whisper."

Kapilla watched him closely. The fire was burning low, and it was overcast and dark. He was lying on the ground, his head propped up with his hands. She couldn't see the other man but was sure he was prowling just out of sight in the trees, seeing that the women behaved themselves.

"I know about you people," he went on with a smirk. "You must be the ones who poisoned your escorts."

Kapilla was stunned. How could they know about them? Unless . . . Yes, that was it. They must have been coming from the hideout, not going to it. Dara spoke up. "So Moreal helped them after all. Did all three of them make it?"

"No. One died." The robber chuckled, then said, "You won't be trying the same with us, so don't get any ideas. It's clear that you're lost—hopelessly lost. We can help you find your way back to Zarahemla."

One of the girls asked hopefully, "Oh, would you do that?"

"For a price," he gloated.

"What's your price?" Dara asked suspiciously.

"That one for me?" he said, pointing across the fire at Kapilla.

"Never!" Kapilla hissed, shocked. "Never! Never! Never!"

"What choice do you have? You'll all die or we'll take you back to the hideout if you don't agree."

"It's either him or me."

Kapilla jerked and looked around. The second man was standing beside a tree behind her, his grinning face leering ghost-like in the shifting shadows.

"Never!" she shouted again.

"Kapilla," Dara said. "Let's be sensible. What choice do you have? I'm afraid the men are right. We'll all die without their help."

"Dara," Kapilla said, suddenly sick at heart. "How can you say that?"

"Kapilla, they have offered to save our lives. All of us, including you, will die here if we don't agree. Don't be so ungrateful"

"But . . ." Kapilla said sharply, then stopped short when she felt Dara's hand on her knee giving her a gentle, reassuring squeeze. Relief washed over her. Dara was buying time. She berated herself for doubting the kind woman. She said, after an awkward moment, "How do you know they can find their way? Maybe they're just as lost as we are, Dara."

"We know our way, Kapilla," the one behind her said before Dara could respond.

"Are you sure?" she asked, sounding defeated.

"As sure as Herdon is your father, we can," the robber by the fire said.

Kapilla gasped. "You know my father?"

Both men laughed. "You don't remember me, do you?" the lounging one asked with a toothless grin.

"No," she said, trying hard to recall.

"I am Amarton," he announced. "You used to deliver stolen jewels for me to your father. He promised me that one day you would be my wife. I intend to hold him to that promise."

So that was what was in the packages—at least some of them. Slowly, Kapilla remembered this man. He was much older than she, and had been clean shaven and well dressed then. He used to have all his teeth and his beard, long greasy hair, and dirty rags had disguised him, but she should have remembered the wide, leering eyes. How could she forget?

"So that's settled, then?" he asked. "If we deliver all of you from the wilderness, you will stay with me?"

"Only if you let us care for Eva," Kapilla answered slyly.

"Do it," he said. "But we can't wait too long before we leave. The army . . ." He stopped speaking abruptly, his eyes looking over Kapilla's head at his companion.

"What about the army?" Dara pressed quickly.

"Nothing," Amarton said, trying to cover his slip of the tongue. "Tend to the girl. Tomorrow we're traveling."

Without another word, Kapilla and Dara built up the fire and turned their attention to Eva. Kapilla's mind raced while she worked. She wished she could confer with Dara, but the men watched them like hawks.

Dara and Kapilla took turns sitting with Eva while the others slept. The men also took turns sleeping while the other stood watch. By sunrise, the sick girl was feeling much better, and by the time Amarton announced that they were ready to leave, she was, with help, able to walk.

Their progress was painfully slow, and several times they changed direction. Periodically, the men argued over which way to go. It was soon apparent to Kapilla that she had been right. They were as lost as the women, but wisely, no one mentioned the fact.

Amarton became increasingly surly as the day wore itself out. Most of his anger was directed toward his friend. After an especially heated argument, Amarton was struck a violent blow by his comrade. He drew his sword and a moment later the other man lay dying on the marshy ground.

"You! Kapilla," he shouted. "Come with me."

Kapilla hesitated, and Amarton grabbed the girl nearest him and held his sword to her throat. It was weak and sickly Eva. About to collapse anyway, she fainted in his grasp. He dropped her and stuck the point of the sword over her heart.

"Amarton!" Kapilla cried. "Don't hurt her. I will come."

"Then move. Now!" he ordered with deadly venom.

Kapilla rushed to his side. He grabbed her arm and twisted it behind her back and, with her body as a shield, backed away. Dara stepped forward. "Don't try anything, Dara," he warned.

She stopped, her face grimaced with grief. As soon as they were out of sight in the trees, Amarton started to run, dragging Kapilla along. It was well after dark before they finally stopped for the night.

Kapilla's heart was heavy. The days in the wilderness had been made bearable only by the positive, cheerful presence of Dara. Now, alone with an evil robber, she felt she would most certainly die in this fever-infested jungle.

"Tomorrow, we will begin our journey to one of the cities by the East Sea," Amarton announced to Kapilla late that night.

"But you said we were going to Zarahemla. Can't you find it?" Kapilla protested weakly.

"Of course I can, my beautiful one, but we are both known there. We will find a new city where we can begin our life together," he said, putting a smelly arm around her shoulder.

She shuddered. Death would be better than living with this despicable man. Oh, Oreb, she thought. Dear Oreb. How she longed for him, but her love seemed an empty dream. She feared that only death could release her from the misery and fear that gripped her soul.

The next morning, she awoke to the cheerful chirping of a variety of gaily colored birds. Her companion echoed their mood. He was whistling and strutting about, adjusting his weapons.

"Are you hungry, my lovely one?" he inquired, favoring her with his toothless smile.

Kapilla threw him a sullen look, but said nothing. He paid no attention to her anger. "I'll have you something shortly," he said, surprising her with kindness and ambition she had not seen before. In her mind, she could still vividly see the sudden burst of anger that had resulted in the slaying of his friend the day before.

"You stay put and I'll be right back," he said. "I wouldn't want you to get lost by yourself out here. I don't want to lose you." She nodded. She had to admit she feared being alone in the jungle even more than being with him, and anyway, she convinced herself, he was certainly acting like a changed man this morning. He was gone only a few minutes before returning with fresh game. He cooked the meat over the open fire and offered the most tender pieces to Kapilla. She gratefully accepted.

They ate in silence, then Amarton said, "We better get on our way, my love. We have far to go."

She forced a weak smile. The depression and feeling of hopelessness she had felt during the night was slowly being replaced with renewed hope and faith. As long as Amarton acted as he was now and made no threatening moves toward her, she would tolerate him, she decided. If he did actually succeed in getting them out of the wilderness and to the East Sea, she would find a way to escape and seek help then.

In the afternoon, her spirits took a nose dive. Twice, she recognized the same stagnant lake as they passed by it. They were traveling in a giant circle, but Amarton did not seem to know it. He whistled and sang off-key, encouraging Kapilla along as if they really were on their way out of the maze of streams, marshes, and lakes. When he finally ordered a stop and set up camp that night, he was genuinely pleased with their progress.

"You are not only the prettiest girl I have ever seen, Kapilla, but the strongest as well. You walk as if you would never tire. How do you do it?" he asked, admiration in his wide, lustful eyes.

Kapilla couldn't mask her surprise. "But Amarton, I'm exhausted. If you hadn't stopped when you did I would have collapsed," she said truthfully.

He grinned his toothless grin again. He was in his favorite position, stretched out on the ground, his bearded chin in his hand. "Well, you sure don't look tired, and you don't slow me up at all. At this rate we'll soon be to one of the cities where we can find a priest and get married," he said.

Kapilla could not believe her ears. As if his failing to realize that he was lost was not ridiculous enough, he actually thought she would marry him.

Perhaps, she decided, it would be safest for now to encourage him in his delusions. She forced a tired smile for him, yearning for Oreb.

CHAPTER 18

It won't be long before it's dark Sam," Oreb said, staring into the long shadows that filled the jungle. "Do you think we should stop for the night?"

"That's for Captain Calno to decide. We are his guests now," Samuel said with a weary smile. "But I think he is getting tired, too. We aren't making much progress, but I guess that doesn't matter. Our job is finished."

"Not quite, Sam," Oreb replied hastily. "Until I see Kapilla safe and sound in Zarahemla, or better yet, in Gilead, I will not be satisfied."

"Oh, she's at the palace, preparing a welcome home for you, little brother, that you won't soon forget."

"I hope so, but I won't rest until I have her in my arms. Don't you miss Ophera, Sam?"

"More than anyone knows. And I miss Jath, too, but I'm thankful I can return to them with good news this time."

"Father and the others must certainly be worried about Nonita. They'll be happy to hear she's safe and well," Oreb said. He paused thoughtfully before looking at Samuel with a worried expression. "Actually, I'm worried about her, Sam. What if that robber, Kerlin, is freed? He would almost certainly come looking for her. He is really a dangerous character."

"Surely that will never happen. These men have caused so many problems for the government and the people. They will never be allowed to go free. I just wish we had captured Gadianton and Kishkumen. They're the ones that worry me," Samuel said.

"They worry me, too, Sam. And so does Herdon, but I worry most about Kapilla. Do you think it would be all right with Captain Calno if we went on ahead to Zarahemla? He doesn't need our help, and Nonita and Enos will be safe traveling with Gadoni and the army."

Samuel glanced at his brother. Lines of worry were etched deep in his youthful face. "Well, maybe . . ." Samuel began.

Oreb was not listening. "I must know that Kapilla is safe. You and I and the twins could travel much faster alone. And they are worried about her, too. She's the only family they have, you know."

"We'll speak to the captain later, Oreb," Samuel said with a smile. "If he says it's all right, then we'll do it."

The company stopped to camp for the night in a large clearing near a meandering stream. The prisoners, including the wounded ones, were placed in the center of the camp under heavy guard. Samuel, Oreb, and the others who were not part of the army were given a spot near the edge of the clearing, not far from the bank of the stream. Moreal, the only woman captive, was under separate guard not far from the other robbers.

While the camp was being set up, Kim and Kib came tearing from the trees and straight to Oreb. "We went out in the jungle a little ways," Kim said, pointing in the direction they had just come from. "We smelled smoke."

Oreb snapped to attention. No fires had been started in the large encampment yet. "Come," he said quickly. "We better let someone know."

Samuel was helping Gadoni pitch a tent and overheard them. "Are you sure?" Samuel asked, instantly concerned.

"Yes," Kib said.

"I'll report it to Calno. It could be robbers that deserted during the fighting," he said, roughing the boys' hair. "You two are good help."

They smiled proudly as Samuel and Oreb hurried off in search of the captain. "Calno," Samuel said after locating him, "there may be some of the robbers camped nearby. Kim and Kib smelled smoke to the north."

"I'll dispatch a patrol," Captain Calno said decisively. "I still feel bad that Kishkumen and Gadianton were not among the dead and captured. With those two still at large, the band will continue to flourish, despite their losses here in the wilderness."

Samuel could not agree more. He knew that pair. More dangerous and satanic men had never lived among the Nephites. He was still convinced that Kishkumen had personally killed his friend, Chief Judge Pahoran. His desire to see him brought to justice had not diminished in the least.

"I'd like to go with your men, Captain," he said. "I know those two and some of the others. I can identify them."

"Excellent idea. Are there any other men you would like to have included?"

"You are very perceptive, Captain. Yes. I'd like Gadoni, Nemti, and Oreb."

"As you wish. Talk to them. I'll have some men ready very soon. We must hurry. It will soon be dark."

Calno gave instructions to the patrol of twenty men before they left. "You are to spy only. Once the number of robbers and the condition they are in is known, send someone back with word. We'll send enough men to safely capture them after that."

Samuel led out. The twins had been right. The faint odor of wood smoke teased his nose before they had gone a hundred yards from the clearing. They followed the drifting smell, encountering numerous obstacles—marshes, ponds, and streams. It was fully dark, with only a waning moon to light their way by the time they had pinpointed the location of the camp.

The men broke up in pairs and approached on their bellies through the dense jungle foliage. Samuel and Oreb crawled side by side, just a short distance from Gadoni and Nemti. The sixteen soldiers were all deployed evenly around the area. "I can hear voices, Sam," Oreb whispered.

"Not many, though," was Samuel's whispered reply.

They moved closer. Samuel could make out four or five shadowy figures hunched near the fire. He touched Oreb's arm and they stopped to listen.

Samuel was surprised when he heard a young woman's voice. "I hope she's okay, Dara. What can we do?"

"Sounds like a girl," Oreb whispered in Samuel's ear. "What could this mean?"

"I don't know," Samuel whispered back, but an icy feeling pricked his skin.

He strained to hear more. "Kapilla is a very smart girl, Eva. She'll take care of herself."

Oreb stiffened at the sound of the mature woman's voice mentioning Kapilla. Samuel grabbed the young man's arm. "Stay put," he whispered fiercely.

"We can't help her if we don't find our way out of this place," the young woman said tearfully.

"We will do all we can," the older woman said. "Amarton will eventually find his way out of the wilderness. Then maybe she can get away from him if someone doesn't find her first."

Oreb started to get up, but Samuel tightened his grip on his arm.

"I'm afraid, Dara. I'm so very afraid for Kapilla. She was so good to me, and Amarton is so bad. He might hurt her."

Samuel had heard enough. Anyway, he wouldn't be unable to restrain Oreb much longer. They stood together and approached the fire. All around the circle, the others took their cue from Samuel and stood. Several gasps near the fire preceded the women jumping to their feet and cowering together.

Samuel was taken aback momentarily by their strange jungle dress of fronds and grass. Recovering, he spoke quickly. "We are your friends. We come in peace. I am Samuel and this is my brother Oreb."

"Oreb!" the one called Eva squealed. "Are you Kapilla's Oreb?"

"Yes," Oreb said, stumbling the few steps to the fire. "Where is she? What has happened to her?" he demanded.

"I am Dara," the older woman said. "I will explain. You are an answer to our prayers." Her voice was choked with emotion.

The story poured from Dara and the others. "Sam, let's go. We can't wait any longer," Oreb said impatiently as the story unfolded.

"We'll take you to our camp," Samuel said and explained rapidly about the army and their victory over the robbers. "You can tell us more later, but Oreb is right. We must find her."

Oreb said very little on the way back to the encampment. Even in the darkness, Samuel could see enough of Oreb's face to know he was seething. It would not be easy to control him while an organized search was carried out.

Kim and Kib listened intently while Samuel and Oreb explained about Kapilla. The light of a small fire danced off their faces and burned in their eyes. Hurt and anger twisted their features, and Samuel saw in them the same fierce determination that Oreb possessed.

Captain Calno had many questions for the small band of women. They were weak, tired, and embarrassed by their immodest dress, but tried to answer the questions in detail. Samuel was astounded at the courage of Dara and the resiliency of the entire group.

Samuel and Calno conferred until late in the night. Oreb tried to help but danced around like he had ants crawling on him. If Samuel had given the word, he would have charged like a bull into the jungle, despite the darkness. Kim and Kib sat quietly, but sleep had fled from their eyes and they devoured every word that was spoken.

They all finally got a little rest, but were up again before the dawn. They ate, packed, and prepared for the day ahead. Samuel, Gadoni, Oreb, the twins, and Nemti were going in search of Kapilla. Calno promised he would safely deliver the others to Zarahemla and would personally see that Enos was delivered to his mother.

"I will send a courier to Captain Moronihah," Calno promised Oreb, "requesting that a search be conducted in every city in the land for Kapilla in the event they have found their way out of the wilderness. If they show up, Oreb, we will get her back."

"Thank you, Captain, but I hope we find her first," Oreb said, his green eyes flashing.

"Well, I hope you do, too," Calno replied and bid them farewell before turning to the task of readying his army to march.

Samuel looked around. Everyone was ready. "We'll be home in a few days," he said confidently to Nonita.

"You've got to find her, Sam," she said. "I can't bear to see the hurt Oreb is going through."

"With the help of God we'll find her, Nonita," Samuel said, touched by her love for Oreb.

Her eyes shifted to Nemti. He smiled. Surprise showed in her dark eyes, and she smiled back, lifting a slender white hand to smooth back her long waves of ebony hair.

"Are you two coming?" Oreb interrupted.

"Yes. Let's be on our way."

"I'll see you later, Nonita," Oreb said to his younger sister. "Nonita?"

She was still gazing at Nemti. For a brief moment the world stood still for the two of them. Her face flushed and she said, "What, Oreb?" breaking the spell.

"I'll see you later," Oreb repeated, the anxiousness on his face broken momentarily by a mischievous grin.

Nonita rushed forward and hugged him, tenderly touched each of the twins, embraced Gadoni, kissed Samuel on the forehead and glanced shyly at Nemti.

Samuel looked back as they walked toward the trees. Moreal was looking past her guard, casting angry darts at Nemti. And then he saw Kerlin, seated near the edge of the bunched prisoners. His eyes, full of lust, never strayed from the lovely figure of Nonita. Samuel shuddered.

CHAPTER 19

"Which city are we going to, Amarton?" Kapilla asked.

"I haven't decided, but we'll find a place you like," he bragged.

She was confident that he had no idea how to get out of the wilderness, and she was equally sure that he did not know they had been going around in a giant circle. She thought about suggesting a different direction several times, but decided not to, even though she was tiring of the facade.

Kapilla was surprised at her strength and endurance. Despite the uncertain diet she had lived on for the past several days, the constant walking had hardened her muscles. The pain and stiffness she had suffered at first were gone. Physically, she felt good.

It was not necessary to beg her captor to slow down or stop to rest because he tired much faster than she did and had to frequently stop to rest. Kapilla would feign exhaustion if he asked how she was doing, but that was only to keep him thinking she was weak.

By nightfall, Amarton was quite restless. He didn't admit it, but from the look on his face, she wondered if he was beginning to realize that they were getting nowhere. To keep his mind off his dilemma she struck up a conversation.

"How long have you known my father?" she asked, eyeing him as he reclined by the fire.

"Several years. I'm really not sure how long," he said without interest.

"Have you been friends all those years?" she persisted.

"Yes. Your father always liked me. That's why he promised you would be my wife someday."

"How long ago did he tell you that?" she asked, shuddering.

He looked up at her. "Oh, maybe four years."

"But I was only fourteen then," she protested.

"He said I'd have to wait a few years, but you were beautiful even then. I have waited patiently, but looking at you now, you were worth the wait."

Kapilla did not like the direction this was going or the look in his eyes, so she attempted to steer the talk back to Herdon. "When did you last see my father?" she asked.

"Before I went to the hideout."

"How long ago was that?"

"Oh, about six weeks ago or maybe a little more. Why do you ask?" he inquired gruffly, sitting up and eyeing her suspiciously.

"I just wondered. Has he been to the hideout?"

"Yes, several times."

"Where is it?"

"The hideout?" he asked, looking surprised at her question.

"Yes. Where is it?"

"That way," he said pointing uncertainly. He furrowed his brow. "No, it's that way." He hesitated again. "Oh, it doesn't matter."

Her chest tightened. They had to get out of this wilderness. He was hopelessly lost. He did not even know where the hideout was.

"What are you thinking about, my beautiful one?" Amarton asked.

"Oh, just how deep in the wilderness we must be. I didn't know it was so big. I've never been out of Zarahemla before," she told him.

Amarton was surprised. "You mean Herdon never took you anyplace?"

"No. I always stayed and took care of the twins. Mother never went anywhere either. She didn't want to, I guess."

"The twins," he said with a laugh. "Now there's a pair. Poor Herdon never could figure out why he was cursed with sons so stupid. He always said if they were half as smart as you, they'd be fine boys."

Kapilla bristled. She had to bite her tongue to keep herself from speaking in anger. She said nothing for several minutes. When she finally spoke, it was quietly. "They are quite smart and can talk as well as anyone."

"What? Who can?" Amarton's mind had drifted.

"My brothers. They've changed," she said with pride.

"I don't believe you, Kapilla. Don't lie to me. My wife will not lie to me," he said angrily.

"I am not lying," Kapilla snapped. "They're not dumb. They're very bright."

"They're stupid. None of our children better be like them. You better not have idiots like your mother did," he growled.

"They're not idiots, but what if I did?" Kapilla shouted, unable to contain her anger any longer.

"Then you'll end up like your mother did, you fool! Herdon did well by killing her. It was her fault the poor man had idiot sons."

Kapilla was seething. "They're not idiots, I tell you! I will be proud to have sons like them," she retorted.

"Be quiet, you stupid woman!" Amarton shouted, jumping to his feet and shaking his grimy fists. "You will bear me strong, brave sons and beautiful daughters. Do you hear me?" he asked insanely.

Kapilla was on her feet. "I'll never marry you, Amarton. You don't have to worry about what my children are like, because they won't be yours!" she screamed.

Amarton came around the fire like a cat after its prey. Kapilla tried to run, but he caught her, spun her around and knocked her to the ground. When she tried to get up, he swung his foot, catching her solidly in the stomach. She doubled over and fell, writhing in pain.

"Stupid woman," he hissed. "Let this be a lesson. You will do as I say from now on, and don't you ever talk back to me again." He paused, and when she did not answer, he poked her with his foot and asked, "Do you hear me?"

"Yes," she choked.

"Go to sleep now, woman. Tomorrow we are going to travel much farther than today, and you better keep up," he threatened.

Kapilla crawled into a thick clump of shrubbery, curled up like a ball, and cried herself to sleep.

* * *

"They're going in circles," Gadoni said, wiping his forehead and staring at a fresh track on the ground. "They have crossed their own trail here. I think this man Amarton is lost."

"Maybe we should split up," Samuel suggested. "If we were in two groups it could save us some time."

"That's a good idea," Oreb said quickly.

The little party of searchers had risen early and by the time the sun had shot its golden rays over the jungle wilderness, they were following the faint tracks they had been on for nearly two days. They had little doubt it was Kapilla and Amarton who were meandering in the area.

"Gadoni, you take Nemti and Kib. Oreb, you and Kim come with me," Samuel said.

"Why split the twins up?" Oreb asked. "They'd both rather be with me."

"I'm sure you're right, Oreb, but I'm trying to even out our strengths. This way we all have the advantage of their skill with a sling," Samuel said with a grin. The boys swelled and he went on. "Gadoni and I will be the trackers and you, Oreb, and Nemti, are the best ones with a bow."

With that settled, they planned when and where to meet under the different circumstances that might occur. "Have we covered everything?" Samuel asked at last.

"Yes, let's get going," Oreb said eagerly. "We're wasting too much time."

"Fine," Samuel said patiently.

By late morning, Samuel signaled with his hand for Kim and Oreb to stop. He carefully studied the ground where the grass and flowers had been stomped flat around a small mound of black coals.

"What is it, Sam?" Oreb asked.

"Something's odd here," Samuel said thoughtfully, dropping to his knees.

"What?" Oreb asked. "It looks like they just camped here, to me."

"Let's see if we can find where they left this area," Samuel said without explaining further.

He held his hand over the fire pit, nearly touching the black coals. "Still warm," he observed. "They were here last night."

Oreb started scouting around. "They went this way, Sam," he suddenly shouted.

"You're right. Like I said, this is odd."

"What's odd, Sam?"

"Have you ever seen the smaller tracks ahead of the big ones?" Samuel asked.

Oreb thought a moment. "Well, no. Kapilla must be following him."

"Not anymore. His track is covering hers in places here. Why would she be in the lead now?"

"I don't know. Is that important, Sam?" Oreb asked, puzzled.

"Yes, it is. I think something has changed, and I don't like it."

Oreb's puzzled face was suddenly worried. "I wonder what's happened," he said softly.

"Could be a couple of reasons," Samuel said as he followed the tracks into the trees. "Maybe she's trying to find the way out of the wilderness, since he obviously can't. That would mean, though, that he's admitted he is disoriented. Very unlikely, I would imagine. Or . . ."

"Or what?" Oreb pressed impatiently.

"Back there," Samuel said, pointing toward the recent campsite, "it looked to me like someone had crawled around the fire and into the bushes. That could mean he's mistreating her—maybe doesn't trust her as much. Anyway, that could explain why she's walking ahead of him. Maybe she won't follow him anymore and he's having to force her."

"Let's hurry," Oreb said, pushing Samuel urgently from behind. "We can't afford to waste time."

They passed through an area so dense that they had to hack at the branches and foliage with their swords. Leaves and branches had been broken recently from those struggling through ahead of them. When they finally emerged into the open they were on the grassy bank of a meandering stream. Samuel plunged in and waded through, Oreb and Kim faithfully following. The bottom sucked at their feet and they stumbled over slimy objects that protruded from the muck.

Samuel found where Amarton and Kapilla had pulled themselves up the bank on the far side. Leaves were stripped from shrubs that had been used as handholds. From there, they had forged straight ahead.

Samuel stopped a few minutes later. "They rested here," he said. "They were just as wet as we are. Look, it's still wet on this log."

"Keep going, Sam," Oreb said anxiously after a cursory glance.

"I think we're not far behind them. We'll keep pushing," Samuel agreed, plunging into another thicket.

A couple of strenuous hours followed. "Does Amarton really think he's getting anywhere?" Oreb asked. "They're heading into harder country to travel in. This is almost impassible."

"Yes," Samuel said, raising an arm to signal a stop. "They could well be doubling back before long, don't you think, Oreb? We better be very alert now. Let's have Kim get between us," he said, peering into the trees ahead.

"Sam, he's gone!" Oreb said with such urgency that Samuel spun like a top.

"He was there a minute ago," Samuel said with alarm.

They swiftly backtracked to a small clearing. "He's gone this way," Samuel said, pointing to a steep, rocky incline to the east. "He's scrambled up these mossy rocks and into those trees up there."

Oreb started up the rock, but Samuel stopped him. "Look," he said, pointing at the ground. "Someone has passed this way since we came by just moments ago. Looks like they were running, from the length of the strides."

Samuel's eyes met Oreb's. A look of concern and understanding passed between them. They rushed in the direction the tracks led. Branches slapped their faces and they stumbled frequently but suddenly broke into the clear. Ahead of them lay a large, shimmering lake.

"Sam!" Oreb whispered urgently and pointed.

Samuel looked. Kapilla was running along the very edge of the treacherous, log-strewn shore several hundred feet beyond them. The shiny surface of the water was to her left, ten or fifteen feet straight down over a precipice.

She was looking back over her shoulder as she ran. Stumbling, she fell dangerously near the edge. Oreb and Samuel rushed toward her. The rocks beneath their feet were jagged and rough, covered with slick moss, water seeping over them. They had a hard time staying on their feet.

"Kapilla," a panting voice shouted. "You stay where you are, you stupid woman."

Samuel grabbed Oreb and they slid to a stop. A man emerged from the trees only a short distance from the cowering girl. He was wielding a sword, shaking it menacingly as he approached her.

"Kapilla!"

Samuel recognized Kim's voice ringing through the humid air. At that moment, Oreb shouted, "Jump into the lake, Kapilla!"

She hesitated, still on her knees. Amarton was almost to her, his sword now high over his head. Oreb and Samuel were both fumbling with their bows. Kim appeared from the trees on a ledge above them, his sling in his hand.

Kapilla had finally gotten Oreb's message and was scrambling to the edge. Amarton's sword started to fall toward the scrambling girl. Kim's arm moved in a swift arc, sending a small missile on its deadly course.

For a brief moment, Amarton seemed to freeze. Then, as Kapilla slipped over the edge of the precipice to the sanctuary of the water below, Amarton's hand came open and the sword fell harmlessly to the mossy rock surface. The big robber's body crumpled to the ground.

Samuel and Oreb rushed toward him. "Kim," Oreb shouted, "we're coming."

The boy looked back and saw them. He waved, a big grin on his thin face. "I saved her," he said, sliding off his high perch and running to meet them.

"You sure did," Samuel said, putting a big arm around the boy's slender shoulders. Oreb dropped his bow and quiver and dove headlong from the ledge and sailed through the air to rescue Kapilla, who was bobbing in the water below. Samuel knelt and examined Amarton while Kim nervously watched Oreb swim toward Kapilla.

Samuel straightened up and stood beside the boy. He smiled when the couple below came together in the water for a joyous reunion. "Hey Kim, let's give those two some privacy, should we?" he asked. "They've been mighty lonely for each other, you know."

Still grinning, Kim said, "Sure, Sam."

"You and I can drag old Amarton into the trees."

"Sam!" Kim exclaimed, gaping at the prostrate robber. "Is he dead?"

"Yes, David, the Gadianton robbers are short one Goliath, thanks to your skilled arm," he said with a wink.

"I'm Kim," the boy said with a puzzled expression. "Why did you call me David?"

"Tonight, Kim, remind me to tell you the story of David and Goliath from the brass plates, then you'll understand," Samuel said. "Now, latch onto that foot and pull. I don't want your sister to have to see this man again."

"Can I have his sword?" Kim asked a few minutes later as they finished their task.

"I guess you've earned it."

Samuel helped Kim strip the sheath from the dead robber and strap it to his side. Kim ran back to the edge of the lake and picked up the long, straight sword and felt its sharp edge. He swung it several times through the air before shoving it into the sheath at his side.

"You two look a little wet," Samuel observed dryly as Oreb and Kapilla appeared, arm in arm.

Kim squealed and threw his arms around his sister. Oreb stepped away, a smile stretching his broad face. "That was close, wasn't it?" he asked, looking around.

"Too close, Oreb," Samuel responded.

"Where's Amar . . ."

Samuel cut him off with a finger to his lips. He pointed into the foliage up the slope. Oreb nodded in understanding and turned back to Kim and Kapilla. Kim was talking excitedly. "I got him, Kapilla. I got him."

"You saved my life, Kim. Thank you," she said, pulling him close, her pale eyes glistening. "And thank you, Sam," she said, looking up. "Oreb told me about all you've done."

"Only with the help of the Lord," Samuel said modestly. "Let's go find the others and get back to Gilead. I have no intention of leaving my family again. Ophera was right in the first place. Oreb and I should never have tried to catch the murderer of Pahoran ourselves."

"But I am glad we did, Samuel, for I would never have found Kapilla if we hadn't," Oreb said with a grin.

"Yes, many times the Lord helps us turn foolish blunders into miracles if we confess our errors to Him. You have gained Kapilla, the boys have gained a new start in life, and I have learned a lesson that I already knew and forgot: if we let the Spirit guide us, life goes much better," Samuel admitted.

"It is still early in the forty-first year of the judges, and I hope that we can make this a better year than the last one, away from Zarahemla," Samuel continued with feeling.

"Yes," Oreb agreed. "I think that if we let someone else worry about Kishkumen and Gadianton, our troubles will be over."

"I certainly hope so, little brother. I certainly hope so."

CHAPTER 20

Nonita felt the tension, like electricity in the air, when she arrived in Zarahemla three long, hard days after Samuel had left with his little expedition in search of Kapilla. Laishita and Ophera greeted her warmly, but warned her of unrest and dissension in the city. "Chief Judge Pacumeni is very worried. The robbers are growing in strength and many people are complaining that they want a different chief judge," Ophera explained.

"Where is my father?" Nonita asked, knowing of his fierce loyalty to the government but needing his love and encouragement desperately.

"He returned to Gilead. Pacumeni insisted that it was too dangerous for him to wait here, so he left us and returned. We were going to wait until Samuel and Gadoni returned before we went back, too," Ophera said, her face drawn with worry and lack of sleep. "But, if it's too dangerous here for Latoni, then maybe we should wait in Gilead, too."

The others agreed without argument.

A short while later, Captain Calno appeared at the palace, asking for Nonita and her sister-in-law. Nonita tensed when she noted his furrowed brow. She introduced Ophera and Laishita, who still held her little son, Enos, possessively in her arms.

"You women are in danger," he stated emphatically. "We have received word from an anonymous source that the Gadianton robbers still seek revenge against Samuel, Oreb, and Gadoni. The guard here at the palace is being strengthened at this very moment, and it would probably be best if you and your children did not leave without an armed guard if you decide to go on to Gilead. The robbers don't know you are here, but they may suspect it and could lie in wait for you to leave."

"Where are the prisoners that were taken in the wilderness?" Nonita asked.

"That, I am afraid, is the other thing I came to talk to you about," the captain said, the lines on his face growing deeper. "Most of them escaped from the prison they were being held in. The robbers somehow discovered where we were taking them, and a plan to get them out had already been formulated."

"Kerlin. What about him?" Nonita asked, trying to hide the fear she felt.

"He's gone. He escaped with the others."

"Oh," she said faintly, suddenly feeling very weak.

"Also," Calno went on, "the Lamanites are said to be preparing for war. Moronihah and most of the army have gone to strengthen the border cities against attack. I have orders to march my men to the city of Moroni, near the East Sea, in a few days. We will leave the day after the Sabbath."

"What about Kapilla?" Nonita asked.

"We have sent couriers to all parts of the land. She'll be found. I must go now, but please heed my warning and stay in the palace until your men return or seek assistance from the palace guard to escort you if you must leave," Calno urged. He whipped smartly around and strode briskly from the palace.

"I would feel better in Gilead while I wait for Samuel to return," Ophera said as soon as Calno was out of sight. "You know how Samuel and Gadoni are, and Oreb is no different. They could search for Kapilla for weeks, and I don't want to be cooped up here for that long."

"But it may not be safe to leave," Laishita said, hugging Enos to her so tight he squealed.

"It may not be safe to stay, either. I think the sooner we leave the safer it will be. Anyway, Chief Judge Pacumeni will give us some men to get us out of Zarahemla," Ophera argued. "We could leave at nightfall and travel in the darkness. I know the way very well."

Nonita studied her sister-in-law intently. She knew her well and recognized that it would be hard to change her mind once she had it set, but she was exhausted and needed at least one good night's rest before traveling again. So she tried. "I want to be with my father, but I am too tired to leave tonight. Let's wait one day. If they're not back by tomorrow night, let's leave then."

"Laishita, what do you think?" Ophera asked.

"I want away from here, too. As long as we have protection, then tomorrow night will be fine."

Ophera smiled. "All right," she agreed, "but if they aren't here by dark tomorrow night, we will leave and travel at night."

Nonita nodded her head and Laishita said, "Let's pray that they return quickly." The stress of the past weeks showed on her dark face, and Nonita's heart went out to her.

Nonita lay that night in bed, tossing and turning, the much-needed rest she had stalled for fleeing before her troubled thoughts. She envisioned Samuel and Oreb in the unfriendly wilderness and it haunted her. The handsome face of Nemti, the young man she hardy knew, danced, smiling, behind her closed eyelids. And, try as she would, she could not keep fearful thoughts of Kerlin away.

* * *

Latoni was up before the birds the next morning. He had slept fitfully, a nagging worry over his family denying him rest. He limped barefoot across the street to his shop, his old war injury aching worse than usual. He hated to admit it, but he was not well.

Latoni made the metal parts for wagons, carriages, and chariots— very strenuous work, especially for a lame man. He sat down in the shop and watched the morning light steal past his dusty windows, casting an eerie glow across the tools of his trade. He barely had the strength to lift them and pound out the hot iron each day. He hoped one of his sons would soon take over his business, for he was not sure he could keep it up much longer.

Latoni was also a priest and directed the spiritual lives of the people of Gilead under the direction of Helaman. He even served as a lesser judge and received compensation for his work. He could live on the small salary and would enjoy the work of the government and the church much more if he was not so drained all the time from the strenuous physical labor in his shop.

A monkey chattered at the door, stirring Latoni from his reverie. Smiling at the little beast, he said, "No worries. You can take each day as it comes and think not of the next. At times I envy you." At the sound of his voice, the monkey scampered away.

Latoni struggled to his feet, stood for a moment rubbing the ache from his leg, limped to the door, and returned to the house. Kamina was still asleep. Their son, Uri, barely seven, was in his room. Latoni peeked in. He also slept, a peaceful smile creasing his small face. Latoni wished with all his heart that all his children, grown though they were, could be lying here, too.

Uri would awaken soon and liven the house with his laughter. So like Samuel in many ways, yet not unlike Oreb, Latoni thought. In looks, he most closely resembled his other grown half-brother, Josh, Kamina's son and the full brother of Ophera. Josh had wavy, light brown hair and was fair complected but sturdy, with a handsome, determined face.

Josh was another source of constant concern. A soldier by choice, he had grown up with stories of his dead father, killed by the Lamanites in battle. Drawn like a moth to the flame, he had always wanted to be a soldier and had left home at an early age to seek his fortunes at war. Peace had been his lot, though, until now. Latoni had heard the rumors, and knew that Josh might be fighting the Lamanites soon.

Latoni returned slowly to the back door. His sandals were where he had left them the night before. He stooped to put them on. Suddenly, the door burst open and Latoni was knocked to the floor, blood spurting from his nose. Two men with twisted, bitter faces stared down at him. He suppressed the urge to shout, not wanting to wake up and endanger his sleeping wife and son.

"We are here for your daughter, Ophera," a short, stocky fellow demanded, holding a knife to Latoni's throat.

"She isn't here," he whispered hoarsely.

"Then take us to her," the young man ordered, jerking Latoni to his feet.

"I don't know where . . ." he began.

A knee was jammed cruelly into his stomach, knocking the breath from him. "We want Ophera and we want Gadoni's wife, too," the other man sneered. "Take us to them or your days will end."

"Who are you men?" Latoni asked, still whispering, even though they were making no attempt at silence.

"It doesn't matter who we are, just get them for us," the first answered, twisting Latoni's arm violently behind his back.

"I tell you, I don't know where . . ." he began but trailed off when his wife appeared in the hallway.

"Latoni, what is . . ." she started.

Before she could finish, the taller man grabbed her long hair and hissed, "Tell us where Ophera and Laishita are."

"I don't know. They aren't here," she said, her eyes wide with terror.

"Liar!" he screamed. "We'll search the house."

"What about them?" the short one asked, still holding Latoni so painfully he thought he would pass out at any moment.

The tall one shrugged his shoulders. "It doesn't matter. They won't talk anyway, will you?" he said to Kamina, who was struggling to free herself from his grasp.

She shook her head. Latoni tried to wrench himself free, provoking a violent knee to his back. The short man's grip loosened and Latoni fell helplessly to the floor. Kamina screamed. The tall man shoved her hard against the wall. She fell across her husband.

"Go search the house, Kerlin," the tall man ordered. "I'll give these two another chance to tell us what they know."

Kerlin ran from room to room, looking for Laishita and Ophera. He knew them only by name. He half expected to find Nonita cowering in one of the rooms. He grinned wickedly, picturing her gazing into the eyes of the young soldier in the wilderness. She'll pay, he breathed to himself. She'll pay.

The last room he looked in had toys scattered about that might belong to a young boy. The closet contained small clothes, and a pair of little sandals lay where they had been dropped on the floor. The blanket on the bed was ruffled, but no one was in it. Kerlin turned from the room. He failed to see the frightened form hunkered down behind the cot, the little blue eyes wide with fright.

Uri stayed in his hiding spot for a long time after the man had left his room. His eyes were red from crying and his little arms and legs trembled with terror. He had been awakened by the shouting in the back of the house and had run there in time to witness the mistreatment of his parents. Fearfully, he had returned to his room and hid, the name "Kerlin" ringing in his ears.

He kept thinking his father and mother would come for him, but when they did not, he finally mustered all the courage he had, climbed out over his bed and crept through the silent house.

Uri's heart leaped, and he fell to his knees when he entered the hallway and discovered his father lying awkwardly on the floor. Blood was pooled around him and his face was white and still. On his hands and knees, Uri crawled toward him, calling, "Father," very weakly, then again louder. "Father."

Latoni stirred and Uri buried his head in his father's chest, sobbing uncontrollably. "Uri," Latoni said in a whisper so soft the boy could barely hear him. "Where is your mother?"

"I don't know, Father," he choked out between sobs.

"Go find her, Uri. She may be outside."

Uri forced himself to his feet. His father's eyes opened slightly, then closed again. "Father, you are sick. Did those men hurt you bad?" he asked in a hoarse little voice.

Latoni's eyes opened a crack again. "Yes, they hurt me. I am very sick." His voice faded and he coughed before going on. "Uri, my son, I love you. I have to go away now. You take care of . . ." He coughed again, his face twisted with pain. "Take care . . . of your . . . mother."

"Don't leave me, Father," Uri said, kneeling in the blood again and pleading with Latoni. "Please don't die. I'll be alone. Please . . . please, Father." His little body shook.

"Uri," Latoni said again, "find your mother . . . and somehow, send . . . someone to find . . . Ophera and Laishita." He coughed again and his body was racked for a full minute before he went on. "And warn them. The robbers are after them."

Latoni lifted an arm and put it around the boy's trembling shoulders. "Uri . . . I love . . . you." He pulled the boy closer while he coughed again. "You've got . . . to be . . . a man . . . now," he stammered weakly. "Will you . . . take . . . care . . . of your . . . mother?"

Blinded with tears, Uri nodded, hugged his father, and sobbed. The arm around his little shoulders relaxed, then slid to the floor. The gentle man's eyes closed. Peace had come to a righteous Nephite in the midst of troubled times.

Somehow, Uri knew his father's spirit had fled. Slowly, he pulled himself to his feet, trembling with grief, and went in search of his mother. He found her on the pathway in the garden. She was pulling herself toward the house, a broken and twisted leg, useless now, hampering her progress. Uri rushed to her, calling, "Mother, Mother, don't you die, too!"

She looked up at him as he knelt on the grass, still moist from the morning dew. "Is your father dead?" she asked, her voice shaking and her face creased with pain.

"Yes, Mother, he's dead. He . . ." Uri couldn't go on. The sobs were coming too fast and hard.

"Uri, help me to the house. Then go get someone to help us," Kamina instructed her crying child.

The boy tugged and pulled, wincing when she screamed out in pain, but obeying her request, as he always did. When she finally lay on the floor beside Latoni's body, she said, "Run now, Uri. Get help."

He obeyed again, fleeing through the front door and into the street beyond. He ran to the nearest house and entered without knocking.

"Uri, whatever is the matter?" a big woman asked when he burst through the door. There was a sudden intake of air when she saw the blood smeared on him.

"Bad men . . . they came . . . Father is dead . . . Mother needs you . . . hurry," he stuttered, wiping his eyes with his hand, streaking his face with his father's blood.

The woman's hazel eyes were big as the moon, but she didn't hesitate. Shouting for her husband, who came into the room almost immediately, she lumbered out the door. Uri led them across the street and into the house. The big woman knelt beside Kamina, her hands working feverishly. Then she stopped, folded her arms across her ample chest and bowed her head. Her husband took Uri's hand, holding him tight. The boy struggled to free himself.

A long moment passed before the woman heaved herself to her feet and faced Uri. The look in her eyes froze him. "Uri, my child, your mother has gone to be with your father," she said gently.

Uri stared at her. "No!" he cried. "No, she'll be okay. I'm supposed to take care of her. I promised Father . . ."

"Come, my child. We'll take you to our home," she urged gently.

Uri bolted from the old Nephite, scampered around the big woman and fell on his mother. There he lay, crying until the tears would come no more.

CHAPTER 21

Darkness descended upon Zarahemla, crowding streaks of faded pink from the western sky. "We will go now," Ophera said. "We'll be safer in Gilead while we wait for the men to return. I told the chief judge that we were leaving and he agreed to give us a large escort until we are into the forest beyond the city," she explained.

"What about the rest of the way? Will we be alone?" Laishita asked fearfully.

"No, two of the men will accompany us on to Gilead," she said. "I know the way, but I am glad we will have someone along to give us protection after all that has happened these past weeks."

It was with a feeling of relief and excitement that the three women and four children traveled the dark city streets under the protection of a dozen armed soldiers. They passed through the gates of Zarahemla and a mile beyond before ten of the guards turned back. Then, accompanied by the two remaining men, they slowly wended their way through the darkness toward Gilead.

* * *

Samuel and the others reached the palace not long after the women and children had left. They did not even take time to rest or eat before getting underway again after learning all that had occurred during the past day.

"Are you sure you want to come, Nemti?" Samuel asked with a grin as the young soldier followed them from the palace.

"Yes," he said firmly. "Captain Calno told me that I did not need to report to the army until you and your family no longer needed me. With Kerlin on the loose again, it seems to me like that time hasn't come yet."

Samuel nodded, still grinning. He had become very fond of the young soldier, and another day or so around Nonita would not hurt either one of them. "Good. And you can still be back in time to leave with Calno and the others for Moroni."

"Will you be safe in Gilead?" Nemti asked after they had picked up Samuel's horses at the palace stables.

"I don't know," Samuel said solemnly, boosting the twins onto the back of one horse while Oreb helped Kapilla onto the other one. "It will be safer than here in Zarahemla, but I wonder sometimes if there is any place in the land that is truly safe anymore, especially with the threat of war again."

"There must be someplace," Gadoni said wearily.

Samuel led his exhausted little group through Zarahemla in the darkness. They met the returning soldiers just a short distance away. After a brief conference with them, they hurried on.

"I wonder why there are no sentries at the gate," Nemti mused as they passed through.

"They must feel that the Lamanites would never dare come into the very center of the land," Oreb said.

"Very unlikely, all right," Samuel agreed. "The biggest threat here is the band of Gadianton robbers, especially since the ones we captured escaped."

"Which way from here?" Oreb asked, anxious to get going again.

"Just follow me. I think I know the route Ophera will follow, because it is how we usually go together," Samuel said, feeling tense and worried.

By shortly after midnight, they caught up with the women and children. Samuel told the two palace guards they could return to the palace, and then much rejoicing and prayers of thanksgiving followed. Too tired to go much farther, Samuel suggested they rest for a few hours before pushing on.

Sometime during the pre-dawn darkness, Samuel stirred in his sleep. Not fully awake, he seemed to hear a rumbling in the ground. His groggy mind drifted back many years. In a dreamlike trance he envisioned the massive Nephite army he had served with marching to battle, thousands of feet pounding the earth until it shook. He drifted into deep slumber.

He was awake again just as the first strains of dawn struggled over the eastern horizon. The memory of a quaking earth and dreams of the army nagged at him. He shrugged it off until his son, Jath, asked, "Father, who was marching in the night?"

His stomach knotted with apprehension. "What do you mean, Jath?" he asked, fearing that he knew the answer.

"I woke up in the dark," the little fellow said, his sparkling blue eyes wide and innocent. "I heard the ground shake. It sounded like lots of people. It sounded like when Captain Moronihah brought the army past the palace," he said, wrinkling his nose. "Only I didn't smell dust last night."

Ophera laughed. "They did stir up some dust when they passed the other day. Jath," she said, turning to her little son, "you had a dream. Did you dream about the army?"

"He wasn't dreaming, Ophera," Samuel said, a chill in his voice.

Everyone looked at him expectantly, their faces registering alarm. "I heard it, too, only I didn't wake up fully. I thought I was dreaming. Gadoni," he said, his voice rising, "come with me. The rest of you wait here."

Without another word, the two friends strode from the camp and through the heavy forest. They did not have to go far before they found where a large army of marching men had passed by.

"Lamanites. They're marching right into Zarahemla, and most of the army of Moronihah isn't even there to defend it," Samuel moaned.

"They are probably taking the city right now," Gadoni agreed.

"And there were no guards last night to even give a warning," Samuel said anxiously.

A few minutes later, Ophera, her face anxious and her voice betraying her fear, asked, "Were there many, Sam?"

"I'm afraid so. It was a massive army. I'm sure Zarahemla will fall quickly under the attack. We must hurry to Gilead." He turned to Gadoni. "Who do you suppose is leading the Lamanites?"

"The head of the Lamanite army is a former Nephite. He's a large and mighty man by the name of Coriantumr. Tubaloth is king, and he too is white. They are wicked and bloodthirsty men. I think Tubaloth would not send anyone but Coriantumr himself to make such a bold move as this," Gadoni said with certainty.

"That is as I supposed," Samuel groaned. "Their purpose will be to control all of our land. I wouldn't be surprised if Gadianton himself is in league with them and behind this invasion."

It was a weary and depressed party that trudged through the muggy forest toward Gilead later that day. Someone had seen them coming and spread the word, for many residents waited near the edge of town.

"My, we have a greeting party," Oreb said with a half-smile.

"Have they missed us that much?" Ophera asked, quite surprised.

Samuel said nothing, but a cold hand clutched his heart. Ophera sensed his mood and asked, "What is it, Sam? Aren't you glad to be home?"

"Something is very wrong," he said slowly. "They never come to greet us like that," he said, quickening his pace.

"Oh, Sam, it's probably just that everyone is anxious . . ." Oreb started.

"No. I can feel it," Samuel said.

Suddenly a young child burst from the crowd and came running to meet them, his wavy hair flying in the wind. Samuel recognized his little brother, Uri. He scooped the sobbing child into his big arms.

Uri grabbed Samuel around the neck and cried, "They're dead, Sam! The robbers killed them!"

A cold hand clutched Samuel's heart again and squeezed unmercifully as he forced the question he did not want answered. "Who, Uri? Who is dead?"

"Mother and Father!" he said, and his tears flowed like warm rain.

Samuel sank to his knees. He held tightly to his brother. He suppressed the urge to shout—to pound the ground with his fists—even to cry. The anger he felt toward the invading Lamanites paled in comparison to the anger, even hatred, that now filled his heart toward the Gadianton robbers.

Gilead was washed with hot tears that day. None were more bitter than those that flowed from the dark eyes of Nonita, for she had lost a husband and now a father and step-mother. But her bitterest tears, ones filled with unspeakable fear, came that afternoon when Samuel asked Uri, "Can you tell me anything about the men who did this terrible thing?"

Without hesitation, Uri spoke one word with high-pitched venom. "Kerlin!"

Nonita leaped to her feet and fled from the gloomy house. Samuel started after her, but Nemti grabbed his arm. "Let me go," he said quietly.

* * *

Nemti spotted Nonita's streaming black hair through a throng of people who were fleeing with their belongings into the forest, fear of the Lamanite army strong upon them. She turned from them and made her way to the shimmering lake that lay a short way west of the city. It was the fun spot of Gilead—the place where little boys fished and played at war and where lovers strolled, arm in arm, on warm evenings.

She didn't stop until she reached an outcropping of mossy rock that hung over the crystal water. Nemti approached with the stealth of a cat and stood watching her for several minutes before walking up behind her and sitting quietly beside her.

Gazing over the water, he said nothing. Nonita's dark eyes shot him a quick look, then she wiped the tears away and stared blankly over the lake. The afternoon wore on, the golden sun turning scarlet as it dipped toward the western mountains. Still not a word passed between them.

Nemti knew the others would be restless and worried about Nonita. He reached out at last and touched her olive hand which was resting on the rock between them. Slowly she turned it over, palm up, and closed it on his.

Silvery fish jumped with vigor, feeding on insects that were careless enough to hit the water. Gaily colored birds floating near the surface dined on other insects swarming there. For several minutes they watched nature at work while it worked on their own hearts.

Finally, Nemti got to his feet, stretched the cramps away, and then helped Nonita up. Her eyes, dark and full of hurt, gazed into his for a long moment. Slowly they softened, and for the first time in many hours she smiled. Shyly, Nemti drew her slender body close and his lips sought hers. They stood there embracing and silent, heart speaking to heart.

Hers told his that she had found someone who could fill the emptiness she felt and soothe her many hurts.

"Thank you—for making it all right," she said at last.

Nemti smiled and gazed at the beauty of her shining face.

When they entered the almost deserted city, the sun had sunk and only a faint hue of fading pink and amber lit their way. Their newfound love touched all those who waited in the gloomy house, so recently tarnished with tragic death. With their love came hope that rallied around them all and lifted their sagging spirits.

Especially lifted that evening was the dampened spirit of Oreb as he found in the pale green eyes of Kapilla his only exodus from bitter grief. He learned, as Nonita had, that love could carry one through the most difficult trials. He pulled Kapilla close and she dropped her head gently against his shoulder.

CHAPTER 22

With the morning came news of the tragic invasion of Zarahemla. Some had escaped the violence and fled to surrounding cities. Those few who passed through Gilead told of the evil Lamanite chief captain, Coriantumr, slaying Chief Judge Pacumeni with a sword at the city wall. Other important and righteous leaders were also slain. The Lamanite army had terrorized the entire city, dealing death to any who dared to resist.

The people of Gilead filtered back to their homes. A few lingered there, but most packed their belongings and drifted back into the forest. The Lamanites had pushed on, away from Gilead and toward the city of Bountiful near the East Sea, but the people were not taking any chances by assuming that Gilead was safe.

Samuel and his family were concerned that danger would soon reach there. Sitting by himself in the well-tended garden of Latoni and Kamina, the early morning sun bearing down on his back, he grieved for the loss of his father and Kamina and for the loss of Pacumeni. He thought bitterly about Kerlin and others of the Gadianton robbers. Not only the Lamanites posed a threat, but the tragic absence of Latoni and Kamina had burned the other danger deep in his mind. The Gadianton robbers hated him and would do anything to him or his loved ones to get the revenge their evil hearts thought was due to them. He knew they blamed him for the deaths of their fellow robbers in the wilderness hideout, and rightfully so, for it was he that led the army there.

Never in his life had Samuel known fear the way he did now—not fear for himself, but fear for his family and loved ones. If it were not for them he would charge right back into the midst of the robbers and seek his own revenge, but his anger was tempered by his concern for those loved ones still living. Instead of seeking revenge, he considered how he might best protect them.

Alone and on his knees, he prayed for divine guidance. Quietly, almost as a whisper in the warm west wind, his answer came. And in his mind a picture, clear as day, burned itself into his memory. It would not be easy, but he knew now what he must do and where he must go.

Samuel was still on his knees, savoring the sweet spiritual experience he had just been granted, when the sweet voice of his little son came softly over his shoulder. "Are you going to go away again?" six-year-old Jath asked.

He turned and pulled the boy in front of him, and holding him by the shoulders, looked squarely into his bright blue eyes. "Why do you ask that, son?"

"Mother said you are very angry with the robbers. Are you going to get them?" he asked with wide-eyed, childish innocence.

"Jath," Samuel said, scooping the boy into his arms, "right now I plan to stay with you and your mother."

"But Father . . ."

"But what, Jath?"

"Who will take care of Uri, now that Grandfather and Grandmother are dead?"

The boy's question brought the pain to the surface again, but Samuel forced a smile. "Well," he began thoughtfully, "that is a very important question. Who do you think should?"

Jath squirmed from his father's grip, squared his little shoulders and said, "I think we should, Father."

"Now there's a good idea, Jath. Do you think he would be willing to go with us?" Samuel asked, grinning at the boy's serious face.

"Go where, Father? Are we going with you?" His face had suddenly lit up like the morning sun.

"Yes."

"Where, Father? Where?"

Samuel chuckled. "Now don't you go and change the subject on me. We'll talk later about where we're going to go. Please answer my question. Would Uri want to be part of our family?"

"Yes," Jath said with certainty.

"What makes you so sure?"

"Because he told me. Last night he said I was lucky to have a father like you. He said you can do anything. I told him I knew that. He told me he didn't have a father anymore. I said I'd share you. He said he'd like that."

"Well, well. I'd like that, too. Let's go find Uri and tell him, should we?" Samuel said, rising to his feet.

"Sure," Jath said, latching on to Samuel's outstretched hand. "But shouldn't we ask Mother?"

"I already have, Jath. She was thinking just the way you were. What do you think of that?"

"I like it."

They found Uri with Kim and Kib. The twins were demonstrating their prowess with their slings at the edge of town. "I wish you two could find the men that hurt my father and mother," Samuel overheard Uri saying. "You would fix them!"

Samuel interrupted. "Kim and Kib really are skilled, aren't they, Uri?"

"They sure are. They could get the men . . ."

"Uri," Samuel broke in, "Kim and Kib have better things to do. Those men aren't worth going after," he said, trying to convince himself as well as them. "Anyway, Jath and I need to talk to you, Uri. Would you excuse us, boys?"

The twins nodded and Uri walked with Samuel and Jath toward the center of town. They went to Latoni's shop and sat on the wooden bench out front. It was shaded from the hot morning sun, but Samuel wiped his face with his hand before beginning.

"Uri," he said, suddenly awkward. "We're all going to miss Mother and Father very much, aren't we?"

The boy nodded and brushed a tear from his eye. He acted like he wanted to talk, but did not. His head bowed with the grief that he was trying to hide.

"I can never replace your father, but Ophera and I would like you to live with us. Would you be willing to do that?" Samuel pressed gently.

Uri looked up. "Oh, Sam, I want to."

"Good. You could be Jath's big brother. He'd like that, wouldn't you, Jath?"

"I sure would," Jath said quickly. "Father says we're going somewhere and you could come with us."

Uri's blue eyes lit up. "Where?" he asked. "I've never been farther than Zarahemla."

"Well, I hope it will be someplace safe, Uri," Samuel said.

"Are you going after the robbers first?" Uri asked, his face darkening and his high-pitched voice suddenly full of revenge.

"No, Uri. I don't think that would be wise. We seem to lose something each time we chase after them. There are just too many of them now, and they know me too well."

"What if they come after us again?" he asked as if pulling the question from Samuel's own mind.

"I hope they don't, but if they do . . . well . . . we'll make them wish they hadn't, that's what we'll do," Samuel said, trying to keep his voice level but fighting the anger he felt toward the evil band of men.

A wedding was going to take place at noon. Oreb and Kapilla had decided before they ever reached Zarahemla that the first step toward lasting happiness for them and the twins was to form a family. They did not want their marriage to wait. One of the refugees from Zarahemla was the prophet Helaman, who was going on to Manti. He had embraced Samuel and then agreed to stay long enough in Gilead to perform the wedding at the synagogue.

Samuel became more tense and worried as the wedding hour drew near. He was anxious to get his loved ones on their way to a safer place, but he was not willing to deny Oreb and Kapilla their wedding at the synagogue.

Mid-day found them gathered at the town's new synagogue, a building constructed under the leadership of Latoni. It was a wooden structure, but decorated with fine tapestries and ornately carved furnishings.

Kapilla was dressed in one of Ophera's finest gowns. She glowed with beauty, bringing a grin to Oreb's broad face that reached from ear to ear. With her hand in his, he waited in the courtyard for the ceremony to begin. Kapilla had asked that they stand amid the flowers and shrubs that were adorned with a myriad of colors and sent forth an aroma that could not have been sweeter.

Helaman was almost through the ceremony when Samuel noticed a movement by one of the buildings across the square from the synagogue. He tensed and watched closely. A man darted through a narrow alley and behind the building. Another followed. Samuel slipped away from

Ophera and nudged Gadoni, whispering to him. Together, they moved silently away.

Ophera and Laishita frowned, but Nemti, also taking notice of their departure, whispered to Nonita and followed, leaving her standing alone, the smile gone from her face.

Samuel had insisted that as a precaution the men wear their weapons, just in case . . . The ceremony was concluded and Oreb was kissing Kapilla long and lovingly when Samuel shouted, "Everyone down!"

The urgency in his voice was all it took. Everyone dropped. A volley of arrows flew harmlessly over them. Before any more were fired, everyone had crawled quickly for the protection of the low stone walls that surrounded the courtyard.

All was still for a moment. Even the children were silent, frozen with fright. A robber leaped to his feet and started across the street. Nemti loosed an arrow before the man got ten steps. His body hadn't hit the street before two more ran out. Oreb shot one and Samuel the other. Still two more came. Oreb and Nemti fired at them.

"Nemti!" Nonita screamed. Samuel saw the young soldier falling heavily, an arrow having passed clear through his side. He tried to locate where it had come from. He spotted an archer on a rooftop to his left, but before he could draw his bow string taut, the man tumbled forward.

"I got him! I got him," Kib was shouting as he loaded another stone in his sling.

"Get down!" Kapilla shouted at the boy.

He sought protection just as Nonita dashed toward Nemti. Another robber appeared on a rooftop and fired an arrow at her. She dropped at Nemti's side a split second before the arrow sailed by and into a clump of evergreen shrubs.

For a moment it was still again except for the cries of the children and Nonita's sobbing. Samuel heard footsteps. Peering over the top of the waist-high wall, he spotted robbers running from several different directions, dodging and twisting as they came.

In unison, Samuel, Oreb, and Gadoni fired arrows. Three robbers dropped, but the others kept coming, screaming oaths and running as if they were half-crazed. As the robbers came over the wall, the three men, assisted by Helaman, met them with drawn swords. A short and bitter battle followed. Three of the remaining robbers died, the fourth fled. As he disappeared he could be heard to cry out, "He'll die, Nonita! If I can't have you, no one will!"

Uri screamed, "Kerlin! Kerlin!" when he heard the voice.

Samuel, blood dripping from a shallow cut on his arm, jumped the wall and pursued Kerlin, but as he rounded the corner of the synagogue, the robber mounted a gray horse and rode swiftly away. Samuel sent an arrow sailing after him, but it missed by an arm span. Angrily swearing that Kerlin would someday regret what he had done, Samuel ran back to join the others.

Everyone's attention was on Nemti. The arrow still protruded from his side. Samuel took over, cutting off the bronze tip where the arrow stuck out of his back. Then, with a firm but gentle tug, he removed the arrow. Nemti groaned, but gritted his teeth and bravely bore the excruciating pain. Blood oozed thick and red from the open wound.

Samuel called for some plantain, which Ophera quickly gathered, as the stringy leafed plant grew wild in the grass. Samuel applied a pulp of the leaves directly onto the wounds before bandaging them with strips of cloth provided by Laishita. With the aid of the twins, he carried Nemti to Latoni's house where Helaman gave him a blessing and left him in Nonita's tender care.

Oreb and Gadoni checked on the robbers they had shot in the battle. All but two were dead. Those two, both quite seriously wounded, were cared for and left with an ample supply of food and water in the town's small jail and told they would have to make it last, because no one knew when the last departing residents would return to Gilead to feed them again.

Samuel told Gadoni and Oreb, "We will leave the jail only loosely locked. I can't bear to have those men, no matter how bad they are, die a lingering death if no one happens to return to care for them."

Gadoni and Oreb nodded in agreement, even though they knew it was more than the robbers would do for them if the situation were reversed.

Helaman called Samuel aside a little later. "Samuel," he said. "The Lord desires that I ordain you to the priesthood before I go on. You must leave Gilead tonight, so I will do it now."

When he had finished, Samuel and Ophera shed tears of gratitude and Samuel offered Helaman the use of one of their horses. Helaman gratefully accepted and rode toward Manti.

"We'll be safer in the wilderness than here in the city if Kerlin leads others back to help him, which he very well may," Samuel told the rest of his clan after Helaman had departed. "We will leave tonight."

"But what about Nemti?" Oreb asked. "He is so badly . . ."

"We'll take him with us. Helaman gave him a blessing. He will be able to travel. Anyway, we can't leave him here."

"What about him being gone so long from his unit?" Oreb asked next.

"He's wounded. Helaman will explain, I suppose," Samuel said. "For now, he goes where we go." He stopped and a smile spread across his face. "We'd have to fight Nonita if we didn't take him."

"How will we carry him, Sam?" Gadoni asked.

"We'll take the horse. Nemti will have to ride it," Samuel said, "unless either of you can think of anything better."

Shortly after dark they were on their way. Nonita rode behind Nemti, holding him on the horse. He winced with pain, but not a word of complaint escaped his lips. Samuel led the way along a little known route that took them into the wilderness. He was grateful when the moon disappeared behind heavy, black clouds, for they promised rain. He hoped that when it came it would be heavy enough to wash away the signs of their passing.

Silently, he prayed, and soon the storm began, steady and light at first, but heavier as it continued. Finally, it fell in torrents, obscuring the evidence of the route they had taken. Silently, he prayed again, offering thanks to God for an answered prayer.

Dawn came, dreary and gray, and still the rain fell. Many miles had been traveled during the night. "We'll be safe here," Samuel announced as he chose a spot near a beautiful waterfall that cascaded between walls of green vines and shrubbery into a small lake below it.

Samuel had been here before with both Gadoni and Oreb while on hunting trips in years past. He knew that a narrow trail led to a shallow but well concealed cavern behind the falls. Even the horse was able to pick its way along the rocky trail and into the large, misty shelter.

Nemti was barely conscious. The trip had been tough on him, but he was soon comfortably bedded down and asleep. Nonita dozed at his side. Everyone else was exhausted, and the children quickly went to sleep.

Samuel reflected on the peacefulness and serenity of this place. If only his heart could be at peace as well. He said to the rest of them, "We will be safe here until Nemti is well enough to travel."

CHAPTER 23

Gadianton called a meeting. He had clearly assumed leadership of the secret society of robbers that had been tagged with his name. Kishkumen put up little resistance. He was a bloodthirsty killer while Gadianton possessed a superb ability to organize, flatter, and keep order that only the strongest personality could do among such evil men as surrounded them.

The meeting was held in the largest of their stone houses in Zarahemla. Gadianton was addressing fifty or sixty of his most loyal men—leaders within the band. "Coriantumr has promised to place us in positions of power," he gloated. "As soon as he, with his army, has destroyed Captain Moronihah and his men, he will return and set up a government here.

"In return for a pledge of support to the Lamanite government of King Tubaloth, we will be given power over the entire Nephite nation. I will be the king in this part of the land, over all who claim to be Nephites. You men, for your faithful service and according to your rights, will be placed in positions of great power.

"The people will crawl to you for the privilege of paying taxes so we can build palaces suitable to our needs. You will all be rich men, for whatever any of you desire, the people will provide it for you." Gadianton paused, his sinister eyes gleaming with evil pleasure. His face darkened and his deep voice rumbled as he said, "Any who are foolish enough to oppose such brave and mighty men as you will be executed publicly to discourage other dissidents from resisting. The church of Helaman's so-called God will be banned from the land and he will be scoffed and ridiculed by the people!"

Shouts of approval rose from the wicked men, but Gadianton subdued them with mention of a sore spot. His face was dark and angry as he spoke. "Men, there is still another problem that must be dealt with. Samuel and his clan are still at large. Kerlin reported that Nemti was shot and would surely die, but Samuel and his brother and that Lamanite friend of theirs put up a cunning fight.

"They must be found and destroyed! Not a man, woman, or child is to be left alive! Some of our strongest men will be sent to find and destroy them. To track them may be difficult due to the storm last night, but they will be using fires to cook. We will have our men watch for smoke, check neighboring cities . . . whatever it takes. They will be stopped!

"Samuel is our greatest enemy with Pacumeni dead, Helaman fleeing in fear, and Moronihah soon to die at the hands of Coriantumr. He has been the cause of much death among our men and he will pay. When we take over the government, we don't want to have to worry about him anymore."

Gadianton's dark eyes swept over his corps of leadership. After a moment of silence, he said, "For the men who are successful in destroying Samuel and his troublesome clan, there will be great rewards."

"What rewards?" one man demanded to know.

"The one of you whose men find and destroy them will be governor over the land of Zarahemla!" he shouted, the veins standing out on his temples and his face scarlet with hatred. His men shouted and clapped each other on the back. When they had quieted down, he said, "And you will have a palace built just for you and your wives." There was more cheering before Gadianton raised a hand to silence them once more. "And finally, you will have your choice of any ten women in the land to be your wives! I want Samuel destroyed!" he screamed.

* * *

The next few days were peaceful and relaxed, marred only by the memory of their recent tragedies and the grave condition of Nemti. Nonita spent most of her time caring for him, but exhaustion forced her to let others take turns.

The men hunted and kept on hand a good supply of meat, fruits, and edible roots. They did not have to drift far from their little sanctuary to find food, for it was abundant. Wood was stored in back of the cave for a cooking fire. Oreb objected that the smoke might give away their hideout, but Samuel demonstrated how that would not happen. The smoke from a fire near the mouth of the cave curled up and mixed with the spray from the falls. Outside, not a trace of it appeared. Even the smell of the fire was washed away by the pristine falls that shielded them.

The children played happily, their shouts and laughter muffled by the roar of the falling water. The men even let the children play outside the cave for a short time each day. They swam in the lake, climbed on the rocks, and watched the wide variety of small animals and brightly colored birds that made their homes in the forest that surrounded them.

Of particular fascination to the children were the monkeys. One day Uri surprised them by bringing one into the cave. It was injured and he had caught it with little trouble. By the time the boy had nursed the wide-eyed little animal back to health, it was tame and refused to return permanently to its own kind.

Munk, as he called it, spent most of the time with the boy. It even slept by him in the cave. Whenever the little monkey would join the other monkeys in the trees, Uri had but to call its name and it would appear. It would swing through the trees, drop to the ground, and bound to the boy, leaping into his outstretched arms.

Everyone was kind to the new pet. Munk would let anyone handle him, feed him, or even pick him up, but if Uri called, the monkey would immediately scamper to him.

It wasn't long before many of the other monkeys would follow Munk into the cave, but they kept their distance from the people there, peering at them with curious faces and chattering constantly. They seemed to know that they were not in danger but preferred not to become as friendly as Munk was.

Nemti, as he gradually recovered, took great delight in watching Uri and Munk at play. The little animal was a catalyst in his recovery. Uri, under Nemti's patient coaching, trained Munk to retrieve bananas and other items. He was even able to teach him to give them to Nemti as well as himself.

Nemti would say, "Uri, I'm thirsty."

Uri would grin and say, "Munk, fetch water," and point to Nemti reclining against the wall. Munk would grab a gourd, dip it in a small pool of water beneath the falls, and carefully carry it to the sick man.

When Nemti was nearly strong enough to travel, Uri became sullen and withdrawn. The boy said nothing to Samuel about his increasingly depressed moods, but he grew ever quieter as each day passed.

When Samuel would ask, "Uri, is something the matter?" the boy would silently shake his head.

Finally, Samuel took Jath aside and said, "Son, I'm worried about Uri. Do you have any idea what's bothering him?"

Jath knew. "He's going to miss Munk when we leave. He told me he would rather stay here alone with Munk than go with the rest of us and leave him."

Samuel laughed and patted Jath on the head. "Well, I can think of a much better solution than that. Let's go talk to Uri."

"Uri," he said a moment later, "We'll be leaving in a few days. Have you asked Munk if he wants to come?"

The boy's downcast face brightened. "You mean I don't have to leave him, Sam?" he asked, barely able to contain himself.

"That's between you and your monkey. If he would rather be with you than his monkey friends and family, he may come."

Uri bounded to his feet and ran to the edge of the falls. "Munk," he called, his voice smothered by the crashing water. In a moment the monkey, his hearing more keen than any man's, scampered into the cave and leaped into Uri's outstretched arms.

* * *

Things were not going well for the Gadianton robbers. Kishkumen was the first to come to Gadianton with the worst news of all. "Coriantumr and his promises are dead!" he reported angrily. "He and his great army suffered defeat to the army of Moronihah. "

"How did it happen? How did his entire army fall?" Gadianton demanded.

"He foolishly allowed them to be surrounded by Moronihah's army, and they were ruthlessly swept down. Coriantumr was a stupid and foolish man. If he had waited for reinforcements from King Tubaloth he would not have been defeated. He should have stayed in Zarahemla instead of marching on as he did, intending to capture all of the Nephite lands."

"And where are those who did not die? Are they prisoners?"

"Fools, they were!" Kishkumen scoffed. "They made oaths that they would leave the land in peace and not make war any more on the Nephites. Moronihah allowed them to go free and they ran like scared rabbits back to their own land. They are cowards!"

Gadianton fumed. "Where is Moronihah?"

"He and his army are nearing the city now. They will destroy the small army Coriantumr left to watch the city before nightfall."

"Call our men together!" he ordered. "We must hide."

* * *

Among those released was Laman, the hateful and angry brother of Gadoni. Having come into the land hoping to see his brother and Samuel dead before he left, he and a few of his men made the oath with Moronihah, but they had no intention of keeping it. They swore a greater oath to themselves: they would see that Samuel and Gadoni died. They would hide for a time in the wilderness, then, when things were calm again, they would find Laman's hated enemies and strike the fatal blows.

* * *

The lofty ambitions of Gadianton and his men were thwarted, and the promise he had made for the destruction of Samuel and his loved ones was empty. No one had been able to find Samuel or his people, and without the promise of power and riches attached to his death, they lost interest in pursuing him.

Gadianton met with his leaders. "It will be very difficult for us to conduct our business in Zarahemla for awhile," he admitted, "but we are not through. They will choose a new chief judge, and when they do, he will die! Many of you are known to the Nephites now," he told his men. "You will build up a new stronghold in the wilderness while the rest of us remain in Zarahemla and begin again to plan a way to take back that which is ours: the right to rule!"

Gadianton was becoming increasingly impatient and ill-tempered. He decided to exert more pressure on his followers. They had sworn secret oaths, and he was about to test the loyalty of a few.

"Men," he went on, his face as dark as the back side of the moon, "the Lamanites failed us. We have no call, however, to let ourselves down as well. We have all taken sacred oaths to conduct our business or forfeit our lives.

"Many of our band appear to have lost courage in the face of increased pressure. The time has come to strike hard at the government. I trust that none of you, my trusted leaders, are among the faint-hearted. Along with you, I am going to make another oath tonight. Any man here who refuses to take the oath or violates it in any manner after taking it will suffer torture and death. But for those who are faithful, great power, honor, and riches yet await you."

A murmur passed through the throng of men seated around the large table, but Gadianton stilled it with a wave of his brawny arms. "All who take the oath must stand," he ordered.

Everyone stood, and Gadianton administered another evil oath. Every man in the room agreed to devote themselves to the overthrow of the government except one. Partially hidden by a large stone column, a spy sent by Moronihah was unobserved as he silently watched the others swear.

Kerlin, Herdon, and five other men were ordered to find and destroy Samuel and all his loyal band. "Your lives, men, depend upon your success, but each of you, when you return with the heads of Samuel and Gadoni, will be paid from our treasury, and great power will be yours when we take our rightful places as rulers of the Nephite nation," Gadianton told them. His eyes were but black slits, and his face was twisted with hatred. "Do not return until you have destroyed our dangerous enemy. Swear to me that you will kill him!"

Gadianton watched them closely. They knew that if they failed he would destroy them. All seven took an oath that they would pursue Samuel and his loved ones, and that they would not return until it was done and they could present the heads of Samuel and Gadoni as proof.

Gadianton smiled a twisted, evil smile, then dismissed them. They feared him and he knew that they would not return until their assignment was complete. Gadianton dismissed his men with a charge to clear the way for him to become chief judge within the next year. They swore on their lives and the lives of their families that it would be done.

CHAPTER 24

Sam, I hate to leave this beautiful spot. It has been so peaceful here these past few weeks. I wish it could go on forever," Ophera lamented, her pretty face upturned to Samuel as he held her in a quiet embrace.

"It has been nice," he agreed, gazing over her head at the starlit sky beyond the falls. "I hope I never have to leave you again, even for a day," he told her, his heart full of love for this elegant woman who was his wife.

She rested her head against his broad chest. Long waves of blonde hair draped over her shoulder and hung like golden threads to her slender waist. For several minutes they enjoyed the sound of the falls behind them and of the forest, alive with the nighttime activities of many creatures, both large and small. Samuel thought of the life and death that went on out there in the dark of night. The weak and unwary died while the strong and alert lived on.

He pulled Ophera closer as he thought how like the animal kingdom his own kind were. The strong preyed upon the weak, and even the righteous, like Latoni and Kamina, died. In this life, he knew, justice would never fully prevail, but in God's own time it would all be made right.

"Was I wrong?" he asked, startling Ophera.

"Wrong? What do mean, Sam?" she asked, tightening her hold around his waist.

"Was I wrong for pursuing Kishkumen? I only wanted to avenge the death of Pahoran. So much of the trouble that has happened since then is my fault."

"Sam, that's not true. You were only after justice. And I heard you say that you only wanted the killing and hatred to end."

"But has it? No! It's only gotten worse. And now my father and your mother are dead. If I had only . . ."

Ophera pressed a slender finger to his lips. "No more, Sam. What you did was right and took courage that few men have. Don't blame yourself. Anyway, if you will remember, they sought your life after Pahoran's death."

"I love you, Ophera," he said quietly, grateful for her faithful support. When he was down, she lifted him with her own special mix of faith and courage. "I hope you're right, Ophera, for if I had to do it again, I'm afraid I would act no differently."

"And I wouldn't want you to." She sighed. "Even though the worry is almost more than I can bear at times."

They clung silently to each other and gazed at the dark night sky. The scream of a jaguar, somewhere not too far distant, reminded Samuel of their precarious situation. They were the prey, and out there somewhere were the jaguars—Satan's own Gadianton robbers.

Ophera clutched him tightly at the hair-raising sound. "I wonder what poor creature just died," she said, her voice suddenly weak.

"Whatever it was, had it only known, it could have been somewhere else," he said thoughtfully. "It could be us if we don't move on."

"Sam, you frighten me."

"I'm sorry, but they are after us again. I can feel it—I know it. I could go meet them, but this time I must take a different road and flee. It is what the Lord would have me do—have all of us do."

"Is it the only way we will be safe?" Ophera asked, her head pressed tightly against his chest. He said nothing and felt her shiver in the warm night air before she asked, "How soon must we leave?"

"Tomorrow. Nemti is strong enough to travel. I have loved this place, but we must move on," he said. "We have already stayed longer than we should. There is another place we must go and it is far," he said with a longing look in his eye.

"Where is that place, Sam?" She had asked him that question before, and each time he had answered the same. He felt her lips moving, mouthing the words as he answered.

"Someplace where it's safe," he said. Then, to her surprise he told her of his answered prayer in Latoni's garden. When he had finished telling her his plans he said, "That is why I was ordained by Helaman."

She smiled and he asked, "Is it all right with you?"

"I promised before and I will again," she said. "Where you lead me, I will follow."

"No one else is to be told until later. Helaman and I spoke of this matter at length, and he said I should wait to tell the others."

She nodded and then, hand in hand, they strolled behind the roaring falls and back into the cavern. It was quite late and everyone was sleeping. Quietly, Samuel and Ophera knelt in prayer, then they too slept.

Samuel awoke with a start. Light was filtering into the cave through the water that shielded them from the world beyond. Munk was tugging at his arm, a stream of frantic chatter pouring from his tiny lips.

"What is it, Munk?" he asked, shaking the grogginess from his head.

Uri appeared beside the monkey. "Someone's out there, Sam," the boy said urgently, a frightened look in his deep blue eyes.

"How do you know?" Samuel asked.

Uri pointed to the excited monkey. Samuel nodded. Gadoni and Oreb stepped to his side. The three of them strapped on their swords, grabbed their bows and arrows and, after sending the others deeper into the cave with Nemti armed to protect them if needed, started along the path through a mist of water to the world beyond.

Samuel held up his hand. The others stopped. Through the mist he saw the outline of a man, bent over, examining the ground near the pathway they were on. When he stood, Samuel recognized him as one of the band of Gadianton: an ugly purple scar ran from his eye to his chin from some long-ago battle. The men stepped into the clear morning light beyond the falls and confronted him. A look of startled fear filled the robber's eyes and he began slowly backing away, his hand clutching the hilt of his sheathed sword.

"Watch for others," Samuel said to Gadoni and Oreb as he approached the retreating robber. "We want to talk to you. Drop your belt and sword, then we'll talk," Samuel shouted above the roar of the falls.

"I have nothing to talk to you about," the robber snarled, baring his teeth like a dog. "I'm leaving now."

"No, in that you are mistaken," Samuel shouted. "You have come to do us harm. You will either surrender or die."

"I'll do neither," the robber said, still stepping backward, unaware that he was dangerously near the cliff that dropped into the base of the falls.

Samuel's sword was in his hand. Oreb had an arrow strung, and Gadoni was surveying the surrounding forest. "You're trapped. Give up now," Samuel warned.

"Never. You are doomed, Samuel," he said with a nasty laugh, taking another step backward, oblivious to the danger behind him.

"Where are your friends?" Samuel asked, pressing ever closer.

"They know where you are and . . ."

Whatever else the robber was going to say would forever remain unspoken. It was driven from his throat with a piercing scream as he fell over the edge and plunged into the churning, thrashing water below. Samuel rushed to the edge and looked down. All he could see was the foaming water where the falls met the lake with ear shattering force. Several minutes passed before the lake spit the dead man to the surface like a piece of driftwood and carried him farther into the lake where he again disappeared beneath the surface.

"He may have lied, but if they have figured out where we are, we could be in grave danger," Samuel said urgently. "We must leave now."

The little group rushed to collect their things and in two hours they were ready. Nemti, who was much better, rode the horse at Samuel's insistence. The children were in a festive mood, seemingly unaware of the danger lurking in the lush green forest.

Munk, riding on Uri's shoulder, went with them, leaving his own kind behind. Some of the other monkeys followed for awhile, swinging effortlessly through the trees, but they soon turned back, scolding Munk all the while.

The route they followed was difficult. Samuel had to find a way that the horse could go while avoiding any traveled routes. The route was rocky and rough on the horse's feet, and it went constantly upward, sapping everyone of their strength. Stops became more and more frequent. Nemti insisted that the women take turns on the horse. They protested, but each in her turn was silently grateful.

Toward nightfall, the horse began limping badly. Samuel lifted a forefoot, then a hind foot. The horse's feet were very tender. Samuel's practiced eye told him the horse would not be much good for very long. The news worried the little group, especially Nonita. "Nemti will get sick again if he has to walk," she moaned.

"Oh, quit fussing over me," Nemti scolded, his brown eyes twinkling. "I'll be fine."

"You'd better be," Nonita said, trying to match his jovial mood.

The horse had to be turned loose to fare for himself early the next afternoon. Samuel picked a lush, high mountain valley. There the lame horse grazed contentedly as the little party trudged on.

* * *

Captain Moronihah and the prophet Helaman were worried about Samuel and his family and friends. Moronihah had been informed by his spy about the order that Gadianton had issued against Samuel's people.

"I wish they were here where we could offer them protection," Helaman said, wiping his brow for the tenth time in as many minutes.

"It is difficult to protect anyone for very long. If my servant can find out the robbers' secrets, then I am sure they can find out ours," Captain Moronihah said, pacing back and forth, his arms behind his back. "Anyway, I fear that the robbers may have already harmed or killed Samuel and his people; we should have heard from them by now."

"They're still alive, Captain," the prophet said, "but they are in grave danger."

Moronihah looked at Helaman in surprise. "How do you know . . ." He stopped, gave an embarrassed smile at Helaman's condescending look and said, "Of course . . . the Spirit . . . Anyway, we must find them before Gadianton's men do."

Helaman told Moronihah of Samuel's plans and then asked, "How many men did your servant say were after them?"

"Seven. Two of them bear particular malice. Their names are Herdon and Kerlin. I fear they will not easily give up their pursuit," the chief captain said, sitting down at the heavy round table that filled half the room.

For a few moments the two leaders worried in silence. "We shall send twenty of our best men. And they will not give up!" Moronihah exclaimed.

"And what of the robbers among us?" Helaman asked.

"We will pursue Gadianton and his men until we have either destroyed them or driven them from the land," Moronihah said emotionally, leaning forward with his elbows on the table.

* * *

A cool breeze carried the pungent scent of mountain sheep across the high plateau where Samuel had called for an afternoon rest. He was concerned that the women and children were being taxed too hard. Nemti, despite earlier worries, was faring quite well.

The sky was crystal clear, and the sun felt good as it bore down on Samuel's back. Uri, Jath, and the twins were resting beneath one of the few trees on the plateau. Of ancient date, the pine was tall, with only a smattering of lightly dotted green branches on the top half of a twisted gray trunk. Munk took the break as an opportunity to explore those few high branches.

High overhead, a large bird glided effortlessly, carried gently back and forth by the changing wind currents. Samuel watched as the boys pointed it out to each other. He let his eyes drift upward and follow the path of the graceful creature. Gradually, it began to lose altitude, slowly at first, then at an ever increasing rate of speed.

Suddenly, it began a rapid dive toward the plateau. Kib screamed, "Uri, call Munk!"

In that instant, Samuel realized what the giant bird's intention was. Uri sat up with a start, "Munk!" he cried at the top of his lungs. "Come down, Munk." The boy's eyes were wide with fright as he too realized that Munk, at the very top of the tree, was easy prey for the swiftly approaching harpy eagle, largest of all eagles and a deadly enemy of monkeys.

In obedience to Uri's call, Munk began to swing gracefully down through the sparse branches. Both twins began to swing their ever present slings as they backed away from the base of the tree.

The shadow of the eagle passed over Munk and he reacted to the danger. He sped around the tree just as the giant bird spread its wings in a braking motion and reached for him with its razor-sharp talons. Munk escaped with only inches to spare. The bird banked and picked up height again, never letting Munk from its sight. Munk screeched in fright and dropped several feet to another branch.

The harpy eagle, in position again, dove in another attempt to crush the little monkey with its mighty talons. In that instant, both twins fired rocks from their sling shots with amazing accuracy. The eagle, stunned, drifted to the ground, landing with an awkward thump only a few feet from another tree where Gadoni and his family were resting. Zera and Limre screamed and Gadoni jumped to his feet, sword instinctively drawn, but the eagle was dazed and for a minute it lay trembling on the ground.

Munk, meantime, finished his descent and leaped into Uri's arms where he tried to hide his wide-eyed brown head beneath the boy's leather vest. Everyone gathered to watch the majestic bird. It began to recover and started hopping dizzily about, sending the younger children squealing to their parents.

"Aren't you going to kill it?" Uri demanded in indignation as he tried to soothe Munk.

"Why should we kill it?" Samuel asked, seizing the opportunity to teach an important lesson.

"Because it tried to kill Munk," Uri answered angrily.

"It didn't know he was any different than any other monkey. The eagle was only after a meal. That's the way nature works," Samuel explained patiently to a doubting audience of offended children. "We should never kill animals or birds just for the sake of killing. The twins were right in hitting it when it was attacking Munk and they saved his life, but he is in no danger now. There is no longer a need to kill or even hurt it worse. Let's watch and see if it can fly away again."

Uri opened his mouth to protest further, but just then the massive bird began to hop along the gently sloping ground. In a moment, its long wings spread wide and, flapping awkwardly, it lifted off the stony plateau and began to fly. Silently, they all watched as it slowly gained altitude and drifted over the dense forests below.

"Now it will hunt again," Samuel said reflectively.

"For monkeys?" Uri demanded, still not forgiving its attempt at taking Munk's life.

"Perhaps, or for sloths, agouti, or other small jungle animals," Samuel explained, suppressing a grin as Uri held the monkey protectively.

The next few days melted together as they crossed the rugged mountain range, ever alert for danger behind them. Nemti, so strong at first, gradually began to lose his strength. It slowed their travel alarmingly.

Samuel frequently backtracked to check for any sign of the robbers, but finding none, listened sympathetically to the urging of the women to seek out a place to hole up for awhile again and let Nemti regain his strength. He was apprehensive, knowing of the fierce determination of the men of Gadianton and the hatred they had for him. Finally, however, he agreed, seeing that Nemti was not going to be able to keep going much longer without a prolonged rest.

He searched out a place where they could easily watch for an enemy and have an alternate escape route if necessary. The spot he chose was deep in the jungle at the base of the mountains. An island, surrounded by shallow but dangerous marshes that were not easy to cross, was what Samuel sought. The men constructed a crude raft from fallen trees, cut to uniform length and bound together with vines. He guided the raft through a maze of meandering streams, finally pulling up to the secluded shore of a modest spot of land surrounded on all sides by the marshes. There the little group set up camp and prepared to wait out Nemti's recovery again.

* * *

It was with considerable care that Moronihah had selected the company of twenty soldiers to go in search of Samuel's clan and provide them protection. Commanded by the wise and experienced Captain Calno, who had miraculously escaped death during the Lamanite attack on Zarahemla, some of the army's best trackers, swordsmen, and marksmen had entered the wilderness.

One of the most skilled men in the company was the younger brother of Ophera. Josh had learned the art of tracking from Samuel and Gadoni, two of the best, and had been schooled in the use of a bow and arrow by his step-brother, Oreb, who could shoot as well as any man in the nation. Moronihah had sought Josh out, not only for his skills, but because the prophet Helaman had requested it. There was not a man in the land who had more incentive and would work harder at finding Samuel's people, because they were also his people.

Josh was a young man of great physical strength and stamina. He had proven himself in combat during the defeat of the army of Coriantumr, both by his ability and willingness to fight and his enduring efforts as he carried wounded companions in his arms to safety from the field of battle. Each time he had heroically returned to fight with renewed vigor.

His dark brown hair dropped to his massive shoulders in wavy curls. He always wore a leather headband that had been his father's. It kept his hair out of his face while giving him a distinctive, intimidating appearance.

Having been raised by his righteous step-father, Latoni, and his kind, gentle mother, Kamina, Josh had grown to love the Lord. He was a young man possessed of great spiritual strength and knew the Lord blessed those who were obedient to His commandments.

Josh loved his family intensely, and was prepared to lay down his life to save them. Captain Calno was grateful to have him, knowing that his courage, strength, and wisdom, as well as his skills, would be an asset in their search for Samuel and the Gadianton robbers that were pursuing him.

Calno had considered splitting his company of twenty into two squads, but success had come quickly, and that had not been necessary. Josh knew of the falls and, putting himself in Samuel's position, felt that was a likely place to begin the search. He remembered Samuel telling him the first time they camped in the cave together while hunting, "Don't ever tell anyone of this place, for it could be a good hideout if ever needed, and the fewer that know of it, the better."

With that advice in mind, he had led the small company to within a couple of miles, then asked them to wait for him. He hiked alone to the falls. There he found that his guess had been right, but it appeared the group had left there several days earlier.

A careful study of the cavern gave Josh several clues. It was obvious that they had a horse. There had also been someone who had been in serious need of being doctored, for a supply of healing herbs was scattered in the back of the cave.

As Josh returned to his company, he spotted a body floating on the far side of the lake. Alarmed, he stripped off his gear and swam across with powerful strokes. He was relieved to see that the decomposing face was unfamiliar to him. He examined the body and could find no wounds of any kind. It presented a mystery to him, but he left it, gruesome and bloated, and swam back across the lake. On his way to join Calno and the men, he looked for any sign or old tracks that could have been made by the man at the lake. He found none.

After he had returned, he reported to Captain Calno. "They were here," he said, "and I know which way they went. I searched for sign of the robbers but found nothing except a dead man," Josh said, going on to explain about the body in the lake. "If we are alert, we may yet find where the robbers have been, for I suspect the dead man was one of them."

Later that afternoon, Josh located a dim trail left by a small party. "It could be the men of Gadianton," Josh ventured.

The next day they found other tracks, including those of a horse. They were where Josh expected to find them. Several miles beyond, the two trails merged, and Josh felt a renewed urgency to catch up with Samuel, for he knew that the robbers were in pursuit of Samuel's people.

They hastened their pace in an attempt to catch the robbers before they overtook the slower group of men, women, and children. Josh and another soldier scouted ahead. It was Josh who noticed that the horse had taken a separate route. He was surprised to see that the robbers had followed the tracks of the horse. The robbers had apparently experienced some difficulty relocating the right trail, for it was two days before he found where the two trails merged again.

The time lost by the robbers in their mistaken pursuit of the lame horse gave Josh greater hope. He urged Captain Calno and the rest of the company to hurry even faster. The urgency of catching the robbers before they caught Samuel and his people was clear to all the soldiers, and they forged ahead with renewed determination.

* * *

Laman had an evil smile on his face. "You are sure it was just a small band of Nephites?" he asked.

"Yes. I got very near them without them knowing that I was there. Their leader is Samuel. Your brother, Gadoni, is with them," Laman's friend and the chief scout for his little band of a dozen renegade warriors said smugly.

"How far away were they?" Laman asked, gleeful that he would finally get his chance for revenge.

"Two days' travel in the jungle," he said, pointing. "They were camped near a meandering stream when I saw them."

"Then we will go with haste. They will die. Gadoni and all his friends will die," Laman vowed.

CHAPTER 25

"You fools!" Herdon chided in anger. "Can't you even follow a perfectly clear trail without losing it?"

"This is a swamp, Herdon. People don't leave good tracks in swamps," one of the other robbers countered. "They must have gone into the marshes."

"Don't be ridiculous," Kerlin said. "We just need to backtrack and try again. We will find them."

Just then one of his men shouted. "Here they are. There are tracks here. We haven't lost the trail. Look," he said, pointing to imprints in a rare strip of bare, moist ground.

"Those are not the tracks we were following!" Herdon snarled after a close examination. "You have led us astray, you idiots."

The others studied the tracks again with great care. "Well?" Kerlin asked.

"It may be different, but who else would be in this smelly, forsaken marshland?" one of them asked.

"We don't care who is," Herdon snarled. "Now, get looking until we find the right trail. We are wasting time."

"I still can't imagine where Terantum went," Kerlin grumbled as they began working their way through the teeming jungle. "He was the only one of the lot of you who could track."

"Yes," Herdon agreed, "and I still wonder if he found Samuel when he was off on his own, and got his fool self killed."

"If he deserted . . ." Kerlin began.

"He didn't desert," one of the others cut in sharply. "Terantum would never desert. He was . . ."

Herdon cut in this time. "He was a good tracker, but a big fool. Gadianton stuck Kerlin and me with a bunch of blockheads! When we finish this job I will report to him what incompetent . . ."

Herdon grunted and tumbled to the wet ground as one of the robbers hit him violently in the back with a stick. Kerlin snarled, "You men will die for this."

Their anger at the two leaders' constant chafing had gotten the best of them and they attacked Kerlin and Herdon, beating and kicking them mercilessly. The four left Herdon and Kerlin lying unconscious in the tall grass and shrubbery and hurried on, following the well-beaten trail through the jungle.

"We shouldn't have done that," one of them said a few minutes later. "Gadianton will . . ."

"We will finish the job alone and report to Gadianton," another said with anger. "Those two will never leave this place alive. Even if the beasts don't devour them, they can never find their way out of here without our help. They called us fools. They are the fools. This is the right trail. These are the same tracks. They have to be the right ones. No one else would be here."

The others laughed and concentrated on following the tracks that they believed had been left by Samuel and his clan. They were so intent on their work that they failed to hear the rustling of the bushes and light footsteps on the grass until it was too late. A bitter but short fight ensued. When it was over, the four Gadianton robbers lay dead on the sodden jungle floor, and Laman and his dozen Lamanite warriors continued to follow the tracks of Samuel and his clan.

"Gadianton will be very angry," Kerlin moaned, sitting up and rubbing his cheekbone where a fist had left it bruised and bleeding.

"Shut up, Kerlin!" Herdon ordered with a more distinct rasp than usual as he carefully felt his bruised and battered body. "I guess there's nothing broken," he said at length, "but I'm too sore to walk."

"Do you think they will continue to search for Samuel?" Kerlin asked, ignoring the older man's insulting behavior.

"They may try, but they will never succeed. They're all morons. Now if you'll be quiet, I'll see if I can get the pounding in my head to stop," Herdon said, as if he were the only one with injuries.

The sun, filtered by the dense, vine-entangled trees, slowly made its mid-afternoon descent through a misty sky. A couple of painful hours had crept by before Kerlin ventured to strike up another conversation. He said, "You look like you might live, Herdon."

Herdon had forced himself to his feet and was limping around the little clearing, moaning loudly about the treachery of his fellow robbers. He was indeed feeling better, but a decrease in pain was offset by his foul mood growing darker. Finally, he snapped an answer at Kerlin. "I'm feeling good enough to know we better look for something to eat and a place to spend the night."

"Tomorrow, will we look for Nonita and her family?" Kerlin asked.

"Forget about that girl, you dunce," Herdon rebuked angrily. "We are going after our men first. They must die for their treachery. Then we will continue after Samuel, and all his family will die as Gadianton planned."

* * *

Nemti improved rapidly. Rest was what he had needed most. He apologized constantly for everyone's discomfort on the insect infested island, declaring emphatically that it was all his fault. Nonita, tender and caring, gently rebuked him each time: "It's not your fault that you were injured," she would say. "It could have been any of us."

Early on the dawn of the third day on the island, Samuel announced, "Today we will begin our journey again. Nemti is strong enough to travel, so we must waste no time." As he spoke, he thought of the urgency of pressing forward if they were to reach the destination that only he and Ophera knew about before they were too late.

Captain Calno and his soldiers were also in the marshy, sodden jungle. "This is most difficult, Captain," Josh told him, shaking his head. "Samuel came into this area intentionally, I'm quite sure. He must intend to find a way to lose the robbers, but if he succeeds, he will probably lose us, too."

"We must keep trying," Calno urged.

Josh nodded his head, the expression on his face telling of his grim agreement as he remembered a promise made to him by Moronihah and Helaman. Deeper and deeper into the jungle he led the men, following a dim trail that twisted like a den of snakes past stagnant ponds, through small clearings, and across little streams. After several hours of silent travel, he stopped and studied the jungle floor with care.

"Lamanites," he said, straightening up and casting worried eyes at Calno's puzzled face.

"Lamanites? Are you sure?"

Josh nodded. "There are prints of moccasins over the sandal tracks. They came from that direction," he said, pointing. "They are following Samuel and the robbers."

"Lamanites?" Captain Calno asked again.

"Yes, a dozen or so. We must hurry. They may have joined Herdon and his men," Josh said with a growing feeling of alarm. "If they are, my family is in much more danger. The Lamanites will track better and more rapidly than the robbers, I suspect."

"Captain, what would a small band of Lamanites be doing roving in such a loathsome place?" one of the soldiers asked.

"I don't know. Captain Moronihah told us after he ordered the survivors of Coriantumr's army released that he was afraid a few of them didn't take the oath of peace very seriously. I wonder if this band we're following has decided to return on their own and harass our people in some of the outlying villages," Captain Calno mused.

"But why would they come into this jungle? It's not fit here for man or beast," one of the other men said with disgust.

Josh was very thoughtful for a few minutes while the others discussed the folly of anyone entering such an area. Suddenly, he interrupted them. "They probably saw Samuel and the others, or even the robbers, and decided they would be an easy target," he said, wiping the perspiration from beneath his leather headband and swatting a mosquito that was growing fat and red on his arm.

Without waiting for a reply, Josh forged ahead impatiently. It was the middle of the afternoon when the soldiers came upon the grisly scene where the robbers had died. The corpses were partially eaten by wild beasts and birds, but there was enough left to tell the tale of their battle with the Lamanites.

"Well, it looks like the only problem left is a few Lamanites," one of the soldiers remarked casually.

"Not quite," Calno said sternly. "Two of the robbers are missing. I am sure there were six, but only four died here. None of these is Kerlin, and I suspect that the other missing one is Herdon. He was the oldest of the band, according to Moronihah's servant, and had gray hair. These were all young men."

Josh spoke up grimly. "Those two are the most dangerous of all. They each have their own private enmity towards members of my family."

"Also," Calno cautioned, his arm sweeping the bloody scene before them, "the Lamanites who did this are bloodthirsty."

"At least now we know they were not working together," Josh observed gravely.

"No, at least these four are not in league with the Lamanites, but we don't know about Kerlin and Herdon," Calno said. He surveyed the scene a moment more, then said, "Move on, men. The Lamanites may be more danger to Samuel and his clan than the robbers were."

"But what about Kerlin and Herdon?" Josh asked.

"We must forget about them for now. We haven't time to figure out where they went. The Lamanites present the greatest risk at the moment. We must overtake them. We'll worry about Kerlin and Herdon later," Calno said.

Late the next morning, the soldiers drew up short on the bank of a sluggish stream that flowed almost imperceptibly through the marshy jungle. They had barely stopped when one of the men groaned and fell forward, an arrow in his back.

"Take cover," Calno shouted, diving behind a mossy log.

It was too late for three of his men, but the rest hurriedly found cover in spite of a flurry of arrows. Calno had picked some of the best soldiers in the Nephite army, and they wasted no time in proving themselves. The fighting was fierce, but Calno's men soon gained control of the battle. They surrounded the maverick band of Lamanites and worked death until only two survived. Those two sullenly surrendered.

After binding their captives securely, Calno ordered his men to tend to the dead and injured. Among the five dead Nephites Josh found his fellow tracker. Others were wounded, but none seriously.

Calno turned his attention back to the captives.

Josh joined him, a puzzled expression on his tired face. He turned to the Captain. "This man looks familiar to me"

"What is your name?" Calno demanded.

The Lamanite grunted and said nothing. Josh continued to study him, then he suddenly spun toward Calno. "I've got it, Captain. He looks like a Lamanite I know." Without further explanation, he again faced the sullen Lamanite.

"Yes, you do look like him. He's much younger, though. And . . . well . . . he's much happier, too. If I didn't know better, I would say you could be Gadoni's older brother."

"Not anymore!" the Lamanite said with anger. "He's a traitor!"

"Then you are his brother!" Josh said triumphantly.

"Gadoni is not my brother. He is a Nephite, but I am a loyal Lamanite."

"What's your name?" Josh asked.

Glaring at Josh with hate-filled eyes, he said, "I am Laman."

Josh nodded. "Ah, yes. I have heard much about you. Gadoni spoke often and fondly of an older brother he called Laman."

Laman's cold eyes betrayed a hint of surprise. "He did?" he asked.

"Yes, he did. He admires you."

"Then why did he betray his people?" Laman asked, scowling.

"His people betrayed him, but he still loves them. He just can't understand why we can't all get along with each other. He has many Nephite friends, too, and can see no reason why you and your people are so determined to destroy them," Josh explained.

"Nephites are liars," Laman said with venomous conviction. "How can Gadoni have Nephite friends and still love his own people?"

"To Gadoni we are all people. He doesn't believe the color of our skin should make any difference. And I agree with him," Josh said sincerely.

"How did you come to know my brother . . . I mean Gadoni?" Laman stuttered.

"My name is Josh," the sturdy young man said, squaring his shoulders. "My brother-in-law is Samuel, Gadoni's best friend."

"Samuel?" Laman asked, shock betrayed in his voice.

"Yes. Do you know him?"

"We've met," Laman hissed. "He's the cause of Gadoni's treachery." Laman spat on the ground in defiance before saying, "We were after Samuel when you came. He led his people out there somewhere," he said, nodding toward the slowly moving stream. "He has been the source of many problems for my family. I will not rest until he is dead," Laman said bitterly.

Calno's face darkened with anger. "Laman, I am Captain Calno. You have committed an act of murder against the Nephite people. You and your friend are now prisoners. I'm going to have you tried and punished for the lives you have taken this day. As for Samuel, he has done nothing to merit your anger and hatred, and I intend to see to it that you never molest him again."

Laman glared at Calno, but the captain went on. "My men will take you to the nearest prison. There you will be held until you can be tried for your crimes."

Captain Calno turned to Josh. "I need to speak with you," he said and led him into the trees. "A very bitter man, isn't he?"

"And determined, too. What do we do now?" Josh asked.

"First we bury the dead, then I will send five of our men to take Laman and the other Lamanite to prison—probably over the mountains to Manti. Then we try again to find Samuel. We can't forget about Kerlin and Herdon."

"That is what I am worried about, Captain. Samuel is going to be difficult to find now. It appears that he has taken his people by raft from this point."

"And I foolishly let my men walk into a trap set by Laman and his warriors," Calno said glumly.

"It was not your fault," Josh said quickly. "How could you have ever known . . ." He let his thought trail off.

"Well, it is done, and we must go on. What do you think Samuel's next move will be?" the captain asked.

"Hole up for awhile."

"Where?"

"Out there somewhere," Josh said, tipping his head.

Calno glanced at the infested waters and beyond. "It's big out there," he moaned.

"Real big," Josh agreed.

"Maybe we should build ourselves a couple of rafts," the captain suggested.

"Maybe, but there must be a dozen channels out there—maybe hundreds. And what if I'm wrong? What if they didn't hole up, or if they are already on the move again?" he asked, slapping viciously at the flies that buzzed around his head.

"What do you suggest, Josh?"

The young man squared his shoulders and looked his commander in the eye. "It would require a lot of walking, but maybe we should get to higher ground and circle around the marshy jungle area. We're more likely to find signs of where they left the jungle than we would find signs of them floating around out there," he said, waving toward the murky brown stream.

"That sounds like a good idea to me. And maybe we'll come across the tracks of Herdon and Kerlin. Yes, that is what we will do," Calno said decisively.

After the dead were buried, Calno sent five men toward Manti with the two Lamanite prisoners and led what remained of his little company of men, ten counting himself, toward the mountains that rose above the jungle in the northeast. He set a blistering pace, determined to find Samuel as soon as possible.

CHAPTER 26

"Are you sure you know where you're going?" Gadoni asked Samuel with a chuckle as they poled their way through the maze of channels that filled the sultry jungle.

The water was not deep, and the men had cut poles to propel and guide the raft. Samuel placed his pole firmly against the murky stream bottom and pushed. "No," he responded, "but we'll figure it out as we go."

"Where are we going now, Father?" Jath asked.

"Out of the jungle, and then to a safe place," he said with an encouraging smile.

Ophera looked at him and smiled. When Samuel was ready to tell the others where he was leading them to, he would. She just hoped they would follow willingly.

For several hours they slowly navigated the confusing maze. The farther the raft drifted, the clearer the water became. As dusk approached, they maneuvered through low-hanging branches and reeds until they had worked their way against the bank. They secured the raft and clambered ashore.

After a good night's rest, they set out again the next morning. In the early afternoon, Samuel steered the raft to the bank of what was now a gently flowing river. "We'll walk from here," he announced.

There were no complaints, for the small raft was crowded and the children had become cranky and restless. Samuel led the way on foot, leaving the raft to float unburdened down the river. He was alert for signs of other people as he parted rubbery shrubs and forced his way through foliage so dense they had to cut a path at times with their swords.

Before the sun painted the sky with colorful streaks that evening, Samuel had led his clan out of the heaviest jungle where the traveling was not so taxing. Had he been alone, he thought to himself, he would have taken advantage of the bright moon that rose as the sun made its departure, but the women and children were exhausted and Nemti was showing signs of faltering, so he selected a likely spot and called a halt for the night.

* * *

Josh was surprised when, mid-morning the next day, he spotted the river flowing gently from the jungle. He scouted the bank with care for several hours. Suddenly he shouted, "Captain Calno, they've been here! They must have let their raft go, but they left on foot, I'm sure."

The captain rushed over and looked at the grassy ground where Josh was pointing. "They couldn't be more than a day ahead of us," Josh said. "If we hurry, we can overtake them by tomorrow sometime." He grinned. "They'll sure be surprised to see us."

"Any sign of Kerlin and Herdon?" Calno asked cautiously.

"None," Josh shouted recklessly as he followed the trail away from the river.

They made excellent time, traveling late into the moonlit night before finally stopping for some sleep. They were on their way at daybreak again, weary but excited that their mission might soon be completed. Josh whistled as he tracked, thinking about how happy his family would be to see him and how proud Samuel would be for his successful use of the skills he and Gadoni had taught him.

Josh was several hundred feet ahead of the other men. The trail led around the base of a small, grassy knoll. On an impulse, he sprinted to the top and surveyed the surrounding forest. He knew he was close and hoped to spot them in the distance, but all he could see was a sea of green grass, shrubs and, a few hundred yards from the base of the knoll, more forest.

* * *

"Sam, come here quickly!" Oreb said urgently.

"What is it?" Samuel asked, hurrying toward his brother.

They had been taking a short rest in a shady mahogany grove near the edge of a large, grassy clearing. Oreb had been assigned to keep watch, a practice Samuel never allowed the group to neglect. Oreb was behind a tree trunk near the edge of the clearing.

"Up there," Oreb said, pointing to the knoll they had passed a few minutes earlier.

Samuel tensed. He easily made out the form of a man standing there, looking, he was quite certain, in their direction. "They must be on our trail again," he said dejectedly. "I thought we had lost the robbers in the jungle."

"Gadianton had better trackers than I would have ever guessed," Oreb moaned.

"And they are persistent," Samuel stressed, a worried crease on his brow. He watched a moment longer. When the distant form moved off the knoll, he said, "Oreb, we better get moving, and we've got to find a way to lose them fast."

Long faces greeted him when Samuel announced the situation to the tired travelers, but they pulled themselves to their feet, a wave of fear passing through them.

"We can do one of two things," Samuel said. "Either we can try to get them off our trail or we can set up an ambush and fight. Not knowing how many of them there are, I would favor trying to lose them again. What do the rest of you think?"

"If we can't get rid of them, then we can fight," Gadoni suggested, "but I don't want to see anymore bloodshed if we can avoid it."

"At least we have the advantage of knowing they're back there," Nemti said.

The others nodded agreement, and Samuel said, "Very well, then. We will have to push hard for awhile. This could get difficult, but we won't have time for much rest. Oreb, you take the rear and I'll take the lead."

Samuel led them at a sharp angle from the direction they had been traveling. They went downhill and into denser forest. He found what he was searching for in a couple of hours. A shallow stream flowed slowly in a westerly direction.

"Jath, climb on my back," he instructed his son. "We'll have to carry the children," he told the others. "We will leave no tracks in the water," he explained as willing hands picked up those who were not already in backpacks. For an hour they waded down the stream, constantly alert for dangers in the water and on the bank.

After a couple of taxing hours, their little stream joined a slightly larger one. "We'll build another raft now," Samuel announced.

They worked rapidly, leaving telltale signs of their hasty construction. They bound logs of uneven sizes with long vines. "Don't worry about making it very strong, we aren't going to use it," Samuel said as they worked.

Ophera turned on him and snapped, "Why not, Sam? We are exhausted and . . ."

"We want them to think that we floated downstream when they find this spot. We'd have done it sooner, but the stream was a little too shallow," he explained patiently.

Ophera was in no mood for patience. "So what are we going to do," she demanded, "if we aren't going to float down the stream?"

"We'll go that way," he said, pointing up the larger branch.

"Up it?" she demanded, a puzzled expression on her face.

"Yes, Ophera. They won't expect us to go that way. They'll hurry down this larger stream, thinking we are on a raft. In the meantime, we'll be going that way," he said, pointing up the new stream.

"I'm sorry, Sam," she said with a weak smile. "You're right."

"I hope so, because if they aren't fooled, it could be serious. I love all of you, and I don't want anyone hurt," he said as they put the finishing touches on the crude raft.

As soon as the raft was on its lonely way, they forged up the larger stream. It was a little deeper and the travel was more strenuous against the current, but raw courage and determination pushed them on. They camped that evening as the sun set.

"I'm going back to where the streams merged and see if the Gadianton robbers took the bait," Samuel told Gadoni in the middle of the night when his Lamanite friend came to relieve him from keeping watch. "Keep a sharp lookout and I'll be back as soon as I can."

Samuel reached the junction of the streams shortly after daylight. He chuckled to himself when he spotted a crude raft with several men aboard floating out of sight several hundred feet downstream.

Believing that he had succeeded in throwing them off his trail, he pulled himself out of the stream, no longer worried about leaving tracks, and hurried back to the others. Worried faces greeted him later that morning, but cheers broke out when he reported their success.

"Where to now?" Oreb asked.

"Northwest, back to where we were before you spotted that fellow on the knoll yesterday," Samuel replied wearily.

By noon the following day they spotted the grassy knoll. From there they traveled west again, still watchful but feeling more secure.

* * *

"That brother-in-law of yours must know where he's headed," Captain Calno said that same evening as they drifted down what was becoming a good-sized river.

"If they're as cramped on their raft as we are on ours," Josh said, "they'll soon tire of this sort of travel."

"Captain, look over there," one of the men shouted, pointing toward the north bank of the river.

Josh and Calno both gaped. "Their raft. It must be their raft!" Josh said in surprise. "Do you think they're on foot again?"

"Looks that way, doesn't it?" Calno responded.

The soldiers steered their raft over and worked their way under the branches of the tree that had entangled Samuel's raft. They briefly examined it. Josh scratched his stubby growth of beard thoughtfully. "This is very poorly built. I'm surprised they made it this far."

"I wonder . . ." Calno mused.

"Wonder what?" Josh pressed.

"Oh, just . . . well, never mind. Let's go ashore and see what we can find."

After several minutes of thorough searching, Calno called the men back together. "They haven't been here, have they?" he asked. The men shook their heads in unison.

"We've been outsmarted again. Josh, do you think this raft was built to carry people, or could it be a decoy?" Calno asked.

"A decoy, sir," Josh said meekly.

"What do you suggest we do now?"

"We need to return to the place where the rafts were built and see if we can figure out where they went from there," Josh said, struggling to hide his bitter disappointment.

"Very well. Men, we'll go up-river on foot. Watch for any sign of anyone having passed through here anywhere," Calno ordered his discouraged company. "And keep a lookout for any sign of Kerlin and Herdon. Those two are not dumb and could be very near."

* * *

Near they were, but alarmed at the presence of a well-armed squad of soldiers. "Somehow, we've got to get to Samuel first," Kerlin said, after he and Herdon had nearly stumbled into the soldiers as they retreated from the river.

"But we don't know any better than they do where Samuel is leading them. And leading them he is. He has something in mind—a destination. We've got to figure what it is," Herdon said impatiently.

"Where do you think they are going?"

"Well, I know where this river will end up, and it gives me an idea. For now, we need to just keep moving, and fast. We don't want them to reach Samuel before we do." Herdon smiled to himself.

Kerlin watched him, but Herdon said nothing more. Instead, he started walking rapidly in the direction the soldiers had gone.

CHAPTER 27

It was a dirty travel-worn and tattered clan that stood high on a mountaintop overlooking an endless expanse of blue sea far below. Silence had prevailed following the first exclamations of surprise and wonder upon breaking out of the trees and having the magnificent view thrust unexpectedly upon them.

The day was clear and mild. The azure sky dipped in the distance, merging with the gently rolling waters of the great deep. Jath, his eyes wide with amazement, asked, "How far does it go, Father?"

The other youngsters looked toward Samuel expectantly, waiting for his answer. He signaled for the rest of the group to come near, saying nothing. Ophera took hold of Jath's grimy little hand. Uri, Munk on his shoulder, stood beside them. Slowly the others gathered, sensing that Samuel was about to say something they did not want to miss.

"Jath," Samuel said at last, "it goes much farther than any of us can even imagine. Only God understands its size." He paused and smiled at the eager faces surrounding him. "What I do know is that there are other lands out there, too far to see from here—much too far. Somewhere there is a peaceful place."

He paused again, gazing beyond the upturned faces at the never-ending blue before him. When he looked back at his loved ones, he was smiling. "We are going to go to one of those places."

Stunned silence greeted his announcement.

Oreb was the first to speak. "Leave our land?" he asked. "Why should we do that?"

Before Samuel could answer, Nonita exclaimed, "Sam, we can't leave all our friends! And what about the Church? We need the prophet Helaman to guide us. Why . . ."

Ophera interrupted. "Let Sam explain. He has known for a long time what he wanted to do."

"Thank you, Ophera," he said, pulling his gaze back from the magnificent view so far below them. "I will force no one to come, but we have many enemies. At least, I do, and for me and my family, to stay in the land of Zarahemla or anywhere that the Gadianton robbers might be, would be very dangerous."

"But Moronihah will destroy them after he has driven the Lamanites from the land again, and he will do that," Oreb argued.

Samuel turned again to the ocean and gazed silently for several minutes. Murmurs continued behind him. Finally, he turned to face his little clan again. When he spoke, all murmuring stopped and everyone listened in awe to the words he spoke.

"We are not going out there," he said, sweeping his arm toward the distant sea, "because I chose to do so. Many weeks ago, while I prayed for guidance to help me keep us from the hands of the Gadianton robbers, the Spirit of the Lord whispered to me.

"'Samuel,' I heard the Spirit say, 'lead your family from this land and I will guide you to a place where you are beyond the reach of your enemies. Go, as Hagoth and others have gone, by ship, and if you are obedient, you will be given a land for your inheritance.'"

Samuel's face glowed as he continued. "The last of Hagoth's ships is at the narrow neck of land. The date for it to sail is fast approaching—if my calculations are correct, it will leave in one week."

"How will we find the ship?" Nonita asked softly, all sign of doubt gone from her face as she felt the power with which her righteous brother spoke.

"It is north," he said. "We must descend these mountains and follow the sea north until we find it. I saw in a dream the lagoon where it awaits us. I will know the place when I see it. Now," he said, his voice softer, "pray, each of you, tonight. Tomorrow, you may let me know your decisions. You may all come, but as I said, I will force no one."

Ophera stepped to his side and whispered, "I promised to go wherever you go. And I know that the Lord is directing you." She smiled at him and put her arm around his waist. "I only wish my brother Josh were here. I will miss him, but Jath and Uri and I will go. Right, boys?"

Jath grinned and nodded, but Uri looked at his feet and stroked his monkey absently. "You may take Munk," Samuel said, and Uri's face lit up like the full moon.

"Sam, Laishita and I can give our answer right now," Gadoni said. He smiled at his wife and she nodded. "Since the Lord told you to go, then we will go with you." No doubt clouded his eyes as he spoke. Gadoni had great faith.

"I'm sorry, Sam," Oreb began with downcast eyes. "It caught me by surprise, but what you propose is good. My family and I will go with you." Kapilla hugged him and the twins' eyes sparkled with excitement.

Nonita spoke next. "You are the patriarch of our family, Sam. I will go. All I ask is that Nemti be allowed to go, too," she said and gazed at the young soldier with fierce longing.

"My father and mother are dead. I have many friends, but none so important as you," he said to Nonita. "I will go if Sam will let me."

"Of course you may go," Sam said with a smile as his little sister rubbed at her eyes self-consciously. "Now, all that remains is to safely reach the ship before it sails."

"What if it's already gone?" Oreb asked.

"Then perhaps we could go northward, beyond inhabited lands, and settle there," Sam answered. "But I think it will still be there."

"What about the Gadianton robbers that are pursuing us?" Nemti asked.

"We have eluded them so far. We will continue to watch for them as we descend these treacherous mountains."

* * *

The two surviving Gadianton robbers had no intention of being eluded. Herdon, after following the soldiers for two days, did some thinking. He would have his revenge. He devised a plan, and he and Kerlin forged swiftly on, murder on their evil minds.

* * *

For two-and-a-half tiring days, Samuel and his people descended the rugged mountain. Many times they had to drop strong vines over ledges and lower themselves. Getting the children down safely was particularly difficult and time-consuming.

The worst was past, but Samuel worried for fear they were taking too long and the ship would be gone. To make matters worse, their periods of rest became increasingly longer and more frequent as the grueling descent wore them down. He entertained doubts about reaching the ship before it departed, but firmly cast them aside and prayed for success.

After one rather short rest, he rose to his feet and said, "We must press on."

Moans followed.

"I'm sorry," he said sternly, "but our only hope of escaping the wrath of the Gadianton robbers is the ship, and we don't want it to sail without us."

"But Nemti," Nonita moaned, casting a worried glance in his direction.

Samuel followed her eyes. The young soldier was weak, but his face was determined. "Of course we can do it. We've come this far. We can't give up now," he said with confidence.

The rest of the day they picked their way toward the shore of the West Sea that beckoned like a welcoming beacon from the distance. Darkness overtook them before they reached the narrow strip of fertile green land that connected the mountains with the sea. Samuel called a halt. "It's too dangerous to go on in the dark," he said. "We will just have to wait until daylight to go on. Rest well and we'll start early. When we reach the shore we will move swiftly north."

The final descent went without a hitch the next morning. If enthusiasm could help them make up for lost time, they had it made. Smiles abounded and everyone pushed forward along the bright strip of green land that bordered the sea.

Samuel looked back up at the treacherous mountainside they had so miraculously descended. His heart lurched. He had caught a fleeting but unmistakable glimpse of a man hanging from a vine far above.

"Hurry," he urged.

"We are," Ophera said.

"Not fast enough," he said urgently, looking over his shoulder again.

* * *

"They camped here," Josh shouted up the hill at the soldiers who were lowering themselves from the vines Samuel had left in place. "The coals of their fire are still warm. And they descended there," he said, pointing to the next series of ledges and the last steep decline before the mighty mountains touched the gentle slopes.

"I see them!" one man shouted, running toward the next ledge.

"Not too fast," Calno cautioned. "I don't want anyone hurt. We are almost up with them, so let's make sure we don't take any undue risks."

The captain's warning went tragically unheeded. Two of his men, without checking the condition of one of the vines that had been left dangling below them, started over a twenty-foot ledge together. The vine, worn from the use Samuel's people had given it, was unable to support the weight of two big men and snapped. They screamed as they hit the slope, bounced a few feet, and dropped over another ledge to their deaths in the rocks a hundred feet down.

When the others reached their dead comrades, their excitement had vanished. A somber Captain Calno ordered the bodies buried. Josh sat on a rock with slumped shoulders. He mourned his fallen comrades and mourned the time that was being lost. His soul ached with the desire to reach his loved ones, but out of respect for those who had died in their aid, he waited and grieved.

An hour passed before Calno, saddened and discouraged like Josh, said, "We must go on now, men, but please, take great care."

* * *

"The ship! The ship!" young Uri shouted so loudly that Munk scurried from his shoulder and cowered like a naughty child on the ground.

A cheer rose from the exhausted travelers. From the top of a short rise they could see a small fortified city tucked against the base of the mountain at a point where a deep, green lagoon glistened, cutting the narrow strip of fertile ground almost in two. Only a few hundred yards of bright green foliage separated the city from the white sands of the beach. They only had a couple of miles to go.

The ship rolled lazily at anchor several hundred feet out in the green lagoon. The time for risk had arrived, and Samuel did not hesitate. There could be Gadianton robbers in the city who might recognize them. He had

Oreb and Gadoni lead the small group of weary travelers into the woods at the base of the mountain while he went on alone and cautiously approached the city.

Hundreds of Nephite soldiers were busy inside, going about a multitude of tasks in an orderly and efficient manner. But Samuel worried when he failed to see many women or children. He spoke to several people. As he feared, the ship was already loaded and ready to sail.

He was introduced to the captain of the company of Nephite soldiers. His name was Josiah. A large, burly man with a heavy beard and thick, curly hair that hung to his massive shoulders, the captain welcomed Samuel warmly.

"Captain Moronihah sent word to be on the lookout for you and your people," he told Samuel. "He greatly loves you and feared for your life."

"We have had a difficult time, but so far have managed to evade the men of Gadianton who pursue us. We seek passage on the ship in the lagoon," Samuel said urgently.

"It sails in a few minutes, but there is space for you. Two other passengers, two men who just arrived a short while ago, boarded just minutes ago. You will be the last, but if you will get your people ready, I will send a boat out to request that Captain Baronihah wait. He will not wait long though, for he hopes to be out of the lagoon and clear of the shoreline before dusk," Josiah said with a smile that barely appeared beneath his face of black hair.

"Captain, we have no money for fare," Samuel said.

"It is not required. Hagoth will have work for you to do to make up for the passage when you reach him. Now hurry, you probably only have an hour or less to be on board."

"An hour!" Samuel exclaimed. "They are clear back there," he said, pointing, "and we have women and children and one wounded man."

"Ah, that would be Nemti, I hope. I am glad to hear he is still alive."

"He is weak, but alive and doing well considering what we have put him through. And that is another matter. I would ask for his release from the army and permission for him to travel with us. Helaman said . . ."

Captain Josiah waved a burly arm and interrupted. "He may go with you, but you must make haste. Tomorrow is the Sabbath and Baronihah, who is also a priest, will not begin a voyage on the Sabbath," he said.

"Thank you, Captain, we'll hurry. Oh, there is one more thing. Will you alert your patrols that we are coming? The Gadianton robbers that have been pursuing us are not far behind, and we don't need any . . ."

"We will be watching for you and give you assistance if necessary," Josiah interrupted, his dark eyes twinkling. "May God go with you."

"Thank you, sir," Samuel said and hurried through the door, his eyes darting about but failing to recognize anyone from his days among the robbers.

As Samuel returned to the waiting people nearly a half-hour later, he saw a small band of men rushing toward him in the distance. Frantically, he ran into the woods and in a moment he and his loved ones surged from the trees and rushed toward the little city. "Run," he shouted, as they drew near the city nearly another half-hour later. "The robbers are almost upon us!"

Fear pushed them like nothing else could. Samuel could not imagine why the robbers would be so bold as to pursue them when the city was full of soldiers and so close ahead, but he did not care to find the answer. To his dismay, he also noticed that the ship in the lagoon was slowly turning until its bow was facing the open sea. Men lined the shore. A squad of soldiers joined them, wiping out the threat from behind, but the ship was slowly drawing away.

Captain Josiah met Samuel at the shore. "Climb in and you'll make it," he shouted, pointing to three small vessels that were pulled up on the sandy shore. "There is not much wind and Baronihah sent word that he had to start out, but it would be very slowly. You won't have any trouble catching up."

A dozen soldiers assisted them into three small boats, and four strong men in each boat rowed them across the gentle swells toward the ship which was slowly progressing toward the mouth of the green lagoon. Samuel, still breathing hard from the taxing run, looked over his shoulder at the receding shoreline. He could not suppress a grin when he saw their pursuers, surrounded by soldiers, dropping their weapons to the ground.

With a sigh he looked forward, determined to put the Gadianton robbers from his mind forever. A moment later, Ophera nudged him. "Sam," she said, "why would Captain Josiah free the robbers?"

"What!" he exclaimed, turning to look. "He is," he moaned. "They are gathering up their weapons."

"Sam, look. One of them is shouting something at us," Ophera said, a look of alarm on her face. "He's running into the water. He's swimming toward us!"

Samuel was stunned. With strong strokes, the swimmer gradually closed in on the laboring boats. No one pursued him. In fact, excited shouts seemed to be encouraging him from the shore.

For the next several minutes, they watched in puzzled fascination as the swimmer would rise with a swell, then disappear from view until he crested another one. He continued to gain steadily on the boats which in turn were gaining on the creeping ship.

Everyone, including the strong oarsmen, were caught up with the gallant efforts of the lone swimmer. By the time they reached the ship the figure had slowed down.

"He's getting tired," one of the oarsmen said with a laugh.

"Swing about," Samuel suddenly ordered the men at the oars. "While the others board the ship, I'd like to see who that is and what he's coming out here alone for."

Without a word, the men steered the little boat in a circle and rowed toward the bobbing figure. As they drew closer, Ophera nudged Samuel urgently. "He's tired, Sam. He's having a hard time. We can't let him drown even if he is a robber."

Samuel nodded. "Faster, men," he urged.

Suddenly, Ophera shot to her feet, setting the small boat to rocking dangerously.

"Sit down," one of the oarsmen ordered roughly.

"Sam, it's Josh!" Ophera screamed.

Samuel recognized Ophera's younger brother about the same time she did. "I'm going after him," he shouted as he removed his sandals and weapons. When he tumbled over the side, he set the little boat to rocking again and the oarsmen fought to keep it upright.

As Samuel swam, Ophera was shouting, "Josh, Sam's coming. Don't give up!"

Josh struggled, and just before Samuel reached him, he slipped beneath the surface of the warm water. Samuel dove and caught him with one strong arm and fought his way to the surface, dragging Josh along. Two of the oarsmen entered the water and helped Samuel tow Josh to the near side of the boat. Willing hands reached for him while others struggled to keep the boat upright. They pulled him, along with several gallons of salty water, into the boat.

Josh coughed and began to struggle. "It's okay, Josh, you're safe now," Ophera said tenderly, cradling his head in her lap.

His eyes opened and he brushed at them with his hand. Samuel, scrambling into the boat beside him, helped him sit up. For a minute Josh had difficulty breathing. He coughed violently. Samuel slapped him on the back and his breathing evened out. He smiled. "You sure are hard to catch," were the first words he said.

Samuel shook his head. "Josh, don't tell me it was you that was following us. I thought . . ."

"Yes," Josh broke in. "Captain Calno, myself, and several other men were sent into the wilderness by Captain Moronihah. Helaman asked the captain to send me so I could go with you to the lands where Hagoth went. I first discovered that you had been to our secret hunting hideout behind the falls. From there . . ." he trailed off when Ophera looked at him with a question in her eyes.

"But the robbers," she said. "Where are they?"

"All but two were ambushed and killed by a band of Lamanites in the jungle. Those two, Kerlin and Herdon, we have been on the lookout for but have not seen."

He gave a feeble grin. "I guess we beat them," he concluded as the boat approached the ship, which was still moving at a snail's pace toward the open sea.

In the ship, evil eyes watched with murderous delight as the new passengers boarded. A hearty welcome was not on two men's minds.

CHAPTER 28

"I am Captain Baronihah. I'm relieved that you made it. I really wasn't trying to leave you, but there is so little breeze this afternoon that I thought I could start out and you could catch us, as you did." He chuckled, a deep, throaty sound, before going on. "We have a long way to go and Hagoth awaits our return." The large ship commander shook Samuel's hand with force that made him wince.

Samuel immediately liked the captain. Not young but not as old as his flowing white beard suggested, Baronihah was as strong and agile as a man half his age. "We thank you for taking us on board," Samuel answered with a tired smile. "By the way, Captain, two men boarded the ship not long before we did. Who were they?"

"I did not see them. Perhaps one of my men . . ."

"Captain Josiah told me they boarded," Samuel interrupted anxiously.

"As I was saying, perhaps one of my men took them on board. I'm sure they are good men or they would not be going where we are," he said firmly.

Samuel had an uneasy feeling but let the matter drop. "I would like to perform a wedding on board. My sister . . ."

"I am a priest, too. Won't you let me have the pleasure?" Baronihah asked.

"Of course," Sam said, silently grateful. Although ordained by the prophet Helaman in Gilead the day of Oreb's wedding, he welcomed the captain's offer.

"Excellent. Now, let's find you all a place to bunk. It'll be crowded, but we do have room. Is this the lucky couple?" he asked, encircling his long, sinewy arms around Kapilla and Oreb.

"We're lucky," Oreb answered quickly, "but Helaman already married us."

"Well, from that grin on your face, I thought sure you were still anticipating the romantic occasion." He guffawed heartily before saying, "At least you two are still in love." His laugh originated somewhere deep in his massive chest, then rolled up his throat like a tidal wave before rumbling from his mouth, blowing the white whiskers around his weathered lips like grass in the wind.

"If it isn't you two, then it must be this handsome couple," he roared, still amused at himself. He had moved over to where Nonita kneeled on the floor beside Nemti, whose head was cradled gently in her lap.

The rumble died and a genuine look of concern appeared in his sea-blue eyes. No one disagreed with him this time, and he bent over, his beard touching Nonita's black hair like a snow-capped peak. "Looks like this young fellow needs a little rest. Let me help you get him to a bunk," he said.

Nemti had given all he had and more to keep up that day, but it had taken its toll on his weakened body. He was too exhausted to even speak. Samuel explained to Captain Baronihah why Nemti was in the condition he was.

The captain grunted and, with what seemed to take no more effort than lifting a small stick, slipped his strong arms under Nemti and picked him up. He did not appear to need help, so Samuel, Nonita, and the rest of the clan followed as he wound his way through a maze of stairwells to a bunk in a secluded corner of the ship. They had descended two decks into the bowels of the vessel where it was dark, lit only by an oil lamp in the center of the small room.

"This will be your quarters," the captain said after seeing to Nemti's comfort. "You should be happy here, even though it's cramped."

Samuel looked around with some relief. They were in tight but private quarters, a wall separating them from the rest of the deck, which consisted of other such rooms occupied by several Nephite families.

Exhaustion overtook them, and except for Samuel, welcome sleep rejuvenated their tired bodies. Even the excited chatter of other people on the deck did not disturb them. But Samuel could not sleep. A nagging worry ate at him and he prowled the deck, his sword strapped to his side. When his family began to stir, he awoke Gadoni and told him of his concerns, then slipped from the room and made his way to the upper deck where he was surprised to discover that it was just turning dawn over the rolling blue expanse which had quietly swallowed the ship while he slept.

He turned at the sound of footsteps and smiled when he saw Josh approaching from the lower decks. "Thank you, Sam, for saving my life," Josh said, looking sheepish as he held the rail and gazed over the rolling ocean.

"Glad to be of service," Samuel answered after an awkward silence.

"I guess it was foolish of me to attempt to swim after you following such a long, tiring march, but Helaman and Moronihah told me I could go if I wanted, and so I wasn't about to be left," Josh said, turning to face Samuel with a big smile. "I'm sure glad you decided to quit running from me, Sam."

"I'm equally glad, Josh, and so is Ophera."

"Ophera told me about your father and my mother. I will miss them," Josh said, his eyes glistening.

"As will the rest of us, but they would have us do what we can to escape the deadly reach of the Gadianton robbers."

The two talked and watched the sun, a large orange ball, rise like a monster from the deep over the eastern horizon, before joining the others for breakfast. The children made faces at the food, but Samuel was stern and soon let them know that they should be grateful for whatever they had during the long journey ahead.

Captain Baronihah was anxious to perform the wedding. "The sooner, the better," he said with his characteristic smile after breakfast. "Today is the Sabbath, so we will perform the wedding then hold services. The celebration must wait until tomorrow. After that, some of you may be getting seasick and not feel like celebrating. Are you feeling well enough for a wedding?" he asked, turning his attention to Nemti.

"Yes, thank you. I'm ready if Nonita is," Nemti said with a weak smile.

"Do you still want to marry this man?" the captain asked.

Nonita smiled shyly. "When can we do it?" she asked.

"Right now," he thundered, the deep rumble starting to roll from his chest again. "There is nothing I'd rather do." His laughter continued.

Nonita brushed her long black hair from her face and rose to her feet. Her eyes sparkled and her cheeks glowed. "Where to?" she asked.

"On the top deck, of course," he said, "where the salty smell of the sea and the beauty of the endless waves will give your marriage a start that will last forever. Not as good as in a synagogue, but second best in my mind. As soon as your little ones are ready," he said, watching Laishita round up her little brood, "then you can all come topside and we'll get started. And bring that monkey," he added, patting Uri's blond head with a large, leathery hand.

Captain Baronihah passed through the open door and out of sight. Suddenly, he roared like a bull, "There's about to be a wedding up on the main deck. Everybody come. Worship services will follow. It's time we all got acquainted proper anyway." He laughed so deep and long that the ship seemed to sway with more force than before.

On deck a few minutes later, their backs to the sun, Nemti and Nonita stood hand in hand, glowing with love. The captain began a lengthy speech. He spoke of the sanctity of marriage and the privilege of bringing children into the world. "Yours will be a special challenge," he said solemnly. "You will be raising your children in a new land. They will have no need to be exposed to the evils we leave behind if you," he swept his hand over the whole congregation, "all of you, strive to always obey the teachings of God."

When at length, having repeated himself several times, he paused, one of his sailors shouted, "You tell 'em, Captain. Only thing I wonder is this: how do you know so much about love and marriage and the like when you've always been a single man?"

The captain cast a dark look his way, then roared with deep laughter. "I remember what my mother used to tell me," he said. "Now, don't you dare question her wisdom."

The sailor said no more, and Baronihah rambled on. Samuel found himself chuckling. It was quite apparent the captain had not performed a wedding for some time and was making the most of it.

Samuel glanced around at his family and friends. Uri and the monkey were missing. He had barely noticed it when a piercing scream rose from a lower deck. The captain stopped in mid-sentence and everyone looked around to see where the sound had come from. A doorway and stairs leading to the deck below were a short distance behind them on the starboard side of the ship. Uri charged through the door, still screaming. Blood was streaming from his nose, and his face was scratched. His eyes were wide with terror.

Samuel caught him up in his arms and the boy began to shout a single word, over and over again. "Kerlin! Kerlin! Kerlin!" he screamed.

"Take him," Samuel shouted, handing the boy to Ophera and dashing to the lower deck, followed closely by Gadoni, Josh, Baronihah, the twins, and Oreb.

Kerlin was stooping beside a bunk just a few feet from the bottom of the rough wooden steps. He cursed and swung his sword wildly beneath the bunk.

"Kerlin!" Samuel shouted.

With a start, the robber straightened up and faced him, his face masked with hatred. He raised his sword, poised for a fight as Samuel approached. As Samuel circled around Kerlin, his own sword drawn, Munk shot from beneath the bunk where Kerlin had been swinging his weapon.

Momentarily distracted by the monkey, Samuel was not prepared for Kerlin's sudden lunge. He twisted away, but blood spurted from a shallow gash in his side. Their swords clanked, and Kerlin's was knocked from his hand and went clattering across the floor. Samuel sprang forward and caught Kerlin by the right wrist and twisted his arm violently behind his back.

A shadow moved across the deck. Oreb took off in a dead run shouting, "Herdon! Stop!"

Kim and Kib darted after Oreb, and Gadoni headed the same way while Josh and the captain struggled with Kerlin, who was shouting and twisting with insane strength. By the time they had him securely bound, Oreb came across the floor, pushing his wicked father-in-law, who was alternately cursing the monkey and Kerlin. The twins, tears streaming down their narrow faces, followed.

"What are the idiots doing here?" Herdon asked with a sneer, looking at his offspring with black eyes.

"Why don't we let them tell you," Oreb said, panting for air.

"We are going with Oreb and Kapilla to a new land where there aren't any Gadianton robbers," Kim said, his voice quivering but clear.

"They love us like you never did," Kib added, meeting his father's dark stare bravely.

Herdon's face went blank.

"You see, Herdon, they are really quite intelligent. Their only problem was your cruelty. Now, I want to know what you're doing on this ship," Oreb said icily.

Herdon said nothing.

Josh spoke up. "After the others in your little band were killed by Laman and his Lamanite warriors, where did . . ."

"Laman?" Gadoni interrupted with a gasp. "Do you mean my brother, Laman?"

"Yes. I'm sorry, Gadoni," Josh said, his eyes lowered.

"Where is he now?" Gadoni asked.

"We took him captive and Captain Calno sent him to Manti to stand trial," he said.

Gadoni nodded sadly as Ophera and Kapilla came down the stairs. "Father!" Kapilla shouted in angry surprise. "What are you doing here?"

Herdon turned away from her and said nothing. Tears streamed down her face. "I thought we had escaped from you and your kind."

"Samuel, you're bleeding!" Ophera exclaimed.

"Not as bad as he's going to be," Kerlin threatened as he struggled in vain against the cords that held him bound.

Others streamed down the stairs. Among them were Nonita and Nemti. She heard Kerlin's threat. "You've done all you're going to do, to him or to anyone else I love. You are such a . . . such a . . ."

"Nonita," Kerlin interrupted with a contemptuous voice, "you will die, and so will he." His eyes swung to Nemti, full of hatred.

"You were mine," he continued. "Kishkumen and Gadianton gave you to me," he said angrily.

"I wasn't theirs to give. They are evil men and someday they will pay for what they've done," she said abruptly and turned away.

"Let's finish the wedding," Samuel said brightly.

"Not until you're cared for," his pretty wife reminded him.

"Here, let me help," a familiar voice said from the stairway.

"Dara!" Kapilla squealed and rushed forward to embrace the good woman who had loved and encouraged her during those long days of terror in the wilderness. "Where . . ." Kapilla started.

"Later," Dara said. "I'll explain later. Right now, I think Samuel needs some help."

As she helped Ophera tend to Samuel's wound, Captain Baronihah ordered everyone back to the upper deck with a promise that the wedding would go on in a few minutes. He also ordered the two robbers to be removed to the hold beneath the third deck.

Kapilla was surprised again when another friend appeared and began to help with Samuel's wound. "Eva is with me," Dara exclaimed with a smile. "She has no family."

"Captain," Dara said, catching the eye of the massive ship-master. "I need some water. Will you get me some?"

"Right away," he said meekly and, to everyone's surprise, went after it.

When he returned, Dara said, "Thank you, Captain," and smiled up at him. The slightest blush crept from under his white beard and made its way up his face, across his broad forehead, and faded away in the bushy white hair that topped his head.

After the wedding and services, everyone stayed on deck to rest in the sun except Samuel, Ophera, Jath, and Uri. They went below. While Samuel rested, Uri explained what had happened earlier.

"I came back down to get my knife," he said.

"Why did you need your knife?" Ophera asked.

"Because Samuel had his sword," he answered, with a look that said that should certainly explain it.

"Oh, and why did you have your sword?" Ophera asked Samuel with a smile.

"Just a feeling I had," he said, then turned to Uri again. "So then what happened?"

"When I got up to the next deck, I heard someone talking. One of them said Nonita's name, so I stopped and listened. Then I heard his voice," Uri said, trembling.

"Kerlin?" Samuel asked.

"Yes. He said he was going to . . . to . . . kill Nemti. I . . . I got real scared . . . I started to run. He caught me and hit me. That's when Munk jumped on him and bit his arm. He let go and threw Munk. That's when I started to scream. I fell . . . and he nearly caught me again. Then Munk jumped on him and started to bite again. That was all I saw before I ran up the steps."

"You're a good monkey," Sam said, patting Munk's head. "I hope there's plenty of monkey food aboard this ship."

Uri and Jath looked at each other and grinned.

CHAPTER 29

Captain Baronihah proved to be right. Rough water caused a wave of seasickness that brought even some of the strongest passengers to their knees. The few who were not affected nursed the ones who were the sickest. Dara seemed to be everywhere, giving encouragement, wiping sweaty brows, and cleaning up foul messes.

The captain finally said to her, "Dara, you need to rest. Someone else can take care of the sick for awhile."

She took hold of his weathered hand, squeezing gently, and said, "No, I can rest later. Why don't you help me for awhile, instead?"

Meekly, he obeyed, and it soon became a common sight to see Dara tending to the needs of someone in a bunk while the massive captain, his white beard and hair shining like a halo, wiped the brow of someone nearby.

One of the sickest passengers was Eva. Kapilla spent a lot of time at the young girl's side. "Why aren't you sick?" she asked Kapilla one afternoon.

"I don't know. I'm just lucky, I guess. Captain Baronihah says some people get sick from the constant motion and others don't."

"Will I be sick the whole trip?" she asked, her hazel eyes full of misery.

"I think not. They say it will eventually pass; you will get used to it and be able to enjoy the trip," Kapilla said with a smile.

"Kapilla, you look very tired. Let me help with Eva." Surprised, she looked up. Josh stood over them. He looked a little pale, but was apparently getting over his own bout with seasickness.

"Thank you, Josh," Kapilla said gratefully, and with a wink at Eva, got to her feet and moved away.

From that day on, Josh seldom left the frail girl's side. Even after his constant nursing had strengthened her and they had sailed into calmer seas, he could usually be found near her. She blossomed like a spring flower, and Josh beamed when she gazed at him with her calf-like eyes.

Two others got quite sick, but were denied fresh, salty air. Down steep ladders to the rumbling bowels of the ship, Kapilla trekked faithfully each day, sometimes several times a day, to take food to her father and Kerlin. Herdon reached through the bars and snatched whatever she offered, never acknowledging her. She searched his face for any sign of softening in his hatred for his own flesh and blood, but Satan had stolen his soul; there was no change.

Kim and Kib accompanied her once, but after enduring just a few moments of his cursing and reviling, Kapilla wisely led them away. "He has given himself to the evil one," she said sadly. "I will feed him, but that is all. You two must try to forget he is here."

Finally, the prisoners asked to see Captain Baronihah. He came down at Kapilla's bidding. "What do you two want?" he asked roughly.

"Off this wretched ship," Kerlin begged.

"The law requires that you die for your crimes," Baronihah said bluntly and left them, deeply disturbed by the duty that was his. Herdon cursed and the captain climbed up from below with Kapilla. "I am sorry, Kapilla. I know that Herdon is your father," he said after they had reached the top deck, "but under the law, they must both be put to death."

"I know he is evil, but he is my father," she said, her voice strained and sad. "If it could just be done off the ship," she begged, looking hopelessly out over the endless expanse of blue sea.

Baronihah scratched his nose then said. "We have been traveling north. It would put us out of our course by a couple of days. Hagoth will be worried. This is the only ship he has left." Captain Baronihah was thoughtful for a moment. "On the other hand," he said at length, "I don't think he'd be too pleased if we showed up with two Gadianton robbers on board, and I must respect your feelings. We'll steer east to the coast and . . ."

He let the thought linger and Kapilla nodded in assent. "Thank you, Captain," she murmured.

Kapilla tried once more to make peace with her father before he was taken ashore. He rebuffed her like a stranger. She shed quiet tears on

Oreb's willing shoulder as she watched a crew of sailors row the two robbers to shore.

When the boat returned, the executions completed, the sailors bore fresh fruit. Much of it was for Uri to share with his monkey. The rest provided a nice respite from the bland diet they had been experiencing.

* * *

For several weeks the ship sailed on glassy seas in a westerly direction. Even the most ill of the passengers regained their strength, and the mood on board was a festive one. Then one day dark clouds boiled up on the western horizon. The ship began to rock on ever-growing waves. The sickness returned. Captain Baronihah directed the ship directly into the storm. "Don't know where this will lead us," he said to Samuel and several other men, "but we must steer into the winds or the ship might flounder. I just hope we can ride this storm out."

The look of concern on the weathered face of the captain gave Samuel cause for worry, and he gathered with his family and sought the protection of the Lord.

For three days they were pounded by the storm. Cracks opened on the upper deck, and water dripped below. From the third deck, the creaking and cracking of the great timbers of the bow threw fright into even the bravest hearts. It sounded as if the ship was about to be torn apart by the violence of the thrashing sea.

Baronihah chuckled when Samuel expressed his concern. "Our only danger is in getting caught sideways of the winds. As long as we keep her headed into the worst winds or with them, we'll be all right. Hagoth himself supervised the building of this ship, and I have nothing but confidence in its strength."

The ship held together but was blown far off course into strange seas. For two more days it was blown about on the angry sea. The morning of the sixth day the winds abated, but the sky was dark and foreboding and a dense fog descended, enshrouding the ship with mist so thick that the top of the mast was lost from sight. Samuel was standing on the deck with Gadoni when there was a terrible crunching sound and they were thrown forward against the rail. For a dreadful moment, Samuel clung to the rail as the ship shuddered and shook, then it slowly began to settle into the water.

"We've run aground," Samuel shouted at Gadoni, who was struggling to his feet.

"Let's go check on the others," Gadoni shouted back.

Water was pouring into the ship from somewhere below the third deck. Samuel and Gadoni had to fight their way through streams of people who were rushing topside in a panic. By the time they reached their room, Oreb had the people organized, and within a few moments they had gathered their weapons and few other belongings and joined the throngs rushing topside.

The ship settled until water had filled the third deck, then, tilted crazily to port, it came to rest. Captain Baronihah wasted no time in calming the passengers. "As soon as the fog clears we'll be able to tell where we are," he said calmly, Dara at his side. "Until then, she seems to have settled as far as she's going to."

In the early afternoon the fog lifted, revealing a sandy shoreline fringed with green. The storm had torn up many of the trees, but the beauty of the land was still a sight to behold. The ship itself lay on a jagged coral reef a scant hundred yards from shore.

Captain Baronihah ordered a small boat, and the rest of the day was spent ferrying the passengers to the safety of the shore. What provisions had survived the shipwreck were brought ashore the next morning.

The captain, as much in charge ashore as on the sea, ordered two small parties of men, including Samuel, Gadoni, Oreb, and Josh, to undertake a journey. One group he sent north, the other south. They were told to travel no more than one week before turning back and returning to report what they had found.

Samuel was in command of the group assigned to go south. Gadoni and four other men traveled with him. Oreb and Josh went with the other party of six men. They set out at dawn, just three days following the grounding of their ship.

Wild game and waterfowl were abundant as were a wide variety of fruits and nuts. Much of the terrain was rugged, but green and beautiful. Water from high mountains inland cascaded over cliffs and fell like streaks of silver into deep pools that became streams, threading their way to the sea.

"Gadoni, I do believe the shoreline is turning constantly. We are going west, I'm sure," Samuel said as they rested and ate some fruit at noon the next day.

"It'll head south again soon," Gadoni said confidently.

It did not. Thirty-six hours later they were trekking north. Samuel was not surprised when, early the following afternoon, they met the group that had been sent north coming south.

"An island!" Oreb shouted with delight. "It's beautiful."

"And far from the land of Zarahemla," Samuel added.

"Did you see any sign of human habitation?" the leader of Oreb's group asked.

"None. Should we head back across the center of the island?" Samuel asked.

"That sounds good to me. The captain will be surprised when we return so quickly," the other man said with a chuckle.

"Maybe," Samuel said thoughtfully.

The land was fairly flat for a couple of miles inland, then began to rise. They climbed and passed over a summit that soared over three thousand feet into the air. It was rugged, but nothing like the mountains bordering the narrow neck of land.

"You're back early," Captain Baronihah said with a smile when the men trekked into the camp just five days after leaving. "I take it that means this is indeed an island. Is it as abundant in food supplies elsewhere as it is here?"

Oreb's eyes glowed. "I've never seen anything like it," he said, fingering his bow and thinking of the wildlife he had seen.

"This is not where we set out to go," the captain said, stroking his long white beard thoughtfully. "By tomorrow we must come to a decision. Either we can stay and settle this island, or we can begin building another ship and go on, hoping we can find Hagoth and his people."

"Can we actually build another ship?" one of the men asked.

"Certainly. Much of the old ship can be used if we take it apart carefully and float the timbers to shore," Baronihah said with confidence.

"How long would it take to build a ship?" one of the crew asked.

"Six months. A year at the most," he said.

"I say we build another ship," the sailor said with enthusiasm.

"I'd rather stay," Oreb said with equal enthusiasm.

Captain Baronihah raised his massive arms in the air. "Talk it over tonight. We'll reach a decision tomorrow."

* * *

Samuel lay on his back studying the unfamiliar sky. "It is so different here," he mused.

Ophera snuggled close to him and yawned. "What's different?"

"The sky. The stars."

"Oh, I thought you meant how peaceful it is," she said.

"Yes, that too."

"Sam."

"Yes?"

"What do you want to do, stay or go?" Ophera asked softly.

He rolled on his side and faced her, running his fingers through her long hair as it reflected the rising moon with a golden shimmer. "What do you want to do?" he countered.

"Sam, I will go wherever you want, but I would be content to settle right here," Ophera said.

"Laishita and Gadoni want to stay. He says they feel so safe here. He's tired of running. I agree. And Oreb already spoke about his feelings. I guess we should check with Nemti and Nonita. Of course, we might get outvoted tomorrow," Samuel said, pushing himself into a sitting position.

"Sam, what if the others want to go? Couldn't we stay, anyway?"

"Well, I don't see why not. If we helped build the ship, they would have no complaint, and they don't need us to sail. We'll talk to the others in the morning," he said excitedly.

"We want to stay," Nemti said without hesitation when the question was directed to him.

"This is home to Kapilla and me already. We're not leaving," Oreb said stubbornly. The twins nodded in delighted agreement.

"Josh," Samuel said. "What about you?"

"If Eva will stay, too," he said with a shy grin.

The girl was seated next to him on the trunk of an uprooted palm tree. She placed her dainty hand in his. "I'm going wherever you are," she said.

"Gadoni, do you still want to stay?"

The sturdy Lamanite bounced his giggling little son on his knee. "Absolutely!" he said.

"That about does it then," Samuel announced. "We will stay no matter what the others decide."

Later in the morning, Captain Baronihah presided over a heated debate. Over three quarters of the people wanted to build a ship and go on, including the crew. Most of the people had friends and loved ones who had gone in years past with Hagoth. They wanted to find them.

Finally, Baronihah called for order and spoke. "We will build a ship, but you are free people. When it is finished, those who desire may choose a new captain from among the crew and go when the ship is ready."

"But you are our captain. Why should we choose a new one?" one of the men shouted.

"Because Dara and I are not getting any younger," he said, and his deep laugh rolled to the surface. After his humor had run its course, he said, "If Sam will perform the ceremony, we will marry and raise a family right here on this island."

Dara, at his side, smiled fondly at him and took his hand. "We will all help until the ship is built," she said, "then those who want to go may do so."

* * *

Samuel and Ophera stood overlooking a beautiful lagoon. A warm breeze rustled the palm fronds and gently stirred their hair. Behind them, the laughter of Uri and Josh rang through the trees. "Thank you, Sam," Ophera said.

"For what?"

"For bringing us to this beautiful place," she answered, laying her head against his chest.

He smiled at her, brushing a lock of stray hair gently from her face. "We have worked hard the past year, but since the ship has sailed, I guess we can get down to our work. Tomorrow we will begin a permanent house. That shack is just not good enough for you," he said, gazing over her shoulder at the little building he had hastily built and they had lived in during the construction of the ship.

"Father! Father!" Jath shouted, bursting from the palms. "Come quickly. You've got to see what Uri and I just found!"

Samuel kissed Ophera on the forehead. "I can hear the baby stirring in the shack," he said. "If you'll see to her, I'll see what the boys have found."

"You better hurry, then," she said, following the darting figure of her son with her blue eyes as he streaked back into the palm forest.

With a hearty laugh, Samuel ran after him. Ophera returned to the shack and picked up their infant daughter and faced the shoreline. She smiled to herself, holding the baby close. A tear dampened her cheek.

Ophera knew peace.

ABOUT THE AUTHOR

Writing is something Clair does because he loves it. He has always been an avid reader, and writing was a natural outgrowth of his interest in books. When his children were young, he used to enjoy telling them "make-up stories" before they went to bed. Now he enjoys the same activity with his grandchildren. He values the helpful ideas that his children and their spouses give him on each new book he writes.

If you would like to be updated on Clair's newest releases or correspond with him, please send an e-mail to info@covenant-lds.com. You may also write to him in care of Covenant Communications, P.O. Box 416, American Fork, UT 84003-0416.